"All material in nature, the mountains and the streams and the air and we, are made of Light which has been spent, and this crumpled mass called material casts a shadow, and the shadow belongs to Light."

Silence and Light
Louis Kahn
Architect, 1901-1974

THE LIGHT OF ALL THINGS

LISA ARRIOLA

ISBN: 979-8-9870587-2-5 (Paperback)
ISBN: 979-8-9870587-1-8 (Hardcover)

Copyright Registration Number: TXu 2-332-940

Although I maintained historical accuracies in most instances, I took creative liberties in others. Any references to historical events, real people, or real places are used fictitiously. Names, characters, and places are products of the author's imagination.

Book design by Michael Da Viá.
Photography provided by Tiziano Zatachetto.

Second printing edition 2023.

www.thefullspanti.com

lisa.r.arriola@gmail.com

lisa_arriola_neidhardt

For Rhett and Archie,

I hope you

Discover your own truths and define your own set of beliefs.

Never stop

Exploring and learning; it's an endless and magical universe.

Remember

Inside of you, shines The Light of all Things.

Dear Reader,

I have included direct quotes from *The Malleus Maleficarum*, a treatise written by Heinrich Kramer, a clergyman of the Roman Catholic Church, in 1486 during the time of the Roman Inquisition.

Perhaps one of the most misogynistic documents ever written, *The Malleus Maleficarum* outlines the procedures to identify, torture, and exterminate witches.

Kramer's first attempt to prosecute a witch took place in Innsbrook against a woman, Helena Scheuberin, with whom Kramer is believed to have had a personal vendetta. Helena was described as an aggressive, independent woman who was not afraid to speak her mind.

During her trial, Kramer's examination became dominated by questions regarding her sex life. It became so uncomfortable and intense, the town bishop ended the trial and dismissed Kramer as "senile and crazy".

In what some believe to be an act of retaliation, Kramer wrote *The Malleus Maleficarum* and submitted it to Pope Innocent VIII, who gave Kramer a papal bull, granting him full approval to use the manual to prosecute what was deemed to be witchcraft.

It was regarded as fact and treated as law.

Lisa Arriola

Italy, 1500's

Family Tree
1523 - 1553

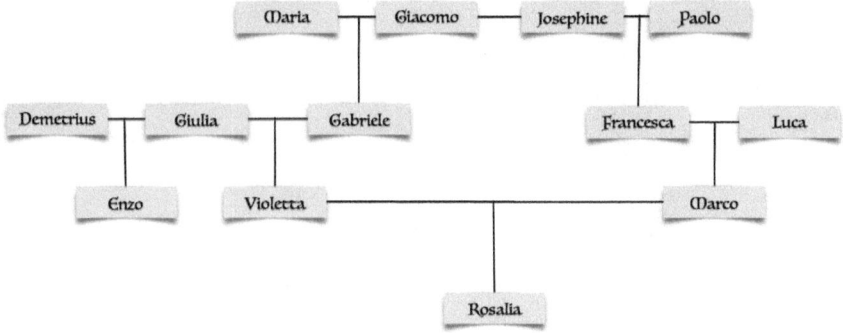

Albergo Pietra Bella, 1523-1557

Iris

"And so in this twilight and evening of the world, when sin is flourishing on every side and in every place, when charity is growing cold, the evil of witches and their iniquities super-abound."

The Malleus Maleficarum, Part 1

Question II

Heinrich Kramer 1486 AD2

Trento

January, 2012

"I've walked by this church countless times as a child, but I never noticed it," Nico said.

"How could you miss it? The entire facade on all four sides is covered. Look," Iris said, gesturing toward the entrance of a small medieval church. "The images depict stories from the Bible for the citizens who couldn't read, which was pretty much everyone at the time."

Nico shrugged. "The town is full of frescos. All of Italy is, if you haven't noticed."

Iris had noticed.

The first time they'd driven through Italy, she was enchanted by the colorful pixels dotting the landscape. Iris adored the ancient buildings, with their cracks and imperfections, and she never tired of looking at the patina on the walls in faded shades of oranges, yellows, and rusts. Years later, the phenomenon of pigment, corrosion, and time still enchanted her. Nico was not as enamoured. He longed for the sleek and shiny high-rises of the modern world. Iris was content to wander the streets of millennia past.

"Wait a minute," Iris said, but Nico didn't hear her.

She could tell by his lack of response that his mind was far away today, but that was not unusual. He was a thinker by nature. It's what he got paid to do, to sit and postulate about an invisible world - the quantum world. Einstein's world of freaky science where the rules of physical reality fall away and dichotomies are the norm. Nico spent his time pondering theories on the origins of life, often into the early morning hours. Iris would laugh and tell him that he needed to be careful.

If he spent his entire life looking for life, he might miss it.

She swept her auburn bangs from her eyes, annoyed at having cut her hair. She liked feeling the air on her neck, but the bangs irritated her while taking pictures with the camera she kept strapped around her neck.

She brought the camera to her eye, zooming in on the hand of a man gripping a spear. Whether wandering through the open countryside or walking the streets of an ancient town, there was always a beautiful statue or majestic cathedral to shoot, but it was the details of these things she liked to capture best.

The sunlight's soft haze shone on the fresco, illuminating the tiny droplets of moisture that spun in the air and danced playfully before the paint's magical glow. She adjusted the focus. If photography had taught Iris anything, it was to look at everything from a new perspective. She found it easy to do with objects and landscapes.

People were more complex.

Iris snapped the picture and hurried to catch up with Nico at the end of the street.

"Come on," he said. "We need to get going if we want to make it to Val di Luci."

The mountains. Iris had forgotten it was tonight.

Val di Luci

January, 2012

Not much happened in the obscure mountain village shrouded in shadows and frost most of the year. But that night, flames born from a heap of wood and discarded rags were frenzied and untamed, commanding attention as they whipped and twisted before the townspeople. The smoke was just as savage but not as vain. It wafted through the field and clung to the hair, skin, and clothes of everyone who had come to witness the spectacle.

The heat from the fire, a hungry hearth in the belly of an unforgiving landscape, warmed Iris on the frigid January night. The flames grew higher and seemed to feed off the shrieks and high-pitched laughter from the adults and children encircling its glow. Iris squinted to keep the sting out of her eyes as she tried to see through the activity that swarmed around her. She had to find Nico quickly.

Soon, it would be time to begin.

Iris finally spotted Nico and pushed through the crowd with two steaming mugs of mulled wine. A group of children stood in front of Nico, squirming in anticipation. He smiled as she handed him a cup. Iris turned toward the fire and took a sip. The sweet liquid coated her mouth with a sugary film. Iris didn't care for mulled wine, but she was grateful for the warmth tonight.

A few minutes later, cheers erupted from the crowd as two men brought the witch out, one holding each of her arms. She was cloaked in black and looked like every conceivable stereotype from a children's fairy tale. A long cape was tied around her neck and flowed over her black dress. Her long stringy hair poked out from beneath the tattered shawl wrapped around her head and tied beneath her chin.

Garish red lipstick stained her lips, giving her the appearance of a whorish clown, and the painted wooden eyes expressed a perpetual state of dull lunacy. She held a long broom in her hand - a stylized prop to complete the ensemble.

A silence settled over a few hundred townspeople as the two men approached the fire. They paused for dramatic effect, and the crowd froze in anticipation. The men tied the noose around the neck. Then, they pulled the rope in one choreographed gesture, and she was yanked upward, suspended above the jovial faces below. The witch jerked and twitched about, dangling like a rag doll above the flames nipping at her feet before being lowered into the fire. Cheers and whistles erupted as the flames consumed the witch. The adults clinked their glasses and threw candy while children raced in circles, grabbing the sweets that fell like confetti at their feet.

Nico put his arm around Iris' waist. "Are you having fun?" he asked.

Iris smiled. "Of course," she said, grateful Nico didn't seem to notice her unease.

Feelings of isolation plagued her, but tonight, she felt like a million miles from civilization. Still, this place held a strange allure, one she could feel but not explain. Now, the image of the burning witch seems to have made raw that which she had come here to heal. Those persistent sensations that would not allow her to rest. In fact, the feelings had worsened since her arrival. The doctors told her there was nothing physically wrong with her, and it was all in her mind, but Iris knew they were too real to be a figment of her imagination. With that thought, a searing burn ignited in her chest, and she fought to ignore what her body was telling her.

Something here was trying to speak to her.

And what more fitting place than this, she thought. Iris knew the town's history well. Although the Roman Inquisition was established in Rome, the people here in the Süd Tyrol region of Northern Italy eagerly embraced its ideals and objectives.

Influenced by the rigid intolerance of the Germans to the north and the religious fervor of the Roman Catholics to the south, the town was perfectly positioned in the foothills of the Italian Alps for the people to carry out the consequences of witchery in a movement that would span over five hundred years. Ultimately, it would kill countless innocent women, men, and even adolescents.

Ignorance, isolation, and fear fed the frenzy. Conformity was paramount if one were to survive within their tightly knit community. Being different was a detriment. Rebellion was not tolerated, and questioning was akin to heresy.

A joyous rumble echoed through the evening as the witch's remains continued to burn. Iris and Nico talked and sipped their wine as the local children ran about, shouting excitedly. Eventually, people began to disperse. It had been an eventful evening, but the crowd was hungry, and it was time to head home to their Alpine houses with the pitched roofs and timber wood construction. Inside, a warm fire, bottles of robust wine, and plates piled high with polenta, cheese, and sausages awaited. The same meal at every table.

The temperature was dropping, and Iris was eager to get home. Nico was immersed in a conversation with a man next to him. They spoke in the local mountain dialect, an unusual blend of Italian and German that Iris didn't understand. He had grown up in Trento, but his entire family was from this mountain town where he had spent the summers of his youth.

"I'll return the cups," she interrupted, and Nico nodded in response.

She hurried to the drink stand, where she placed the cups on the counter and waited to collect her deposit. She smiled at an older woman standing next to her, but the woman shifted her attention to the man behind the counter pouring a beer.

Iris wondered to what extent the psychological wounds of the Inquisition persisted. There was an insular quality to the way of life there, one that families were intent upon preserving, albeit at a lesser cost. People were typically quiet and reserved, avoided eye contact, and kept their shutters tightly closed. Nico told her it was to keep out the cold, but she suspected it was to keep out prying eyes.

The man handed Iris her coins, and she met Nico back at the bonfire. "Are you ready?" Nico asked.

"I'm ready when you are," she replied.

As they walked to the car, a child ran past. "That was awesome," he exclaimed.

"Yeah," chimed in his friend who was trailing from behind, "we saw Befana buuuuurn."

Iris felt a surge of heat course through her veins. It vanished as quickly as it came.

"Hey, slow down, guys," Nico yelled after them. "The sidewalk's icy. You'll crack your heads open."

"Come on, let's hurry," said Iris. "I'm freezing."

Iris sat in the car's passenger seat and watched the dark road snake in front of them. "Are you okay?" Nico asked, putting his hand on her thigh.

"I'm fine, just cold." Iris adjusted her scarf tighter around her neck. "You know, the Czechs used to blame the cold weather on witches. They believed that witches lost their powers when the warm weather came, so the people believed they would cast spells to keep the temperature cold. Then, if winter lasted too long, the townspeople would burn women in the town square. It was a big spectacle. Everyone would come to watch, even children."

"Wow, what an uplifting story to end the night," Nico said.

"I thought it was a fitting story to end the night." Iris knew this could be headed toward a fight but continued anyway. "I mean, this coming from the guy who postulates that we're nothing but microorganisms devouring a larger, unknown biological system, like bacteria in a gut. Talk about uplifting philosophical conjecture."

"Hey, why so serious? I just came here to enjoy an evening of mulled wine and some innocent witch burning."

"*Innocent* witch burning? Is there any other kind?" Irritated, Iris turned the heat up. The chill seemed to be lodged deep in her bones.

"Relax, it was just a puppet." Nico laughed. The one where he opened his mouth, but no sound came out, the one that annoyed her. "Here, burning Befana is a symbolic way to release the past year's troubles and embrace a new beginning. It's full of positive overtures."

"Ah, what beautiful symbolism to wrap up all of your troubles in the form of a woman and set her on fire. It's really kind of sick if you think about it - and we call that entertainment?" Iris knew she should probably let it rest, but she didn't feel compelled to stop. Not yet. "You know the story, right? Astrologers knocked on her door, looking for Baby Jesus. Later, feeling guilty for not helping, Befana decides to look for Baby Jesus on her own, and she follows a bright light in the sky. She brings along a bag filled with candy and a broom to help the new mother clean. But she never found the baby, and she's still searching for him. And that's her reward, being burned at the stake - after all the candy has been delivered."

Nico chuckled. "I'm familiar with the story. But when you put it in those terms, yes, it does seem a bit—"

"Barbaric?"

"Harsh."

Iris wasn't sure if he was being agreeable or if he was trying to appease her, which irritated her all the more. She hated it when Nico dismissed her.

"Which makes it all the more troublesome. It's scary to think how many things people do, giving no thought to why they are actually doing them. And that's how these things start, you know—just blindly following the masses. If I was the only person disturbed tonight, we are all doomed." Iris knew she sounded dramatic, but she couldn't shake the nerves that were making her shiver beneath her thick down coat.

Nico squeezed her leg gently. "Well, then, it'll be up to you to save us all."

She turned and looked at his profile. Iris couldn't tell if Nico was smiling or smirking.

"I didn't get the job," Iris said flatly.

"Which job?"

"Which job? The only one I've interviewed for."

"Well, that's okay. They weren't paying you very much anyway, right? It was more like volunteer work."

"Volunteer work? No, actually, it was a real job, with a real paycheck," she replied.

"Well, there's always your old job waiting in Boston."

"It isn't about the money. And it isn't about Boston. It was something I thought I would be passionate about. You know, passion, right? Or have you forgotten the concept?"

"You'll find something else," he said. "And no, I haven't forgotten about passion," he added.

She looked down at his hand resting on her thigh.

She tried to conjure up a feeling of excitement, but she only felt a dead weight on her leg. Iris feared she had forgotten about passion too.

Iris loosened her scarf around her neck, not because she was hot, but because suddenly, she felt trapped. Trapped in the car, trapped in these mountains, trapped in this relationship. She gripped the door handle and furrowed her brow. Iris realized they seldom agreed on anything. It was as if they were living in two different worlds. According to Nico, that was precisely what they were doing. He said no two realities were the same because each person experiences his own version of reality.

She knew he was right.

"Milena, the woman I interviewed with, told me that her no is a yes to something else. I thought that was a strange thing to tell someone. But it kind of makes sense."

"What makes sense?" he asked.

"Nothing," she replied.

Iris turned her attention out the window.

Giant rectangular mirrors dotted the ridge of the mountain. During the day, they tracked the sun and reflected sunlight down onto the town buried in shadows most of the year. Tonight, the mirrors reflected the moonlight, and they glowed like lanterns of a lighthouse, illuminating the path over the mountain.

The car snaked to the left and right, winding its way through the valley, down the mountain. Iris checked her phone.

"I'm not getting reception. How far are we from Trento?" asked Iris.

"We should be coming up on Alpinella. So, probably another twenty-five minutes," replied Nico.

"I'm starving," she said, tossing her phone in her purse. "So, how's your research going?" she asked.

"It's going nowhere. That's where it's going," Nico said, sounding dismayed.

"What do you mean?"

"We know the heart has an electromagnetic field that generates a certain level of electricity. But I want to conduct my own research, move beyond what we already know, and start developing ways to harness the energy inside our bodies."

"To power nano devices implanted in our bloodstream to track us?"

"Yes, among other things."

"I don't know. It worries me. It's like you're reducing us to machines."

"That's basically what we are, Iris."

"There's nothing basic about us. Just because we generate electricity doesn't mean we're machines. The heart is more than a battery. Ancient civilizations believed the heart was the center of intelligence, and now we have the science to back it up. The heart communicates. It has a memory and wisdom. In transplant patients, the heart carries memories, preferences, and personality traits of the original person."

"I'm familiar with the studies," he replied, keeping his eyes on the road.

"Well, the heart isn't just studied in laboratories. The heart was the only organ the Egyptians left in the mummified body because they believed it was the center of wisdom, not the brain. The heart has an electromagnetic energy field five thousand times greater than the brain. Now, there's evidence that the heart and brain are connected, and it's the heart that supplies the brain with energy, not the other way around."

"It looks like you've been doing your research."

"I didn't just look at pretty art all those years I spent in museums," she replied, unamused.

"Of course, you didn't."

"Well, all I'm saying is the heart has a significant influence on the body down to the cellular level. So, I don't think your partners are wrong in studying this, especially if you plan on inserting foreign objects into the bloodstream."

"We have studied all of this and are using all of our money to rehash it. It's time to move forward."

"So, say the heart is a battery and is generating a certain amount of electricity, what's the point?" she mused.

"What do you mean?"

"I mean, where is all of this electricity going? Is it just keeping our bodies alive?"

"Pretty much."

"So, you think we can really use it to generate nano machines?"

"That's what I'm hoping."

"Well, that seems a little self-serving to me. What if you can take the energy and do something more?"

"Like what?"

"I don't know, like transfer to other people who need energy."

"Need energy?"

"Yeah, like people who are sick or something."

"I don't think it works that way. There's no way to transfer it."

"Well, energy travels well through a conduit such as water."

"Yes."

"Aren't we mostly water? And isn't salt water the best conduit? We have lots of salt in our bodies. So, what if the energy produced inside our heart, the battery inside our chest, can be transported?"

"Conducted," Nico corrected.

"Conducted through the water in our bodies and somehow channelled externally? What if we were designed to share our energy? That sounds more interesting than powering nano chips."

"Well, I think it's generally accepted that we consistently exchange our energy with one another."

"Yes, but we do it so haphazardly. What if—"

The car hit a patch of ice and slid across the road without warning. Nico slammed the brakes as the car went careening into a shallow ditch and stopped with a forceful jolt.

He hit the steering wheel with his palm. "Damn it," he cursed.

"Are we stuck?"

Nico put the car in reverse, and the tires spun beneath them. He unbuckled his seatbelt and opened the door. "I'm going to take a look."

A moment later, he opened her car door. A burst of frigid air hit Iris in the face. "Looks like we're stuck. And we don't have cell phone reception."

"I remember seeing a sign about a half-mile back that pointed to an inn. Maybe there's someone there who can help us?"

"You stay here in the car. At least you'll be warm."

"No way," Iris shook her head. "I'm not going to be road bait for some serial killer. I'm going with you."

"I doubt a serial killer is lurking on this mountain road on the off chance he comes across a woman sitting in a car."

"That's exactly how it happens," she said, stepping out of the car.

"All right. Come on, let's go."

They walked down the road until they came to a wooden signpost that read *Albergo Pietra Bella*. Iris wrapped her scarf tightly around her neck and pulled the hood to her coat over her head. They soon came upon a clearing where the moon cast its glow upon a small shimmering lake. On the far side was the outline of an inn.

"I don't see any cars," Iris said.

"Maybe the owner is home," Nico said, taking her hand as they made their way across the frozen lawn, the frozen blades of grass crunching beneath their boots.

"I'm not sure about this," she said uneasily. "It doesn't look like anyone is here. What if squatters are living inside?"

"You should really stop watching those crime stories."

Nico knocked on the door, and they strained to hear a sound inside.

"Damn it, no one's home," she said, peering through the window.

"Hold on. Maybe there's a phone we can use inside."

"Who would we call?" she asked. "I doubt anyone is up this late."

"If nothing else, maybe we can find some blankets we can borrow." He turned the knob and pushed the door open. "It's unlocked. Hello," he called out.

Iris followed him inside. "It's freezing in here," she whispered. "Clearly no one's around."

They stepped into a small dining room off the entry and turned on the light. A threadbare oriental carpet covered the floor, and landscape paintings and portraits hung lopsided on the walls. A fireplace stood at the far end of the room with a heap of ashes inside. Iris relaxed. It didn't look like a squatter's abode after all.

"I don't think this place has been open for a while," Nico said.

Iris walked over to the bar. "Shall I pour us a drink?"

He opened the door behind the bar and peered inside.

"Well, I'm having a drink," she said, taking a crystal glass from the shelf. "Let's see if we have running water." She walked over to the sink and turned on the faucet. "Look at that," she exclaimed, "crystal clear mountain water." Iris turned to inspect the row of dusty liquor bottles on the shelf.

"I'm going to have a look upstairs," Nico said.

"Can I offer you a drink, Sir?" she asked a second time.

When she turned around, he'd already disappeared up the stairs.

"One drink coming up," she mumbled under her breath.

Iris poured a whiskey into the crystal tumbler and walked over to the fireplace. A pile of long matches lay scattered beside a stack of wood on the floor. She was considering lighting a fire when she heard steps coming down the stairs.

"The rooms are pretty empty. Furniture is pushed against the walls. It looks like it's been ages since anyone has been up there," Nico said, dusting off his pants.

"Here, take mine," she said, handing him her glass. "I'll fix another one. I think we're going to need it."

Just then, the front door opened. Startled, Iris and Nico turned to see a stout man with wavy silver hair walk in.

Nico stepped forward: "Hello. I'm Nico, and this is my girlfriend, Iris. We're sorry to disturb you, but our car broke down, and we were trying to find someone to help, maybe make a call…" his voice trailed off.

Iris shook her head.

Nico was always so awkward when it came to meeting new people.

"I'm Giuseppe," the man answered in a gravelly voice. He shot Nico a stern look. "Have a seat, and allow me to fix a drink for the lady."

Iris raised her eyebrows at Nico, who stared back at her with a bewildered expression on his face.

"Is this your inn?" Iris asked, trying to lighten the mood.

Giuseppe placed a glass down in front of her and poured the whiskey. "It is now. The inn belonged to my parents, and I took it over when they died."

"And do you still operate it?"

"I continued to run it for a while," he took a deep breath, "but my mother was the heart and soul of the place. Besides, it takes a lot of work. And people are getting more and more demanding each year. My patience runs thin these days."

He handed Iris the glass.

"Thank you," she said. "I bet this place has a fascinating history. How old is it?"

"The earliest record we found is from the early 1500s. It stayed in the same family for many generations. It was vacant for about fifty years. Then, in the mid-eighteen hundreds, it was purchased by a man from Tyrol who turned it into a hunting lodge for the gentlemen in the surrounding cities. It was pretty successful, judging from the books. Then the Germans occupied it during the first and second World Wars. You can still find the marks on the walls upstairs, counting the days."

"This area is known to have had a pretty big resistance movement during the Second World War," said Iris.

"There was. It was quite effective. You can usually find some sort of monument in every town."

"It's late," said Nico. "We're sorry to have disturbed you, and we certainly don't wish to occupy any more of your night. If you could just help us call for a tow truck, we can be on our way."

"Don't be ridiculous. There aren't any tow trucks around here this time of night. You'll be staying here."

"That's very nice of you, but we really don't wish to intrude."

"Intrude? A little late for that," he chuckled and took another sip.

"We don't wish to be a bother," Nico said.

"Listen, it looks to me that you don't have any other option other than spending the night on the side of the road. Temperatures are below freezing tonight."

"That's very kind of you," Iris said, shooting Nico a look. "Of course, we will accept."

"There's a room at the end of the hall that my mother always kept made up. You can sleep there. It may be a little dusty, but it's comfortable."

"It sounds perfect," Iris said. "We are so grateful."

"I live in the house out back, if you need anything. Otherwise, I'll see you in the morning." He left, taking his whiskey with him.

Nico and Iris lay in bed that night in the small room at the end of the hall. It was tidy, and ample blankets were piled on top of the bed.

"It's like he knew we were coming," Iris said.

"I'm just grateful not to be sleeping in the car tonight."

"We lucked out for sure," she said, running her hand down his stomach. "A cozy inn, whiskey, and nice warm bed. This is turning into a romantic getaway."

"Iris, we are not on vacation. We're stranded. And I'm exhausted."

He put his arms around her waist and pulled her close to him.

She closed her eyes, but as usual, sleep did not come.

Early the following morning, Iris sat on the porch step and stretched her legs out. A fat tabby lay next to her, soaking up the morning sun. It stretched its paw out, inviting her to scratch her side.

"Cats are good at living in the moment. When they're hungry, they eat. When they're happy, they purr. When they're tired, they find a nice sunny spot and sleep," Giuseppe said.

He stood in the doorway, dressed in navy pants and a white button-up shirt. His hair was slicked back from his face. Iris thought he looked younger in the morning light.

"I wish I could be more like a cat," Iris said and then laughed.

"What's stopping you?" he asked. "Come inside. It's cold, and I have breakfast ready."

Nico was speaking rapidly on the phone, as they walked past him in the lobby. Inside the dining room, a basket of bread, boiled eggs, and an assortment of jams were laid out on the crisp white table cloth. Giuseppe placed two white ceramic cups filled with steaming espresso and frothy milk on the table. "This is so nice, but it isn't necessary," Iris said.

"It's a pleasure to have guests finally. Be sure to try the jams. This one is frutti di bosco. I made it myself."

Iris spread butter on a slice of bread and then dipped her knife into the jam pot. "So, do you have plans to reopen the inn?" Iris paused. "I don't mean to pry. This is just such a special place. It would be a shame not to reopen it."

"I'm afraid there isn't much tourism for a rundown inn on the outskirts of a no-name Italian village."

"There's a market for everything," said Iris. "It's just a matter of zeroing in on your niche. In fact, there are plenty of people who are tired of mainstream travel and are looking for something a bit more authentic. Like this place."

"Maybe so, but I won't be around to see it. I'm not getting any younger, and it's a lot of work to run an inn, even a small one like this."

Nico walked into the dining room. "The tow truck is on its way. It should be here in twenty minutes."

"Have a seat and eat some breakfast," Giuseppe said.

"Thank you, but we've taken enough of your time. We should get going. Come on, Iris."

"But, I'm not finished with my breakfast. Have a cappuccino at least," Iris said, gesturing toward the cup and saucer.

Nico took a seat, and Iris tried to ignore the impatient expression on his face as she finished her breakfast.

Giuseppe opened the door and they stepped onto the porch.

"Thank you again," Iris said, putting on her coat. "You saved us."

"Don't mention it. And please, come by any time," he replied, looking at Iris.

Nico and Iris walked down the road. "What a lovely place," she said. "Giuseppe is such a nice man. We need to bring him a gift."

When she didn't get an answer, Iris looked at Nico. "Did you hear me?"

Nico looked at his watch. "Yes. He's not a serial killer."

"Definitely not a serial killer. But isn't this place incredible?"

"Yeah," said Nico, holding up his phone, "still no signal."

"It's probably your carrier. I told you not to get the cheapest one. You know the Italians say that carrier is for the immigrants."

"You're an immigrant. Come on," said Nico, and he walked ahead toward the main road.

Iris laughed and glanced back at the sunlight streaming through the leaves and dancing off of the water.

Trento

January, 2012

Nico wandered into the kitchen and stopped in front of the table. "Nice basket. Who's it for?"

"Giuseppe." Iris beamed him a smile. "I'm bringing it to him this afternoon."

She tied the lavender-colored ribbon around the handle and adjusted the linen napkin inside. Then she arranged lemon scones next to the beeswax candle.

"And what's that?" Nico asked, pointing inside the basket.

"It's a matchstick holder. I found it at the antique market. I thought he could hang it in the dining room next to the fireplace. I noticed his matches were scattered around on the floor."

"That's very thoughtful." He smiled. "You always have a way of picking up on the details." He snatched a scone from the basket.

"Hey, those aren't for you, but I made extra."

Iris walked over to the counter and picked up the plate piled high with scones. By the time she turned around, Nico was gone.

Iris looked at her watch. It was a quarter past ten. Not that it mattered. Giuseppe told her to come by anytime today. She got in the car and turned the volume up on the radio.

As she drove along the winding country road, she gripped the steering wheel and accelerated, not because she was in a hurry, but because driving felt good today. The weather was chilly, but the skies were clear, and she was looking forward to seeing Giuseppe again. She had felt a unique kindred spirit with him she had not felt with any others she had met here.

Iris slowed down as she approached the sign to the inn. She parked in front of the porch and stepped out of the car. The inn looked brighter and more welcoming than she'd remembered. The empty wooden planter boxes in the window caught her eye. She imagined how they would look, bursting with red geraniums in the spring, framed by the faded green shutters.

Balancing the basket in one hand, she knocked on the door. Judging by the weathered wood and heavy hardware, she guessed it was original. Giuseppe opened the door and smiled warmly.

"This is for you," Iris said, handing him the basket. "Not nearly enough to repay you for helping us the other night, but I wanted to thank you."

"I don't remember the last time someone baked for me. Let's sit in the dining room, and I'll make us a cappuccino."

Iris followed him inside. She noticed he had dusted the tables and mopped the floor. The rug that had seemed worn and faded now looked charming and cozy on the wide wooden planks.

"Can I help you with anything?"

"You can get the plates and napkins. They're in the cupboard," Giuseppe said, pointing to a large kitchen cupboard against the wall.

Iris didn't notice it the other night and wondered how she could have missed it. It looked as if whoever made it either had a strange sense of humor or was trying to see how skinny he could make the legs without it collapsing.

"Wow, this is quite an imposing piece of furniture. An antique, I presume?"

"We found it in the back of the cellar. I find it rather unattractive, but my mother liked it for some reason. She said it looked sad and just needed some love, so she restored it."

Iris took three dishes and closed the door. She caught her reflection in the glass, and a sharp chill ran down her spine. A mix of longing and fear overcame her. She pressed the door firmly closed as if she could keep something inside from getting out.

"So, it could be original to the inn?"

"Possibly," Giuseppe answered. He sat the cups on the table. "Now, I'd like to try one of these scones."

A fog entered her brain that made her head spin like a toy spindle as she sat down. Her fingertips burned as she dug them into the edge of her chair.

"Are you okay?" Giuseppe asked.

"Fine," Iris said, smiling, trying to sound nonchalant. "I think I just need to eat something."

She twisted the napkin on her lap in a slow rhythmic motion that matched her breathing. It was a trick she had learned over the years to calm her nerves, and within a minute, she relaxed.

"Here you go," he said, placing a scone on her plate. He sat back in his chair and interlocked his hands over his belly. "So, Iris, what brought you to Italy?"

"My boyfriend, actually. He got a job here."

"You're a long way from home. Do you miss America?"

"Mostly the people."

"So, how do you like Italy so far?"

"I like it. There's something about this place. I just need to find my footing and do what makes me happy."

"What's stopping you from doing what makes you happy?" he asked, and took a bite of his scone.

Iris was surprised by his candor. "I guess the big thing stopping me is other people's ideas and expectations of me."

"That's a lot of wardrobe changes if you were to please them all." He leaned slightly forward: "I say to hell with expectations and proprietary. You don't owe anyone a damn thing."

Iris took a sip of water and cleared her throat. "I think men are better at the not pleasing and conforming. Take Nico, for example. He has no problem telling his boss that he disapproves with his project's direction. On the other hand, I am jumping through hoops at interviews, responding to questions based on what I think ought to be said, regardless of whether I agree.

It infuriates me. But I don't feel like there are many options here, so I sell myself short and play the game."

Giuseppe chuckled softly. "Don't envy men. Believe me, we have our own set of societal pressures placed on us."

"What about you?" Iris asked. She spread some honey on top of the scone.

"What about me?"

"Have you ever wanted to venture out? Live someplace new?"

Giuseppe shifted in his chair. "I've had a good life. Of course, there are things not in my life I wanted as well."

"I see," she said.

"But not all things are possible," he continued. "Not here anyway. Sure, things are changing in the larger cities, but traditions are deeply rooted in these parts. For me, it was get married or join the clergy. I couldn't see myself in the clergy," he laughed.

Iris laughed along. "I can't either." She wiped her mouth with her napkin. "I thought I had everything figured out. My life was on track. But then something happened, and for some reason, I can't even rationalize, I just up and left my job in Cleveland. It was like I felt an impulse, and I followed it. So, I moved to Boston and went back to school to earn a master's in Renaissance Art.

I've always been fascinated with European history. I studied in Sienna for a semester, and one day, I wandered into the Museo Tortura. What an experience. The whole museum was filled with these horrific torture devices. It is truly awful to think how humans have inflicted such atrocities on each other."

Giuseppe raised his eyebrows: "You know, most people come to Italy to see The Last Supper or David."

"I know. I'm probably a little odd in that regard. Anyway, there was a room inside the museum that described the history of the Holy Inquisition. Of course, I was aware of what had happened, but there was something about seeing the torture devices in person that deeply affected me. It was horrifying to think that women were actually brutally tortured with them. And believe me, they were brutal. The iron maiden still haunts me." She shook her head quickly back and forth. "So, that day, I changed the topic of my thesis to study the Inquisition and how it continues to shape women's inequality and perpetuate misogyny in the modern world."

Giuseppe rubbed the stubble on his chin: "I see, and where did Nico fit into all of this?"

"I didn't meet Nico in Italy. I met him at a lecture in Chicago." Iris waved her hand in the air. "Completely unrelated to any witch burning. That is, until he took me to one a few nights ago."

"I'm assuming you're referring to Befana."

"Yep, the night we broke down."

"Funny how things are sometimes connected, isn't it?"

"It is."

"So, now the two of you are here."

"Shortly after we started dating, his work visa expired, and he had to return to Italy. I had just started a job at a museum, but I decided to quit, and I followed him here."

She twisted the napkin in her hands under the table. "I guess that sounds pretty reckless."

"It's not reckless. Change is good for the soul and allows you to evolve. Without change, you remain stagnant, and that's not a very exciting place to be." He looked at her intently, and Iris swore she saw flames dancing in his eyes. "You, my dear, are currently hunting. Enjoy the hunt. Let it fill you, and let it challenge you. But most of all, let it change you. You'll be back home resting by your hearth soon enough."

Iris raised her eyebrows. "We all speak from experience, don't we?"

"Yes, we do." He stood up. "Do you have time to let me show you around?"

Iris was in no hurry to get back. "I would love that."

"Come on. I'll give you the grand tour."

She followed him through the front entry. He pointed to a small room with a plush green sofa and Turkish rug just beyond the stairs. "That's my favorite room. It's nice to read a good book and look out over the lake."

"It's very lovely."

"You've seen the upstairs. Let's go out back," Giuseppe said, leading the way out the back door. "The grounds need a bit of maintenance this spring."

"Maybe you could hire a gardener," suggested Iris.

"It starts with a gardener, then pretty soon I'll need a carpenter, a painter, and a candlestick maker."

Iris gestured toward the far end of the yard. "What's over there?"

"It's a seating area. A great place to spend summer nights and enjoy a glass of wine."

"I bet you can see every star in the sky out here."

"And, every star can see you," he winked.

Iris paused and looked at the wooden bench with an iron back. It reminded her of the ones along the tree-lined boulevards in Paris. Then, she noticed something peculiar—in front of the bench. There was a circle of half-buried stones and a rusted iron pulley.

"What are those stones? It looks like a mini Stone Henge."

"That's just the top of an old well." Giuseppe paused for a second. "Come on. I'll show you the lake."

The sun was setting when she pulled into the driveway of her home. Grateful to be back, Iris searched through the bathroom cabinet for the pills to soothe the rash that had spread across her torso and spread down her legs on the drive home.

She made a cup of herbal tea and tried to relax on the sofa, but her thoughts were racing with the events that had transpired over the last several days. She picked up her phone and scrolled through pictures she had taken of the inn: the lovely facade with its faded shutters and heavy wooden door; the dining room with the blackened stone fireplace; the tattered rug and a painted portrait on the wall. Iris paused and squinted her eyes. Then, she zoomed in closer to the painting of a man hung on the wall. His long hair fell in waves around his angular face. His dark eyes held a steady gaze ahead and seemed to be looking at something or someone just behind the viewer's shoulder.

"My God," she gasped. "That looks exactly like—"

A second later, her phone beeped, and a message appeared on the screen, causing her to drop the phone from her hand.

"Damn it," she cursed, bending over to pick it up.

The screen was lit with a message across the top:

I know it's been a while, but I've been thinking about you lately.

"We can't start this again," she whispered aloud.

Boston

2006

"I can't deal with this anymore. The long-distance thing isn't working for me," Ben said.

Her heartbeat pounded in her temples as she grasped at understanding the words ringing in her ears. Still, she remained calm and didn't expose the quakes erupting beneath the surface.

"Ben, we agreed. This is only for a short time until I finish my research, then we can decide the next step." Iris tried to contain the panic she felt rising inside her chest.

"I'm sorry," he said flatly, and she could hear the resignation in his voice.

"That makes two of us," she replied bitterly, and hung up.

She stood in the middle of the room as it seemed to spin out of control. She focused on a large horizontal canvas hanging on the wall in front of her, and waves of memories came rushing back to her. The sofa. The fire. The snow falling outside the window. The easel that concealed his face as he worked through the night.

What once was a source of happiness, now filled her with a deep despair.

She tightened her grip on the phone.

Then, she let out a cry and hurled it against the painting.

Trento

January, 2012

At the razor's edge of dawn, conscious thought awakened Iris once again. She gripped the sheets and gasped for breath as she opened her eyes. Beads of sweat dotted her chest. She was in her bed, her room, her house.

Alone.

The blurring of realities had deceived her senses once again.

Her phone beeped.

Call me.

Call him? Call Ben? She hadn't heard his voice in six years.

She sat up in bed and waited for the swimming in her head to subside before she started typing.

Give me fifteen minutes?

She recalled Giuseppe's words. She had an impending sense a hunt had begun. She only wondered who was going to be the hunter and who the kill.

Iris dressed and went downstairs. She opened the gate and stepped onto the sidewalk. A swirl of white smoke wafted from the chimney across the street, and she inhaled the intoxicating aroma of rosemary, garlic, and red wine. She imagined a cast iron pot with wild boar simmering in a rich sauce on the stove and a crunchy baguette next to a bottle of olive oil and red wine sitting on the table, a hearty meal for this cold, damp day.

Suddenly, a shadowy figure peered down from the upstairs window.

Before she could discern if it were a man or woman, the shutters slammed shut.

She turned her attention toward the hills. The sun penetrated the morning fog and cast a steely glow over the vineyards surrounding their houses. Slowly, a constriction gripped her chest. Then, the familiar heat burned in her fingertips.

"Not now," she told herself.

Iris zipped her jacket to her neck and hurried in the direction of the fields.

She made her way along the rows of twisted vines. This time of year, it seemed that the landscape was trapped in a state of perpetual dormancy. It was difficult to imagine how the bare branches could explode into a canopy of lush leaves and grape clusters in just a few months. For now, there was nothing to do but wait.

Iris took the phone from her jacket pocket and scrolled through her contacts. I can do this, she thought. Surely, enough time had passed. Suddenly, the sound of sirens in the distance caused her to pause. She waited for the disruption to pass, but they stopped instead of fading in the opposite direction. Curious, she circled back to the road where she saw an ambulance parked in front of the neighbor's house.

Iris placed her hand over her heart. She tried to will it out of her mind, but she knew it was useless. The distinct pricks of pain would not relent. The fractured images would be coming soon, and the jumbled words that demanded her attention but never made sense.

Her phone beeped.

Are you still calling?

She couldn't do this, not now. She put her phone in her pocket and hurried back to the house.

The next evening, a somber wreath hung on the gate of the neighbor's house, its black ribbons streaming down like streaks of mascara over flushed cheeks. A light wind occasionally stirred, grasping weakly at the pale blue ribbons hanging from the adjacent wreath, announcing the arrival of a baby boy.

Iris tried to go about her day as if nothing was happening, as if she weren't splitting herself in two. But she had split herself in two. One half felt like a role she was playing, as formless as fog. The other half felt solid and sure. It surprised her how effortlessly she flipped back and forth, like two faces of the same coin.

Her phone dinged, interrupting the music blaring through her headphones. She stopped running and looked at the message.

Can we talk now?

Iris still hadn't called Ben. While she was assertive in some ways, she was cautious in others.

Finally, she took a deep breath and hit the call button. He picked up on the first ring.

"Hello."

"Hey, it's Iris."

"Thanks for calling," Ben replied.

"Of course," she tried to sound casual.

"Wow, it's been what, five years?"

"Six," she replied, cringing at how quickly she had responded. "So, how have you been?"

"I've been well. I work for an investment firm in Seattle."

"Seattle? How's that?"

"It's an interesting city. Great food."

"Nothing about the weather."

"Excuse me?"

"Usually, whenever you ask about Seattle, the first thing people talk about is the weather."

"It's not terrible. How about you?"

"I'm living in Italy."

"Italy? How did that happen?"

"Let's just say it was a hunting accident."

"Excuse me?"

"Nothing. My boyfriend got a job here."

"I see. So, it must be serious?"

"I take every relationship seriously." Her voice came across sharper than she intended.

"Fair enough."

"So, do you still paint," she asked, eager to change the subject.

"I haven't painted in years," his voice suddenly heavy with regret.

"Why not?"

"I can't find the time, I guess."

"That's too bad. You were excellent."

"I'm a better banker."

"Banking is what you do. It is not who you are. You're an artist."

"Yeah, well, my family didn't spend that amount of money on my education so I could end up painting landscapes on a sidewalk in New Orleans."

"You wouldn't be painting landscapes."

"Thanks."

"Caricatures. You'd be much better at caricatures."

"Very funny."

"Or, perhaps tiny pictures on grains of rice?"

"Okay, I get the point."

"My point is, at the end of your life, no one remembers or cares what you did. It only matters that you were happy doing it."

"Well, I don't have that kind of freedom. People expect things from me."

"You're saying that no one expects anything from me?"

"I mean, everyone knew what I would become. Three generations of bankers before me laid that foundation. You, on the other hand, your future is still TBD. Don't take that freedom for granted."

She heard the resignation in Ben's voice. The flat, even tone when he spoke. It was the same tone he had used the day she answered a call, out of the blue, that changed the course of her life, or at least the path she had mapped out.

"I should go," she said.

"Of course. I need to get back to work, too."

"Working on your debut, perhaps?"

"I'm afraid not."

"You should consider it. I mean it when I say you are really good."

There was a long pause. Iris sensed there was something more he wanted to say, but the silence persisted.

"Goodbye, Ben."

"Iris."

"Yes?"

"Can I call you again sometime?"

She took a long pause. "Sure. That would be nice."

Iris opened her old wooden trunk and stared at the bundles of old letters, photographs, and scrapbooks. At the bottom, she spotted a rolled canvas. Carefully, she laid it out on her bed and moved her hands across the rough painted surface. She stared at herself, frozen in time. She was lying on her side, her head resting on her bent arm. She appeared pensive as she gazed at the flames from the fireplace that reflected in her eyes. She was naked, but she remembered the brown suede sofa was soft and warm against her skin. Ben had painted her body in warm earth tones - a stark contrast to the snow covered landscape outside the window. He had painted her through the night, and when she awoke the following morning, he was still sitting behind the easel, lost in a world of his own creation. A cashmere blanket covered her body.

She traced her fingers along the edge of the frayed canvas. Suddenly, a thought occurred to her. It was daring and reckless. She knew she was standing on the edge of fidelity, toeing the line between loyalty and betrayal, but she wanted to do it.

Iris wanted him to remember.

She closed the door and looked around their bedroom. Their bedroom. They had stopped sleeping in the same bed months ago. Maybe longer, but she had stopped keeping track. Just as she had stopped keeping track of how frequently or infrequently they were having sex. Nico blamed it on lack of sleep, stress, and work. He told her that he slept better on the couch. He assured her it was only temporary. She believed him. There wasn't any reason not to.

Iris looked at her phone. It was eleven in the morning. She calculated the time change in her head. Ben would be sleeping. She tapped on her photos and found his picture. He was lying in bed, tousled hair and bare-chested. She remembered the taste of his neck, like a fresh mix of salty sea and damp moss. She could still smell his chest, especially after a night wrapped in those luxurious sheets.

Daylight was streaming through the window. The room was bright. Too bright. Iris walked over to close the shutters. She glimpsed an older woman leaning out her window, shaking her rug vigorously up and down. Iris waited until she disappeared back into her house.

Italian neighbors could be notoriously nosy, possibly stemming from when metal boxes were mounted to the outside of churches for citizens to drop a note informing the Church of illicit activity they had witnessed, heard, or suspected. It was no wonder there remained a thread of paranoia running through the fabric of Italian society. Sometimes, Iris got the feeling she, too, was under surveillance.

Iris closed the shutters half way and stepped back from the window, reading the message on her phone one more time. She needed a drink, something strong.

Stepping into the downstairs office, she saw Nico sitting at his desk, buried behind his monitor. "How is your research coming along?"

"Look at these idiots," he said, pointing to the screen.

"What is this?"

"The accounts and passwords of our neighbors. The fools think they are protected, but all their information is right here."

"How did you do that?" she asked, alarmed. "Isn't that illegal?"

"No."

"But, you're breaking into their accounts," she exclaimed.

"I'm not breaking into anything. I'm just accessing the server that receives the information. But I could if I wanted to. "

"You're crazy. Close that now."

"I'm not doing anything illegal."

"I'm sure they wouldn't see it that way."

"Fine," he said, closing the window, a bored expression on his face.

"So, how's your research going?"

He leaned back. "I'm not getting anywhere. I think I need to go back to America and get a job that actually uses my skills."

"Well, do I have a say, or have you decided this on your own?"

He was staring at his screen. "You're not working here," he said, "I thought you'd be happy to return."

"I'm happy here. Does that count?"

"Well, it's not decided yet. I haven't heard back from the interview."

"Interview. What interview?"

He glanced up. "It was a phone interview. I'm just testing the waters."

"I can't believe you haven't told me any of this."

"Because nothing will probably even come from it." Nico took a sip of his coffee and turned his attention back toward his monitor, tapping the eraser of his pencil on the table.

Iris eyed the decanter. "I'm going to refill this," she said, picking it up from the bar cart.

The grinding of wood and flint in the sharpener whirled behind her as she walked out of the room.

Upstairs, the whiskey warmed her belly, and a pleasant tingling sensation washed over her body. She felt relaxed and in control. Propping her phone on the antique dresser, Iris pressed the red circular button at the bottom. Then, she climbed on the bed, faced the screen, and took off her clothes.

The following day, she opened her eyes, and a wave of regret sickened her stomach. She cursed herself for being so reckless.

There was a new message on her phone.

I loved it.

I feel like I cheated.

You haven't cheated.

Yes, I have.

We haven't even seen each other.

Isn't this the same thing?

No.

It feels the same.

Iris kicked the covers off her body. She needed to move her body and clear her mind.

The orchards were dotted with bright orange fruits dangling from twisted bare branches. Iris had always considered persimmon to be just another shade in a pretty autumn palette, like cinnamon, pumpkin, or spice. She never knew it was also such a delectable fruit. The subtle flavor of persimmon could stand alone or blend effortlessly into any dish, sweet or savory. Today, she would make a sauce to go with pork shoulder. The persimmons hanging on the lowest branches over the road had already been plucked, probably from random by-passers like herself. However, the best ones were still growing a little higher up.

She could tell they were at their peak ripeness, large and soft in her hands. Persimmons, or cachi, as they are called in Italian, are a temperamental fruit that require time to ripen. Then, once they reach their peak, there is a small window before they turn into a ball of mush. The timing was everything. She held them gently, taking care not to squeeze or bruise them. Too much pressure and the delicate skins would break open, allowing the gooey inside to spill out, rendering them useless.

When she returned home, she placed the persimmons on the kitchen counter and circled back to the entry, where she hung up her coat and pulled off her rain boots. She slid her feet into the shearling slippers she kept by the door and walked back to the kitchen.

Iris preheated the oven and placed three pots of water on the stove - one for pasta, one for potatoes, and one for the persimmons. She added salt to the larger pots and sugar to the smaller pot. Placing the persimmons on the cutting board, Iris cut them into quarters. Then, she gently ran the edge of a spoon over the delicate skin, removing the sticky pulp. As she worked, her thoughts began to wander. Iris thought about the pictures she'd sent to Ben. She was feeling the same sense of liberation she had felt that cold January night eight years ago. The first night he had painted her until dawn. A rebellious smile swept across her face. She scraped the pulp into the small copper pot, sprinkled red pepper flakes over the top, and then gave it a quick stir. Soon, it would thicken into a sweet and flavorful sauce.

Iris wiped her hands and reached for the bag of spaghetti. She held the long pasta in both hands above the boiling water. Nico told her never to break the pasta in half. He said it was a sin against the pasta itself. She'd asked him why. Nico had replied it just wasn't done.

Iris wanted to know why it wasn't done. He said his grandmother told him that they wouldn't be long enough to twist around the fork if you break them in half. Iris said she never had a problem wrapping the spaghetti around her fork. He said one had to respect tradition and do things a certain way, the *right* way.

She gripped the pasta tighter and applied a steady downward force, snapping the bundle in half. Then she tossed the pieces into the pot and watched the thin sticks sink into the boiling water.

The steam rose from the pots as she wiped her forehead with the back of her hand. She walked over to the window where heavy beads of moisture were sliding down the panes. Without warning, a series of sharp stabs rippled through her torso, and a feeling of nausea washed over her. She turned the brass latch and pushed the window open. Closing her eyes, Iris let the cold air wash over her cheeks, cooling the nape of her neck.

Suddenly, her eyes flew open. She froze, terrified she would miss it or, worse, dismiss it as a figment of her imagination. It had been two weeks since the fragrant herbs wafted through the street. Two weeks since she heard the bellowing cry of sirens fade into the distance—the same amount of time with no signs of life from across the street. But now, she heard a new sound, the puncturing screams of a newborn crying out for his mother. The cries pierced her ears, and her stomach twisted in response.

She looked across the street, and, to her surprise, the green shutters were open. She strained to see if she could catch a glimpse inside, but a gossamer curtain hung in the window, creating another barrier behind the layer of fog.

A minute later, the crying subsided, and the only sound came from the gentle thrum of boiling water. The baby had been mollified, but she didn't know by whom. Then, a flash of green and the wooden shutters slammed shut. The house fell silent and the ivory facade blended into the fog, blurring the lines between solid and ether.

A chill invaded her body, dissipating the heat she had felt a moment before. She closed the window. But, unlike the neighbor, she left her shutters open.

Iris walked to the sink, drained the pasta, and then transferred it to a ceramic bowl. She caught her reflection in the window as she stirred in the sauce. Walking over, Iris pressed her palm to the antique pane and her fingertips burned. This time, she didn't fight it. Images of the witch, the ambulance, long black ribbons, and the bonfire appeared before her. A man's words floated towards her.

Don't take that freedom for granted.

Iris knew how far she wanted to take it.

Father Lucien

Alpinella, Italy

September, 1533

"Father Lucien, my son is a smart boy," Demetrius pleaded.

"I understand he is smart, but it takes more than a certain degree of intelligence. Enzo has no vision. God's work requires, above all else, vision," the priest replied.

"If you could grant me this one request," Demetrius persisted. "You know I've been a very generous supporter of the church over the years."

The priest glanced around the empty piazza. There wasn't much money flowing into the church these days. Times were difficult, and the donation plate was getting lighter each week.

He didn't care for the kid. He couldn't put his finger on it, but something about Enzo made him uneasy, and he got the sense the boy was never completely forthcoming in his confessions. The father wasn't much better, but he had deep pockets.

The priest only cared for the mother. Giulia had been shy and reserved when she first arrived to live in their small town, but over the past year, she had blossomed. She seemed more relaxed and wore a warm, contagious smile. It were as if she held a secret the rest of them didn't know. Intrigued, the priest had often tried to coax it out of her during confession; but each week, she only recited the usual menu of minor offences against God.

Now, God only knew what had happened to her. Giulia disappeared one day without a trace. When people inquired, her husband had claimed she had gone mad and run off with the devil. Her husband was a respected man, so no one questioned his word.

But the priest didn't believe it. He'd been judging people for forty years, and there was nothing mad about Giulia. The boy, on the other hand, was another matter.

The priest sighed. He didn't want to do it, but it wasn't always about his preferences. He had to think of the survival of the Church and put its needs above all else. So, against his better judgment, he relented.

"Enzo can join the Order."

"Thank you, Father." A rush of relief washed over Demetrius' face.

Demetrius

"Blessed is the man who has a virtuous wife,"

Malleus Maleficarum, Part 1

Question VI

Heinrich Kramer, 1486 AD

Alpinella, Italy

September, 1533

Later that evening, Demetrius sat alone at his dining table and poured himself another glass of wine. He rarely indulged in drinking, but tonight he would make an exception. He would finally be rid of his son, and along with him, another memory of his wife would be erased. Demetrius took a slow sip and allowed the memories he kept locked away to reawaken in his mind.

His son had always been an odd boy, an odd baby even, abnormally attached to his mother. He clung to her with a ferocity that disturbed him from the beginning. His wife told him babies were like that, and he would grow out of it. But he didn't grow out of it. In fact, it only got worse with each passing year.

The day arrived when his son entered school. The hours Enzo spent at school were a welcomed reprieve for them both. Demetrius would retreat into his office, and Giulia would leave the house and not return until well after lunch.

Giulia was a loner by nature. She didn't have many friends, and he liked that about her. She also didn't have any close family. He liked that too. Giulia's family perished in a fire when she was a teenager. Her father had a love of scotch, and after a few too many one night, he fell asleep and knocked over a candle, engulfing the house in flames as the family slept. Giulia was the first to wake that night, but it was too late. Realizing her family was doomed, she saved herself by breaking a second-story window with her fist and escaping down a tree.

She inherited her father's jewelry store in Amsterdam. That was where he had met Giulia. Demetrius was working on legal work for a friend who had moved to Amsterdam to cash in on the trade boom that had erupted, making merchants rich overnight. He had wandered by her shop one afternoon and glimpsed her in the window talking to a patron. He was immediately drawn to her gentle demeanor and how her eyes sparkled as brightly as the gemstone bracelet in her hand. Demetrius waited until the patron left, then entered her shop, where he purchased a ring for his mother.

Over the next two weeks, he returned to purchase three more items until he finally got the courage to ask her out. Demetrius learned her story and decided he wanted to rescue her from the life she had inherited. She would not have to worry about selling jewelry with him, and she could leave behind all the worldly matters that were meant for men.

"Any woman in this town would have been happy to marry me," Demetrius said bitterly. He poured another glass. "But I had wanted her."

So, he'd asked her to marry him. It was a simple, straightforward proposal. He was not an extravagant man. He presented her with a single gold band. She accepted, and he was pleased.

She sold her father's jewelry store, which provided him with the required dowery, and they packed up her belongings in two suitcases. Giulia didn't own much, a few dresses and a collection of jewels that had been passed down in her family for generations. Demetrius didn't protest. He allowed her to take them with her. Although he warned her that she wouldn't be wearing them when she arrived in his town. It would be immodest for a woman of her position to flaunt such wealth.

Instead, he hired a local carpenter to build her a jewelry case to house her collection. It would be her wedding gift. He designed the case himself. It stood on carved wooden legs, six feet tall, with red velvet-lined shelves. The case had a glass door that locked with a small brass key. It was the most frivolous piece of furniture he had ever purchased, but her happiness was worth it.

They left Amsterdam one bright spring day when the tulips were in bloom. They drove past her family's plot of land on their way out of town. Nothing remained amongst the scorched ground and scattered ashes of what was once a home.

Demetrius recalled a collection of old books from her father he had kept in his office. She had pleaded with him to take the books with her, but the Church was tightening its grip on heretical material and it would be a hassle to obtain the required permits to transport books across regional lines. Besides, she would not be reading them. Everyone knew it was dangerous for a wife to read. Such activity was sure to elicit impure thoughts and corrupt a woman's mind, thus corrupting her soul. The Church's prudence on such matters was well justified. Oblivious to the look of despair upon his wife's face, the books he told her would stay.

"She was lucky that I found her," he said to his glass.

Demetrius ran his hand through his long wispy hair. He knew he was journeying into dark territory with these memories, but he was defenseless against the resentment that seemed to suck him down a bottomless well.

He looked back on those first years of marriage and struggled to recall a clue, any clue that would have alerted him to the devil lurking beneath. But she had given nothing away. Her demeanor remained calm and unwavering.

"She was happy in her new life," he swore. "The one I gave her. She performed her duties with obedience and steadfastness. She always greeted me with a smile and never seemed perturbed by the daily inconveniences that life inevitably brings one's way."

He could feel his chest tighten. "The corruption must have occurred later, perhaps at the birth of our son," Demetrius spoke to the empty room. "Yes, the boy must have infected her body in some way. He was not good, but he was the one who had informed me of her corruption. Without him, I may never have known what demonic activity she was engaged in all those long hours spent away from the shelter of our home. *My* home."

Demetrius twirled the gold ring on his left pinkie with his thumb, a habit he'd developed over the years. The ring had become an extension of his body - yet another thing he claimed as his own.

He looked down at the two gold bands on each of his fingers resting side by side, just as they should have been together, until death. "I should never have given her the freedom to wander out into the world alone," Demetrius took another sip of wine, "and I should never have given her a warning."

And with that final thought, his heart raced out of control. He gripped his chest, his heart tightened and released one last time, and he fell face forward onto the table, spilling the wine. Freed from the confines of the glass, the red liquid assumed its natural state and flowed over the edge of the table, pooling on the floor and staining his boots.

Giulia

Alpinella, Italy

April, 1522, Eleven years prior…

Demetrius yanked the black sheet away in one sweeping gesture and smiled broadly. "What do you think? It's your wedding gift. I had it made especially for you."

Giulia stood in front of the jewelry case in disbelief. It was big and ugly, and she instantly hated it. The proportions were off. It was top-heavy, and the four spindly legs appeared as if they would collapse under its massive weight.

She managed a smile and replied, "How thoughtful of you."

She reached for the handle and tried to open the glass door.

"I have the key," Demetrius said.

"Where is it?"

"It's in my office safe," he said dismissively as he folded the black fabric neatly into a square. "Isn't it lovely? All of your family jewels are neatly organized for you to admire. I even had everything polished for you." He looked satisfied, as if this single act had guaranteed her contentment for the rest of her life. "I have some work to do. I'll see you at dinner." Demetrius kissed her on the forehead and left her alone in the bedroom.

She laid her hand upon the glass door and stared at the monstrosity in front of her. Generations of priceless family jewels were all locked away in what looked to be a child's dollhouse. Except, unlike a child, she couldn't play with her treasures. Instead, she was on the outside looking in on the memories of her past. Everything she owned, her necklaces, rings, and bracelets, were now under lock and key.

Her lock, his key.

She clenched her jaw. But, there was one thing she'd brought with her she had kept hidden and vowed he would never touch.

Giulia lifted her hand from the door and studied the ghostly print that remained. Then she held up both of her hands and laid them down repeatedly, covering every inch of the glass.

That evening she lay on her back. She felt a soft mass move above her and a rectangular object pressed between her shoulder blades beneath her. She tried to block out the sight of his face as he rocked back and forth on top of her. Giulia didn't care for the grimace contorting his mouth, so she turned her head and patiently waited for it to end. He always had trouble and told her not to move. So, she would lie still, and eventually, he would let out a grunt that reminded her of the hogs at her grandmother's home, and she knew it was over. Then he would roll over and go to sleep, and she would pull her nightgown down around her legs and think of other things.

That night, like so many others, sleep evaded her. She lay on her side and gazed at the jewels locked away in the case.

She wondered if she'd made the right decision to marry him, and she wondered what fate awaited her in this tiny village.

Eventually, she grew tired and closed her eyes.

Alpinella

November, 1532

Giulia felt no connection to her son. How could one feel a connection with someone like him? So detached and uncaring. The faraway look in his eyes, the constant need for control, and the abnormal obsessiveness dominated every aspect of their lives.

At the age of eight, it was clear her son was unique. But not unique in the sense that he possessed exceptional talents setting him apart and making him special in the eyes of his mother. No, this child was something else. He wasn't just different. Something darker and more sinister was lurking beneath. It wasn't anything he'd particularly done that disturbed her. It was the way he was. His mere presence could cause her unease.

Clearly, other people felt the same. He had no friends at his school, and the teachers complained that, although he grasped the academic lessons with ease, he lacked compassion and empathy. They warned her that her son would have a troublesome life ahead if he didn't change. They urged her to find a way to change him.

Change.

Change was for seasons or clothes. Not for people. Giulia knew people did not change. They weren't butterflies, after all. People were born the way they were born, and no amount of pleading or bargaining could alter them.

So, like any good mother, she tried to see only the good in her son. But a mother always has a keen understanding of her offspring, and she couldn't escape what she knew deep down in her bones. The boy was not good.

It had been a long and painful birth, and when she finally held him in her arms, she was shocked at what she saw. Or, rather, did not see. There was no light surrounding him, and she always saw the light around everyone, no matter how brilliant or faint.

As Enzo grew, more problems emerged. Smaller and less physically capable than the other boys his age, he was often the target of relentless bullying. Eventually, he retreated into a world of his own making—a world where he could control the outcome of the mental games he set into motion. A world where he answered to no one and everyone did as he commanded—a world where people feared him.

Giulia had heard tales from the villagers about the odd boy who spent long hours alone in the woods catching small prey and conducting experiments on them until they eventually succumbed to death. Then, disappointed in their lack of resilience, he would toss them aside and begin work on the next. She had never seen the scattered animal remains, and could not allow herself to believe that any child could commit such an act.

Grateful that her son was finally attending school, she was free to leave the confines of her house. She ran errands and chatted with the local women, although she never cultivated close relationships with any of them. Giulia was content in the solitude of her own company.

On some days, she would take the long way home and walk along the river, collecting stones that she would line along the windowsill in the kitchen. Stones that, unlike her jewels, she could touch.

On one particular day, she took a different path down a road she'd never ventured before. It was a path covered in a blanket of moss that meandered through the woods and led to a small inn on the edge of an emerald lake. The lake was famous amongst the locals, but her husband had never taken her to see it. He didn't believe in squandering time when there was work to be done instead.

That day she decided to go.

The sun was high above the mountains when she arrived at the inn. It was small, well kept, and inviting. The busiest time was in the summer when people came to enjoy the lake and escape the oppressive heat of the overpacked cities. But now, it looked vacant except for a few lazy cats sunning themselves on the front steps. After the long walk, Giulia was tired and thirsty, so she decided to stop for tea before heading home.

Next to the front door, hung a wooden sign that read, *Albergo Pietra Bella.* As she opened the door, a brass bell swung back and forth and made a delicate tinkering sound. She stepped into the dining room that smelled of cloves and ashes. It was modestly adorned with several tables draped in ivory lace and wooden chairs. A single taper candle in a brass candle stick was lit at each table. A fire was burning in the fireplace, and a collection of family portraits hung on the adjacent wall.

She took a seat by the window and gazed out across the lake. The sunlight danced off the water and sparkled like the crystal-encrusted cloaks she had seen draped over the women at Carnivale. Her father had taken her to Venice once as a child, and she remembered it vividly. The colors, jewels, and masks were unlike anything she had ever seen. She felt like she had entered into a fantasy world, a world existing in another time and place.

Giulia thought about her life in Amsterdam. She remembered the hours spent with her mother, reading by the fire to pass the long winter evenings and the summers spent with her father in his shop, watching him make beautiful jewelry pieces for the wealthy patrons. Giulia tried desperately to keep the details of her memories alive, but time was steadily dissolving the past into a faded dream.

Then, the fire happened and changed the entire course of her life. Another thing that can change: the course of one's life.

A door opened behind the bar, interrupting her thoughts. She looked up to see a man enter the dining room and approach her table. "I'm sorry, I didn't realize someone was here. We usually don't get many travellers this time of year."

He took a step closer.

"I'm Gabriele." The single flame from the candle danced in both of his eyes.

It was late afternoon by the time she left. Giulia had spent longer at the inn than planned, but she didn't care. She was happy. It wasn't that something profound had occurred. They had talked about the mountains, the inn, and the snow. The man had asked her questions.

Giulia wasn't used to people asking her questions, especially a man. He'd put her at ease, and he seemed genuinely interested in her responses. So, Giulia loosened her tongue and found, much to her surprise, that her mind held many ideas about things she had never considered.

Giulia was sad to leave, but he had asked her to come back. Anytime, he said. And she knew he meant it.

As she walked home, Giulia noticed subtle changes happening inside of her. A lightness filled her entire being. She noticed that her feet didn't feel so heavy, her heart fluttered in her chest, and her lips decided they felt better curving up toward the sky.

When Giulia arrived home, the sun was setting behind the mountain peaks. It was shaping into a long dark winter, but she didn't feel the impending cold. She was blinded by the light reflecting off the snow.

Gabriele

"They can bewitch them by a touch and a look, or by a look only..."

Malleus Maleficarum, Part 2
Question I
Heinrich Kramer, 1486 AD

Albergo Pietra Bella

March, 1532

"But why are you leaving so soon, Gabriele?" Francesca asked. A look of disappointment crossed her face as she placed her hands on her swollen belly. "It's not even Easter. I thought you would be staying through the summer."

"I know, but there's some business I need to tend to with some shipments."

Francesca looked skeptical. "But can't Rico take care of it? Isn't that why you made him a partner? To oversee the business while you are gone?"

"I won't be long. Three or four months at the most."

Francesca sighed, "I understand, but I was hoping you would be here to meet your new niece or nephew."

"Don't worry, we will have plenty of time to get acquainted." He stood and playfully rubbed the top of her head. "Don't look so sad, sister. I'll be back before you know it."

Gabriele walked upstairs and entered his small bedroom at the end of the hall. He took a small leather satchel from a drawer and tossed it on the bed. He looked inside the drawer. There wasn't much to pack, a few sweaters and some trousers. It could wait. He slammed the drawer shut and plopped on the bed, crossing his hands behind his head.

He wasn't thinking about the trip back to Constantinople. He knew the journey well, having traveled it many times, running trade shipments between Italy and the East. Besides, he never worried about travelling alone or losing his way. No matter where he journeyed, he had a map above him in the sky and keen instincts in his bones.

He stared up at the ceiling. It was thoughts of Giulia that raced through his mind.

Following the death of his parents, he returned to help his half-sister and her husband run the inn. With Francesca bedridden most of the pregnancy, her husband was grateful for the help, and Gabriele welcomed the chance to enjoy a simpler life on solid ground. Life at sea was physical, and working at the inn was a pleasant respite. He enjoyed the simple daily routines and entertaining the guests with tales of the sea and far-off places he had visited.

And then, one day, a guest entered the inn. He knew he was swimming in dangerous waters. She was married to a prominent clerk in the region, and the last thing he needed was a scandal at the inn. Still, he could not resist asking her to come back and see him.

Weeks passed, the sun lingered a little longer in the sky, and winter was slowly releasing its grip. Giulia had come each week to have tea and talk with him. He looked forward to those days with anticipation. As she talked, he listened to her voice that rose and fell along with her emotions. He memorized the faint freckles speckled across her nose and cheeks and he liked the way the sunbeams danced off the copper highlights in her hair.

He had spent years studying the current beneath his oars and mapping the stars above his head. He relished the rush of adrenaline and sense of power that came from steering a ship through choppy seas and navigating torrential storms. But now, for the first time, he knew how the tide felt when it surrendered to the moon. And it was making him uneasy. He did not know women, but he knew the sea; and Gabriele sensed in her an underlying current that he knew could turn into a riptide and carry him away.

So, he would be leaving sooner than planned. It was for the best, before he was caught in a storm from which he could not find his way out.

He would tell her this afternoon.

Giulia

"A rebellious and sinful spirit of life is subject to an obedient, pious and just spirit of life. And those Creatures which are more perfect and nearer to God have authority over the others."

Malleus Maleficarum, Part 1

Question IV

Heinrich Kramer, 1486 AD

Albergo Pietra Bella

March, 1532

Giulia watched as a woman with a full belly walked into the dining room at the inn. She felt an incredible pressure in her head and a ripping in her chest that felt like her heart was breaking away, falling to the floor.

The woman had dark circles under her eyes, but her face was glowing like a woman filled with the promise of new life.

"Why are you up, Francesca?" Gabriele asked. "I told you that you've done enough today and should be resting. The doctor said you must rest."

"I know, but it's been months, and I'm sick and tired of being in bed. Besides, baking a pie isn't going to kill me. And now, I would like to enjoy a piece." She looked down at the two of them sitting at the table by the window. "I'll bring three pieces. And a match for the candle." She smiled brightly and turned toward the kitchen.

"Let me help you at least," he said, hurrying after her. "I told you not to overdo it."

Giulia's head was swimming. She had to get out. Standing up and heading toward the door, she wanted to be gone before he returned. Giulia hurried across the lawn. Her eyes stung with tears, that she fought desperately to keep back. She felt foolish and naive. Of course, he had a wife. He wasn't living in this world alone, not a man like him. But people see what they want to see and believe what they want to believe. She wrapped her cloak tighter around her chest and headed across the lawn toward the cover of the forest.

"Giulia!" she heard Gabriele calling her name behind her. She quickened her pace, but she heard her name again, and this time it was closer. Feeling a hand on her arm, Giulia twirled around.

"Where are you going?" he asked.

She tried to hide her face under the hood of her cloak.

"I remembered I have to get home. I'm sorry, but I'm very late."

She turned to leave, but he was still holding on to her arm.

"But, you can't leave without trying the pie first."

"I really need to get back."

"But my sister will be very disappointed if you don't at least try it."

She looked up, perplexed. She wasn't sure if she had heard him correctly.

"Your sister?"

He stared deeply into her eyes, and she knew he could read her thoughts. He casually offered, "Well, step-sister, to be exact. My father remarried when my mother died. Anyway, she spent all morning baking it, and you can see by her condition that that was no easy feat," he said, chuckling.

"But… who is her…."

"Luca, our groundsman."

Suddenly, she had another thought. It was a thought she had never had before. It was daring, dangerous, and bold, and it felt like the best thought she had ever had. She took Gabriele's hand and led him deeper into the woods.

They came to a small clearing in the forest. Turning to face Gabriele, she untied her cloak around her neck and spread it on the ground.

Her heart was racing, but her hands were steady as she unbuttoned her dress and let it fall to the ground at her feet. She reached up, wrapped her arms around his neck, and kissed him. His mouth melted into her, and they fell upon the cloak and continued undressing one another.

She wrapped her legs around his waist. Giulia ran her fingers through his hair and down the nape of his neck. Her body oscillated between waves of release and tension as deep moans and gentle sighs escaped her lips, coming from somewhere inside her she didn't know existed.

They continued moving at a steady and rhythmic pace until, eventually, her entire body shook uncontrollably, and she let out a cry. As she screamed, she felt the outer layers of herself crack open, and she finally broke free of the shell that had contained her for so long.

She gazed beyond the treetops and into the endless blue sea above them. She couldn't be sure if she felt it in her heart or imagined it in her mind, but Giulia was sure she saw the sky explode into a million tiny prisms and rain down upon them.

Entwined in each other's arms, they lingered in silence, listening to the sounds of the forest, when suddenly, they heard a snap, then another. It was the sound of footsteps. She bolted up in time to see a young boy, carrying what looked like a bloody stick, dart into the woods. Her blood ran cold. She caught only a fleeting glimpse, but she knew who it was.

They both fumbled to put their clothes back on. Giulia pulled her dress over her head, and without bothering with her shoes, she ran after him, calling his name and begging him to stop, but he had disappeared into the forest's shadows.

She ran further into the woods and found a small area between three large trees. She covered her hand to her mouth to stifle the screams. In the middle of the circle, dozens of small animals were piled on top of one another, their bodies mutilated into bloody, mangled masses. She bent over, willing herself not to faint. Then she felt two arms encircle her from behind.

Her head spun, as a wave of sickness overcame her. Gabriele steadied her, but she pushed him away, breaking free from his arms, and ran home.

Three days had passed. Giulia and Gabriele sat on the edge of the bed in the guest room at the end of the hall.

"You can't stay. It's too dangerous. He's too dangerous." Gabriele's voice was grave, and the creases in his forehead deepened as he waited for her response.

She knew he was talking about the boy—her son. The eight-year-old boy who tortured innocent creatures in the woods.

"I know. And I have a plan," Giulia replied slowly, rubbing her hands on her thighs. "I decided to leave."

"Where will you go, back to your family in Amsterdam?"

"I have no family. Not anymore. Besides, my husband would look for me there," she said. "There's a small village further north, by the sea. My grandparents had a cabin there."

He placed his hand over hers. "You can come with me."

"Where? What about the inn? Your family? You can't just leave them. Your sister needs you."

"I had never planned to stay here. I came here to help Francesca after my father died. I always planned to return to Constantinople and continue my trade business."

"I didn't know you were from Constantinople."

"I didn't say from. I moved there to work in the trade."

"I guess there's a lot we don't know about each other."

"I know all I need to. We could go to a port city, take a boat to Cyprus, and then head to Turkey."

"Isn't it dangerous there? Aren't the Italians fighting with the Turks?"

"It's no more dangerous than it is here. I promise, once we get settled, you'll be safe."

"I don't know what to say. I have much to consider."

"Just say yes. It's only a matter of time before your son tells your husband what he saw. He could report you to the Church," his voice wavered. "They've killed women for far less."

"Give me a few weeks. I need time to think. To plan."

"What if you don't have a few weeks?"

"Please, I'm just asking for a little time."

"So your answer is yes?"

"It isn't no."

The days dragged on and Giulia became more anxious. Her stomach lurched at the mere thought of food, and her nights were filled with a mixture of both dread and anticipation.

But the following week, Giulia awoke to sunlight streaming through the window and birds chirping in the trees. She lingered just a bit longer in bed, enjoying the warm sunlight on her skin coming through the window. She had reached a decision. She wasn't afraid of the unknown; she had started over once before.

Walking into the kitchen, she walked past her son sitting at the table eating breakfast. He didn't look at her. She poured herself a cup of tea. The boy walked over and placed his plate on the counter in front of her. She looked at the toast on the plate. He had torn the bread into tiny little pieces and covered it with strawberry jam. It reminded her of the scene from the forest.

He looked straight into her eyes that bore into her like hot daggers and walked out.

She turned and wretched into the nearest pot. Slowly, she wiped her mouth with the back of her hand. She looked out the window across the green pasture. It wouldn't be long now, and she would be on her way.

Out of nowhere, she felt a blow from the back of a hand hit her on the side of her face, knocking her to the floor, and the world turned black.

She blinked, and the room came into focus, but she couldn't remember why she was lying on the floor.

"You," a voice bellowed from above her.

Her head swam in a sea of confusion. Giulia struggled to stand, but Demetrius put his boot on her back and pushed her back to the floor.

"It has come to my attention that you're more comfortable down there."

He applied more pressure with his boot.

"I could never understand what was wrong with our son, and now I know. It's your blood that runs through his veins. You tricked me, hiding the devil beneath that pleasant smile."

She didn't say a word, terrified so much as to breathe.

"But now I know. I'm going make sure you burn for this." Demetrius applied a bit more pressure before lifting his boot. "Just like your family."

He put his coat and hat on and then walked toward the back door. Then, without turning around, he said, "You've made me late for my appointment."

Giulia waited until she heard the door shut. Then she stood, holding herself steady on the counter, trying to slow the thoughts racing out of control in her head. Giulia had heard the stories of other women in the region being arrested. What had been done to them. She knew she had to leave now.

Giulia turned to go upstairs and saw her son standing in the doorway with his satchel and staring at her with those cold vacant eyes.

"Go," she demanded, "you're late for school."

Giulia brushed past him, staggering toward the stairs.

She watched from her room until she saw the boy leave down the winding road that led to town. She breathed a sigh of relief, and suddenly, a sense of calm descended upon her. Knowing what she had to do, Giulia hurried to implement her plan.

She grabbed her leather bag from the top of her armoire and dusted it off. Giulia scanned the contents of the bedroom. There wasn't time to go back downstairs. She opened her armoire and looked at the dresses hanging neatly in front of her. Removing a brown wool dress from the hanger, Giulia wrapped it around her hand. Then she walked to her jewelry case and stood in front of the doors. She caught her reflection in the glass. Giulia was no longer the young girl who had first stood in front of it all those years ago, unsure and obedient - the one who placed her hands upon the glass, too scared to take what belonged to her.

Today, she saw a different woman. She saw a woman who had uncovered new facets of herself and was no longer afraid to take what was hers.

She saw a woman who had changed.

Giulia remembered the fire in her house. She remembered putting her fist through the window without a second thought.

Smiling at the woman in front of her, she lifted her fist, and for the second time in her life, she shattered a pane of glass to save herself.

Working as quickly as she could, Giulia piled her jewelry into the leather satchel. She took every piece except one. It was a butterfly pendant her father had made for her when she was young. A piece of the delicate wing, in every color of the rainbow, was encased inside glass and sealed around the edge with gold. She had never taken it off, hiding it beneath her clothes so no one would see. Removing it from around her neck, she placed it in the center of the shelf. Instinctively, she ripped the gold wedding band from her finger and placed it over the butterfly.

Then she turned back toward the bed and dropped to her knees.

Reaching her arm under the bed, Giulia pushed aside the mulberry branches used to keep the fleas at bay, and searched beneath the mattress and bed beams. Her hand felt the familiar wooden surface and pulled it out. She laid it on top of her jewels and buckled the satchel, now heavy with metal and gemstones - the currency for her new life.

Swinging the bag over her shoulder, she ran downstairs and out of the house. As fast as her feet could carry her, Giulia headed in the direction of the inn.

Demetrius

"…they distract the minds of men, driving them to madness, insane hatred, and inordinate lusts."

Malleus Maleficarum Part 1

Question II

Heinrich Kramer, 1486 AD

Alpinella, Italy

March, 1532

Demetrius was the first to arrive home that afternoon. The meeting with this client had gone well, despite the interruption he had experienced that morning. Afterwards, he had gone to visit the priest, but by the time Demetrius had arrived, it was well past lunchtime, and the priest had retired to his home for the rest of the day. Unperturbed, he headed home. Another day would not make a difference.

Demetrius knew the priest would be sympathetic to his plight and remedy the situation promptly. There had been a dozen trials in the area in the past year, so he knew the process was clear-cut. The priest would prepare the necessary documents set forth by the Holy Inquisition, and his wife would be arrested on charges of witchcraft. The trials were conducted promptly to spare the men further pain and humiliation. His son, although odd, would be a reliable witness. A conviction was assured. He could put the entire matter behind him and move on with his life, confident that he had done his duty. He had not only saved his family but also saved the community by ridding it of the devil's insidious grip. He was a good man and pleasing in the eyes of God.

The house was quiet when he arrived home. He hung up his coat and walked into the kitchen. All the activity had left him thirsty.

His son would be home from school soon, and he assumed his wife was upstairs in bed, where she had been for the past several weeks. He knew she would be trying desperately to come up with a way to beseech his forgiveness. But it was too late for that. Everyone knew that once the devil has taken hold of a woman, the two become entwined, and only a priest could exorcise him from her body. There was nothing he could do.

He finished his tea and headed upstairs. When he opened the door to the bedroom, he was surprised to see the bed was empty. Then he saw the jewelry case and felt as if his head would explode.

Enzo

"And we read often in history of children whom their mothers, in some passion or mental disturbance, have unthinkingly offered to the devil from the very womb, and how it is only with the very greatest difficulty that they can, when they have grown to adult age, be delivered from that bondage which the devil has, with God's permission, usurped to himself."

Malleus Maleficarum, Part 2

Chapter XIII

Heinrich Kramer, 1486 AD

Alpinella, Italy

March, 1532

When Enzo arrived home from school, the house appeared in order. He sat at the dining table, slicing an apple and thinking about the girl he saw each day on his way to school. She never paid him any attention, avoiding his gaze whenever he tried to catch her eye. He thought about how wonderful it would feel to take a pair of scissors and cut off her long blond ponytail that swung like a horse's tail when she walked. Then, he could braid the strands of hair into small ropes to put around the necks of his tiny animals. Strangulation fascinated him the most.

He swallowed his last bite of apple and climbed the stairs to his mother's room. He wanted to find her sewing kit and see if she had a pair of scissors that he could hide in his school satchel.

Enzo walked toward the room at the end of the hall, where the door to the bedroom stood open. He found his father sitting on the bed, his shoulders hunched over. He heard glass grind beneath his boot as he made his way around the bed, causing him to stop. He looked toward his father, who was staring blankly ahead at the empty jewelry case, rolling a gold band between his thumb and forefinger.

The realization hit him. His mother was gone. The boy's entire body trembled uncontrollably. Then, a shiny object resting on the shelf caught his eye. He stepped toward the case. The butterfly pendant.

He studied it closer. He had seen it once before, hanging around his mother's neck that day in the woods.

Slowly, he bent over and reached for a shard of glass lying at his feet. He squeezed it until blood trickled between his fingers. Enzo felt a sudden urge to hunt some prey.

Giulia

Albergo Pietra Bella

March, 1532

Giulia arrived at the inn breathless, her cheeks flushed and sweat on her brow.

Gabriele met her at the door. "My god, what happened to your cheek?" he asked.

Her body was coursing with adrenaline. "He knows. My son told him."

"I have everything ready. We should leave immediately."

The journey to Venice had been slow and arduous, but they finally arrived at his Aunt Maria's home, where they could stay before boarding the ship to Cyprus.

Both Giulia and Gabriele were trying their best to ignore the fact that she was growing weaker each day and unable to keep food down. His aunt sat Giulia down by the fire and covered her with a blanket. Then she took her nephew aside and spoke in a whisper, "She doesn't look well. How long has she been in this state?"

Giulia heard them whisper in hushed tones and could only make out a few phrases.

"She is not well… should not travel until she is better," she said.

"That is not possible… must leave tomorrow… make it…."

Giulia stood up, but she immediately felt lightheaded and dizzy. Cursing her condition, she sat back down. She couldn't believe the timing that she should be this ill now. She was never sick. The last time she had felt this bad was when she... her head spun as she calculated the days in her mind—since the day in the woods. There could only be one explanation.

Gabriele walked over to Giulia and knelt down, a troubled look crossed his face. "Do you think you can make it aboard the ship tomorrow? The seas are calm, but if you have never been on a ship before, it could be difficult for you," Gabriele said.

"I'm sure I will be fine. I just need a good night's rest," Giulia replied.

"My aunt offered for you to stay here with her until you are recovered. I can go on to Turkey to get everything settled and then come back for you."

"I promise I will be better in the morning," she assured him.

His forehead furrowed and he didn't look convinced.

"Why don't you go to bed. You need to rest. My aunt made the bed for you."

"I can make the journey, I know I can."

"It will only be for a month at the most. And then I will be back for you." Gabriele squeezed her hand. "You need to regain your strength."

The next morning, she stood on the sidewalk, her arms crossed tightly in front of her, shivering.

"You need to go back inside and get warm," Gabriele said.

"There's something I need to tell you before you go. I'm pregnant with your child."

She waited for him to fill the silence that engulfed them.

He smiled broadly and replied, "Now I have two things to hurry back for."

She struggled to hold back a flood of tears as she watched his grey figure slowly disappear down the canal.

Suddenly, a subtle tingling sensation overcame her. She put both hands on her stomach. Expecting the usual wave of nausea, she swallowed hard, willing for it to pass. Instead, she felt a wave of heat rise from her belly and settle in her heart.

The canal was quiet that morning except for a young couple walking past her arm in arm; an older woman shaking a blanket out of her window, and a man passing in a gondola. None were aware of the beam of light that shot out of her heart, cut through the fog, and shone like a beacon onto Gabriele's back. When she could no longer see his outline, the heat in her chest subsided. She gasped for breath and let the tears flow freely down her cheeks.

On the other side of the canal, one girl with eyes the color of indigo did see. She peered through a window and smiled at the spectacle of light she had seen dance between the man and a woman, whose tears continued to fall despite the rainbow of light dancing all around her.

Francesca

Albergo Pietra Bella

May, 1533

The brass bell rang above the front door, alerting Francesca of the arrival of a guest. She sighed in exasperation. Another guest. She had just sat down to feed her baby for the third time, and she was interrupted yet again.

"I'm so sorry, little one." She gently stroked the baby's cheek and stood up. "Magdalena," she said, turning toward the maid stirring a steaming pot of polenta, "could you watch him while I tend to the guest?"

Magdalena wiped her hands on her apron. "Of course, signora."

Francesca walked into the dining room, where a man and young boy were standing next to the fireplace.

"Good afternoon," Francesca said warmly. "Welcome to Albergo Pietra Bella."

She studied the man. He held a hat in his hand, but did not carry any luggage with him. His hair was disheveled. Seeming agitated, his eyes twitched nervously from side to side. The boy's stoic expression ran shivers down her spine.

"If you want a room, I'm afraid we have none available."

"I'm not in need of a room. My name is Demetrius, and this is my son, Enzo." He fidgeted with his hat, and looked around the room. "I'm looking for a man."

Demetrius turned his uneasy gaze toward her. Francesca's eyes immediately darted to the portrait of a young man hanging on the wall. The rapid-fire glance went unnoticed by the man, but not the boy, whose eyes she felt narrow in on her.

"He would have been traveling alone, about a year ago," pressed Demetrius.

"As you can imagine, many travellers come through the inn over a year's time."

"This man could have been with a woman. A local woman."

She did not like where this stranger's comments were headed. "I do not recall such a man. I'm sorry I can't be of any help, but I need to get back to work if there's nothing else."

Demetrius straightened his back. "Of course, and I apologize for disturbing you. Come along, Enzo."

The boy shot his father a sideways glance, which Francesca could see was filled with disgust, but he did not respond to his father.

"It's no problem at all," replied Francesca, desperately wanting them to leave.

The man laughed nervously and put his hand on the boy's head. "I think it's time we head home for lunch. Does that sound good?"

The man and the boy turned and walked toward the door. She heard the boy mumble to his father as they closed the door behind them, "How could you give up so easily?"

Francesca watched them through the window as they walked down the road. She pulled the lace curtain tightly over the window and returned to the kitchen.

She sat at the wooden table and tried to steady her hands as she raised the spoon full of smashed peas and polenta to her baby's mouth. She cursed herself for having hung Gabriele's portrait back up on the wall. But it had been over a year, and she missed the comfort of seeing her brother's face in the dining room.

Violetta

"And it should be noted that there was a defect in the formation of the first woman, since she was formed from a bent rib, that is, a rib of the breast, which is bent as it were in a contrary direction to a man. And since through this defect she is an imperfect animal, she always deceives."

Malleus Maleficarum, Part 1

Question VI

Heinrich Kramer, 1486 AD

Venice, Italy

January, 1553

Carnivale was approaching. The time of year when the city became the
backdrop for flamboyant costumes painting the grey city with bold
strokes of purple, red, crimson, and gold. A time for decadence,
drama, and transforming into someone else.

"This one for our party!" Violetta exclaimed, laying the gold and silver
brocade gown on her mother's bed next to the five other ones she'd
spread out over the silk coverlet.

Violetta pictured herself dressed and dancing the night away. It was her
favorite time of the year. Everything about the week-long celebration
was magical, and she wanted to make the most of it.

Picking up the royal purple dress covered in intricate needlework and
crystals, she held the velvet bodice up to her chest and twirled around
the floor. "And this one is for the Doge's Ball."

"Violetta, you won't be going to any ball if you don't finish your
studies." Giulia took the dress. "Now go on. Your tutor is waiting."

"But mother, how can I possibly think of studying right now? When
everything is just getting started."

"Studies first, then you can think about your dresses." Her mother
smiled and motioned for her to leave her room.

Violetta turned to leave and paused at the portrait of a man she had
never met. "Do you think father would have enjoyed Carnivale?"

Giulia hung up the dress and looked at the portrait of Gabriele. Then
she turned toward her daughter's expectant face and smiled. "I think he
would have liked celebrating with us very much."

That look crept into her mother's eyes, the way it always did when Violetta mentioned her father. Seventeen years had passed, and Violetta noticed her mother had finally begun to speak about him in the past tense, but the small painting, mounted inside a simple wooden frame, still hung next to her bed.

The house was filled with art in every room, but in her mother's bedroom, only this one piece adorned the walls - the portrait of her father. The artist had worked for months, transferring the image of her father's face from her mother's memory onto canvas, and she vowed never to take it down until the day he returned.

Violetta turned around at the door. "Could I ask one more favor?"

"Of course, darling."

"Could you pick out a necklace from the shop to wear with the purple dress?"

"I promise I'll find something nice. Now hurry along, your tutor is waiting."

Giulia

Venice

January, 1553

Giulia turned the key and pushed open the heavy wooden door to her shop. A small silver bell tinkered as she closed the door behind her. She had long since grown accustomed to the way the sound of a bell resonated through her ears, then passed the knot in her throat, and stirred memories resting in her heart.

She walked across the stone floor and over to the long case on the back wall. She knew exactly which item she needed. Giulia pulled the black drape off the top and peered through the glass. In the center, a necklace was displayed on a red velvet cushion. It was the only one in the shop that was not for sale. An emerald and diamond choker her grandfather had made for his wife's birthday. Giulia turned the lock and reached for the necklace. She held it up and admired the alternating pear-cut diamonds and emeralds. Her grandfather said he had chosen emeralds because they shone like the green flecks in his wife's eyes, and she remembered wishing she had green eyes instead of blue. As he fastened it around her neck, he explained how, rather than hang, he had designed it to fit like a crown around her neck.

She held the necklace up to the light and smiled. It was the first piece she had sold to Sahadi, a local spice merchant and close friend of Gabriele's aunt. It had been an ambivalent gesture to help her get started, with the understanding that she would buy it back from him one day.

Her plan had been uncertain, but she continued to find buyers for the jewelry pieces she had brought with her. Soon, she had enough money to open a modest store and workshop in a lively Bohemian neighborhood where the best courtesans in Venice lived. Not only was the rent more affordable, but it proved to be an auspicious location for wealthy men to purchase a gift on their way to call on their favorite courtesan.

She placed the emerald necklace in a silk drawstring bag and closed the glass case, locking the lid. Then she went into the back room to retrieve some cash from the metal safe she kept hidden behind a stone in the wall.

She hummed to herself as she removed the stone and opened the door to the safe, where she saw the wooden box lying on the left. She reached in and took a small stack of cash from the pile. Just then, she heard the silver bell ring. She quickly closed the safe and replaced the stone.

"You're in early today," Giulia said, stepping back into the shop, expecting to see the young apprentice she had hired to make her custom designs.

She gasped when she entered the room, and the necklace and cash fell to the floor. She reached for the case to steady herself.

"I've been trying to find you for a long time," he said, taking a step in her direction.

Giulia put her hand over heart. "Gabriele, you're back," she exclaimed in disbelief.

They sat in the dining room. The maid delivered a silver tea tray and placed it on the table.

"Is there anything else you need?"

"That will be all, thank you," replied Giulia, and the maid quietly left the room.

Giulia took the cup from the tray and placed it in front of Gabriele.

There were so many questions, but for the moment, she couldn't seem to find words.

She grabbed the sugar bowl nervously, and he reached across and put her hand over hers.

She sat back in her chair and looked at him. "Tell me everything," she said.

Slowly, he began to recount the years of his absence.

"I left you that morning and boarded a ship to Cyprus. When we entered the bay, we encountered a Turkish ship, and fighting broke out. They seized our ship, and we were taken as prisoners. I spent five years in a Turkish prison. I eventually escaped, along with two other prisoners. I returned to my aunt's house to find she had died. I was able to track down her lawyer, but he refused to divulge the details of her estate. So, I went back to the inn. I thought Francesca may have known where I could find you, but she said she had not heard from you."

"I didn't want to put her in danger," replied Giulia. "You never saw Demetrius or my son?"

"No. I did not want to stay long and raise any suspicions. So, from there, I went to Amsterdam. I made countless inquiries, but no one had seen or heard from you since you had left. I felt I had exhausted my options for the time being, so I went back to Turkey to continue work and rebuild my trade business."

"So, what made you come back to Venice?"

"Well, I thought you surely would have left Venice, especially considering that my aunt had died, but something kept nagging at me that perhaps you had stayed. It's an easy place to disappear. So, I came back frequently, looking for you. One day I was walking down a canal and passed a jewelry store, and it hit me. It made perfect sense. So I went to the local consulate and requested a register of every jewelry store in the city. I scoured the list, looking for your name, but found none. Then it occurred to me that you probably changed your name. So, I took the list to my aunt's lawyer and asked him to see if any of the names were familiar. He said he could not divulge any information. He said he had signed papers at the request of my aunt not to reveal the names or any information regarding her will. He was sorry, but it was sealed. My aunt obviously thought me to be dead and did not want anyone to find you."

"Your aunt was very kind to us. She helped me with our papers, and even left me money to help us get by."

"I wasn't sure if you had remarried, and perhaps it could be under your husband's name. So, I searched marriage records and death certificates and left no stone unturned. Then, one day, I was sitting in a cafe when a courtesan approached my table. I explained to her that I was looking for a woman and a child who could own a jewelry store, and she gave me the name of your shop."

"I can't believe it. And now here you are." Giulia stood up and held out her hand. "You must be tired from the journey. Let's go sit in the library."

She opened the wooden doors to the library.

"Have a seat," she said, motioning toward the sofa. "I'll be right back, I have to quickly run upstairs."

Violetta

Later that evening…

After weeks, the winter rain was finally relenting, l'aqua alta was receding from the piazzas, and a dense fog blanketed the canals. It was late in the evening, and Violetta's breath hung heavy in the air as she walked along the footbridge that led to her house. The dampness clung to her clothes, and the cold crept into her bones, but she did not mind. She was accustomed to wet Venetian winters.

Violetta climbed the steps to her front door. She removed her long cape and gave it a good shake before hanging it up inside. Next, she removed her sodden slippers and ivory silk stockings and left them by the front door, regretting that she had not worn her heavier wooden clogs. She walked barefoot over the Turkish carpet that stretched from the front door to the large arched window overlooking the courtyard. The courtyard was barren, but come springtime, jasmine, roses, and daffodils would blossom into a colorful bouquet and fill the entry with intoxicating scents.

In the middle of the entry, a colorful Murano chandelier hung high above a black and gold circular marble table. On top of the table, stood a tall blue and white porcelain urn that the maid had filled with yellow irises from their small greenhouse in the courtyard. The urn was a treasured possession, a gift from a friend who had spent years traveling the Silk Road. Yellow irises were her mother's favorite flower.

Violetta paused briefly in the dining room, where she noticed two place settings for tea and a fire burning low on the hearth. The fireplace was perhaps the most unusual and impressive part of the house. It was made of stone and carved into the head of Brizo, the Greek goddess of sailors and interpreter of dreams. Long waves of hair fell around the face and cascaded down to the floor, creating two pilasters on either side. Her lips formed around the firebox where smoldering embers burned inside her open mouth. Two wide eyes painted aqua blue kept silent watch over all who entered the house.

Violetta was unaware that her mother had company today, but their home was always open to guests stopping by for a visit. They often enjoyed a cup of tea in the dining room and then retired to the library. The library was to the left of the grand entry, and it was Violetta's favorite place in the house. Floor-to-ceiling bookshelves lined the room's perimeter and were filled with literature from around the world.

"Books contain chapters that make up a story like our own adventures make up the chapters of our lives," her mother had spoken gently. As a five-year-old, Violetta cuddled closely to listen to her mother read her favorite story. "And, if we are very lucky, each chapter is as adventurous, magical, and mysterious as the ones written in these books."

Violetta decided to have a hot cup of mint tea and continue reading the story of Genghis Khan before dinner. The hot desert and mysterious men riding camels captured her imagination. Having never ventured outside the jigsaw of manmade islands that made up her own city, it was difficult for her to imagine an endless sea of sand and sunshine.

But first, she was eager to see which necklace her mother had selected for her to wear to the Doge's Ball.

She ran swiftly up the marble staircase and flung open the door to her mother's bedroom. She spotted a red silk bag on top of the dresser. She untied the satin cord and removed the necklace tucked inside. Violetta gasped. It was the emerald and diamond choker. She pulled her hair back and held it up to her neck, gazing at her reflection in the mirror. The emeralds sparkled alongside the green specks in her eyes, and a smile beamed across her face.

Suddenly, something in the mirror caught her attention, causing her to drop the necklace. On the blank wall behind her, a small rectangular shape several shades darker than the surrounding paint jumped out at her.

She hurried back downstairs, bumping into the maid as she ran out of the room. "Clarissa, where is mother?" she demanded.

Alarmed, Clarissa tried to appease her, "She's in the library resting. But she asked not to be disturbed," Clarissa called after her, but Violetta had vanished down the stairs.

Violetta opened the door and entered the library where she saw the back of a man's head with wavy hair sitting on the green sofa. Her mother's head was resting on his shoulder. Violetta was compelled to step closer.

Just then, a young maid rounded the corner into the library and ran directly into Violetta, sending a tray of crystal and silver crashing to the floor.

Giulia bolted up from the sofa and turned toward the door.

"Violetta," her mother cried.

"I'm sorry, Signora. I was clearing the tea from the dining room and wanted to check if you needed anything. I didn't know your daughter had returned," stammered the young maid.

"No need to apologize, Paola. Everything is fine," said Giulia.

Paola bent down, placing the shards on the silver tray, while Violetta's eyes remained focused on the man who had turned around to meet her gaze.

"Please, leave that for now. We would like a moment alone," said Giulia.

The man stood up. His towering presence filled the room, but there was a calmness about him that alleviated any sense of alarm within her. Violetta studied the man with his broad shoulders and defined jawline. His nose was narrow and aristocratic, and his brown eyes were made up of concentric circles that, if looked at closely, could be read like rings of a tree trunk.

"Violetta, I would like for you to meet your father."

Violetta's jaw dropped as she turned toward her mother in disbelief.

Venice, Italy

February, 1553

It was Carnivale, and the house had been teeming with activity all week. Her mother busied herself overseeing the preparations for the party she hosted each year. Floors were scrubbed. Furniture and silver polished. Menus were prepared, and crates of food and wine were delivered, sorted, and stored. Gambling tables were set up in the library, and spaces were cleared in the grand entry for musical performances. In one week, the house would be filled with guests dressed in elaborate costumes and masks made from porcelain and glass and adorned with beads, crystals, and feathers. But tonight, it was the Doge's Ball - the main event that kicked off Carnivale season.

Only a select few were invited inside the palace walls, but the entire city, no matter position or rank, gathered in the Piazza San Marco to celebrate the tight rope act.

Violetta and her parents were dressed in festive costumes as they made their way through the crowded streets to the Piazza San Marco, where everyone was gathered. A Moretta covered Violetta's face. The mask was black velvet with only two holes cut out for her eyes. It did not tie around the head like other masks. Instead, it was held in place by biting a button sewn on the inside, preventing the wearer from speaking. A coy and flirtatious mask, it allowed for the woman to completely ignore an undesirable suitor by not having to respond to his advances.

Her mother leaned in toward her father and whispered something in his ear that caused him to laugh.

"It's not exactly my scene, but I'm happy to be here with you," she heard her father respond.

Violetta removed her mask. "I'll meet you at the palace later. I have to find Franco."

"I thought you two were meeting at the ball later tonight?" inquired her mother.

"I want to surprise him before the tightrope act," Violetta said excitedly.

She put her mask back on and disappeared into the crowd.

A kaleidoscope of colorful fabrics, streamers, and music swirled through the piazza and up toward the spires of St. Mark's Cathedral. Violetta waded through a brocade sea of fabric and made her way toward the tower where a rope stretched from the belfry of St. Mark's Cathedral bell tower to the balcony of Palazzo Ducale.

Violetta had to find Franco quickly if they were to watch the acrobat walk the rope to the balcony, where he would present the Doge with poems and flowers. Violetta knew she could easily spot Franco. All she had to do was look for his family's gold lion crest on his cape. She reached the tower and scanned the crowd, looking for the shiny gold lion's crest with ruby red eyes.

Jewel encrusted capes swept through the crowd in disorientating waves. Violetta turned her head, straining to see beyond the maze of frozen faces. Suddenly, the crowd erupted into cheers, and everyone's attention turned toward the belfry. The acrobat emerged and waved to the excited crowd. Then, he squared his shoulders, lifted his chin, and held his balancing stick in front of him. Placing one foot in front of the other, he began his long and tedious ascent toward the Doge's balcony.

Violetta arrived at the colonnade across from the Palace. She scanned left and right, but could not find Franco. When a man in front of her moved, she saw a small child, no older than six, staring straight at her with a pair of piercing indigo eyes.

Violetta put her hand on the child's shoulder, and briefly removed her mask to ask, "Are you lost?"

The child nodded and took off in the direction of the canal.

Violetta followed the little girl up to the water's edge. The child turned around and ran, disappearing into the crowd.

Confused, Violetta turned back toward the water, and standing directly in front of her was a man in a black cape. On his lapel was the unmistakable gold lion's crest. She breathed a sigh of relief and started towards Franco but stopped. He wore a black porcelain mask with red and orange flames painted around the eyes. But his eyes were not looking at her. They were staring directly into the eyes behind another jewel-encrusted mask. She could see their necks outstretched and lips open as their mouths met. Violetta's cheeks burned hot as embers. She released the button between her teeth, and her mask fell to the ground just as a thunderous gasp swept through the piazza. Violetta snapped her head up to see a stick fall through the air and the sinewy figure on the rope twisting and contorting his body, fighting to counterbalance gravity's pull. His knees locked, and his torso folded. His outstretched arms made desperate circles, trying in vain to push against the air as he plummeted to the ground.

Violetta turned her head and closed her eyes. Silence engulfed the piazza for the briefest moment. Then, anguished cries shattered the crimson-streaked sky. Violetta stood frozen in the chaos that erupted around her. She felt two hands grip her arms and spin her around. A pair of dark eyes encircled by flames stared back at her.

Violetta broke free and ran.

"Bitterness will cripple you," her mother's voice, usually such a source of comfort and reassurance, fell flat on Violetta's ears.

Violetta sat on the couch next her mother. Tears stung her eyes, blurring the flames dancing in the fireplace before her.

"But mother, you don't understand what I saw."

"You saw a horrific thing tonight."

"You're not listening. I saw Franco. He was with-" Violetta was unable to finish her sentence. "You won't believe it. But I'm going to make him pay."

"Darling, you will learn that revenge walks with a hunched back, always staring at the ground and missing all the beautiful possibilities surrounding it and, most importantly, what is in front of it. I'm telling you, daughter, walk with your back straight. Look forward and up, never down or back, no matter the hand you are dealt, no matter the pain that is inflicted upon you, however unjust. Your life lies ahead of you, not behind you. Please, whatever this is, whatever you thought you saw. However hurt you may feel in this moment, let it go."

"He wasn't who he said he was. And now, how do I forget all the dreams I had for us?"

"Because that is precisely what it was, a dream. It was a fanciful illusion of a future you created in your mind. It may have felt real, but it was not. When you understand this, you will find that you are not walking away from reality, only a version of it you had hoped to have. I know it feels very real now, so don't fight it. Instead, remember the times you shared in fondness, knowing you will experience those things again. And then you'll see that today you have lost nothing."

"I feel like that will never happen now."

"It will. And you will value it all the more. Your father and I would love for you to join us tonight, but it's up to you. I'm sure he will understand either way."

Violetta had forgotten her father in all the commotion. There were so many changes in such a short amount of time. Now, necklaces and dancing seemed trivial and insignificant. She looked at the rows of books lining the walls of the library and felt the warmth of the fire on her face.

"I think I'll stay home."

A rainbow of light glowed around her mother's face, but it appeared dimmer this evening. She looked tired and, for the first time, older than Violetta could remember.

"I understand. Just remember, books are treasures, but the best stories are the ones that are lived." She walked quietly out of the room and shut the coffered doors behind her.

Violetta sat on the velvet sofa and stared at the fire. Anger brewed inside of her, a burning hole in the pit of her stomach. Violetta wished she could be more accepting like her mother. But she was not.

Her brocade house slippers sank into the plush Oriental rug as she walked along the bookshelf, running her hand mindlessly along the smooth spines. Violetta reached the corner of the room when a rough surface pricked her finger. She pulled her hand back and stared at the small splinter sticking out of her skin. Violetta pulled it from her finger and looked at the shelf. There, in plain sight, was a book slightly unlike the rest. Strange, she had never noticed it before. It was dark brown and blended in with the others, but its surface was flat with squared-off edges. Violetta pulled it from the shelf and was surprised to see it wasn't a book after all, but a box. She tried to open it, but the lid was tightly fitted. She walked to the writing desk and pried the lid with a letter opener.

She gasped and sat down in the desk chair. Inside, there was a book unlike any Violetta had ever seen. The leather cover was tooled and embossed with an intricate floral pattern. Gold metal covered the front and back like a cage and capped the edges and spine. Tiny pave-cut jewels covered the front.

Her hands were trembling as she gently opened the book. Confused, Violetta stared at the page covered in strange writing. She had never seen such writing before. Violetta turned the page and the next.

All the same, words she did not recognize in a foreign language unlike she had ever seen. Violetta skipped to the middle of the book and breathed a sigh of relief. Latin. Latin was one of her better subjects.

Violetta began to read, the blood pumping in her temples. Suddenly, she heard the front door open, and her father call for a maid.

Violetta closed the book and placed it back in the wooden box. Scarcely breathing, she rushed to the empty slot on the shelf and slid it back into place. Then she stepped out of the library. Her father and the maid were helping her mother up the stairs. She looked pale and weak.

Violetta ran over to them. "What happened?" she asked.

"Not to worry. I'm only tired. With all the activity going on, I'm sure I just need to rest," her mother assured her.

"Let me help you."

"Don't worry, we have her," said her father gently. "I'm going to help her to bed."

A wave of panic rushed over Violetta. It wasn't like her mother to succumb to fatigue. She could not remember her ever being sick. A panic sweated through her. She had heard stories circulating around the city—whispers about the return of the Black Death. A cold chill ran through her body. Violetta pushed the thought from her mind. Only rumors, Violetta told herself, and she retreated back into the warmth of the library.

Violetta lay on the sofa and pulled a blanket on top of her. Her eyes fell on the wooden box sitting on the shelf.

A tingle of excitement coursed through her body. Where had this book come from? Violetta had been in this library countless times and knew every book on the shelves. She had dozens of questions running through her mind. Did her mother know about it? Surely she knew. But why had she never mentioned it?

Violetta decided not to tell her mother about finding the book. It would be the first thing Violetta would keep from her, but she decided she was old enough to have a few secrets of her own.

The heat from the fire warmed and relaxed her entire body. Her eyes grew heavy as she relaxed into the sofa and drifted off to sleep.

Her dreams were muddled and violent. Her body lay cold and shivering, pinned to a dirt floor, unable to move. Metal objects lay scattered across the floor, the sharp points nipped at her limbs. The silhouette of a man lurked in the background. Desperate for him to come closer, she called out to him, but as hard as she tried, no sound escaped her mouth. Then, a dense fog rose from the floor, and the man evaporated before her eyes, pulling her with him. Soft grass replaced the dirt floor. As she lay on her back, staring at the sky, the man stepped beside her, blocking the sunlight. She squinted to see his face, but it was nothing but a dark shadow against the brilliant sky.

A sense of calm overcame her, and she heard him whisper, "Adolphina."

Violetta bolted awake. She was drenched in a cold sweat. Her eyes darted around the library. The fire had burned down to embers.

Relaxing, Violetta settled back on the sofa, pulling the blanket tightly around her. She would stay there until morning. The room was warm, and there was something that she wanted to protect.

Exhausted, she closed her eyes. She wanted desperately to reconnect with the mysterious man in her dream, but he never came.

Venice

March, 1553

There were two possible outcomes, recovery or death.

Her mother had been in bed for weeks and showed no improvement. She had grown delirious from the fever and could not eat. Her father had not left her side. Violetta walked around the house in a daze, distraught with fear. She couldn't lose her mother. She had only just found her father. They were supposed to be a family now.

Violetta wandered into the dining room and secured the curtains back with the long silk tassel.

"Clarissa," Violetta called out to a maid, "light more candles. Why is it so dark in the house?" Everything in her life felt so dark, and she could feel the hope draining out of her.

Violetta crept slowly up the staircase, careful not to make a sound. She was not allowed to see her mother. The doctor said it was not safe until her fever broke. Still, she had to be near her mother.

Violetta tiptoed up to the door to her mother's room. It was slightly cracked so that she could see inside. Violetta could hear her mother and father speaking in hushed tones. She sounded breathless and tired, but her voice held the urgency of someone trying desperately to get her point across. Her father sounded distraught as he tried to calm her. Violetta strained to hear what they were talking about but could only pick up every other word.

"Should tell her…"

"we can't… everything… put her… danger."

"… know… inn by lake… take her if… your sister… only family…"

"must rest... time..."

"... deserves to know... her...."

"the book... hidden in... the store..."

Violetta heard a rustle behind her that caused her to jump. Clarissa was walking down the hall carrying a box of candles.

"I lit more candles in the dining room. Is there anywhere else you would like for me to light them?"

Violetta tried her best to hide her guilt. Clearly, she had caught her eavesdropping, and she felt ashamed.

"No, thank you. That will be all," Violetta whispered.

Clarissa nodded and made her way down the corridor.

Violetta remained standing at the door to her mother's bedroom. She wanted to know what they were talking about. Did her father have a sister? What was so important about the inn by the lake? And why was her mother talking about a book? Was it the one in the library she had found? Violetta strained to listen, but the room had fallen silent. Violetta gently pushed the door open a tiny bit more. She saw her mother lying in bed, pale and thin as a skeleton. Her father sat on the bed next to her holding her hand, a mask covering his face. Connecting them was a cord formed out of a million tiny points of light popping in and out of existence, like fireflies in the night. Her parents seemed oblivious to the lights, but Violetta could see it clear as day.

Then something shifted. It was subtle at first but became more apparent. The lights would disappear, but fewer and fewer were returning until, eventually, only a handful twinkled between them.

Violetta bolted into the room.

"You mustn't be in here. It isn't safe," her father said, walking toward her.

Violetta brushed past him and stood before the bed. Her mother's face was peaceful. Violetta thought she had fallen asleep, but her eyes were still open. She took her hand and stared into her eyes.

They looked the same, but Violetta knew she was gone.

Violetta turned to look at her father and gasped at what she saw. She could see a light cord stretch from him to her mother. Then, suddenly, the cord unravelled and stardust floated up to the ceiling. It danced above them, like tiny strings quivering to a symphony of music, before disappearing.

The next day, her father took her to her mother's shop. He said he had to give her something. Violetta couldn't imagine what he would have to give her. Violetta now owned everything in the cases. But he walked past the cases and into the tiny back office. He removed a large stone from the wall. She watched as he unlocked the door to a metal safe and swung it open. There was a pile of cash and a few loose gemstones. He reached inside and felt around. A look of confusion crossed his face.

"She said it was in here."

He felt around again and looked inside.

"What are you looking for?" Violetta asked.

He ran his hand through his hair. "Your mother told me there was a book in here. She wanted you to have it. She made me promise to give it to you."

"A book?"

"She said it was in this safe, inside a wooden box, but it's not here."

"Did she say what the book was about?"

"No, only that it was from her family."

"Father, I think I know where it is."

Violetta pulled the wooden box from the library shelf. She sat down on the couch next to her father and placed it on her lap. Violetta removed the lid and took out the book. His eyes grew big, and a wave of relief washed over his face.

"She said it was special, but I had no idea," he said. "But how did you know where it was?"

"I found it right there on the shelf the night of the ball."

"It must have been the fever. She must have forgotten."

Violetta sat next to her father in silence.

He took a deep breath and continued, "There's something else she wanted you to know. It's about your past, your family."

Her father died a month later. The doctor informed her that God had not spared him from the Black Death, but Violetta thought otherwise. God had delivered him straight into the arms of her mother.

The Plague was spreading quickly. Funerals were forbidden. Victims were burned per government mandate. The ashes couldn't be retrieved, but it made no difference. Violetta felt their light on everything they had touched, and occasionally, she would catch a glimpse of two orbs dancing in the library.

Violetta sold the jewelry store to her mother's young apprentice, save one piece, the diamond and emerald choker.

As for her future, Violetta felt the force of life tugging at her heart and inviting her to venture down uncharted roads. There were so many adventures, and she knew it was time for her to leave. She was her father's daughter, after all.

She rolled up the deed to her father's trading business. She would go east to Constantinople and continue his work, exactly as he wanted. But, first, she had many questions, and only one place held the answers. She looked down at the piece of paper lying on the table. The name of a small village, Alpinella, was written across the top. Violetta placed the choker, money, and the book at the bottom of her bag.

Clarissa and the other maids met her at the door, and tears filled their eyes. They had known her since she was just a small child. They were her family. Violetta tried to sound strong, but her voice trembled like a child's.

"I promise to return before I leave for Constantinople," she told them.

Violetta opened the front door, and followed the maids down the steps as they carried her trunk to load onto her gondola.

To her surprise, standing at the bottom of the steps, was Franco. "My mother said you were leaving," he shifted awkwardly. "I called on you many times."

"I know," Violetta gripped the strap to her bag tighter, "but there was a lot to deal with."

"I understand," he said slowly. "So, it's true. You're leaving."

"I am," replied Violetta.

"For how long?" he asked.

"That remains to be seen."

"Listen. What happened at Carnivale was all one big dare. It was just a game," he said, the words rushing from his mouth.

Franco shifted uncomfortably, and Violetta waited for him to continue.

"But we both have obligations to our families to continue what we started."

"I don't have a family anymore," said Violetta flatly.

"Then we have an obligation to one another."

A few sparks of light flew off of his chest, bright and vibrant. Violetta could hear her mother's whispered words: we all have a wild streak that longs to be released.

Violetta hoped one day, he would learn to direct all of that fire in his heart. For now, he was a boy, reckless and full of life. She also saw murky colors swirling at the top of his head. Confusion, her mother had taught her; it occurs when a person's head conflicts with his heart.

"My obligations lie elsewhere now," she said, walking past him toward her gondola.

"When you return, we *will* pick up where we left off," he said sternly.

Violetta only smiled in response. She did not feel the need to inform him that she had different plans. She hugged the maids one last time, and he helped her in.

Violetta did not look back, but she could feel his eyes on her as she departed. They had known each other since they were children. Although she was leaving, she understood that they would remain connected. Her mother had told her when a light cord is formed, it never breaks. It only changes. Some bonds may be stronger and others more tenuous; and they even change back and forth over time, but the light cord is always there.

She had never told anyone about the Lights, not even Franco. Her mother said it was important to keep it to herself. When she asked why, her mother told her that it was dangerous. How could something so beautiful be dangerous? Violetta had pressed. Because, her mother said, truth and beauty usually are. Not because they themselves are dangerous, but because humans are filled with fear, so their first instinct is to destroy that which they do not understand.

The city faded behind her; and although Violetta had never seen another city, she knew that Venice was the most beautiful in the world and one day she wished to return. But, hearing her mother's words echo in her ears, she feared it might one day be destroyed, too.

Violetta put her hand to her chest. Like her mother, Violetta, remembered seeing the Light since she was very young, when a child's heart is most open.

She could feel the Light in her chest now, and it filled her with courage. She did not know what awaited her, but she was eager to get there.

Aster

"All wickedness is but little to the wickedness of a woman. What else is woman but a foe to friendship, an unescapable punishment, a necessary evil, a natural temptation, a desirable calamity, a domestic danger, a delectable detriment, an evil of nature, painted with fair colours!"

Malleus Maleficarum Part 1

Question VI

Heinrich Kramer, 1486 AD

Venice

May, 2110

The Church had fallen, but the churches still stood. They served as a reminder to the people that power over instead of power with is not power at all. It is enslavement. It was also the general consensus that they were too beautiful to tear down. So, two dozen committees had been formed to oversee the task of converting them into museums, exhibition halls, galleries, restaurants, and discotheques. Individuals with a taste for the macabre had transformed several into soaring residences.

Aster's job as Director of the Roman Historic Preservation Committee was to preserve the historical integrity of buildings while embracing the spirit of innovation and contemporary artistry. At least, that is what it read in the job description. In reality, her job was far less glamorous. The day-to-day activities mainly consisted of her acting as a mediator between ego-driven architects and neurotic city officials in combative meetings that would conclude without reaching a conclusion. It was exhausting and tedious work, but all of that changed the day she got a call from the Director of The Revival and Beautification of Venice. She had been selected as the Lead Archivist for the Venice Conversion Project, or the VCP.

The petrified piles driven into the lagoon stood firm, impervious to the decay that had slowly engulfed the crumbling palazzo above. The building was designated to be torn down. Synthetic grass would be laid on top, and four benches arranged in a square would be placed around a concrete monument honoring the old artisans of Venice. The Board agreed it was a good idea to bring greenery into the city where possible; people responded well to nature.

Demolition robots had arrived early in the morning to clear the wreckage and remove piles of sewage-soaked debris. Broken chairs, tables, and soggy cardboard boxes filled with discarded items littered the sludge-covered floor. The rooms were bare of chandeliers and copper fixtures that had been looted ages ago. Faded frescoes, now speckled with mold, were but whispers of a once opulent and colorful past.

Aster entered the building and stepped inside the room off of the entry. The crew was on the top floor clearing the items she had designated for removal. She put on her gloves and mask. This was the last floor she needed to survey, and judging from its looks, she did not think it would take long.

A small wooden door in the back of the room caught her eye. She stepped around a pile of wood and broken bottles and pushed down on the rusty door handle, but it would not budge. She placed her other hand on the door and gave it another strong shove. It gave slightly. Encouraged, she raised her boot and kicked at the door. It creaked and groaned and gave way enough for her to peer inside. She took the flashlight from her belt and shined the light inside the room. It was a small room, the size of a large walk-in pantry. Wooden crates lined the wall, and a small desk and three filing cabinets were shoved up against the far wall. She pushed the door open a few more inches and squeezed inside. She shone the light around the room. Papers lay scattered on the floor. She picked one up, a payroll from the 1920s. She walked around the wooden desk. Stacks of folders and binders, yellowed and brittle, covered the top. She opened the middle drawer. More documents. She turned toward the file cabinets. Aster selected the one on the left and pulled at a rusty drawer. It creaked open. She picked up a catalog and flipped through the brittle pages.

Masks stared back at her, adorned with jewels, feathers, and elaborately painted designs. It must have been the last of the great mask makers from Carnivale, a celebration lost to the tides of time.

She took out her red tape and made a large X over each cabinet. They would be taken to the warehouse to be cleaned and cataloged for the museum collection. She scanned the rest of the wall, sweeping the light along the blackened stone. She pointed the light in the corner and stopped. One stone caught her attention. It was larger than the others and protruded from the wall. She ran her hand along the perimeter of the stone. Then she gripped the edge with her fingers and wiggled it back and forth. The stone moved. It did not seem to be grouted to the surrounding stones. She placed the flashlight on the desk and used both hands to try to loosen it, but it would not budge any further. She took a knife from her tool belt and ran the blade along the edge of the stone, driving it further into the crack. She worked the blade around each side of the stone. She grabbed the corners and slid it from the wall.

To her surprise, it was half the depth of the other stones in the wall. She laid it down on the ground and reached for her flashlight. Leaning forward, she peered inside the opening, where she spotted a black box covered in dust. She pulled it out and laid it on the desk. It appeared to be a small safe. It was rusty, and the hinges were broken. She pried them off and removed the door. Inside the safe was a wooden box. "Probably another ledger," she mumbled to herself.

She removed the cover of the box and gasped.

"Are you in here?" a man's voice boomed through the doorway, causing her to jump. "Sorry," he said, "I didn't mean to startle you."

"It's ok, Ivan," she said, quickly placing the lid on the box.

"We're almost finished on the top floor. If everything is ready on the second, we can begin after lunch."

"Yes, everything is ready."

"What a mess," he said, looking around the room. "There's not much worth salvaging around here, I guess."

"Only those filing cabinets," she gestured toward the back wall. "They contain some catalogs I would like archived."

"Sounds good. We should be able to finish up today."

"Great, I'm late for a meeting, but I'll be back this afternoon," she replied.

She waited until he disappeared. Then she slipped the box inside her satchel and headed out the door.

Aster climbed the steps to the palazzo. Originally the home of a jewelry merchant, as part of the new plan, it was redesigned as a hotel for visiting dignities; for the time being, it was her home. She walked through the entry and into the library, where an imposing pink marble fireplace commanded the room. She settled into a Louis XVI-style chair with upholstered arms and a plush velvet seat cushion.

She ran her fingers over the gold metal rose on the cover, tracing the details along the edges of each petal that seemed to have budded from the leather itself. She opened the book and scanned the first page. Luckily, she had an entire library of ancient texts at her disposal, she thought. From the looks of it, she was going to need it.

Aster heard footsteps coming from the corridor, startling her out of her thoughts. Quickly, she closed the book. An older woman with a rounded back and a pleasant smile entered the library. "Good evening, Signora Bauldine." She was holding a tray with a bowl of pasta and a glass of red wine. "I thought you might be hungry."

"I didn't realize you were still here," Aster said, placing a hand over the box. "You can leave the tray in the dining room. I'll eat in there tonight."

"Very well," she said. "Don't forget. You need to eat," she replied, giving her a stern look.

"I will, and thank you."

Aster waited until she heard the front door close before standing up. She held the box to her chest and tried to think.

Rows of books lined the shelves on either side of the fireplace. She ran her fingers along the spine of *Star Wars*. Over a century had passed since Lucas dreamed of interstellar travel, and still, there were no signs of extra-terrestrial life. Only silence. Only us, she thought.

The clock on the mantel chimed, causing her jump. It was an antique relic from the past intended to make guests feel as if they have traveled back in time. Aster sighed. Time travel was just another far-fetched fantasy.

She turned to leave and then stopped. Slowly she walked back to the shelf. *A Study in Scarlet* and *The Hound of the Baskervilles* - she would hide it between her two favorite Sherlock Holmes novels.

Venice

June, 2110

William, the head of the Roman Oversight Committee smiled. "Thank you again for this incredible discovery. There's no doubt it will be an added draw for the museum, which, of course, means more revenue for us."

Aster clenched her jaw and fought to swallow the anger rising in her chest. Her worst fears were confirmed. It had been a mistake to turn it over. Damn, it. Why didn't I keep it a bit longer, she cursed to herself.

"But don't you think it should be studied a bit further?" she asked.

"What do you mean?"

"Wouldn't you agree that it's a little more than a relic? It's not exactly a piece of pottery to be displayed in a case."

"But, it is a historical relic," he replied, glancing at his watch.

"Yes, but it is also a piece of literature, possibly even a religious text, from an ancient society that we have just discovered. I think it needs to be studied in more detail. Have you read any of the translations? There are some very revolutionary ideas contained in this book."

"I'm sure there are, but unfortunately, we don't have time. We need to keep moving forward, and so do you. A lot of work still needs to be done before the opening. If you like, perhaps at a later date, you can make a copy of the book and conduct your research from that."

"I don't like working from copies. Details get lost. I prefer the original." Aster stood up. "How about you grant me access to the book after hours? I don't mind working at night."

He crossed his arms, and the side of his mouth twitched. "I appreciate your...enthusiasm. But the museum opens in a few weeks. The statue we uncovered has received worldwide attention. Now, we have this book.

Well, it's the icing on the cake. I understand your academic background. Believe me, I do. But, this is business. People aren't coming here to learn. They are coming for an experience. To take pictures, drink wine, and brag to their friends about their vacation. If they wanted to learn, they'd go to school. We aren't a school. We are here to make money. And this," he said, pointing to the book, "means more money. Money for you to get paid so you can continue your work here. We all have our role, Aster. Now, if you'll excuse me, some things require my attention."

He paused at the door. "Listen, if you want, you can choose the page that will be displayed." He gave her a weak smile before closing the tall glass door behind him.

Aster stared at William standing on the other side of the door. He was still holding on to the handle, and she swore she saw his arm tremble. He turned his head around, and their eyes met through the glass. She forced a smile, and a startled expression crossed his face. He turned and quickly walked away.

She sat back down at the desk and turned another page, but she could not concentrate. She began to close the book when she noticed a butterfly flattened near the spine. Gently, she picked it up with her tweezers and scales from the wings scattered across the page, "A moth," she whispered. She held it up to her desk lamp and a brilliant rainbow pattern shone on its wings. She could not believe it, she was holding a Madagascan sunset moth. She had studied this species during the year she worked at the Natural History Museum in Cairo cataloging a collection of African lepidopterans. She remembered this moth in particular, not only for its colorful wings, but because she was surprised to learn that not all moths lived in the dark, some lived in the light. Because of the colorful markings and the fact that it is active during the day, people often mistake it for a butterfly.

She rotated the moth under the light, admiring its rare beauty. Unlike a butterfly whose wings are made of honeycomb shaped cells, a moth's wings are composed of scales, like a fish. The scales of the sunset moth are clear, and, in subdued light, the wings appear dull and unremarkable, but due to the curvature of the scales, light refracts in different angles, giving a kaleidoscope effect. Their rare beauty can only be seen in the light.

"But, what is a moth from Madagascar doing in this book," she wondered aloud. As far as she knew, these were not migratory insects. They are found only on the lush, volcanic island off the coast of Africa.

The door opened, and the junior security officer poked his head into the room. "I didn't know anyone was still here."

"Hi, Peter. I was just finishing up," Aster said.

"No problem, just make sure everything is in order when you leave. There's been chatter coming from Rome about security threats."

"What kind of threats?"

"Oh, you know, the usual - fanatical lunatics who disagree with what we are doing. They're threatening to sabotage, steal, and bomb - the usual litany of destruction and mayhem. Of course, the threats have been unusually high since we are nearing the opening, so they want us to be extra vigilant. Of course, they also don't want to send extra security either. Cheap bastards."

Aster shot him a look, and the man stammered, "I'm not talking about Theo, of course. He's at the mercy of Rome, just like the rest of us."

Ignoring his last remark about her boyfriend, Aster asked, "But this archive room is secure, right?"

"Of course. The entire city is secure, but being on an island, there are always weak entry points. One more thing, the security team will be troubleshooting in the next few weeks around the clock. There are some issues with several exhibition halls. You'll be receiving a schedule of the checks and shutdowns in the morning."

"Pretty butterfly, by the way," he commented.

"Actually, it's a moth."

"Well, we don't want those around. I can call the exterminator tomorrow and let them know."

"Actually, it's ok. I found it in an old book. It came from Madagascar."

"Sounds exotic."

"It is. They are considered mythical creatures there. The Malagasy people use the word 'Lolo' for "butterfly", "moth", and "soul". They believe the soul of ancestors appear in the form of a moth or butterfly. To attack it is to attack your ancestors. Unfortunately, not all people respected them in same way. This one in particular was highly coveted by jewelry makers for its wings." She laid the moth back on the page and closed the book. "I think we'll leave him be. I have enough enemies around here already."

"Right," he chuckled. He looked around the room one last time. "I'm headed out. You should go home too. Don't worry. All the problems will be waiting for you tomorrow," he said, shaking his head and closing the door.

Exhausted, Aster decided to call it a day. She folded her piece of trace paper covered in red, yellow, and blue markings and placed it inside the book. As she closed the cover, a smile swept across her face, she knew she was getting close to figuring out the location of the cave. She covered the book in parchment and closed the lid to the container.

Then, she walked over to the wall and placed the box inside a metal drawer, alongside other artifacts. She gently pressed the drawer, and it slid into place, locking with a click.

Aster slid her notebook and pens into her brown leather satchel. She preferred to write her notes by hand. Something about the act of writing on a piece of paper made her thoughts feel more real. She slung her bag over her shoulder and grabbed her coat before turning off the lights.

Aster was the last person to leave the building that night, but she never felt alone surrounded by the past. The past did not feel dead to her but very much alive - sometimes, more alive than the living.

She made her way through a room filled with dozens of marble statues. In a single pose, each told a story of strength or weakness, dominance or submission, love or fear. She walked across the shadow of a bed of snakes. Above her, a man held Medusa's head high like a trophy, her gnarled face frozen in anguish. Behind him, Zeus wrestled a lion for its pelt. To his left, Psyche held a lantern above her God. Jealousy, revenge, lust, the same human dramas unfolding time and again. Perhaps William was right, she thought. We all have our roles.

Ironically, immersing herself in the past brought her to life and made her want to live fully in the present. She saw how people spent their days immersed in technology, only to have it dull and deaden their senses. Preferring sedation to the human condition, they begin their day with pills to erase that which is the very essence of what makes them alive. One chemical sequence removes sadness, while another eliminates anxiousness, loneliness, and regret. Once those feelings are exorcised, they take a pill to fill them with happiness, ease, or confidence, or at least a synthetic version of what feels like those things. Ignoring their bodies' natural rhythms, they look instead to the clock that tells them when to take the next pill so they can deal with their boss, fuck again, or just go to sleep. Gradually, all definition and detail of the original is lost, and they become walking copies of copies.

At the end of the Great Hall, next to an imposing black granite statue of Osiris, Aster passed a tall Christian altar gilded in gold, an impressive acquisition from Naples. It was ornately carved and reached to the ceiling. It shone brilliantly and made her pause briefly at the foot of it. She recalled similar alters she had prayed before as a child, but those rituals were not to last. She recalled the uprising that ensued and the rebels' justifications for destroying them: what had begun as religious freedom had become religious self-righteousness, which had turned to religious intolerance. It was their duty to rid the world of intolerance. So, after another Great World War, many battles, and countless lives lost, the religious establishment was overthrown. All evidence of the past had been destroyed, converted, or relocated to museums. In a single stroke, another creation story had been wiped out, and Christianity took its place alongside prior religions, which had also succumbed to the title of *Mythology*.

Aster wondered which Mythology would come next...

"Things were supposed to improve with overthrowing the religious establishment," she muttered. Yet, despite their promises, she had seen little advancement. The people who took power decided on a different approach to control the masses and replaced faith and fear with knowledge and reason. But, although the tree had been cut down, the roots remained intact. Once again, it was fear disguised as freedom. And once again, the same ideas were pounded into the minds of the people: we are weak and inherently flawed, and it is better to deny who we are than to feel the totality of that which is our very nature. And, her personal favorite: we know better.

They tell us that they know better. And we believe them, Aster thought bitterly. But she saw the deceptions in their declarations and traps in their teachings.

She knew the real danger was truth; the greatest threat was thinking for oneself.

But these thoughts were dangerous, which was why she kept them to herself and did not share them with anyone except with one person waiting for her at home.

The Great Hall opened into an expansive auditorium designed to look like an outdoor amphitheatre. It was the crowning jewel of the museum. Aster stopped in front of large composite blocks arranged like Greek amphitheatres. Floor-to-ceiling fabric panels surrounded the stage and provided a graphic backdrop for presentations and plays. Holographic images of actors from around the world would appear on stage, performing for the audience in real-time. The dome ceiling, covered in constellations, twinkled above and gave the impression of being outdoors. Designers and engineers made the stars change along with the seasons. Aster wondered if all the time and effort were worth it. She doubted if anyone knew what the stars looked like at all, much less in any season.

Suddenly, she felt cold. The room unsettled her. It was a collision of the ancient and modern worlds trying to coexist in the same space, and it didn't work.

She put her coat on and headed toward the exit. She was eager to get home. Peter was right. All the problems will still be there in the morning.

William

Museum of Art and Culture, Venice

June, 2110

A small, rectangular placard hung outside an office at the end of the hall in the administrative wing that read, *Roman Oversight Committee*, in Helvetica Script. It was brushed stainless steel, making it difficult to read the engraved letters unless one looked at it from a specific angle. There was no name.

Inside the windowless room, William Blankship tapped his fingers on the desk. An average man who blended in with his surroundings, he was neither tall nor short, neither fat nor thin, and his hair was either brown or blond, depending on the light. Always unsure of himself, he would never fully commit to a side. He had learned to speak and act through others, thus sidestepping the responsibility that his position afforded him, which wasn't much. It was this skill that had gotten him to where he was today.

Now, much to his dismay, he found himself in an undesirable position, one that required action. He did not like the conversation he had had with Aster. He knew he could never persuade her to let go of the book. She had invested too much time and was too passionate about its contents. But his instructions were clear. Rome did not want the specifics of the book known. He had been told to dumb it down and keep things at a superficial level.

He picked up his government-issued communication device, which, like everything in his life, was owned by someone else and called his second in command. He believed he had reached a solution, and he was excited to tell someone.

"The day of the opening, I want you to pull Aster's security clearances. All of them."

"Sure thing. Do you mind my asking why?"

William thought quickly. "Let's just say, I know a security threat when I see one," he said, pleased with the tone of authority in his voice and relieved not to have to explain things further.

"Very well, consider it done. Where shall we redistribute her?"

William paused. "I'll get back to you on that."

"Ok."

"One more thing, I don't want her boyfriend to catch wind of this. We need him to finish the job."

"Got it. Anything else?"

"That will be all."

William stared blankly at the bare wall in front of him. His heart beat faster and pumped more blood to the extremities of his body, causing him to feel lightheaded. His breath became shallow and small beads of perspiration dotted his temples, his body's natural reaction to a combination of excitement and nerves. He reached for the bottle on his desk, removed the lid, and shook two pills into his hand. William searched for his water bottle but remembered leaving it downstairs in the archive room. He looked at the two purple capsules in his palm and hurled them against the wall. They were the last two, but he didn't care. He would have a crushing headache whether he took them or not.

He ran his hand through his hair, which was now damp with sweat, and he could feel the familiar pressure mounting in his head. He opened the top drawer of his desk and took out a sheet of paper. Carefully, he placed it in front of him and ran his fingers over the surface. He felt the subtle texture of the pulp, and his heartbeat slowed. The paper was handmade and very rare. Paper of that quality was increasingly difficult to find due to the limited production. Young people had little interest in carrying on the trades of the past, but there were a few old artisans in the countryside who still made it if you knew where to find them.

He picked up a pencil given to him by his mother for his birthday.

It was a simple gift, but one heavy with meaning. He dragged the point along the paper in long, even strokes. The sound of graphite on paper was pleasing to his ears. He drew another curved line, completing the form. Then, he began filling in the details with quick, featherlike movements. He cast shadows and shined light upon the subject he had memorized to the smallest detail. Slowly, a form emerged that rose from the confines of the two-dimensional space. His mind was freed as his hand and eyes took over, working in unison. The pressure in his temples released, and he remembered back to the days spent as a boy lying on the floor, his sketchbooks laid out, covering every inch of carpet in his room. He would lose himself in his drawings for hours until his mother called him for dinner.

As the years passed, his love for drawing grew more intense. He studied anatomy and read books about the masters who came before him. When it came time to choose his path of higher education, he took the exam and applied to the Academy of Classical Arts. He passed easily and received his acceptance letter. Only then did his mother inform him that there was no money to send him. There was, however, a scholarship available to another school for a degree in art curation and management. He would not be a classically trained artist, but he could at least work in their world. She was sorry, but it was the best she could do. He then learned a bitter lesson: although you can do something, it does not mean you are free to.

He went on to study and filled his head with things he did not care to know. But mainly, he learned that education is available to everyone who can pay. Of course, the Ivory Elite weren't entirely without a conscious. Occasionally, they made an exception for the extraordinarily gifted, those with a certain level of pigmentation in their skin, or a specific chromosomal combination. Unfortunately, he didn't fall into any of those categories. Nevertheless, it was good PR, because education was foremost, a business.

So, William learned the business side of the art world, and gradually, he adopted their ideas as his own and forgot all about that little boy lying on the floor with his sketchpads, except in moments like this.

He laid his pencil on the desk and looked at the drawing of Aster. It was remarkably good. The lines were confident and bold and conveyed the raw emotion he could only express through his art.

But he did not see it that way. He thought the proportions were off, and the shading was heavy-handed. If only he had been formally trained. He crumpled the sheet of paper into a tight ball and tossed it in the trash bin.

Before he left, he stopped by the archive room and retrieved his water bottle. It was shaped like a faceted jewel with a picture of a penguin sunbathing on top of an iceberg. He flipped open the bottle and downed the last drops. Then he stuffed the bottle in his bag. It was too pretty to throw away.

Suddenly, a sense of powerlessness overcame him. He felt the urge to break free; but he didn't know from what, and he didn't know where to go if he did.

He was eager to return to his apartment. It was small, but he didn't mind.

Humans have always had a way of putting things that are formless and free, like dreams, ideas, love, and even themselves, into confining little spaces.

Theo

Later that night…

In an apartment across town, Theo watched William exit the museum. "Mr. Blankship, you poor forgotten fool. If you weren't such a pathetic romantic, I would have gotten rid of you months ago."

Then, he turned off the monitor screens in his office. The side of his mouth curled upward, and he shook his head. It never ceased to amaze him how insecurity and stupidity always went hand-in-hand. He leaned back in his chair and took a sip of wine. The good thing, was William would not be messing with his clearances. Not that he depended on them anyway, he thought.

Suddenly, he felt a hand run through his hair and pull his head back. "Sorry, I'm late," Aster whispered in his ear.

A lopsided grin crossed his face. "That's ok. I was just finishing up some work."

He stood up and followed Aster out of the room. She was already naked.

Aster

"All witchcraft comes from carnal lust, which, in women, is insatiable."

Malleus Maleficarum, Part 3
Question VI
Heinrich Kramer, 1486 AD

Venice

June, 2110

Ten crescent moons pierced his shoulder blades and streaked down his back, fading like a comet's tail as they rounded the contour of his ribs. The cries that shook the night came not from him but from the woman tethered to his chest. He did not break his rhythm until she had stilled her body and steadied her breath, entering into a state of lucid relaxation. Only then did he release his own tension and empty his life force inside her.

Moments later, they lay entangled, his body depleted and eager for sleep, hers full and content, having captured the code to unlock his being. A gentle smile braised her lips as she stroked his back. Eventually, she closed her eyes and drifted off to sleep—a lock unto his key.

As they lay atop the bed, pinned to a rock that spun through the night, a million points of light swarmed inside her. But, one, in particular, shone brighter than the others. Forging ahead, its brilliant light illuminated a path that it did not remember but seemed familiar in some way. It would be the first to reach the center of her private universe, where photons collided, and stars were born again.

The Museum of Art and Culture

Venice

2110

Three Months Later…

A beam of light sliced through the darkness and landed in front of a pair of black boots that walked stealthily across the terrazzo floor. The svelte figure made its way past ten naked men with skin as cold and white as freshly fallen snow. Their muscles were flexed in a state of readiness, each one gripping a spear that pointed toward the heavens. Their penises had broken off and were lost long ago. The men lined the corridor, silent and watchful, where a heavy coffered ceiling loomed overhead like the lid to a coffin.

The figure reached the end of the corridor that opened to an expansive room with a dome ceiling. In the center of the room, an imposing statue, three times the height of an average person, stood atop a circular pedestal. Her face tilted upward, gazing into an oculus that served as a portal to the infinite beyond. Tonight, a full moon bathed her face in a warm glow. Her long arms stretched outward in a cradling gesture, an offering of comfort and inspiration to the people in a time when she had held center stage in her beloved city. Her round belly protruded, bursting forth with life, and her breasts dripped with milk that ran down her thighs like a meandering river. The embodiment of the dueling nature of the universe, she was approachable and untouchable, serene and bold, maternal and empowering. What she was not, was fearful.

Her name was Rieta.

Beneath the water, piles, sludge, and debris of what was thought to be the oldest version of Venice, lay the remains of an ancient civilization, one that predated the Christians, Romans, Greeks, Etruscans, and every known patriarchal society across the planet. What they found was a civilization that told the story of a time when the female was worshipped as the Universal Life Force on the planet.

A beacon of humanity for both men and women, Rieta represented equality, tolerance, and education. Her temple stood atop a hill, its five black granite walls mortared with gold. Silver-plated torches, fifteen feet tall, lined the perimeter of the roof and could be seen all the way to the sea, where maritime battles raged amongst man and beast.

Inside, torches mounted on the walls illuminated rows of writing desks in the main hall, where the scent of sage and parchment hung in the air. Here, inspiration born in the hearts of poets, philosophers, and seekers was captured on paper and freed again in the mind of the reader. Expansion was expected. Boundaries drawn were to be breached, and limits were treated as illusions. They believed the human brain could hold and transcend the sum of all ideas conceived by man.

Rieta demanded neither praise nor obedience. In her temple, one did not kneel at the foot of a superior and serve an unseen force who remained hidden behind a veil of ambiguity and contradiction. In her temple, each was expected to stand tall as an equal before the Creator, and discover oneself staring back.

Atop the temple, concealed behind the blazing torches, stood a circular room enclosed by seven pearl-inlay columns. Here, a woman had sat at a desk in the middle of the night, her long white gown whipping in the wind as her hand flew across the page, ink splattering and staining her fingers. She knew this was only the beginning of the story. There was so much more to tell, but she had to hurry. Climbing the hill, ten men with torches of their own were fast approaching the temple, the first with shackles slung over his back.

Inside the duomo, the dark figure climbed the marble steps up to the statue of Rieta and stood in front of a glass case sitting atop a wooden podium.

A low hum swirled through the air as a small rotary blade cut a rectangle around the perimeter of the book that lay inside. A white-gloved hand lowered the cut piece of wood to the floor, closed the book, and placed it inside a leather satchel.

Seconds later, the cameras blinked to life, and dozens of lasers zigzagged across an empty room.

Outside the museum, the damp air cooled her face. She felt woozy but hastened on, careful to keep her head down. Only a handful of personnel had access to the city, but that didn't mean there wasn't surveillance everywhere. Cameras, drones, and AI robots monitored the canals and construction sites around the clock. She rounded the corner in the direction of the delivery gate and ran headfirst into a boulder of a man.

"Where are you headed in such a hurry tonight?" His voice sounded like a chicken bone was lodged in the back of his throat.

She steadied herself and looked at the man's face. His bushy eyebrows, the only hair on his head, strayed in every direction. A flap of skin hung loosely around his neck and formed a diagonal line from the tip of his chin to the center of his clavicles.

"I've just come from the security systems check," Aster replied.

He eyed her suspiciously. "In a hurry to get home to your man?"

She ignored the remark and stepped to the side, but he shifted his weight in front of her. A subtle yet aggressive gesture to let her know he wasn't finished talking.

"And how did it check out? Are we up and running?"

"All systems are working," she smiled.

He looked her up and down. "Nice bag. My grandmother had one very similar when I was a kid. She used to keep a pair of binoculars in it, and I pretended I was going on a safari."

"Sounds fun," she said evenly.

"Really? You don't look like the safari type to me."

She knew what he was thinking. She was overdressed for a security check in a black sweater, leather leggings, and over-the-knee boots. She pulled the brim of her felt hat down over the side of her face.

"Well, I have that man waiting," she said, eyeing the building to her right.

There was no way of knowing when the security team would discover the book was missing. It could be tomorrow morning or sooner.

"Too bad. I bet you'd look great in a safari costume," he said, leering at her chest.

"I guess we'll never know," she retorted.

Safaris had been outlawed in the midst of a public outcry against poaching and environmental upheaval.

His wristband lit up. "Hmm, looks like there's been some sort of disturbance in one of the wings. It's probably just another false alarm. The rats are wreaking havoc on the ventilation systems. I'd better go have a look," he said, puffing up his chest. He gave her one last once over and smirked: "I hope you run into me again some time. The name's Jack, by the way. Jack Grossman."

"Good night, Jack," she uttered through clenched teeth.

He turned and walked toward the museum.

Aster breathed a sigh of relief and hurried through the gate.

Jack

Venice

September, 2110

Jack was first to arrive at the entrance to the Gucci Gallery, named in honor of the famous Mario Gucci, inventor of the first electric espresso machine for automobiles. It was a radical, wildly successful innovation that allowed Italians to take their 'pausa' in their cars. Sadly, it was a short-lived experiment, as most cars in Italy were still standard shifts. Still, it had made him a rich man overnight, and, after settling numerous lawsuits involving accidents and third degree burns, he still had enough money left over to be a generous patron of the arts.

Jack opened the door and stepped inside. He was the first to arrive, not because he had rushed, but because he was closer than the others. Jack had a naturally lazy disposition, which is why all of his pursuits in life, both professional and personal in nature, involved sitting. This is also why, instead of feeling a mild surge of adrenaline over the security breech, he mostly felt annoyed.

Nothing exciting ever happens in this tomb of a city, he told himself, as he walked down the long corridor toward the duomo, where he had been given instructions to meet the committee members. A 'breach' was all the information he had been given. It was typical for them not to provide him with any further details. He was the night watchman, a symbolic presence to lend a human element on site. The AI robots had higher clearances than he did.

"Pompous bastards," he cursed aloud as he walked into the center of the room. "They have me running around here like a monkey," he said bitterly.

He didn't know anything about art, and he didn't have a degree or a fancy title to his name. It didn't mean he didn't know a thing or two about people. He had plenty of street smarts, and he could be quite resourceful when he needed to be.

Jack looked at the statue. He was too distracted by the breasts to notice the empty podium in front of him or the rectangular piece of wood lying on the ground beneath. "Nice tits," he said aloud and gave a laugh that sounded more like a wheeze. Then, he circled around toward the back of the statue. "Let's see if the ass is just as good."

A clamour of footsteps and voices filled the corridor. The commotion grew louder as a group of five men entered the duomo and walked to the podium, gesturing wildly. Jack circled around and stood next to the men. It took them a moment to notice he was there. "It had to have happened during the security check when the system was shut down," one man said.

Another man turned his attention toward the guard. "Did you see anything suspicious?"

Jack attempted a serious expression. "That depends," he began, pleased that the attention was now on him. "What exactly are we looking at?" He pointed his chin toward the case, and the flap of skin that hung from his neck stretched like a sail in the wind.

"A book has been taken from this case," replied the man in a dark suit. "It pre-dates the Romans by hundreds, maybe even thousands of years. Not that it means anything to you," he said, waving his hand dismissively. "In simple terms, it is irreplaceable and must be recovered."

Jack may not have possessed a grasp of ancient history, but he certainly knew a slight when he was dealt one, and he was sick and tired of pompous, aristocratic men, who had been handed everything in life, ridiculing him. "Well, can you give me a more accurate description of the book? Size, color, thickness?"

Irritated, another man in a dark suit let out an exasperated breath. "As you can see, there is a cut-out in the podium. That would be the size of it," he said, shooting him an annoyed look. "What makes this book so unique, aside from its valuable contents, is the cover. It is covered in emeralds, diamonds, and rubies. Have you seen anyone around tonight? Anything suspicious whatsoever?"

Diamonds. Well, well, now they're speaking my language, Jack thought to himself. Now it all fit. The bombshell in the black catsuit. The satchel. If he played his cards right, this could prove to be very promising, indeed.

"Not a soul," Jack responded, rubbing the stubble on his chin thoughtfully. "It's been dead around here," he made a high-pitched snort, "not even a rat."

Jack cleared his throat, "Emeralds, diamonds, and rubies. This wouldn't have anything to do with the old country?"

The men looked at him with blank expressions.

"You know…green, white, and red. The colors of the old Italian flag?" Jack pressed, sure that he was coming across as erudite and sophisticated.

The men turned back toward one another and entered into a heated discussion. "Let's get back and review all the data from tonight. I don't want any detail missed. Rome is going to have our balls for this."

"You," said a stout man dressed more casually than the others in jeans and a white tee shirt revealing unusually large forearms and hands. He looked more like a boxer than a museum administrator, "don't touch a thing. The city is blocked off. It was obviously an inside job, so this will be an internal matter for the moment. Do you understand?"

"Yes, sir," replied Jack.

I understand basic commands, he thought angrily.

The tallest man with a parrot-shaped nose and beady eyes stepped into Jack's personal space. "Good, and before you leave, have one last visual check of the room. Make sure everything is in order and secure. Let us know if you find anything."

The men turned and exited the room.

"Oh, you can be sure I'll find something of value. But I won't be handing it over to you bastards," he mumbled under his breath.

He kicked the piece of wood across the floor as hard as he could. It hit the ground with a pitiful thud that echoed weakly around the room.

His footsteps were heavy, and his breathing labored as he headed toward the door, but his heart was fluttering with excitement over the twist of fate he had encountered tonight. His luck had finally turned, and his future would be set. He knew people who worked on the black market. Underground places where deals were struck and fortunes made. All he had to do was find the woman with green eyes and olive skin. He knew exactly where to look. Luckily, his clearances allowed him access to certain information.

The dark hollow eyes of the statues watched as Jack plodded down the corridor. Their bodies stood poised and ready, loyal guardians unto their master. As he reached the end, the last two statues fell forward, silent as owls hunting prey, crushing him beneath them. One shattered his pelvis, the other his skull.

Inside the duomo, the full moon moved into the center of the oculus, and Rieta's pupils adjusted in response. The moonbeams danced off the crystal flecks in her eyes that glowed like smoldering embers—a show only the heavens could see.

The next morning, Jack's body was sent to a morgue, where he was placed inside a stainless steel drawer marked B-52. The two fallen statues were repaired by the museum's top preservation specialists and returned to their podiums. Nothing unusual was found other than several drops on the glass case that were the consistency and color of wet plaster. Samples were gathered and taken to the lab for analysis.

In the end, nothing had been captured on surveillance, and the lab work was inconclusive. The only witnesses to the events that had unfolded that night were the ten men standing in the corridor. But they could not speak. They were only statues.

Aster

Venice

2110

Aster crept across the bedroom floor and placed her palm over a glass plate on the chest. Two clicks and the door slid open. She looked over her shoulder to check that Theo was sleeping soundly, then placed the book and her hat inside the drawer.

She slid beneath the covers. Staring up at the ceiling, her mind raced. The floating city that had been home to millions of people for centuries was being turned into a museum. In a matter of months, all the canals would be drained. The wooden piles that had been the foundation of the city for centuries would be reinforced with rebar and steel braces and concrete poured on top. The only clue to the canal's existence would be holographic images of water projected onto the streets. It would be one more novel attraction for hordes of tourists to check off their list. Well, she would not be around to see it. As soon as her work was complete, Aster would leave. Climate change had scorched the lands and cleared the forests, creating new deserts where ancient cities were being uncovered. These cities were rewriting the story of human history, and she was going to be a part of it.

She listened to Theo's even breath rising and falling next to her. She had considered asking him to come with her, but Aster doubted he would leave. His family were Venetians twenty generations back, probably more. He was firmly rooted here. It's just as well, Aster thought. Just because two people meet, didn't necessarily mean they were headed in the same direction. Sometimes, they were moving like an arc, starting on opposite ends and meeting briefly at the top, before bypassing each other and moving on to their destination. She could see her destination on the horizon.

Aster looked at the silhouette of his body. She had missed him. His trips to Rome were growing more frequent. The new government was relentless in its demands for updates on the progress in Venice. They did not want any detail overlooked. The world was watching and everything had to be perfect. Aster rubbed her temples in small circular motions, but the tension in her head did not budge.

She could feel the heat emanating from his skin that was hot and dry as the desert. Suddenly, a fierce tremor coursed through his entire body. It lasted just a second and was gone. His breathing never faltered as he continued to slumber. She rolled over onto her side and placed her hand on his chest. She did not want to sleep. She wanted to be the woman in his bed that night who was driving him crazy. She bit her bottom lip. Her only desire was to transfer the heat inside of her to the furnace raging inside of him. She slid beneath the sheets, past his naval, and began stroking his penis with her tongue. She wrapped her mouth around him in a cocoon of warm wetness, teasing it to life. Feeling his cock grow hard excited her. With each slide of her mouth up and down his shaft, she grew intoxicated with the power she derived from being the source of his pleasure. She worked with great eagerness. Aster noticed the subtle trembling of his hips as the intensity of his sighs grew more frequent. His hand gently stroked her shoulder and moved up her neck to rest on the top of her head. His touch felt grateful and reassuring. It drove a tingle down her spine.

Aster knew she could stop, climb on top of him and have the most vulnerable part of him penetrate the most vulnerable part of her. Instead, she drove him further to the back of her throat. She wanted him to remember this long after it was over, so she used her lips and her tongue until she felt him shake and the warm salty taste of his eruption filled her mouth.

She rolled over on her back. "Sorry, I didn't mean to wake you."

"I'll let it slide this time," he said. "But don't make a habit out of it."

She gently smacked his chest with the back of her hand. "Go back to sleep. I need you rested for in the morning. I'll want you then."

"Not now?"

"It's been a long day. I'm tired, and I don't have an orgasm in me, I'm afraid."

"I'm sure I can find one somewhere," he said, reaching under the covers.

But she did not respond. Exhaustion overcame her, and she closed her eyes.

Theo

Venice

October, 2110

Theo opened the door to the closet and reached on the top shelf. He swept his hand from front to back and right to left, but it wasn't there. He stepped back and ran his hand through his hair. Where had he put it? He thought. The long chest on the opposite wall caught his eye. Of course, the chest. Aster had put all the chips to upload security clearances and travel pass renewals in one folder and locked it inside the drawer - for safe keeping, she had said. She was right - these clearances were highly sought after on the black market, and people were paying big money for the security chips that would allow them access into the world's most talked-about city—some out of curiosity, some out of nostalgia, some to steal.

He walked across the room and placed his hand on the glass screen. He heard the lock click, and the top drawer slid open.

A black wide-brimmed hat with ivory trim lay inside the drawer. The same hat he had uploaded into the system, projecting it onto every holographic notice board in the city. It was the only lead they had to catch the person who had stolen the book, and it was in his bedroom.

Beneath the hat, lay a wooden box. He removed the lid, exposing the dazzling jewels sparkling inside.

"Shit, Aster."

Iris

"If he wishes to find out whether she is endowed with a witch's power of preserving silence, let him take note whether she is able to shed tears when standing in his presence, or when being tortured. For we are taught both by the words of worthy men of old and by our own experience that this is a most certain sign, and it has been found that even if she be urged and exhorted by solemn conjurations to shed tears, if she be a witch she will not be able to weep."

Malleus Maleficarum Part 3

Question XV

Heinrich Kramer, 1486 AD

Vinci, Tuscany

June, 2012

Iris sat at a cafe on a cobblestone street in a village on the outskirts of Florence where five hundred years ago, an illegitimate baby with neither name nor noble blood brought his light into the world. Nestled among the Cyprus trees where the Arno river meandered through the rolling Tuscan hills, a young Leonardo da Vinci was left in the care of his imagination. Nature would be his inspiration and curiosity, his teacher; although abandonment and betrayal hammered at his soul throughout his life, like a block of clay, he would take his pain and transform it into a thing of beauty.

Although she was alone this bright summer morning, Iris did not feel lonely, for she was in the company of one of the greatest geniuses the world has ever known. The town was small and modest, yet, like the soft-spoken artist himself, a gentle, unassuming energy could be felt on every street. Iris took a sip of the cappuccino that had cooled over the hour she had spent filling her notebook with thoughts and ideas that bubbled up faster than her hand could write. There was so much inside of her that she wanted to get down on paper. She pushed the cappuccino aside and ordered a mushroom pasta and red wine for lunch.

Later that afternoon, she climbed the steps that led to the entrance of a church. She opened the heavy doors and was met with a welcomed burst of cool air. She walked down the nave and admired the simplicity of the inside. The smooth stucco walls were in the soothing color combination of ivory and pietra serena, a greenish-grey stone favored by the likes of Brunelleschi and Donatello. To her left, in a small circular room with a marble pedestal in the center, she was transported back in time to when an anxious young mother soothed a wriggling baby boy as holy water was sprinkled atop his head.

She imagined the fear and uncertainty a fifteen-year-old unmarried servant must have felt over the future for her son born under such circumstances.

Iris walked back outside and sat down on the church steps. She gazed beyond the lichen and moss speckled rooftops, past the neat rows of olive trees that formed rectangular patches over the sloping hills, and out over the hazy blue horizon. Iris thought how Leonardo's mother had stood on the same steps, not ever knowing the life and legacy her son would come to live. She would die too young.

Iris closed her eyes and took a deep breath. She often dismissed it as figments of her imagination, but today she wanted to believe the unseen was more real than the reality before her. So, she willed herself to stay in this place of silent knowing and relaxation, because when she did, everything flowed more easily. Slowly, the words took shape. They floated freely, pulsating gently. Each word had its own color, size, and vibration. As she relaxed deeper into a state of suspended alertness, the words arranged and rearranged themselves, coming together in a tightly knit bundle, and then exploding outward in a burst of color, sending ripples through the space around it. The words continued to flow, stringing together to form thoughts and ideas. She would have no trouble remembering them later - they were born of her.

She need only to write them down, making the unseen visible, at least for the one person she trusted enough to read them.

Ben.

She hadn't thought of him all day. Suddenly, a sense of anxiousness enfolded her, and the words began to swirl into darkened blurs. Her mind conjured up scenarios, and her body followed, willingly living out the drama as if it were actually happening. Feelings of guilt swept through her, and she felt herself sinking lower into despair.

Suddenly, a scream shattered the silence. She opened her eyes and saw two young boys running in circles. They darted down the steps, stopping briefly at the bottom. The taller boy stopped and bolted back up the steps, a cascade of blond curls bouncing around his face. He tripped a few steps below her, catching himself with his hands. He looked up at her and their eyes locked for the briefest moment. Something about the color reminded her of the Van Gogh paintings in Paris. In a split second, he was standing up again.

"Are you ok?" she asked. But he only smiled and ran off, the other boy fast on his heels.

She left the church and walked down the hill. Near the bottom, a small bookstore with an ornately carved wooden storefront caught her eye. Intrigued, she ventured inside. The store was narrow and deep. Shelves of books rose all the way to the ceiling and wooden ladders rested on metal rolling tracks.

"Buongiorno," a friendly voice greeted her. A tall woman wearing a white linen dress and circular black glasses that gave her an owlish quality appeared holding two books.

"Buongiorno," Iris replied, smiling pleasantly.

"The English section is on the back wall," she said, switching to English.

Iris nodded and walked down the aisle toward the back of the store, where she examined the titles. On the shelf near the corner, she spotted a cover that caught her attention—*Discovering the Real Mona Lisa.*

She was reaching for the book, when a voice behind her interrupted, "That's an excellent choice," stressing the word excellent. She didn't need to turn around to know it was the woman who had greeted her. "A fascinating read on the real La Gioconda," she continued.

"La Gioconda?"

"Certo, Mona Lisa. The *real* Mona Lisa," she said, with a knowing look.

"I always thought her identity was a mystery."

"No! Of course, she was real. She was a Florentine, mother, and wife to a wealthy silk merchant. Her name was Lisa Gioconda. Here in Italy, she is simply known as La Gioconda."

"I never knew. Sounds interesting," said Iris, taking the book from the shelf. She turned it over in her hands and smiled. "I'll take it."

Iris stepped onto the sidewalk clutching the package to her chest when her phone rang.

"Hi," she said.

"Hey, how's your trip?" asked Nico.

"Great so far. I visited Vinci today."

Iris walked down the street in the direction of her parked car.

"Ah, the famous Leonardo. How was it?"

"It's incredible, actually. I'm glad I came. It took my mind off the job situation. How's London? Did your meeting go well?"

"As well as to be expected."

"You sound stressed. Is everything ok?"

"Are you staying in Tuscany or headed back home?"

"I'm headed back. I can make it home before dark."

"You should visit Lucca first. It's an interesting town not far from Pisa. I think you would like it. Besides, what's one more day?"

"Hmm. Sounds nice. Maybe I'll check it out."

"I have to go, but call me later and let me know you arrived."

"I will. Bye."

Later that afternoon…

Iris walked along the lush footpath atop the medieval wall that encircled the town. She found a shady spot beneath a tree and took a seat on the bench. She unwrapped the book and studied Mona Lisa on the cover. Unlike other portrait artists of his time, who altered the subject's appearance to appear in the most favorable light, Leonardo painted his subjects as he truly saw them. His gift was capturing the person's essence -a much more difficult feat.

She turned off her phone and began to read.

Iris stretched her back that was stiff from sitting on the bench. She folded the corner of the page and closed the book. Then she turned her phone back on to check the time. Her phone beeped three times, all the messages from Ben.

Hey. I've been trying to call, but your phone is off.

She clicked on the next one.

I have an art show in Amsterdam coming up. I'll tell you the details later, but a friend hooked me up with a friend who owns a gallery. I hope you can make it.

The last message was the invitation to his opening.

Iris smiled.

So, he had started painting again.

On the drive home, Iris thought of Lisa Gioconda, the real Mona Lisa, and the life she had led. By all accounts, it was a typical life of an upper-class wife. She dutifully tended to the daily routines of the household and raising her children, who not all would survive beyond childhood. Like too many women before her, she was a mother who had been touched by grief that comes with the loss of a child.

Life would go on, as it does, and the years passed as she functioned within the constructs of Florentine society. Yet, the rigid society with its rules and hierarchy could not contain her. Somehow, she would managed to wade through the mundane and immortalize herself in a single painting.

But Leonardo was not the only man to have been enamoured with her essence. In her husband's last will and testament, he made specific mention of his dilectum uxorem, beloved wife's, "free-born spirit" - that wild streak that revealed itself in her mysterious smile, knowing and untamed, and enchants us all in perpetuity.

Iris parked her car outside the house and rolled her small suitcase up the sidewalk. Inside, she removed her shoes and slipped her feet into her slippers. She walked into the living room and was surprised to hear Nico's voice coming from the kitchen. "Surely he could not have gotten back from London this soon," she muttered.

She walked into the kitchen where she saw another man she did not recognize. "Nico," she exclaimed. "I thought you were in London?"

The color drained from his face as he stood up. "Iris, I thought you were in Lucca."

"I decided not to spend the night and come home instead."

Iris turned to the man with grey hair, dressed in a green cardigan and khaki slacks. "I'm sorry, I don't believe we've met. I'm Iris." She held out her hand. The older man shook it, but did not speak. "And who do we have here," she asked, leaning into the baby he was cradling in his arms.

"Iris, come with me. We need to talk." Nico turned to the man: "If you will excuse us?"

The man nodded and brushed past Iris without a word, carrying the baby with him.

"Nico, what is going on?"

"Iris, sit down."

"I don't want to sit down. I want you to tell me what's going on. You are supposed to be in London. I just spoke with you a few hours ago. You were in London. Now you're here."

"I am so sorry."

"Don't. Don't start with an apology. Start with the truth."

Nico ran his hand through his hair. "Iris, that baby is mine."

Trento

June, 2012

Iris emptied the dustpan into the trashcan, filling it with broken shards from the wine glasses Nico had given her. Glasses he had brought back as a gift from one of his trips to London. She had not noticed that they were made in Murano.

It had been five days since she had returned to Trento from her trip—five days since she had thrown each one against the tile floor, then told him to leave. She had yet to shed one tear.

Iris carried the bin to the recycling container at the end of the street. On her way back, the front door opened to the cream colored house. Nico stepped out, pushing a stroller. Iris felt a sickness come over her as she took in the view.

"Iris. I was just taking the baby out for a walk," Nico stuttered. Iris stared at him. "Actually, I saw you walking down the street, and I wanted to see you."

Iris noticed the stroller and a blanket covering a sleeping baby. An illegitimate child born to a married man with neither name nor title. She had felt so much compassion for the child and mother that day in Vinci. It had never occurred to her how the wife must have felt.

Iris' phone beeped in her hand. It was Ben.

I haven't heard from you. Are you coming to the gallery opening?

Iris put the phone in her pocket and took a deep breath. "Let's go for a walk," she said to Nico.

They walked down the street. "How did you not know she was pregnant?" Iris asked.

"She never told me. I can only guess she called it off when she found out."

"And you never saw her again?"

"Never. Not even a glimpse. It's like she evaporated into thin air. I assumed she was avoiding me or had left town. I never knew she was hiding the pregnancy."

"So, if your name wasn't listed on the birth certificate, how did her father know you were the father?"

"She had a sister. They were close, and she told her about us."

Iris kept her gaze forward. "How did she die?"

"Complications. The baby was premature. That was all her father would say."

He stopped and turned toward her. "I swear, I was just as surprised as you were. It lasted for just a few months, and I thought it was over."

Iris looked at the stroller. "It looks like it's just beginning."

A cry came from the stroller, and Nico removed the blue blanket.

"I guess you're right." Nico cradled the baby in his arms. "But of all my sins, this one is the sweetest."

"I didn't think you were religious."

"I'm not. But how can you look into those eyes and tell me there isn't something out there bigger than us?"

Iris smiled for the first time in a week. "I can't argue with that. Speaking of us, did you ever think how this would affect me?"

"I didn't think that far ahead. If there's one thing I know, it's that you'll be fine. You'll never belong to anyone, Iris. You never truly belonged to me, and sometimes I don't think you even belong in this world."

She turned her head away, pretending to study a crow that had landed on a tree branch nearby.

"So, can I ask you what your plans are?" he asked.

Iris put her hand in her pocket and wrapped her fingers around the phone. "I'm going to take a trip.

"Where to?"

"Amsterdam."

Amsterdam

July, 2012

Iris' heart raced as her suede boots clicked along the cobblestone street. She passed rows of colorful bicycles, stacked next to each other. The canals were bustling with tourists and locals, soaking up the summer nights before the long dark days of winter bore down.

Iris turned down a street and stood in front of the first shop. The brass numbers on the top of the door read 210. The gallery was just two blocks away. She caught her reflection in the window and was startled to see the woman staring back at her. She was wearing more makeup than she was used to. A dramatic smoky liner played up her eyes. Her lips were stained a deeper shade of their natural color. Her crimson knit dress was fitted and fell just below her knee. The low neckline exposed her collarbones and framed the necklace, a delicate gold chain with an enamel butterfly pendant she had purchased at a local antique market. It felt good to be dressed up again, and shed the jeans, sweaters, and boots she had lived in the past winter. For the first time in a while, she felt like her old self.

Iris checked her watch. She was running late, but it didn't matter, he was not waiting for her. She had not RSVP'd on the gallery's website, although she'd logged on to take a look. Written across the homepage was the title of his opening, TuBeD —'Debut' spelled backwards. The TBD in capital letters had not missed her attention, all a clever nod to their previous conversation.

Iris stood up straight and squared her shoulders. Ben towered over her by a good four inches, but with heels on tonight, they would be eye-to-eye.

Iris walked passed a trendy coffee shop with people sitting at long communal tables, staring at laptops. Just beyond the coffee shop, a group of well-dressed men and women were gathered on the sidewalk, holding glasses of wine and chatting casually. She could hear a mix of Dutch and English grow louder. Soon, Iris was standing at the entrance to the gallery, peering inside the stark white space beyond the window. There, hung on the wall, were six giant canvases framed in neon lights.

Of her.

Iris' eyes were transfixed on the images in front of her. Suddenly, she spotted a woman wearing a brightly colored kaftan with a bold floral motif talking to Ben. Wearing gold hoop earrings that skimmed the tops of her shoulders, the woman turned her head and glanced at Iris. A flash of recognition crossed the woman's face. She shifted her gaze back toward the canvases, then back toward her. Iris turned and hurried back down the street toward the canal.

She spotted a cafe on the other side and crossed the street.

"Iris," a male's voice shouted from behind. "Iris!" the calls of her name got closer.

She felt a hand on her shoulder, stopping her dead in her tracks. She turned around to face him.

Ben smiled at her. "Adena said it was you."

"I was just…" she tried to think of something clever to say to hide her embarrassment.

"I'm glad you came," he said, putting her at ease.

"Thank you for inviting me."

"How about we grab a glass of wine?"

"Don't you need to be at the gallery?"

"They won't miss me. Besides, everything is sold, so my work is done. Adena, the gallery manager I told you about, can handle the rest."

"Everything sold?"

"You sound surprised."

"No, it's just that it's your first show. That is quite an accomplishment."

"Thank you, but I can't take all the credit," a sly smile crossed his face.

"Your friend did a great job setting this up for you."

"I wasn't talking about her." He took her by the arm, "Come on."

Ben led her inside a small cafe with exposed brick walls and crystal chandeliers. The far wall was covered with paintings of Dutch still life that imitated the masters of the Dutch Golden Age. Iris studied them while the waitress prepared their table. The scenes depicted the glory and new-found wealth brought about by trade in this maritime nation. But, if one looked beneath the layers of wilted exotic flowers, overturned crystal vases, silver, and cracked shellfish scattered atop a table draped in silk, a darker tale emerges: a single fly feasting on an apple warns us of the traps of decadence and earthly desires; a gold pocket watch reminds us of the impermanence of life; while a skull resting on the edge of the table serves as a grim caveat of our fleeting mortality and the certainty of death.

They took a seat at a small table near the back and ordered two glasses of wine.

"So, why didn't you come into the gallery?"

"I didn't want to steal the show," she said slyly.

"It's too late for that. You're plastered all over the gallery walls," he smiled.

"So, about that," she ventured cautiously.

"Yes?"

"The paintings. They are the pictures I texted you over the last months. Of course, I wanted to inspire you," she laughed nervously, "but..."

"Are you surprised? I used to paint you before."

"Well, to tell the truth, yes. Mainly because you never mentioned it." She sat her wine glass down. "I remember when you used to paint me. Those were some of my happiest times, me lying on the sofa and you behind the easel. I remember the way you would get lost in the canvas, the way your eyes would light up when I would know you had gotten it just right. That, of course, was my motivation for sending you those."

"And here I was thinking you were trying to seduce me."

"Maybe a little of that too," she smiled.

"Well, I hope you are not upset."

"No..."

"I mean, the way you darted away from the gallery..."

"What did you expect? Maybe I was just expecting some sort of a warning," she said.

"I thought it was something you had to see in person. To fully understand."

"I mean, I gave the pictures to you, but I intended them to be only for you. I'm a big girl, though, and not totally naive. I knew you could use them for inspiration or a weapon."

He chuckled, "You thought I would use them as a weapon? You really think I'm that sinister?"

She shifted her gaze to the flame flickering on the table.

"You were always my muse, Iris. In many ways." He reached for her hand. "Come on."

"We haven't finished our wine."

"There's wine at the gallery. I want to show you the paintings."

Iris stood with her arms folded in front of her, staring into her own eyes. The pupils swirled outward into a green vortex. It was a tranquil green - somewhere between the color of shamrock and olive. She could feel Ben's eyes on her as she studied the painting.

He reached over and unfolded her arms, placing them by her sides.

"It's important to be open. Especially when you look at art," Ben said.

Words, painted in shades as subtle as the tones of flesh, emerged from various parts of her body - the torso, a breast, the side of her face. The skin seemed to breathe them in and out in soft, gentle whispers. She knew the words because she had written them. Her private thoughts were now on display for everyone to read. At that moment, she felt more naked than her body on the canvas.

"You kept the letters I wrote you?"

"I did."

"I don't know what to say."

"You told me there was an artist inside of me. Well, there is a poet inside of you. Your words transformed me. So, I merged them together. The words and their creator. This," he said, gesturing toward the wall, "is the result."

"You're right. I needed to see it in person."

"Well, what do you think?"

She turned around and faced him. "I think we need to leave," she leaned in and whispered in his ear. "Now."

Iris opened her eyes and reached for her watch on the bedside table next to the empty glass of wine. She tried to read the time, but the hands had stopped at 3:53. Then, a pair of warm hands encircled her waist and pulled her close. She let go of the watch, and it fell to the floor.

"Stay with me," Ben said.

"I have a plane to catch."

"I mean, stay with me, like we used to be."

"Why would I do that?"

"Because I want you to."

"Until you don't."

He pulled her in closer. "You don't know that."

"I know I've worn that dress before, and it doesn't fit." She took his hand and laced her fingers through his. "I think we both do better with a certain amount of space in relationships. Besides, I need to feel free again. That'll take some time."

"So you're saying you need time and space?"

"Time. Space. You're talking about infinity and the infinite. We don't even have a clue as to what those things actually are. Maybe we are not even moving through time, but rather, time is moving through us."

"Have been into the sci-fi genre lately?"

"That sounds very condescending. Maybe I'm tired of people making references to things they know nothing about."

"I don't mean to be condescending. I find it all very interesting. So, forget time and space. But, I am interested in one thing at the moment. What am I to you?"

"I can't answer that."

"Why not? You can give me a speech on the space-time continuum, but you can't answer a simple question."

"I can't answer it because the word does not exist…yet."

"You're not making this easy," he laughed. "So let me ask you differently. What would it look like if we could be any way you wanted us to be?"

"It would look like freedom."

"Freedom?"

"Freedom from worrying about what the other person can give us. We don't realize what the magnitude of placing such a burden is on the other person - how selfish of us to find someone and then say to them, 'Here is my heart. Now you are responsible for my happiness'.

When it should be the opposite, we should ask how we can empower the other and what we can give to the other. We should be striving to make each other independent, not dependent. To me, that is freedom. Freedom to act as I choose and be responsible for myself." She reached for the bottle of water on the nightstand and took a sip. "Of course, all of that is easier said than done."

Ben rolled over onto his side and propped his head on his arm. "I think we've been fed this lie that tells us that falling in love will cure all our ails. And the other person is the one who will do it for us, magically, almost." Ben pulled the cover up over them and slid his hands beneath the sheet. "Then how about we not force it. And let's just see where it goes, naturally."

It was mid-afternoon by the time Iris crawled out of bed and showered.

"Do you have time to eat before you go?" Ben asked.

"I have to get to the airport. I'll grab something there."

She picked her watch up off the floor and fastened it around her wrist. Then, she leaned in close and kissed him goodbye. Grabbing her suitcase and purse, Iris walked out the door. She didn't have to turn around to know he was smiling.

Trento

August, 2012

They sat at the table in the kitchen.

"Thanks for coming," Iris said.

"You would have done the same for me," Catrin replied, pouring her a cup of tea.

"I never saw this one coming. Alone in a foreign country. Making a mess of my life."

Catrin laughed. "Hardly a mess. More like an adventure."

"Some adventure," Iris moaned. "I have to figure things out. And I only have two months left on our lease."

"My suggestion is to leave the past where it is. The only question at the moment is, where do you go from here?"

"I don't feel qualified to make such decisions anymore," she laughed.

It was the first laugh she had had in a while, and it felt good.

"Just look at the blank canvas in front of you."

"Don't talk to me about canvases," said Iris, rolling her eyes.

"Right," Catrin bit her lower lip. "By the way, have you talked to Ben since you saw him in Amsterdam?"

"No. I but I do think I need to talk to a fortune teller."

"No, you don't. The best way to predict your future is to create it. Now come on, what is it you really want to do?"

"I'm not sure. I mean, I have some ideas, but... I don't know. They all seem sort of impossible."

"Impossible is a great place to start. Keep going," urged Catrin.

"You should add life motivator to your resume."

"Maybe I will," Catrin said, lifting her chin in the air.

Iris laughed and took a sip of her tea.

"I'm not worried," she said, placing her cup on the saucer. "I always manage to land on my feet."

Catrin grinned, "Why land, when you can just keep flying?"

Iris raised her eyebrow. "Flying or free-falling?"

Catrin shrugged. "Either one."

Suddenly, an idea occurred to Iris, not so much an idea but an impulse. She stood up. "Come on, let's get in the car. I'll show you my blank canvas."

Catrin turned up the volume on her Beatles playlist, and started singing along.

Iris looked at her sitting in the passenger seat. Catrin had a paisley print scarf tied around her head, holding back her loose blond waves. Round, oversized sunglasses covered half of her face.

She wore a suede vest with long fringe that lined the armholes, her faded blue jeans, and favorite pair of broken-in cowboy boots. Iris wondered if she had somehow landed in the wrong decade.

Trees flew past the windows as the car weaved up and over the mountain, eventually arriving at a small unmarked road on the left. Iris put her turn signal on and waited for a car to pass before turning down the narrow lane.

"Great, I inspired you to bring us to the Bates Motel?"

"As usual, you're never too far off."

They passed the emerald green lake on their right. "Ok, definitely not the Bates Motel. This place is gorgeous," Catrin exclaimed.

Iris pulled the car around and parked in front of the old inn. As expected, it was quiet, with only a few cats lying lazily in the sun.

"So, will you tell me why we are here?"

"We are here," Iris said, turning the engine off, "to change my life."

"Well, by all means. Let's do it."

Iris opened the car door and stepped onto the gravel pavement. She checked the front door of the inn, but it was locked.

"I'm guessing no one is expecting us?" Catrin asked.

"Come on," Iris said, stepping off the porch. "Maybe he's in his house around back."

Just then, the door to the inn opened and Giuseppe stepped out. "What a surprise," he said. "Please, come in."

They stepped inside and stood in the small lobby.

"So, what brings you all the way out here on this beautiful day?" he asked.

"This is my friend, Catrin. She's visiting from the States," Iris placed her hand on Catrin's arm. "Sorry to just drop in, but I wanted to show her your place."

They sat around a circular table in the middle of the room, and Giuseppe poured three glasses of wine. Iris glanced over at the fireplace. The brass holder she had given him was mounted on the wall. She was pleased to see it was filled with long matches.

"So, tell me, what's been going on?" Giuseppe asked. "But wait, first a toast." He held up his glass, and the three chinked their glasses.

"I wanted to talk to you about something. I've gone through some unexpected changes lately."

Giuseppe shrugged. "Change is an inevitable part of life."

"It's just a crazy idea, and I will not be offended if you say no." She took a long breath and continued, "I was wondering if your inn were for sale? Because if so, I would like to purchase it," Iris said.

Catrin clasped her hands over her mouth. "Oh my god," she exclaimed.

A surprised look crossed his face. He leaned back in his chair.

"Listen, I appreciate your offer, but you have no idea what you would be getting yourself into."

"What if I bought the inn from you, just the inn - you would keep your house in the back and the surrounding grounds. But I could purchase this main building and renovate it."

"This place needs a ton of work to get up to code. Everything needs to be updated. And don't get me started on permits - the whole thing would be a nightmare," he said, putting his hands up. "And even if you did renovate it, I doubt anyone would come."

"I understand it will be quite the undertaking, but I am more than willing to do the work. I can't explain it, but I felt a connection to this place. I have the vision to restore it and bring people here again."

"It's an incredible amount of work, more work than one person can handle on their own. My wife and I had several workers, and it still nearly killed us. You have no help."

"Yes, she does," Catrin blurted.

Iris turned and looked at her. "What?"

"She has help. Me," Catrin said again.

Iris stared at her incredulously, holding her wine glass in midair.

Catrin jutted her chin in Giuseppe's direction. "You heard him. You need help. I can move here for a few months and help you get started. When else will I ever have an opportunity to live in Italy and run an inn with my best friend?"

"Well, it looks like I have a partner," said Iris slowly, raising her glass higher. Catrin reached across and clinked their glasses together.

Giuseppe shook his head. "I appreciate your interest in the inn, but I think you'll be very disappointed in the end. No one travels out here anymore."

Iris leaned forward in her chair. "Listen, we don't have to reach a decision today. All I ask is that you think about it."

He shrugged. "I'll think about it," he replied.

They left the inn and reached the main road, but instead of turning right, Iris turned left.

"Where are we headed?" Catrin asked.

"To town. I thought we could grab some lunch and take a look around."

"Iris, I can't believe you want to buy that inn."

"Do you think it's a crazy idea? Have I completely lost it?"

"Are you kidding? I think it's the best idea you've ever had. If he agrees, I think you could turn the place into something really special.

Do you think he'll agree?"

"It's hard to tell. I think we caught him by surprise, but I'm hoping once he has time to process it, he'll think it's as good of an idea as you do."

"I would think he would be happy to sell it to someone who genuinely cares about it."

"I know it sounds totally insane, but I almost feel like I've been there before. Like I belong there in some way. Have you ever felt that way about a place?"

"I've always felt that way about Italy in general, but I guess many people feel drawn here."

"Well, it's an ancient country. I guess it only makes sense that most people would have lived at least one past life here," Iris laughed. "Look at this place," she lifted her hand off the steering wheel, "who wouldn't want to come back again and again?"

A small town surrounded by a medieval wall came into view.

"We probably aren't allowed to park inside the wall," Iris said.

"Just park on the side of the road here. We can walk the rest of the way."

She pulled off onto the shoulder.

"It's so picturesque," Catrin said, stepping out of the car.

They walked through the imposing stone archway and up the cobblestone street.

"I could eat something. I'm starving," Catrin said.

"Me too. Let's find the piazza."

"All roads lead to the piazza," Catrin said, pointing straight ahead and picking up her pace.

The piazza was quiet except for two older men sitting on a bench and a group of young mothers chatting while their children ran in circles shouting and laughing.

"That looks like a nice place," Catrin said, pointing to a cafe with a small wooden door.

"Perfect, let's grab a table."

"Let's sit under the umbrella," Iris said, pointing to the one off to the side. "I forgot to put my sunblock on today."

"Why is everyone staring at us?" Catrin asked.

"I have no idea. But I'm sure it has nothing to do with your cowboy boots and fringe," said Iris, rolling her eyes and laughing.

A waiter, dressed in black pants, a buttoned-up shirt, and a crisp white apron, approached the table. "Can I take your order?" he asked, giving them a subtle once-over.

Iris glanced at the selections on a chalkboard by the door: pasta con ragu; carbonara; gnocchi; or pasta with leeks and sausage. "I'll take the gnocchi and a red wine, please."

"Make that two," added Catrin.

"So," began Catrin, "you were awfully quiet in the car."

A woman sitting on the stone steps of an old well was busy tossing breadcrumbs to a group of eager pigeons. The stone steps were worn smooth around the edges, and Iris wondered how many people it had taken, sitting and stepping on the stones, to wear them down to a polished surface. Then, suddenly, a wave of emotion swelled inside her chest.

"Iris?"

"I'm sorry. What did you say?"

"You're grieving. The end of a relationship is a death of sorts. And you were handed quite a shock. And now Ben and the art show." She shook her head and moved her sunglasses to the top of her head. "Give it time."

"It's not just that. I can feel something else going on. I just don't know what it is."

The waiter placed two glasses of red wine on the table and walked off. Catrin looked at Iris. "Do you think you should go back to the States for a while? Maybe you need to be around familiar surroundings, your friends and family."

"That's the thing. This place feels familiar. I can't explain, but this place feels safe, like a cocoon. Does that sound ridiculous?"

"Not at all." Catrin held up her glass. "To changes, uncertainty, and whatever comes your way."

Iris took a slow sip, savoring the bouquet of flavors before swallowing. "Maybe you're right. Maybe I should go back to the States for a while."

"My flight leaves next Monday. You can fly back with me."

"Ok, maybe some distance is all I need. An inn might have been a bit much."

"I admire your gumption. It was a bold idea."

Iris picked up her phone. "I'll check the flights. What airline are you on?"

"Hold on, I'll bring up my info," said Catrin, reaching for her purse.

Iris' phone rang.

Catrin looked up from digging through her purse and shot her a mischievous grin. "Would that be your artist calling?"

Iris rolled her eyes, "He wouldn't be calling at this time." She looked at the screen. "I don't recognize the number. I'll ignore it." She looked back at Catrin. "Can you find anything in that giant purse?" she asked impatiently.

"I know it's here somewhere. Ahh, here we go," she said, pulling her phone out dramatically.

"Hold on," Iris said. "It looks like they left a message."

Iris listened to the message, and astonishment crossed her face. "Oh my god."

"What is it?" Catrin asked.

She put the phone back on the table. "That was Giuseppe. He wants to talk."

"Are you serious?"

"Dead serious."

"Well, change of plans." Catrin held up her glass again.

"Talking is not buying," Iris said cautiously. "This is Italy. These things don't happen overnight."

"You're buying an inn," exclaimed Catrin. "And, I'm moving to Italy!"

"Let's not get ahead of ourselves. We'll see what Giuseppe has to say."

"So, what are plans for decorating? I know you've thought about it," said Catrin excitedly.

Iris laughed and relaxed. "Well, of course, I have."

They ate their lunch and sipped their wine. As they chatted, they did not notice the woman with curly copper hair and golden eyes sitting at the well stand up and straighten her linen skirt. She walked across the piazza and past Iris, who glanced up and smiled. The woman did not smile back.

Violetta

"When a woman thinks alone, she thinks evil."

Malleus Maleficarum, Part 1

Question VI

Heinrich Kramer, 1486 AD

Alpinella

April, 1553

It was an austere piazza with no hint of grandeur or foreign influence. There were no carved marble arches with intricate lace patterns and pointed tips that reminded Violetta of royal crowns, no painted frescoes depicting biblical scenes, or stained glass windows casting prisms onto marble floors. Even the church looked bulky and severe - a brutalist mass against a gentle rolling landscape.

In the center of the square, a woman lowered her bucket into a well that was set atop a stone pedestal. Three mothers sat on the steps chatting while their children ran in circles singing a nursery rhyme. To the right of the well sat a lone man. His forearms were resting on his knees as he looked straight ahead. Even across the piazza, Violetta could see his Light shine like a comet from the center of his chest and radiate outward in every direction. He was strikingly handsome with chiseled features and broad shoulders.

His head slowly turned toward the church, and Violetta followed his gaze.

A priest had emerged from the church, then walked across the piazza. He didn't seem to notice the man sitting on the steps as he passed the well. Violetta stood beneath a tree and saw how the priest lumbered with an uneven gait and how his black cloak hung sloppily over his sloped shoulders. It gave him the appearance of being older than his face suggested. His round belly bulged, making his cloak hang shorter in the front than at the back. Violetta watched as he reached the tavern on the other side of the piazza. His eyes darted suspiciously back and forth, and then he entered through a small wooden door. Violetta's attention then turned toward the handsome stranger who had stood up.

He walked briskly past her, without so much as a glance, and disappeared inside the tavern.

I'm here not even an hour and already witnessed an intriguing encounter, Violetta thought to herself, quite amused. Maybe this would not be such a dull place after all.

Then, she straightened her back. Her mother had warned her not to meddle in other people's affairs. Her mother's words echoed in her head: "All you need to bother with is keeping your side of the street clean. That's enough work."

Violetta checked the small gold pocket watch that had belonged to her grandfather. It was getting late. She would take a room in town and find the inn tomorrow morning.

The next day, Violetta gripped the handle of her small satchel nervously. She reached for the handle on the inn door when, to her surprise, the door opened, and the man from the piazza stood before her. Immediately, a flash of recognition ignited a current that swept over her entire body. Violetta smiled and hoped he had not noticed how her legs faltered for a split second, causing her to sway ever so slightly.

"Hello, my name is Violetta Santori. I sent a letter three weeks ago."

The man said nothing, and suddenly, Violetta was painfully aware of how she must look dressed in her silk dress and sheer veil covering the top of her head in the middle of the country. No wonder everyone in town had stared.

Her confidence wavered, but Violetta tried again. "I wrote to inform you of my arrival from Venice - but I never received a response.

Perhaps if I spoke to the person in charge?" Violetta finished.

"I read your letter," he replied.

"Well, then, I apologize for not receiving your response. It must have-"

He interrupted her, "There was no response."

The man stepped aside, opened the door wider, and gestured toward the small desk inside. "Wait here. Daniella will be in shortly to see you to your room."

Violetta laid her bag on the wooden floor and turned around to ask him if he could please tell her footman to unload her things, but he had already disappeared out the door.

Beads of sweat pooled at her nape and trickled down her spine. She shifted back and forth. Her swollen feet ached in her shoes.

"Good morning," a voice came from behind her.

"Good morning," Violetta replied, facing a smiling young woman with a mouth full of yellow crooked teeth.

The woman's eyes darted quickly up and down her. "You must be Violetta. Marco told me you would be arriving today." Daniella walked over to the small desk and flipped to a page in the middle of her registry. "We have your room ready. I see your footman will be staying one night and you for five?"

"That is correct."

"Please, follow me," Daniella said as she snapped the book shut.

Violetta held up her hand. "I just need to tell my footman to bring in my trunk," Violetta said, looking back toward the open door.

Coming up the steps was the footman carrying her trunk. He laid it down and stepped inside. "I assume everything is in order, Signora. The gentleman told me to bring in your things."

"Umm, yes, Giacomo. Everything is in order, thank you."

"Very well. I'll unload and deliver the rest of your things to your room."

"Thank you," she replied, trying her best to appear confident and in charge.

Violetta followed Daniella up the narrow staircase that creaked with each step and down a dimly lit hall. She instantly liked Daniella's warm charm, crooked smile, and all.

"Welcome to your home for the next few days," Daniella said, smiling warmly.

Stepping into the sunny room, Violetta's eyes lit up.

"It's not our biggest room, but it is my favorite," Daniella said, walking over to the window and pulling back the lace curtain. "There's a beautiful view of the lake."

The room was simple and modest. On the bedside table, a small white vase held a single yellow iris and it made Violetta smiled.

"Is there anything else you need?" Daniella asked.

"Yes, there is one thing. Is it possible to speak with the owner of the inn? I believe her name is Francesca."

The crooked smile disappeared from her face. "I'm afraid that won't be possible," she said.

"Well, I don't mean right at the moment, just whenever she has time," Violetta smiled politely.

"You don't understand," she said, taking a few steps closer, "the lady of the inn is dead."

Albergo Pietra Bella

April, 1553

Word had spread.

A lone female traveler had arrived from Venice.

Several diners cast suspicious glances in her direction. Violetta fidgeted with her linen napkin under the dining table but kept her head high and expression serene. She knew she didn't have to say a word. Her presence alone had the power to make them uneasy. For the first time in her life, she didn't particularly mind. This was her journey, and she wasn't going to let anyone interfere with her experience of it.

A sturdy woman dressed in a black dress with a crisp white apron tied around her waist filled her glass with wine and kept walking. Violetta took the glass in her hand. There was a loveliness in its simplicity, so different from the colorful hand-blown glasses her mother had used for dinner parties.

She could still picture her dining room and the long banquet table stretched out before her. Porcelain plates with gold rims piled high with mutton, pigeon, roasted duck, wild boar, and Venetian-style liver her mother had always urged her to try—just one bite. Violetta preferred fresh fish and seafood, classic baccala spread atop thick slices of rustic bread and drizzled with olive oil, cuttlefish, pasta with anchovy sauce, and fried soft-shell crabs. Fourteen courses were served to guests - stews, pasta, rice, vegetables, and herbolata - a soft cheese pie baked with savory herbs, her favorite.

Dinners began late and lasted well into the early morning hours. She would grow restless, but she did not want to miss the plates of delectable pastries that arrived at the end. So, she sat and let her imagination roam free, transforming the dining table into a mysterious, far away land, adrift in a sea of aqua mosaics. The mirrored ceiling above the table reflected the magical places she longed to journey.

Silver bowls filled with mounds of colorful ground spices transformed themselves into desert islands concealing hidden treasures. She watched as the octopus rose up from its plate and whipped its tentacles violently about grabbing a hold of the pirate ship, an oblong bowl filled with fruit, and dragging it to the depths of the ocean.

Across the table, a battle raged between man and squid. Following a long and bloody fight, the squid ultimately succumbed to the sword of man, perishing in a pool of its own ink.

Three silver candelabras towered high above the landscape - watchtowers that stood ablaze. On the highest rim, a woman dressed in white, her hair whipping in the wind, stared out over the wilderness of slain beasts, wondering if anyone would ever notice the flames burning brightly above.

Violetta closed her eyes. It pained her to think of those days, safely cocooned in her world, the only world she had ever known. She gripped the glass tighter. The pressure from her thumb caused a tiny crack near the bottom of the glass to expand upward, weakening, but not breaking the delicate vessel.

She finished her meal and retired to her room.

Late in the night, a loud pop reverberated down the hallway, jolting her awake. Disoriented, Violetta strained to make out the contents of the room. The outline of a dresser, a lumpy mattress, and the scratchy bed linens, she remembered she was at the inn.

The silence persisted, and she was unsure if the sound had been real, or was part of a dream. It seemed everything was becoming increasingly blurred. She faintly recalled climbing the stairs and falling onto the horsehair mattress. Exhaustion had overtaken her as she drifted into an abysmal sleep.

Now, she lay awake, a traveler in an unfamiliar land. Except, she no longer felt like a traveler. She was a wanderer with neither destination nor purpose, and it seemed even the stars had grown dim in the light of her uncertainty.

Violetta rolled over and closed her eyes, but unsettling thoughts needled at her mind. Three weeks had passed since she had left Venice. As she traveled further from home, she felt her connection to her home fading and the details becoming less vivid, to the point she wondered if it had all been a dream. It surprised her how little time and space was needed to feel a chasm of separation from what was. Even the shock she felt over Franco was slowly dissipating, and, although she owned her house - the stones, beams, floors, and everything contained within the four walls, she wondered if the only thing that determined possession of place or person was one's proximity to it. Further still, she wondered if possession were even possible at all.

That night, she imagined an array of outcomes for the journey.

What she did not foresee, was that, in three years' time, the Black Death would overtake her beloved city, forcing the occupants to flee. Left in the dominion of thieves and squatters, her home would be ransacked, erasing any trace of her prior occupancy, save seventeen black lines that laddered up the far wall of the library, marking her birthdays.

But all of that was vaulted away into a future place. For now, something more threatening than the plague and more sinister than thieves was brewing on the horizon. And, this time, fleeing was not an option.

When she drifted back to sleep, her dreams imparted disturbing images. Were they heralding events that lay ahead? Although she felt a sense of unease when she awoke, piecing together the fragmented images, she dismissed it as merely a dream.

Violetta lingered in bed a bit longer the following morning. Images of the mysterious man from the piazza filled her head. She did not understand why this man, so rugged and aloof, inflamed her so. Violetta ran her fingertips across her naval. Exasperated, she rolled over onto her side. She had more important things to accomplish. She could not be running about the countryside pining over a stranger. She had learned her lesson with Franco. Remaining sensible, she needed to put matters of the heart aside. She must focus on uncovering what had happened to the inn's owner and make sense of the map she found in the book. Daniella was not forthcoming, and Violetta did not wish to press her. However, there was someone who could give her the information she needed. Daniella had called him 'Marco'.

Violetta stretched her arms above her head and smiled.

She was famished and eager to start the day.

The woman with the short sturdy calves and clunky leather shoes served her a cup of steaming coffee and sliced bread. She gave her a half-smile but still did not speak to her. Violetta sipped the coffee. It was weaker than the coffee in Venice, but at least it was steaming hot. She spread butter on a thick slice of bread and took a bite. Surprised, she looked down at the slice in her hand. She had no idea butter could taste so sweet. She took another small bite. Although hungry, she willed herself to chew slowly. She was hoping to see Marco pass through the dining room. Perhaps this time, she could introduce herself properly. But, after finishing the second cup of coffee, she never glimpsed him. So she decided to take a stroll around the lake to pass the morning.

As she walked along the path, her slippers slid into the mud, covering them in brown sludge. Violetta was used to walking the wet canals of Venice, but the mud was something new. Disgusted and feeling foolish, she lifted her dress off the ground and made her way back toward the inn. Violetta made her way up the steps and through the door into the lobby, where she once again bumped into the handsome man.

Violetta stared at him, unsure what to say, but he wasn't looking at her. His eyes were fixed on her shoes. She looked down at her mud-covered slippers. Realizing she was exposing her legs, she dropped her dress to the floor.

"Daniella," he called out to the kitchen.

"We haven't been formally introduced. I'm Violetta. I arrived from-"

The door swung open, and Daniella leaned her head out.

"Can you be so kind as to sweep the floor in here? Our guest has wandered into some mud and tracked it in," he said, his eyes now staring directly into hers. "Would you like for Daniella to clean those for you?"

"Clean my shoes?" Violetta asked.

"And your stockings."

"My stockings?"

"They're muddy," he said.

Violetta reached down and took off her slippers one by one. She could feel his eyes studying her as she laid them on the floor. Then she began to reach for her stockings.

"You can take those off in your room. Daniella will pick them up later," he said.

Embarrassed, Violetta was only able to nod. He brushed passed her with no further word and made his way out the front door.

She stood in the room, unsure of what to do. Then, her embarrassment turned to anger. Although he had not done anything offensive, she was offended. Violetta put her shoes quickly back on and turned and ran outside to catch him, not yet knowing what she would say.

Outside, he was adjusting the bit and bridle on his horse. "Come with me," he said.

"With you?" Violetta laughed incredulously. "Why on earth would I come with you on that horse. I don't have proper shoes, remember? And besides, I don't know how to ride."

"That's right. There are no horses in Venice. You're used to being escorted around on a gondola."

She remained stoic, despite his sneer. Not wanting to give him the satisfaction he was getting under her skin, she lifted her chin.

"Well, you won't find any singing gondoliers here, which is why you should learn to ride," he said. "I'm headed to town, and they have stores there, believe it or not. You can buy some shoes. They won't be custom, but they'll be better than what you have."

"I have shoes. They just need to be cleaned."

"Those aren't shoes, they're slippers. And they may be fine for dancing on the marble floors in a Venetian palazzo, but they are useless here."

Violetta looked at him, trying to understand just who this man was, daring to ask her to ride into town with him on a horse.

"It's your decision, but I have things to do today." He climbed upon his horse and made a clicking sound with his tongue.

"Wait!" Violetta ran down the stairs and reached up.

He pulled her onto the horse. Violetta sat in front of him side-saddle, exactly as she had seen other women do.

"You said you've never been on a horse before."

"First time," Violetta said.

"Then you should ride with your legs like me," he said. "It'll be easier for you."

"But, I've never seen a woman ride like that," she scoffed.

"What difference does that make?"

"It's not proper. People will stare," Violetta said.

"They're already staring."

"Staring at what?" But she already knew the answer.

Slowly, Violetta swung her leg over and straddled the horse.

"Ready?" he asked.

"Ready," she said.

"My name is Marco Agosti. It's a pleasure to make your acquaintance."

He gave the horse a quick kick. Violetta felt the horse's stride move in time beneath her. Eventually, she fell into the rhythm of the stride. Violetta felt his chest press against her back and his breath on her neck. It was the closest Violetta had ever been to any man before, and never before, had Violetta felt so much excitement course through her body. She had stolen kisses from Franco many times, but their bodies had never touched in this way. Now, she looked down at this stranger's arms encircling her and inhaled his scent. She wanted to get even closer.

They arrived at the outskirts of town, and the horse's pace slowed to a canter that was more jarring than the smooth gallop. He stopped the horse on the side of the road in a grassy spot and turned his head. "You should go back to side-saddle," he said.

"Why?"

"It's best if you don't draw negative attention to yourself," he replied.

"But I thought you said I shouldn't care what people think."

"You shouldn't. But I didn't say that. I said they were already staring, and so it's best if you don't draw any unnecessary attention to yourself.

This isn't Venice. People here are not used to outsiders. They aren't bad people, they're just not accepting of anything that is different from what they know. Take my word for it."

His voice had taken an ominous tone that alarmed her. She swung her leg back over and adjusted her dress.

"Ok," Violetta said, straightening her back.

She noticed several people walking along, their faces long and pale.

A few people glanced up at them as they rode past, but quickly cast their eyes down.

He dismounted and led the horse to a pole outside a leather shop. As he tethered the animal to the ring, he looked up at her. "Did you enjoy your first ride?" he asked casually, tying the rope into a knot.

Violetta could only nod as she felt her face burn hot as coals and she resented the deep crimson she knew was blushing her cheeks.

"Is that the shoe shop?" she asked, pointing toward a store.

He walked around the horse and stood at her side. He held up his hand and helped her down. "No, the shop is across the piazza, next to the tree you were standing under the other day."

"I'll meet you back here in an hour," he said.

Violetta watched as he walked away, then made her way to the shop.

"You must be hungry. I'll bring us some food," he said as they entered the empty dining room.

Violetta sat at a dining table. She leaned forward and lifted the bottom of her dress to expose her new black leather shoes. They were rather masculine, unadorned, and allowed her toes to wiggle. A broad smile swept across her face.

Daniella approached her table, holding an envelope in her hand.

"This came for you."

She smiled, exposing the jagged tips of her teeth.

Violetta instantly recognized the writing scrawled across the front. Her hands trembled slightly as she opened it and pulled out two sheets of paper - one folded neatly with a crisp crease and one that appeared to have been crumpled up, then pressed flat and hastily stuffed into the envelope. Violetta opened the crumpled one first and read the neat handwriting.

when you see the dark, I once filled with light

when you feel the chill, I once filled with heat

in the absence of my presence

you'll meet an emptiness that runs still and deep

and one day

you will know how lucky you were

to be loved by me.

Franco

Violetta took a deep breath and laid the paper aside. Then she unfolded the other sheet.

Dearest Violetta,

I pray that you come to your senses, stop this childish rebellion, and return to Venice at once.

You are obviously upset because of what happened that day in the piazza, but Violetta, I assure you, you are mistaken in what you think you saw. It was merely a carnival whim, a drunken dare, during a time when we are allowed to let ourselves go and become someone else.

You know that is not who I am, and you cannot go on punishing me like this. I have given you time to sort out your feelings, but this nonsense must stop now. You must come back to Venice and resume your responsibilities.

Your mother worked hard so that you may have the life she dreamed for you. I know it was her deepest wish for you to marry me, and I am confident we can move forward and put this matter behind us.

We must carry out the duties that our families and destiny have laid out for us.

Keep in mind that a man of my station cannot wait forever. I await your response.

Franco

She caught her reflection in the window. Long strands of hair hung long and loose around her face. She had transformed into someone she did not recognize in only a few weeks. She was far from the girl in Venice, dressed in jewels and brocade dresses, drinking exotic coffees and eating from gold leaf plates. This place was its own Carnivale of sorts and was transforming her into someone untamed and free. Someone who finally resonated with her heartbeat. She wondered if that was how Franco felt the day of the Doge's Ball.

Violetta closed her eyes. She could see them both clearly. Franco, kissing the tall, lithe figure in a red silk gown. She could see the large bulge on the front of the person's neck, the curly dark hair peeking out from the dress's neckline, and broad shoulders - too wide for a feminine build.

She shuddered.

Perhaps it had been a carnival dare.

But, something inside of her told her otherwise. And she could not have lived with that question hanging over her head.

Marco entered the dining room and placed a plate of cheeses and meats in the center of the table and sat down. "You received mail?"

Violetta stuffed the papers back into the envelope.

"It must be important if it's been delivered out here," he said, piling some cheese atop a piece of bread and holding it out for her. "I hope it's nothing serious."

Violetta tossed the envelope into the fire. Its edges turned black and began to glow. "It isn't serious at all."

She swept her hair behind her ear. Then she took the bread in her hand and sunk her teeth into the soft, tangy cheese.

Alpinella

June, 1553

Five days had turned into five weeks. Although Alpinella lacked the vibrant chaos of Venice, the town had its own quiet pulse. Violetta sat on a bench and watched as people went about their day, purchasing vegetables from carts and chatting with neighbors.

She did not find the answers about the book that she had come here to learn, but she had found something else she had yet to name. And, when Marco had offered for her to stay longer, she had agreed on the condition she could make herself useful. So, she organized cupboards, straightened rooms, and did the shopping in town. Violetta soon found her way around town, recognized faces, and, slowly, the unfamiliar was becoming familiar. For the moment, Constantinople could wait.

Violetta spotted a peculiar lady with her bucket, always alone, passing through the streets unnoticed by those around her, always wearing the same somber dress, always averting her tawny eyes that reminded Violetta of wolves from her childhood books.

She studied the woman as she lowered her wooden bucket into the well, and noticed the way she looked straight ahead as she cranked the bucket up.

"She has one too. Hers is just hidden," a small voice interrupted her thoughts.

Startled, Violetta turned to see a boy standing next to her.

He lowered his voice. "Some people are too scared to let it out."

"Let what out?" Violetta asked.

He swept his bangs to the side, revealing two deep pools of indigo.

"Their colors."

Violetta leaned forward and smiled at the boy, "You see them too?"

He turned and ran to join the other boys who were laughing and chasing each other with sticks.

Violetta heard a crash and turned to see the woman had fallen, spilling her bucket of water across the stones. She rushed over and grabbed her arm to help her up. The woman did not say a word as she steadied herself on her feet. Violetta refilled the bucket from the well and then walked over to where the woman was rubbing her wrist. "I'll carry this back with you," Violetta offered.

They crossed the piazza and turned onto a narrow side street, where they eventually stopped in front of a small wooden door. The woman pushed open the door and stepped inside. Violetta hesitated before entering her home.

It was relatively vacant except for a small iron bed in the corner and a table with two chairs.

"My name is Violetta."

The woman laid the bucket of water on top of the table. Then, she walked over and added a few pieces of wood into the hot oven. Filling a pot with water, the woman placed it on the stove. She motioned for Violetta to sit at the table.

"I know who you are," said the woman, brushing aside her copper locks.

Violetta glanced at the footprints in the dirt. The woman appeared to live alone.

"Of course. Word travels fast in—"

"A place like this," the woman finished Violetta's sentence.

The woman took two cups from the small cupboard and placed them on the counter. Then she opened a tin, scooped a spoonful of tea leaves into each cup, and poured the hot water on top.

"I meant, in close-knit communities, like this one," Violetta said.

"The only thing close in this community is bloodline," said the woman. "A word of advice: trust no one here. It may look like a close-knit community, but everyone here has his own agenda. The winters here are harsh. The people harsher."

She brought the tea to the table.

Violetta reached for the cup and took a sip. She looked down in surprise. The tea was the perfect balance of bitter and sweet, with hints of jasmine, orange, cinnamon, and honey. It reminded her of the specialty teas in Venice.

The woman gave her a knowing smile. "Reminds you of home, doesn't it?"

"Yes. It reminds me of the tea my mother would buy from Sahedi. He was a spice merchant and a close friend of my mother."

"I don't buy my tea from a spice merchant. I dry my own leaves and make my special blend."

Violetta could feel herself blush, imagining how that must have sounded.

"I don't believe I caught your name," said Violetta as she lowered the tea cup to the saucer.

"My name is Chiara."

Surprised, Violetta's hand jerked, spilling tea onto the table.

"Are you ok?" asked Chiara, grabbing a cloth.

Violetta set the cup on the saucer. "I'm sorry. That is the name of my favorite tutor. I haven't thought of her in a while…" her voice trailed off.

Chiara's face softened.

"And did you grow up here?" Violetta asked, eager to change the subject.

"Heavens, no. I grew up in Venice," she said.

"Venice? That's where I am from."

"So I've heard."

A slight chill ran through her body. She wondered how this woman came from Venice only to end up alone in this tiny room.

"I followed a man," she said, as if reading her mind.

"A man?"

"Yes. He was a fisherman in Burano. My parents did not approve. Said I was falling beneath my station. So, we decided to leave. We stopped here," a trace of disgust exposed itself, "and he found mining work. I was very young." She took a long sip of her tea, then continued, "Women are born with two choices in this world: we can serve God and become a nun or we can serve a man and become a wife."

"In Venice, there is another choice. You can be independent and become a courtesan," replied Violetta.

"They may be educated, but they still serve the needs of many men. And most are not treated kindly once their prime has past. It is then a man's true colors always show." She leaned forward. "They say men are not what they seem. But I tell you, men are exactly as they seem. A man will always reveal his true nature from the first 'hello'."

Violetta's thoughts went straight to Franco. How there had been whispers and rumors among their circle. The long hours spent with his best friend. Violetta swallowed hard. She had not seen the other person's face when they were kissing, but she knew it was Paolo. Deep down, she had always known.

Violetta wanted to stay and talk. She missed good conversation, but she set her cup on the table, not wanting to overstay her welcome. "Thank you for the tea. It was delicious."

"Come by any time. It isn't often I get guests. Especially a fellow Venetian."

The moonlight shone through the window casting a soft glow on Violetta's face as she sat deep in thought. She could not get the meeting with Chiara out of her head. She felt a certain amount of sympathy for the woman's journey, which seemed to mirror her own in some ways. Something about her made her slightly uneasy, although she could not say for sure what it was.

Marco stepped into the dimly lit room off of the entry. "I hope I'm not disturbing you."

"Not at all. I was just thinking about a woman I met today on the piazza," Violetta said. "Her name is Chiara. I went to her house and had tea."

Marco stepped forward. "You had tea with her?"

"Yes. She's a very interesting lady. So, what is her story?"

"No one really knows. There's a lot of speculation, but it's mostly idle gossip. I wouldn't get caught up in it."

He turned to leave.

"Well, now you've piqued my curiosity. You have to tell me," pressed Violetta.

He exhaled and ran his hand through his hair. "As I said, they are just local rumors, and I don't want you to get caught up in it," his voice grew louder, and it alarmed her. She had never heard him talk with such force before.

"I didn't mean to upset you," Violetta said. "I was just curious about her story, her past."

Marco took a seat next to her on the small settee and lowered his voice, "Listen, there's not much I know other than what I've heard in passing, and I never put much value on that, but supposedly her husband left her after the birth of their son… who died at birth."

"How terrible," Violetta said.

"The husband accused the midwife of killing the baby, but the midwife said the baby was born dead. Of course, no one believes a midwife, not these days. So her husband, a drunk, reported the midwife for witchery. He tried to accuse both of them of killing his son. But Chiara had family connections in Venice that kept that from happening."

"Dear God."

"Chiara couldn't save the midwife, though. Her husband was determined that someone would pay. So, the midwife was taken into custody, tortured, and burned."

"What happened to her husband?"

He looked at her with those steady deep eyes. She thought about what Chiara had told her about men revealing themselves and knew any question she asked would be answered earnestly, but only the part he wanted her to know.

"What should have happened to him," he said flatly.

Violetta waited for him to continue.

"Some hunters found his body. He was a drunk, probably lost his way and froze out in the woods."

"Why doesn't she speak to anyone?" Violetta asked.

"She spoke to you."

"To anyone in town. I think I'm the first in a very long time."

"Maybe she has nothing to say to anyone. It's not like anyone here came to her defence."

"Now she's completely alone?"

"As far as I know."

"Why did she stay? Why did she not go back to Venice to be with her family?

"Supposedly, they didn't want her. She was a tarnish on the family crest, so to speak."

Violetta put her hand on Marco's arm. "I think we should help her. You should see the house where she lives."

"Violetta, I can't be taking people in off the street."

"She could work here. She can clean in exchange for a room and a small salary. You need the extra help. Marco, she has no one."

He looked uneasy. "I'm not sure if it's a good idea."

"My mother didn't know anything about our maid when she took her in either. She was an old Courtesan who had been tossed out and had nothing. My mother said always to trust your intuition about people, and Clarissa proved to be a loyal and trusted servant. She became like a grandmother to me."

He rubbed his chin slowly and replied, "We could use the extra help."

"I'll go see her tomorrow."

Chiara

"We must not omit to mention the injuries done to children by witch midwives, first by killing them, and secondly by blasphemously offering them to devils. The greatest injuries to the Faith as regards the heresy of witches are done by midwives."

Malleus Maleficarum, Part 2

Question VIII

Heinrich Kramer, 1486 AD

Alpinella

July, 1553

Chiara did not own a travel bag because she had never traveled. Her last trip was when she had left Venice, so she packed her few belongings in a small wooden vegetable box.

She looked around the room and felt a surge of relief. All the things in her home that had been collected over the years had born witness to her pain. They would be left behind, and she felt lighter already.

Chiara opened the bottom drawer to her chest. There was a purple shawl that had faded to pale lilac, tattered rags and mismatched remnants. She picked up the shawl. Although faded, it still had a few seasons of wear left in it. That's when she saw the small ivory mirror that had belonged to her mother. Chiara had stopped looking in mirrors the day her son died, unable to bear the sight of herself.

It was easy to do. Chiara put her mirror in the drawer, avoided looking into windows, and kept her gaze forward when she raised her bucket from the well. Trembling, Chiara brought the small mirror to her face. Startled, she thought there must be some mistake. Another woman was staring back at her - a stranger she did not recognize. Tears ran down her freckled cheeks, turning them the color of burnished gold. She ran her fingers along her face. The skin resembled tree bark - dry and rough, starved from a lack of touch.

When she became pregnant, Chiara thought her fortune had finally changed, and God had rewarded her for her suffering. But, when the baby was born on the harvest moon, he came out silent and blue. As the midwife loosened the cord from around her son's neck, she thought how terrible a person she must be. The baby would rather have strangled himself than have her as his mother.

Chiara took her dead baby and pulled him close to her chest, the cord still attached to her body. The midwife wrapped her arms around her and her baby and held them tight. A howl escaped Chiara's lips that traveled to the moon and back. Upon hearing it, a pack of grey wolves howled back in reply.

That night, silver streaked her copper hair, her eyes took on a yellowish hue, and her lips fell silent. Her husband, disgusted by his wife, quickly lost interest, not even caring to administer his weekly beatings unless he was drunk. This was just as well.

Upon his disappearance, she was forced to endure a new and difficult type of punishment - the stares and whispers of her neighbors when she ventured out.

After the death of her son, followed by the midwife's trial and her husband's abandonment, everyone was under the consensus that she was bad luck and it was best to avoid her. Each day, she felt the heavy weight of their judgment upon her. Chiara didn't particularly mind. She had grown a thick skin over the years to protect herself against the pain of other people's ridicule. Life had taught her to rely on herself and not expect anything from other people - until now.

The lady at the inn had been the first person to smile at her in years, and she felt compelled to finally speak. But Violetta was new in town and did not know her past. Unlike the man she lived with at the inn. He knew everything. And she was surprised he had agreed to invite her to work for them.

Chiara placed the mirror and a pair of scissors on top of her belongings in the box and walked into the kitchen. Then, she filled a tin pail with water and put it in the corner of her wooden box. Without bothering to lock the door behind her, she stepped onto the street. The sun was shining on her back as she bent over, cut a bundle of yellow and white daffodils, and placed them in the pail. Half of them would be placed on a tiny grave on her way out of town, and the other half would be a gift to her new employer.

She tossed a bag of bulbs in the box as well. There was plenty of garden space at the inn to plant her favorite flower.

As Chiara walked across the grass, the sunlight reflected the silver and copper in her hair and the gold in her eyes. She carried her small wooden box up the porch steps and put her hand on the doorknob. A shock ignited at her fingertips, making her jump. A contented smile lit up her face. It was the first time she had felt alive in years.

Violetta

Albergo Pietra Bella

November, 1553

Violetta quietly knelt and reached under her bed to grab the box. She had an hour that she was able to read without being disturbed. The last guests of the season had left that week and then the inn would be closing in preparation for the winter.

Violetta tiptoed down the hallway, avoiding the creaky floorboards as she walked downstairs.

She put the kettle on the stove and went into the dining room to light the fire. Arranging several logs and placing some smaller twigs and leaves around the bottom, Violetta prepared the fire. Then she took a long match from the brass matchstick holder nailed to the wall. Striking the match, Violetta lit the wood. She watched the small flames slowly spread to the other logs and grow in intensity. Satisfied, Violetta got up and went to the kitchen to pour her coffee.

Violetta sipped her coffee at the table by the window. She read each passage slowly, committing it to memory. Just then, she heard the front door open and footsteps approach from behind, causing her to jump and spill the hot liquid down her chin and onto the book. Quickly, Violetta grabbed a napkin to dab at the pages.

She looked up to see Chiara standing by the table alongside a priest.

"You startled me. I didn't realize anyone was up," Violetta said.

"Excuse me for interrupting your reading," the priest said, eyeing the book.

"It's okay. It's just a book my mother gave me," trying her best to sound casual.

"Is that Latin?" the priest asked, leaning in closer.

Violetta noticed a small cut caked with blood on the side of his freshly shaven face. "Yes, actually it is," Violetta replied.

"And where did you learn to read Latin, may I ask?" he asked suspiciously.

"From my tutors," Violetta replied cautiously. "Education was important to my mother."

"That looks like a very fancy book."

"My family were jewelry makers. I believe my grandfather made the cover."

Violetta caught a spark fly from the priest's eye. It was the only light Violetta had seen come from him.

"Jewelry makers," responded the priest, scratching his chin.

"Yes, in Amsterdam."

"Amsterdam. Are they still there?" his tone had shifted.

"They are all dead - the Black Death," Violetta added quietly.

The priest's eyes were dark and unsettling.

"What brings you out to the inn today?" Violetta asked.

"Oh, yes." He straightened his back and continued, "I was out for a morning walk. I used to play in these woods as a child," he explained, gesturing out the window. "Anyway, I heard a newcomer was at the inn, so I thought I would stop in and introduce myself. I'm Father Enzo," he smiled, his thin lips forming themselves into two straight lines. "I have not seen you in Church?"

Violetta looked at Chiara, whose eyes were fixed on the book.

"Yes, Father, I apologize for not stopping by the church yet. I've only recently arrived, and there's been so much work to do. Also, I'm not here permanently," she added. "I am only helping out for a bit."

"I understand. And, what brings you to these remote parts, if I may ask?" he said, looking around the room.

"Many people have left Venice to avoid the Black Death."

"Yes, I heard the situation is quite dire at the moment." He clasped his hands behind his back and shook his head. "Although, it's no wonder, with all the debauchery there, running like sewage through the canals." He wrinkled his nose. "But we can count on God's wrath always being just and true."

Violetta was surprised to see not a somber expression but one that revealed what she detected to be an eager satisfaction.

She could feel her pulse quicken with alarm.

"Well, I won't keep you. I'm sure you need to get back to your reading. It was a pleasure meeting you, and I hope you enjoy your stay."

"Thank you for stopping in, Father."

He nodded as he put on his hat and as he turned to leave. "One last thing. The new owner of the inn, I haven't met him yet either. Tell me, does he come from Venice too?"

"No, he's from Switzerland, but I am not sure the exact town." It wasn't exactly a lie, Marco had mentioned he had gone to school there, and she thought it best to be as vague as possible.

"Well, tell him I stopped in."

"I will, Father. Chiara, please show Father Enzo out."

She nodded and they turned and walked toward the door.

Violetta hurried to the stairs to hide the book and ran directly into Marco. "You scared me!"

"What did the priest want?" he asked, eyeing the door.

"Apparently, he had heard there was a new owner here. I guess priests wake up early in these parts." Violetta glanced back toward the door. "He's not exactly a warm person."

"What's in the box?" Marco asked.

"It's just an old book from my mother."

He furrowed his brow. "Did the priest see it?"

"Well, yes. Is that a problem?" Violetta asked. "Surely women are allowed to read around here."

"This isn't Venice, Violetta. Things are different here. That book can get you into a lot of trouble. If you want to read, do so in your room."

He continued down the stairs and out the door. Violetta exhaled sharply and hurried off to her room.

The Priest

Alpinella,

November, 1553

Father Enzo narrowed his hawkish eyes and pursed his lips tightly closed. His patience had paid off. He knew he had found her. It had to be her. The resemblance was uncanny. And it all fit - the family of jewellers from Amsterdam. Of course, his mother had fled to Venice. She could easily disappear into the city unnoticed.

The fallen leaves crunched beneath his feet as he crossed the lawn. He had to think. He made it to the small clearing and stopped. His mind wandered back to the day all those years ago when he had seen his mother spread out on the forest floor with a man on top of her. So, that young woman was the spawn of their union, he thought to himself. How perfectly this was all playing out - better than he could have anticipated.

His mother and the man, Violetta's father, were both dead; but the girl was alive, and she had been delivered straight to his doorstep. And that book, written in Latin, no less. No woman had any business reading Latin. That alone was a reason for a conviction. Yes, this was playing out so easily in his hands. First, he had to prepare the necessary papers, and an arrest would be made. And then, she would be at his mercy.

He could hardly contain his excitement as he walked into the forest. Eventually, he arrived at the place between the three trees. He had not been there since he was a boy. He sat down on the ground and crossed his legs. Then, he picked up a stick and started poking the end into the dirt, carving out a little hole in the ground, thinking of all the ways he would extract the devil from her.

Violetta

"Secondly, if she has a maid-servant or companions, that she or they should be shut up by themselves; for though they are not accused, yet it is presumed that none of the accused's secrets are hidden from them.

Thirdly, in taking her, if she be taken in her own house, let her not be given time to go into her room; for they are wont to secure in this way, and bring away with them, some object or power of witchcraft which procures them the faculty of keeping silent under examination."

Malleus Maleficarum Part 3

Question VIII

Heinrich Kramer, 1486 AD

Albergo Pietra Bella

November, 1553

Violetta walked into the lobby where the priest held papers in his hand and was looking angrily at Chiara.

"Is there something I can help you with?" asked Violetta cautiously.

He turned toward Violetta and shook the papers in her face. "Tell me, where is it?" he snarled into her ear.

She stared at papers and said nothing. This can't be happening, she thought.

"Never mind then. I do not need it to arrest you. My word is good enough. Still, Violetta, I am curious to know what is in the book."

Just then, Violetta glimpsed Chiara dart silently up the stairs. She must know where the book is, Violetta thought. Her legs felt as if they would give way. What a fool she had been to trust the older woman. What a fool she had been not to leave this place.

The priest looked toward the stairs, but Chiara had already disappeared.

"You have no right to arrest me. I have done nothing wrong," said Violetta.

He turned his attention back to her. "You have invoked the Devil with the written word."

"I told you, they are innocent stories - children's stories from my family." Her voice was shaking.

"Well, if they are so innocent, why don't you let me have a look?"

Violetta could see darkness engulfing his chest that seemed to absorb all the light surrounding him. Violetta knew the book could not fall into his hands.

"No," she replied defiantly.

Chiara descended the stairs and stood on the last step, her eyes wide and unblinking. The priest grabbed Violetta's arm and walked her toward the front door.

He stopped and glared at the older woman. Violetta could feel his arm grip her tighter.

"Do you know where the book is?" he demanded, spit flying from his mouth.

Chiara stared ahead.

"Too bad you can't talk. Then again, we've been down that road once before, remember?"

He smirked and addressed the nervous young man he had brought with him: "Search this inn from top to bottom. Find that book!"

"Yes, Father," the young man replied and hurried up the stairs.

As the priest pulled Violetta out the door, she yelled, "Please, tell Marco what's happened."

Chiara placed her hand to her heart, and Violetta saw a vortex of color swirl out toward her.

Chiara

"And what, then, is to be thought of those witches who in this way sometimes collect male organs in great numbers, as many as twenty or thirty members together, and put them in a bird's nest, or shut them up in a box, where they move themselves like living members, and eat oats and corn, as has been seen by many and is a matter of common report?"

Malleus Maleficarum

Part 2, Chapter XIII

Heinrich Kramer, 1486 AD

Alpinella, 1553

Chiara stepped into Violetta's bedroom. Clothes were flung across the floor, drawers were pulled from the chest, the contents emptied—all her clothing strewn around the room. In the middle of the room, the overturned mattress lay on the floor, stripped of its sheets.

She stepped over the mattress and made her way to the window, unlocking it, flinging it open wide. She removed the two clay flower pots filled with red geraniums from the ledge and set them on the floor. Then, she picked up the wooden box that she had hidden on the ledge and dusted off the dirt.

Chiara ran downstairs to the kitchen storeroom and found a metal box. She wrapped the wooden box in layers of linen rags and placed it inside.

In the far corner of the back garden stood an old abandoned well. It had fallen into disuse and filled with dirt, leaving only a circle of stones exposed at the top. Ivy had grown over the rocks and twisted up the iron pulley.

Chiara laid the metal box on the grass and began to shovel out the dirt from inside the well. She had lived through this experience before with her midwife and was fully aware of the outcome. Once arrested for witchery, unless there was some miracle or a large sum of money paid under the table, there was little hope for an acquittal.

Chiara placed the metal box at the bottom of the hole and covered it with dirt. Then, placing a few bulbs inside the circle of stones, she covered them with the remaining soil and leaves. Dusting off her skirt, Chiara picked up the shovel and hurried back to the inn.

Father Enzo

"For a certain man tells that, when he had lost his member, he approached a known witch to ask her to restore it to him. She told the afflicted man to climb a certain tree, and that he might take which he liked out of the nest in which there were several members. And when he tried to take a big one, the witch said: You must not take that one; adding, because it belongs to a parish priest."

Malleus Maleficarum

Part 2, Chapter XIII

Heinrich Kramer, 1486 AD

Alpinella

November, 1553

Although he did not remember, the priest entered the world through a dark tunnel of flesh and blood. At the end of the tunnel was a light to which he was drawn. He resisted each push, but life only moves in the motion of forward, so there was no choice but to labor on. Finally, upon entering the light, he let out a painful and high-pitched scream.

And, even though the light would shine on him many more times during his life, he found its intensity too difficult to bear. So, like the far side of the moon that faces a cold and eternal night, he too turned his back on the radiance of life and lived out his days shrouded in deep darkness.

He liked it there. And it's there he wished to stay. Still, he couldn't help but sense his days were numbered.

The priest knew his body was failing him, but he didn't know why. He blamed his father, his diet, the cold, damp winters, or anyone and anything except himself. He did not understand the simple mechanism by which one creates their own version of hell. He didn't see how, unable to break the coded memory of a single event from his past, he had given revenge permission to penetrate his mind and body. Like rust on a nail, it had worked its way into every crevice, eventually corroding his vision and causing him to worship blindly at the altar of an unreal reality.

He squinted his eyes, trying to block out the morning light streaming through the window. It was a beautiful autumn morning, but he didn't notice. He was irritated because, in all the excitement, he had forgotten to close the shutters before going to bed. He groaned alongside his body, which creaked as he stood up.

He stumbled across the room, shielding his eyes with his hand. Grumbling to himself, he opened the window. A burst of cool air rushed in, and he cursed. He reached for the shutters and slammed them shut, flooding the room in darkness. It was still early, and he could sleep a few more hours before starting his day. So, he crawled back into bed and pulled the covers tightly over his shivering body.

Despite his effort to sleep, his body continued to twitch and ache beneath the threadbare covers as his mind raced. Exasperated, he flung back the covers and got up once again. It was hopeless to try to sleep, so he decided to get dressed. Besides, there was much that awaited him that day.

He fastened the gold chain around his neck and dropped the diamond-encrusted cross inside the collar. It felt cold on his neck before disappearing into a tangled nest of chest hair. He buttoned his shirt and adjusted the collar, then tucked the shirt into his pants, his fingertips briefly brushing the tip of his cock that had been hard since he opened his eyes.

A hot flash coursed through the network of veins inside his body, causing him to feel a thrill he had not felt since the day he heard the unusual screams in the forest. He was accustomed to the various wails and screeches his animals released during his experiments. These screams were entirely new to him, so he had decided to investigate.

He followed the sighs and moans until he came to a small clearing. That's when he saw her. His mother on the ground with a man on top of her moving violently back and forth. Although he couldn't see the man's face buried in her chest, she was screaming and looked to be in incredible pain. He knew he should probably help her, but he couldn't move. And it wasn't because he was scared. It was because he felt a tingle in his pants that was new. Once the strange screams had subsided and he saw them lying entangled together, a smile upon his mother's lips, it was only then that he realized what had occurred, and he swore one day she would pay. He had heard of such accounts at church, of how the Devil could invade women's bodies and corrupt men's souls, driving them to act in mad and animalistic ways. He also knew what the Church did to women who befell such evil.

Much to his dismay, he had never gotten the chance to see her pay the price for her sins. But now, God had given him another opportunity, and he wasn't about to squander it, especially given that she resembled his mother so much in every way. He sucked his belly in and cinched his belt around his waist far tighter than his belly would like, but he was too distracted to notice. He knew she would be waiting in her cell, and he hoped she had not slept. Sleep deprivation always added another layer of torture for the victim.

He finished tying the long black cloak around his neck and went downstairs to make himself some toast and jam.

It was the same breakfast each morning. He had never learned to cook. He felt his time was better spent on more important matters, not indulging in the carnal pleasures of the palate.

He was content consuming mounds of pasta and oil; stale bread; vegetables that he would inevitably boil for too long, draining them of all color and nutrients; and the occasional fish, depending on the religious holiday. He never touched meat.

Since he ate alone, he did not think it was necessary to set a proper table. His mother had been meticulous in arranging a beautiful table, but when she disappeared, she took all sense of propriety with her. His father abandoned the notion of a family dinner, so the crockery gathered dust on the shelves. It had not mattered. He could not remember anyone ever entering their house for a visit, much less dinner. So, he had grown accustomed to eating alone and living in isolation.

He picked up the knife and dipped the blade into the jar of red jam. He scraped up the congealed fruit and spread it across the bread in one quick swipe. Then he picked up the bread and sunk his teeth into it. Crumbs fell from his mouth, tumbled down his beard, and landed on the table. A bit of jam stuck to the hairs above his upper lip, but he didn't bother to wipe his mouth. He had not brought a napkin to the table, and there was no one around to see it anyway.

The priest had convinced himself long ago that he didn't need anyone and behaved accordingly. Yet, it was precisely what he thought he didn't need, that he needed the most. Still, he rejected this truth and never gave it a second thought. He was desperate for something else. Deep down, beneath his frigid and detached facade, the priest craved recognition and approval foremost. Both of which always come from an external source.

He swallowed the last bite of toast and licked his fingers. Then he poured some milk into his cup of tea. The milk curdled in the steaming liquid, but he didn't care. He gulped it down anyway. It was a sin to waste.

Violetta

"The Judge should act as follows in the continuation of the torture. First he should bear in mind that, just as the same medicine is not applicable to all the members, but there are various and distinct salves for each several member, so not all heretics or those accused of heresy are to be subjected to the same method of questioning, examination and torture as to the charges laid against them; but various and different means are to be employed according to their various natures and persons."

Malleus Maleficarum Part 3

Question XV

Heinrich Kramer, 1486 AD

Alpinella

November, 1553

The room was dark and windowless, with dirt floors and stone walls stained black from mold and smoke. Instruments of torture were arranged on the table before her. They came in an assortment of shapes and sizes, each one designed to extract the traces of corruption embedded in her soul: one for the longing in her eyes; one for the quickening of her pulse; one for the saliva upon her lips; one for the breath that swelled her chest; and another for the heat that rises from her flesh.

Violetta felt as though she would faint. But instead, vomit poured from her mouth, ran down her dress, and onto her shoes that were soaked in a puddle of urine.

A man whose face was concealed behind black cloth dragged her to a chair in the middle of the room and forced her to sit. She was grateful for the four legs that supported her in the pit of darkness.

Violetta knew what was coming. Everyone had heard the stories, and every literate citizen had read Malleus Maleficarum's manual. Due to the invention of the printing press, fear and paranoia could be released like toxins into the water supply, seeping into the hearts and minds of every household, clouding judgment and contaminating rational thought. The manual was written by the Holy Roman Catholic Church's lead inquisitor. His sole duty was to justify, identify, and exterminate witchery.

But in reality, it was a vengeful treatise written by a small and vindictive man in response to an unresponsive woman.

However childish the motive, the implications were treacherous. The blood-soaked document was declared law, and it was also written that if one did not believe in its doctrine, that too was an act of heresy, punishable by death. It was as ironclad as the vices used to hold the maidens.

Violetta knew her fate. The only way to eradicate a witch was to kill her. A confession was not a pardon but merely a formality that gave an air of legitimacy to an otherwise fraudulent proceeding.

Her eyes rested on the flame flickering on the wall over his shoulder. Her mother had encouraged her to read people's Light from a very young age, when children see Light as easily as they see rainbows. She had taught her that there are people who generate their own Light and shine brightly like the sun, and there are those who reflect other people's Light and glow softly like the moon. Then, some are incapable of either producing or reflecting Light. They are dark, and they are dangerous.

Violetta knew the priest was such a man.

She heard heavy footsteps enter the room and approach her from behind. Her eyes darted from side to side, and she felt sweat run down her temples despite the sharp chill in the air.

The priest circled her slowly, his hands clasped behind his back and not speaking a word. He was a man who relished the job bestowed upon him. After completing his third circle, he stopped directly in front of her.

"Shall we begin?" he asked.

His long bony hands ripped open her dress, and he began searching. "Where is that mark of the devil?" he sneered. "Let's see, a birthmark, a mole, or a freckle. Any of these will do."

He began the interrogation slowly. His questions flowed forth, each word, pause, and inflexion meticulously rehearsed for increased dramatic effect. The pinpoint pupils in his eyes darted wildly about, and his breath panted in shallow, unheeded rhythms.

Despite her compliance, physical pain was inflicted per the instructions laid out in the Malleus Maleficarum. She did not know how many hours she had been tied to the chair. Every blow or twist or cut administered made each second fester for what seemed like an eternity. Her body began to fail, her vision blurred, and her eyelids lowered. Violetta became suspended in darkness, a welcomed reprieve. Suddenly a wave of lightness rushed over her. She exhaled, and her body released, freeing herself from the world of density.

She hovered close to the ceiling and looked down at her body slumped over in the chair. Violetta did not recognize the woman with the battered face and tattered clothing. She was alert yet calm; she did not want to be there.

In a flash, Violetta found herself in her lover's bedroom. Marco lay in his bed, bathed in sunlight. He pulled her close to his body, and she fell fast asleep.

She was still in her lover's arms when she awoke, clinging to his body. Violetta was unaware of the passage of time, as it did not seem to exist in this realm. Rapture replaced hours, and their cries of ecstasy waxed and waned along with the moon.

They were suspended in eternity and cradled in heat only two bodies as connected as theirs could generate.

"Why are you smiling?"

Violetta could hear the muffled words, but they sounded too far away for her to care. Instead, she buried her head in her lover's chest and inhaled deeply. She was intoxicated by his mossy citrus scent that reminded her of the forest floor. He pulled her closer to him. She could feel his arms flex as he gripped her tighter.

"I said...why are you smiling?" The menacing voice repeated, only this time it was closer.

She couldn't breathe. The words had sliced through her eardrums and drilled a hole inside her head. She recognized the voice, and terror coursed through her body. Her lover wrapped both arms around her and held her close, but he couldn't save her from the dark force pulling her back. She felt a blow to her cheek. The taste of rust filled her mouth and her vision blurred once again. Her lover, the bed, and his smell all dissolved before her. She reached for him, but her hands felt the wooden chair beneath her once again.

She slowly opened her eyes.

"There you are. I thought we had lost you for a moment."

The inquisitor leaned in, and she could smell his breath, as foul as waste floating in the lagoon. "It seemed like you were having the sweetest of dreams." He poked his finger into her forehead. "We must explore that in more depth."

He touched her bottom lip and waited for a reaction, but she had none to give. The edge of his mouth curled into a snarl, and his eye twitched.

"A little later, perhaps."

He turned toward the assistant: "Take our dear Signorina back to her quarters. And this time, stay with her. Give her only what she needs, so she doesn't die. We don't want her leaving us before she has had time to fully repent, now do we?"

The assistant did not respond. He didn't need to. His body stood erect and poised, ready to carry out the command.

The priest stretched his back and placed his hands on his stomach. "God's work has left me hungry. I'm headed home for dinner."

Violetta stumbled back to her cell, where she collapsed onto the dirt floor. Her body was shaking and wracked with pain, but she was too tired to care. Blackness engulfed her.

Father Enzo

"Besides, since impotency in this act is sometimes due to coldness of nature, or some natural defect, it is asked how it is possible to distinguish whether it is due to witchcraft of not. When the member is in no way stirred, and can never perform the act of coition, this is a sign of frigidity of nature; but when it is stirred and becomes erect, but yet cannot perform, it is a sign of witchcraft."

Malleus Maleficarum Part 1

Question VIII

Heinrich Kramer, 1486 AD

Alpinella

November, 1553

Father Enzo sat in his favorite chair by the fire, his stomach bloated. He had continued eating that night, ignoring the signals his stomach sent to his brain telling him that he was full. Putting his feet on the stool and loosening his belt, the priest let out a long belch. His body was not what it used to be. The fat around his belly used to jiggle along with his movements, but now it had hardened like pieces of gristle. He had grown stiff over the years, his bones and joints slowly fossilizing, making it increasingly difficult to administer God's good grace. Hence, the assistant. All good Inquisitors needed one, and he was lucky to have run into him that day in the tavern.

Something about the reserved loner of a man piqued his curiosity. He admired his aloof, detached nature. He was strong, yet seemed passive and agreeable. He said little, which he liked because he preferred to talk and for the other person to listen. It was an ideal situation. So, he had made him an offer. And he was glad that he did. His hunch had proven correct, as usual. The young man had demonstrated himself to be a quick student, effortlessly grasping even the most complex techniques designed to inflict maximum pain while being careful never to cross the line over to death. It was a fine balance.

Most importantly, he was taking over the physicality of the work, except for today. Violetta had surprised him when the assistant walked her through the door.

Her resemblance to his mother was uncanny. It nearly took his breath away. He was excited, but he had to be careful.

"That was close," he thought. "Too close. I lost control, and I was careless. That can't happen again. I nearly lost her. I must remember to be like my assistant, precise and deliberate. I had taught him that. I had taught him many skills that he had already mastered beyond my abilities; still, he possesses an understanding beyond what I had taught him. There are those lessons that cannot be passed from master to pupil.

He understands instinctively that the elicitation of information is unique to the individual you are trying to extract it from, and your approach should be carefully tailored to their psychology. Sure, one can grasp the concept, but implementing it under pressure was something else entirely. Yes, he was good, but the assistant would not touch her. This one was his, and he will hold onto her for as long as possible. Her hair, her eyes, and the voice. So much like...."

The veins in his neck pumped violently, erupting within him an angry howl that shook the night. Then, enraged, he looked down at the cock lying soft as a snail in his hand.

The Assistant

"The Judge should also take care that during that interval there should always be guards with her, so that she is never left alone, for fear lest the devil will cause her to kill herself."

Malleus Maleficarum Part 3

Question XIV

Heinrich Kramer, 1486 AD

Alpinella,

1553

The assistant was sitting on a stool in front of the gate in the dimly lit cell, looking down at her with a steady gaze. For several hours, he had watched her body twitch and shiver, making sure her breath that hung in the cold, damp air did not cease.

He waited. His body was neither rigid nor relaxed, and his face did not betray the raw emotion raging beneath his skin.

He had been well trained. Too well, perhaps.

For the priest was unaware of the traitor who served at his feet.

Violetta

"...shall take her from the place of punishment to another place under a strong guard; but let him take particular care not to release her on any sort of security; for when that is done, they never confess the truth, but always become worse."

Malleus Maleficarum Part 3

Question XVI

Heinrich Kramer, 1486 AD

Alpinella, 1553

Violetta jolted awake. Her body was soaked in sweat. She didn't know where she was or how long she had been asleep, but the rotting stench that filled her nose brought back the horrifying memories.

Her tongue circled her lips which were caked in blood. She opened her eyes and searched for anything that would relieve the stinging burn in the back of her throat.

It was then that she noticed him sitting on a stool in front of the gate.

"Marco," Violetta stammered in a whisper. "What are you doing here?"

Iris

Albergo Pietra Bella

January, 2013

"Here are your keys. Congratulations, you are now the owner of an inn," Giuseppe said, smiling warmly.

"Only a steward for a brief time," said Iris, taking the keys in her hand. "This inn has been here long before we arrived, and it will be here after we are gone."

"I think this calls for a celebratory toast," Catrin said, clapping her hands.

"I'll get a bottle of Prosecco," Giuseppe offered.

"And I'll get the glasses," Iris said. "Where are the Prosecco glasses?"

"They're in the cabinet behind the bar."

"So, when do you expect to have this place operational?" asked Giuseppe.

Iris took three glasses from the shelf. "Well, I guess the first step is figuring out what renovations need to be done. I don't want to change the existing charm, so I want to keep the construction to a minimum and work with what we have. I'd also like to do most of the work myself, if possible."

"I can't wait to go furniture shopping," said Catrin.

"That'll be the fun part," said Iris, setting the glasses on the table. "We'll hit up the vintage stores in Milan. I'm envisioning an Italian midcentury vibe, Missoni meets Achille Castiglioni. I'm sure we can find a used ARCO floor lamp somewhere."

"I'm just not sure we can make it fit," laughed Catrin.

"Not to worry. We'll just cut a hole in the ceiling," quipped Iris.

"Oh boy," said Giuseppe, "I'll be staying out of these decisions."

Holding a long knife in his hand. He swept the blade swiftly upward along the neck of the bottle, causing it to fly from the bottle with a loud pop.

Robinia

Alpinella

May, 2013

Robinia slept most of the afternoon, as she did each day. In her sleep, she ventures down roads that lead to places where physical matter dissolves into a pink mist. As in her waking hours, she travels the road alone because satisfying the God-hunger that dwelled inside her is solitary work. All the while, her body remains in a heightened state of awareness, responding to subtle stimuli within her environment: the snap of a twig; the screech of a hawk; and the movement of a small animal through the grass. She was born with keen survival instincts, but her strongest instinct resided in her gut. It was her gut that led her to this place.

She was born into an influential family, or so she had been told. Her father was an ambassador, and her mother was an accountant. Their house was pretty and large and filled with all the things that a big house required. There was a leather sofa in the living room, televisions in every bedroom, and a dining table surrounded by twelve chairs which remained empty except for two dinners a year. There were stacks of kitchen drawers filled with shiny utensils and gadgets, and volumes of books in the library, all bound in burgundy covers with gold titles embossed on the spine.

In her father's office stood an antique brass telescope next to the Palladian window. One night, eager to gaze at the rings of Saturn, she crept into his office to have a look. Her father walked in and reprimanded her - the telescope was expensive and not to be touched.

She asked him if he could find Saturn for her. He said he did not know where Saturn was, but he had work to do, and dismissed her with a wave of his hand.

Restless, she wandered the labyrinth of canals. The city was crowded and dirty, and there was no grass on which to walk barefoot. She longed to watch the sun melt into a sandy sea, but she saw only walls everywhere she looked. So she looked up toward the moon. Try as she might, she could not see the flags she had been told were there. She did see craters, and that offered her some sense of comfort.

Robinia spent most of her days alone. She would have been well-liked by her classmates if she had made more of an effort to fit in, but she had little in common with the girls her age. Robinia didn't understand their complex social hierarchy or psychological mind games. That left the boys in her class, but she didn't understand how they could be so loud yet have so little to say. She also did not care for the way they smelled like a wet kitchen sponge.

There had been one boy who was a year younger. His name was Clark. He was shorter than she preferred, but he smelled nicely and taught her how to play blackjack. His head was also filled with interesting ideas she had never before considered.

They would sit on the floor in his bedroom, and she would listen as he talked about his plan to move to Las Vegas and become a card dealer in a big casino.

He was drawn to the bright lights, excitement, and promise of fast fortunes. Clark urged her to come with him. She could be a cocktail waitress, and they would live in an apartment off the Strip.

Robinia was not so enamoured with the idea. She thought the casinos sounded more like prisons than an oasis. She wanted to see the desert, but she did not want to experience it from inside a bell jar. Robinia wanted to stand with her feet in the sand and look out on the horizon, where the earth bends like a bow, and imagine which star would be her target.

But, it was the duality of the desert captivated her most: the prolonged droughts and torrential rains; the baked earth and colorful cactus blossoms; the scorching heat of the day and bitter chill of the night. The same extremes shifted and swirled inside her. As she grew older, more primal emotions arose within her, and her skin would burn like magma or harden into a glacial mass, depending on her attraction to her mate. For her, it was consumption or repulsion. Indifference never entered her experience.

For every emotion, its opposite exists in equal measure. For some people, the pendulum swings moderately, revealing an even-temperedness. Their blood runs lukewarm in the midst of both love and disdain, triumph and tragedy.

Of this, she could not fathom. Not to bear your teeth at your opponent in a moment of fury or claw your lover's back in a moment of abandon, for her, was the same as rolling over and playing dead. Her pendulum swung to its highest points.

The rain streaked down the window one dismal Sunday afternoon as Sammy Davis Jr. played on the stereo. "I have an itinerary of my own I've been working on, eight countries so far," she said, but Clark was not listening to her. He was busy shuffling the cards to deal the next hand.

She didn't mind. She sipped her soda and waited for her cards. She knew they would never share a common fate, but they did share a common impulse, and she was eager to explore this new territory. So, that day, she let him kiss her and slip his hand under her bra. He fumbled her breast clumsily, and her nipples only hardened because his fingers were cold. She thought she might feel something more if she let him put his hands below her waist. She guided his hand to the divide between her legs - the only physical clue to her inner duality, but he rubbed his fingers vigorously back and forth as if trying to start a fire, which mostly felt uncomfortable.

Unimpressed with foreplay, she decided that sex might be more satisfying. So, she lay naked on her back, and he crawled on top of her. But, before she felt anything, he made a sharp grunting noise, and she felt a warm liquid drip down her thigh. He rolled onto his back, turned off the radio, and stared at the ceiling, oblivious to the thoughts racing through her head.

What a fool, she thought. He probably thinks when you turn off the radio, the sound waves also disappear.

Always left with the same dissatisfaction, she eventually stopped returning his calls and taught herself solitaire instead.

The rest of her upbringing was uneventful. People called her family lovely and her city the most beautiful in the world, but she saw things differently, and she felt crowded in both. So, she waited. She was good at waiting. And, when she turned eighteen, much to the dismay of her parents, she cashed in her college fund and informed them that she had other plans.

The next morning, she set off with only a backpack, a deck of cards, and her list.

For the first time in her life, she felt a sense of belonging in the world.

On the first night of her journey, her train pulled into a fog-covered station. She checked her ticket. Her connecting train would depart in twenty-two minutes, enough time to grab a coffee.

Across the station, a man with black hair and chiselled cheekbones stepped off a train and looked at his watch. Then he put on his hat, pulled his trench coat around his neck and made his way across the platform.

As she passed him, the hair on her neck stood up. She glanced back at him as he disappeared into the crowd of passengers, unaware that, even though the two of them went in opposite ways, their compasses were pointed in the same direction.

Robinia yawned and stretched her back, lifting her chin high. She got up, added kindling to the logs, and grabbed the box of matches from the mantle lined with river rocks. On her walks along the bank, she liked to fill her pockets with stones.

But she only brought home the ones that were shaped like hearts.

She lit the fire, and held out her hands, allowing the heat to travel up the length of her arms and settle in the center of her chest.

Sometimes, she saw his face in the flames, and seven years of memories would come rushing back to her. A man, a marriage, a child - all gone on a drive home one dark and snowy night. A tragedy so sudden, not even her deck could foresee. Before she could stop herself, she would reach out to touch his face in the flames, but the fire would scorch her hands, causing her to recoil. The man she passed on the train platform that night still had the ability to burn her to the core. So, she would shuffled her worn deck of cards and lay them out in the shape of a pyramid. It took a few rounds, but eventually, their memory would recede and leave her in peace.

She took a sip of bitter coffee and stared out the window. Left over from the morning brew, it had grown ice-cold, but she hardly noticed. Her eyes were focused on a small movement she detected several kilometers in the distance.

She walked to her window and grabbed the binoculars she kept hung on her telescope. A man was walking along the top of the mountain where the peaks pierced the sky. Then, he dropped down and disappeared into the shadows.

Robinia knew the mountain well, and she knew there was only one place the man could be going. She placed the binoculars back on the telescope and grabbed her coat before heading out the door. Robinia had stopped wearing shoes years ago. She did not like blindfolds on her feet.

The sun was dropping low on the horizon, but this did not slow her down. Her eyes adjusted well in the dark. She walked through the meadow and then zigzagged her way up the mountainside.

Her toes gripped the rocks as she made her way toward the shed. The stone building was intended as a shelter for cows and sheep during the harsh winters. The tightly stacked stones and the sturdy slab roof kept out the cold night air. Cigarette butts and footprints were scattered around the remains of a fire. She crouched down.

Her body stiffened as a man appeared outside.

His dark wavy hair fell down the nape of his neck as he hunched over to light a cigarette. He took a slow drag and shoved the lighter into his pocket.

Pietro

Alpinella

May, 2013

Pietro leaned against the door to the shed and stared blankly at the darkening horizon as he took a long drag of his cigarette. He did not like being alone, and the long nights and solitude were getting to him. Pietro preferred the company of friends at the bar and his family sitting around the dinner table. Above all, he liked the company of Alice. It had lasted only one summer, but that was enough for her to leave her imprint on his heart. He tried to imagine her living in New York City. He wondered if she was still holding onto his promise of joining her there or if she had moved on and forgotten all about their plans. I'll find out soon enough, he thought.

He tossed his cigarette on the ground and exhaled as he crushed it with his boot, grinding it into the dirt with more pressure than was necessary and disappeared inside the dwelling.

Inside the shed, a makeshift pallet of blankets lay in the corner. The rest of the space was sparse except for a pile of clothes folded and stacked on the floor next to a book on the history of Italian marble and stone, given to him by his grandfather, who hoped one day to pass along his quarry to Pietro so he may continue the centuries-old family business. But Pietro had no interest in the quarries.

As a teenager, he had worked alongside his father and grandfather high in the Alps cutting the stone out of mountainsides.

It was difficult and dangerous work, and he did not like anything about it. He preferred to hang out with his friends in the streets, shouting and vying for girls' attention.

Sometimes, when his grandfather was busy, or to get out of having to work, he would wander off through the cavernous spaces, deeper into the interior of the mountain where the air was cool and the light did not so easily reach. He would pick a rock ahead of him and dare himself to make it that far. Making his way toward his goal, with heavy breath and tentative steps, he would try to suppress the fear rising inside of him, but no amount of determination would allow him to go further into the cave. Goosebumps on his arms and prickles on his neck would alert him to the fact that he was alone. He hated being alone. The fear would inevitably overcome him, and he would turn and run back.

He lay down on his pallet, covered himself with a blanket, and went to sleep. The flashlight remained on.

The next day, he wandered around the shed. He did not plan to venture out, preferring to go over every detail of the plan in his mind. He could not mess this up. By the late afternoon, his muscles still held tight to the tension that had accumulated in his neck and back during the night before. Pietro tilted his head to the left and right, but the long muscles in his neck remained tight as ropes. He cursed having to sleep on the hard pallet like some barnyard animal. He grabbed his pack of cigarettes and headed outside.

He held a smoke in one hand and massaged the side of his neck with the other. The sounds of cricket and birds filled his ears but did little to fill the vacuum in his chest. Another dream.

Another day. And he still could not shake the image of her that lingered long after he opened his eyes.

Sour bile rose up from his gut and mingled with the taste of tobacco in the back of his throat. He tossed the cigarette in front of him and stomped it out.

He walked back inside and placed his clothes on the blanket, rolled it tightly into a cylinder shape and stuffed it in his backpack. Then he picked up the book and opened it to the page bookmarked with a thin envelope. On the left page, was a picture of a large block of white marble sitting on a conveyor belt. Water poured down from above, and spilled over the edges as a giant spinning blade sliced through the stone, bisecting it into two smaller blocks. He took the envelope in his hand. There was no writing on the front. It was never meant to be mailed, but the detailed letter inside contained a secret as old as the inn he was about to visit. He knew if he could somehow get inside, there was a chance he could find the book that Antonio, an ancestor from hundreds of years back, had written about all those years ago when he went with a priest to arrest a witch. A book covered in jewels that the priest had given him orders to search for, but he was never able to find.

In the letter, Antonio recounted the events of that day and the days following, ending with the priest mysteriously committing suicide. Antonio tried countless times throughout his life to find the book, even breaking into the inn on several occasions, but found no trace of it. He took the secret of the lost book to his grave, having only the letter tucked away as the only remaining proof that the book, according to him and the priest at least, existed.

And now, nearly five centuries later, Pietro had found the letter, hidden in a stack of papers in his grandfather's office he discovered the day after his funeral. He did not know how many of his ancestors before him had searched and possibly failed, but Pietro knew if he succeeded, it could change his life. Sure it had been handed to him by fate itself, he felt that the past was speaking to him from across time and space, and he was listening.

Pietro closed the book and slid it into the backpack, slung it over his shoulder and opened the door to leave.

Standing before him, he nearly bumped into a woman with golden eyes.

"Hello," he said, his body stiffening.

"I noticed a fire. I wasn't aware anyone was living here," she said, glancing inside.

"Just passing through. I'm leaving now, as a matter of fact." He shifted his weight to block her view. "Do you live around here?"

"Yes. I live in the cabin down the hill."

He looked down at her bare feet. "Well, as I said, I was just leaving."

"This is my husband's property," she said flatly.

He was taken off guard. "Your husband's property?"

"That's right. Do you know him?"

"I'm sorry, I don't. I was only…"

"My name is Robinia," she interrupted.

"Pietro," he said, extending his hand. "I apologize for the intrusion, but —"

She looked at his outstretched hand and then down upon the green valley. "Follow me. You must be hungry."

He followed her down the mountain path in silence and across the meadow to her house.

Once inside, she gestured toward the kitchen table. "Have a seat," she said. "I'm going to light the grill."

She returned to the kitchen and began slicing tomatoes. "You can open that bottle of wine on the counter. The opener is in the drawer, and the glasses are in the right cabinet."

She arranged the tomatoes on the platter, and then plucked some basil from the pot on the window sill.

"You read tarot?" he asked, uncorking the bottle.

She glanced over at her deck of cards sitting on the counter.

"Sometimes," she responded, placing a slice of mozzarella between each tomato.

"Care to read mine?"

Pausing briefly, she shifted her gaze upward. "Sure," she replied.

She topped the salad with basil leaves, wiped her hands on a towel, and set the platter aside.

Robinia turned around just as Pietro reached for the deck of cards.

"No," she said sharply.

He stopped and looked at her.

"Never touch someone else's deck."

"Sorry," he said, putting his hands up and stepping back.

She walked over and took the deck in her hands. "We leave our mark on everything we touch. And everything we touch leaves its imprint on us." She looked up at him: "Come on, let's sit down."

Pietro followed her to the table, and they sat across from one another. She stared straight at him as she shuffled the cards, and he shifted awkwardly in his seat.

"So, you said this is your husband's property," he remarked. "Is he still around?"

She laid five cards on the table in the shape of a square, four in each corner and one in the middle. "Not that I have seen," she said evenly.

She flipped over a card and laid it on the table—the Fool.

She could feel her body tense. She flipped another card over—the Thief.

"What does it mean?" he asked.

"You are on a journey to find something."

She flipped over the third card—the Tower.

"You have encountered some sort of upheaval, broken pride. You have a fear of suffering."

"Doesn't everyone?" he retorted.

Ignoring his remark, she moved her hand to the last corner and flipped the card.

It was the Death card.

"That one doesn't look good," he said.

She bristled at his remark. "Death can mean many things. It all rests on the next card in the center." She flipped it over.

"Well?" he asked expectedly.

"An upright High Priestess. She represents the intuitive unconscious mind and the divine feminine. She's also known as the gatekeeper at ancient temples."

"What does that have to do with me?" he said, looking dismayed and bored.

She swept the cards into her hand and stacked them into a neat pile. "Don't worry," she smiled. "Your fate is sealed."

She stood up. "We should put the steaks on. How do you like yours?"

"However you like yours," he replied, standing up.

"I take mine rare."

She opened the grill, and smoke billowed out. Pietro stood next to her. "I can help you with that." He reached for the pair of tongs hanging from the side of the grill.

"I've got it," responded Robinia, quickly grabbing the tongs from the hook.

Pietro took a step back and crossed his arms. He glanced around the field toward a large elm a few yards away. The sun's golden rays trickled through the branches of the tree and shone upon two simple wooden crosses sticking up from the ground.

"You should go inside," said Robinia.

Pietro turned toward her with a puzzled look.

"The mosquitos are coming out." She placed the steaks on the grill. "They'll eat you alive."

"What about you?"

"They don't bother me." She closed the lid to the grill. "A few minutes, and I'll be in."

Pietro walked toward the house and then glanced back as he reached the front door. Robinia was staring toward the elm, a pensive expression on her face. She waved her hand in front of her face as if swatting something away. Perhaps a mosquito. Perhaps a memory, he thought. He opened the door and stepped inside the house.

They finished eating, and they brought the dishes to the sink. He turned on the faucet and reached for the soap.

"You don't need to do that," she said.

"It's the least I can do for not turning me in for squatting on your property," he laughed.

"Listen, I just need to take care of something. I'll be right back."

"No problem."

He hummed a country song from his favorite western he had watched as a child as he washed the dishes. He placed the last plate on the drying rack, then wiped his hands and tossed the towel on the counter. As he looked up, he caught Robinia's reflection in the window above the sink. She was standing just behind his shoulder. He turned the faucet off and turned around to face her.

"I didn't hear you come back," he said.

"Where did you say you were headed?" She opened the cabinet and took a glass from the shelf.

He stepped aside. "I didn't. But I'm actually headed to New York."

She filled the glass with water. "New York. Do you have family there?"

"No, no family. I just want a new adventure," he crossed the kitchen and walked to the dining table. "I don't see my backpack," he said, looking around.

"I moved it by the door for you," she said casually. "It's on the bench."

"Well, thanks again for dinner but I should be going."

"It was a pleasure." She cocked her head to the side. "Just one more thing. You never told me why you were sleeping in an old animal shed."

"My lease was up, and my flight didn't leave for a couple of days." He shrugged his shoulders. "My family already thinks I'm a jerk for leaving and not helping with the business. Pride's a bitch."

They walked toward the door and he picked up his backpack.

"What business?" she asked.

He slung his backpack over his shoulder.

"Sorry to pry," she offered. "I'm just curious what business you would choose to leave here."

"My family owns a marble quarry."

"That makes sense; there are quite a few in the area." She smiled, "Good luck in New York."

She opened the door.

"Thanks," he replied.

He brushed past and she closed the door behind him.

Pietro checked his watch. The meal had taken longer than he planned, but it was still early, and there was still plenty of time to make it to the inn before dark.

Over the mountain, in a small clearing in the forest, Pietro sat behind the wheel of his truck and went over the plan in his head.

A common introduction would not do. He needed to make a dramatic entrance. Fortune did not favor the faint of heart.

Iris

Albergo Pietra Bella

May, 2013

Iris pulled up in her old Volkswagen stuffed to the brim with second-hand furniture, art, and accessories.

"You've been busy," Giuseppe said, opening the car door for her.

"Do you have any idea how many amazing vintage stores are between here and Milan?" she exclaimed. "It's incredible, the art, mid-century furniture, even clothes, and don't get me started on the handbags."

Catrin jumped out of the passenger seat and opened the back door. "Wait until you see the chairs we are having delivered this week. That dining room isn't going to know what hit it," she said, taking out a stack of small paintings and prints.

"Giuseppe, do you mind grabbing the table lamps out of the trunk? I'm going to help Catrin unload the rest of this stuff in the backseat."

He walked around to the back of the car and popped the trunk. "I put the flyers for our yard sale up in town today."

"Great, we posted on our social media accounts as well. Whatever doesn't sell here, I have a few interested dealers who could take the rest off our hands for us. They'll even arrange for the pick-up. We'll get rid of it one way or the other."

"Out with old and in with the not-so-old," Catrin said, carrying an armful of Turkish pillow covers up the steps.

"Just put everything in the first room for now," Iris called after her. "We can sort it out later."

She carried a wooden box filled with accessories inside, and placed it on the bar counter.

Catrin walked into the dining room holding a white ceramic vase with bright yellow daffodils painted on it. "I love this vase," she commented.

"It's very retro-chic," Iris said. "Where shall we put it?"

"Maybe it can go in one of the bedrooms? We could keep fresh flowers in it for the guests. A room with fresh cut flowers always adds a little something extra."

Iris scanned the room. The old tables and chairs were piled in the corner, ready to be put out on the lawn the next day. They kept a few old paintings—portraits of what they thought could have been the owners at some point in the past. But most of the items were ready to be sold.

Suddenly, a shooting pain stabbed through Iris' temple, causing her to wince.

"Are you all right?" Giuseppe asked.

"Fine. Just tired. So, what do you think?" Iris asked. "How do you feel about seeing everything go?"

"It feels really good," he said without hesitation. "It clears out the old ghosts."

"We probably brought in a few new ones with all that stuff," she said, pointing to the pile of furniture.

"You know, Italians are very superstitious. I have known people who have moved houses because a house was unlucky," he said.

"So, why did you keep that one room at the end of the hall, the one we stayed in that night, made up, even when the inn was closed?" she asked.

"Sentimental reasons, I guess." He took a cloth and started wiping down the bar counter. Iris imagined him behind the bar, a younger man, preparing drinks and talking to guests. "Most Italians grow up and live in very old buildings and don't give it much thought. But when my wife and I moved in, we cleared out the cellar and discovered, behind a wall, a trunk filled with old files and records. One piece of paper, in particular, intrigued her immensely - it was a written family tree of sorts, tracking the marriages and births of a family who lived here, one of the earliest owners of the inn, if not the original owners. She became very intrigued by the family, mainly because of the intricacy of connections between the members."

"What do you mean?" Catrin asked. "Like, were they inbred? It was fairly common back then to marry cousins."

"It was more than that," he continued. "There were splits and jumps between the people, marriages, and siblings. Second marriages and half-siblings. But they were all connected somehow, including a notorious priest."

"Oh, now the story gets good," Catrin said.

"We did some investigating, and it turns out that the priest was not only the local priest, but he was also the lead inquisitor who conducted the trials and executions for the Holy Inquisition in the area."

"The Inquisition," Catrin exclaimed. "This is your area of expertise, Iris."

"There were a lot of records written on the man, mostly about the trials, but the most curious fact was that the priest hanged himself in the very cellar he held and tortured his prisoners," continued Giuseppe.

"Why would a priest hang himself?" asked Iris, perplexed. "Suicide is a mortal sin."

"Apparently, there was a note he left, denouncing the trials and asking for forgiveness from his victims. But the most intriguing thing of all is that there was no record of him holding any prisoner at the time of his death."

"Why would that be so strange?" Catrin asked.

"Because we found, in the box, an official letter from the town church, with an arrest warrant for a Violetta Sartori, signed by the priest himself, a few days before his death. But, that's not all. It turns out that Violetta was his half-sister."

"Wow, that is fascinating. So what happened to her?" asked Iris.

"She married a man who owned the inn, had one daughter, and lived to a ripe old age of 72, or so the town records show."

"So, maybe she was never actually arrested, and he killed himself before she was taken in. Maybe the priest would rather have killed himself than murder his own sister," Catrin suggested.

"That's how it appears," Giuseppe said, "but you'll find that Italy is a country of plot twists and deceptions, illusions and contradictions, and nothing is taken at face value."

"So, what's the surprise ending?" Catrin pressed.

"It turns out that the accuser listed on the document was, in fact, the priest. This is virtually unheard of, as most accusers were neighbors or community members with a vendetta to fill."

"That's incredible. So the priest, Violetta's half-brother, was the one who accused her of witchcraft? But, why would he do such a thing?" Iris asked, taking a seat on the bar stool.

"He accused her, but then he killed himself? That makes no sense," Catrin interjected.

"It seems the answer might lie in the family tree we found. You see, Violetta's mother…"

Suddenly, a thunderous crash came from the front. Outside, a truck crashed into the side of a large tree. Behind the wheel, a man lay over the steering wheel, unmoving.

Iris ran outside and tried to open the door, but it was jammed and would not budge. "Try the other side," she yelled.

Catrin was on the other side, pulling on the door handle. "I've almost got it."

Catrin yanked on the door, and it flung open. "He's breathing. But I don't want to move him if his neck is injured. Call an ambulance."

"Giuseppe is already inside calling them."

"I wonder what happened?"

"He may have passed out," Catrin said.

"If this had happened on one of the winding roads, he could have been killed."

Just then, the man began to groan and lift his head from the steering wheel.

"What happened?" he said. A trickle of blood ran down his cheek.

"I'll get the first aid box," Catrin said, hurrying inside.

Iris waited for Catrin to return. The man began to moan and opened his eyes, and lifted his head.

"Giuseppe called the ambulance, but it's going to be thirty minutes or more for them to get out here. He called a tow truck as well," Catrin called, rushing back outside toward the truck.

Iris leaned inside the truck. "Do you think you can get out of here?"

"I'm fine," he said, unbuckling the seatbelt. "It's just a bump on the head, that's all."

"Let's go inside, and I can get you some ice," Iris said.

The three of them walked toward the front door of the inn. Inside, Iris gestured toward the small sitting room off of the entrance. "Have a seat on the sofa. I'll get you some ice and something to drink."

Iris returned a few minutes later. "You'll have to excuse our mess," she said, handing him an icepack. "As you can see, we're renovating."

She sat the cup of water on the side table.

"So, you must be the new owners," he said, placing the ice on his forehead.

"Yes, something like that," she said, taking a seat across from him and Catrin. "I've purchased the inn. Giuseppe lives in his house out back."

"You're a brave woman. We don't get much tourism around this area."

"That's what I tried to tell them," interrupted Giuseppe, stepping into the room.

"Well, we are hoping to change that," she said, smiling. "I'm Iris, by the way, and this is Catrin, and this," she said, pointing toward the doorway, "is Giuseppe."

"I'm Pietro, the delivery man who crashed into your tree."

"Do you remember what happened?" Catrin asked.

"No," he said, running his head through his hair, "it's so strange. I guess I took a wrong turn. I remember driving by the lake, I saw the inn and your car parked out front, and the next thing I know, I'm leaning over the steering wheel."

"Well, the medics will have a look at you when they get here."

"Cancel the ambulance. I said I'm fine."

"Well, you can't drive with a possible head injury. You can stay here tonight. We have plenty of room. Then we can see about getting you back home tomorrow." Catrin said. "Where do you live?"

"Oh, well, I'm actually in-between places right now," replied Pietro hesitantly.

"Well, we can arrange all of that tomorrow," suggested Iris. "Keep that ice on your head. I'm going to start preparing dinner."

Later that evening, they sat around a table filled with plates of fresh cheeses, olives, meats, and breads.

"So what kind of work do you do?" Catrin asked—turning her attention to Pietro and swirling her wine glass gently in her hand.

"My father owns a quarry. I was delivering some marble samples today."

"What kind of marble?" Iris asked.

"It's the typical stone found here in the area called Pietra Rossa. I'm sure you've seen it. It comes in various shades of pink."

"Well, maybe you can cut us a deal. We are starting renovations," Iris suggested.

"I'd be happy to. I also do light construction and renovations. If you need any help, I have a good crew."

Iris poured everyone more wine and held up her glass. "To new beginnings, Salute!"

Giuseppe cleared his throat. "Speaking of new beginnings, I decided to leave and do a bit of traveling."

"Really?" said Iris. "This is a surprise. Where are you going?"

"I have a few places I'd like to visit and never got the chance."

"We're going to miss you," said Catrin.

"I'm confident this place is in good hands. There's an old acquaintance I've lost touch with I'd like to see again." He looked at Iris. "A bit of hunting," he said, giving her a wink.

Iris held up her glass. "Here's to a successful hunt."

Giuseppe

Albergo Pietra Bella

June, 2013

Giuseppe finished packing his suitcase. He put on his shoes and his trench coat, and then walked over to his bed. He pulled out a Bible he kept in his nightstand and opened it. He picked up the photograph that lay inside and tossed the Bible on the bed. Two young men in their twenties, lying in their swim trunks on the beach, a pretty girl in a bikini lying on either side of them. The girls were smiling brightly into the camera, a rosy flush across their cheeks, hair flying carelessly in the wind. The two bronzed men were gazing sideways at one another with their hands buried beneath the sand, the tips of their pinkies overlapping.

Giuseppe took a pair of scissors from the drawer and carefully cut the sides of the photograph, and the two girls fell to the floor.

He tucked the picture inside his wallet, grabbed his suitcase and walked out the door.

Iris

Albergo Pietra Bella

June, 2013

Iris took a sip from her coffee cup and evaluated the condition of the backyard. It needed some general maintenance, weeding, and new plantings. She walked along the pebble path toward the far end of the garden. There were old terracotta pots scattered around the perimeter. Some were chipped, others turned on their sides, speckled with algae and moss in a manner only time could render.

She wandered through the garden, taking a mental inventory of the number of plants she would need to fill the pots.

"You're up early," Catrin's voice called from behind.

Iris turned to see Catrin carrying a hoe across the lawn toward her. "Good morning. I thought I would start work clearing the garden, so I'm taking a look around. "

"Looks like we both had the same idea."

"So, this is an old well," Iris said, pointing to the circle of stones. "The top of it anyway. It's shown in an old drawing from when the inn was a hunting lodge. There were flowers planted in the middle. Daffodils, I believe. White and yellow."

"Just like the vase we bought," Catrin remarked. "How about we go to the nursery and buy some today?"

"That's what I was thinking."

"Have you heard from Giuseppe?" asked Catrin.

"Not yet, but he said he'd reach out once he got settled."

"I'm so happy he's taking the trip," said Catrin.

"I am too. Better late than never." Iris put her arm around Catrin's shoulder. "Let's go buy the flowers. This place needs some color back here."

As Iris and Catrin pulled up to the inn, they could hear the phone ringing from inside.

"You grab the phone and I'll unload the flowers," said Iris, opening the car door.

Iris grabbed a box of flowers and succulents from the back and walked around to the well. She walked to the shed and retrieved her gardening gloves, tools, and wide brimmed straw hat. She tied the hat under her chin and put on the gloves, then began cutting away the grass and weeds from around the circle of stones. After pulling the overgrown vines that had grown up the iron pulley, she knelt on the edge of the well and began digging out the weeds and dirt. She drove the small spade into the dirt, turning it over, loosening it bit by bit. The firmly packed soil was difficult to break, from years of being compacted by rain.

Iris wiped her brow with her sleeve and then drove the spade into the dirt again. This time, the tip of the spade hit a solid object. She lifted it again, and drove it into the dirt. Again, it hit a hard surface.

She worked, clearing away the dirt with her gloved hands, eventually revealing the top of a large stone. It was too large to remove with her small spade, so she stood up to retrieve a larger shovel.

She switched on the light and walked down the steep stone steps that led to the cellar. The cold dampness and musky odor of the cellar ran shivers down her spine. She reached the bottom of the stairs and quickly walked across the cellar floor to the stone wall at the other end. She rubbed her arms up and down, trying to ward off the chill that hung in the air as she scanned the tools. Saws, pruning shears, rakes, and a pitchfork all hung neatly on hooks, but she could not find the shovel. "Pietro must have used it," she thought to herself. "This will do," she said to herself, reaching for a large spade.

Suddenly, a loud crash came from the other end of the wall causing Iris to jump. She cursed, clutching her chest and exhaling sharply.

She took a few steps in the direction from where the sound had come. A small rusty ax lay atop a cracked mirror. Iris picked up the ax and hung it back on its hook, then picked up the small Venetian mirror. "What a shame," she muttered, placing it upright against the wall.

She turned back to retrieve the spade when a painting that had lain beneath the mirror caught her eye.

She leaned down and, to her surprise, recognized the portrait of the man staring back at her. It was the same man in the picture she had taken on her phone the day she had visited the inn. She picked it up and examined it closer. Mercurial waves that she could not tell were longing, dread, or a mix of both, coursed through her veins. She glanced around the cellar, the single lightbulb overhead cast sharp shadows over the furniture and boxes stacked along the perimeter wall. "God, I hate cellars," she said aloud, grabbing a hammer and hurrying back up the stairs with the painting under her arm.

Iris entered the kitchen and placed the painting on the counter. She studied the man's face. Something about his gaze drew her in. She stepped back and crossed her arms. She would hang it in the upstairs corridor alongside other paintings she had saved from the dining room. She opened a drawer, searching for a box of nails. Finding the box, she opened the top and took a nail and picture hook, then headed up the stairs. Halfway up, she dropped the nail as she stepped onto the squeaky stair. The nail rolled through the crack of the floorboard, disappearing with a clink that sounded to Iris, like metal hitting metal. Curious, she leaned down and placed her hand on the wooden plank. She stood up and pressed her foot firmly up and down on the step, causing the plank to give slightly. Intrigued, she took her hammer and pried off the board, exposing a compartment beneath. What she found inside made her gasp.

She stood in the kitchen staring at the metal box resting on the counter. She tried to removed the lid, but the top was rusted and distorted making it difficult to loosen. She took a knife from the counter and placed the tip under the lid, moving gently up and down, working her way around the box until it popped open. Eagerly, she removed the lid and peered inside, only to discover layers of old faded rags.

Curious, she reached under the rags to reveal yet another box, only this time it was wood instead of metal.

"Okay," Iris whispered under her breath. "Here we go."

She slowly opened the lid to the wooden box and gasped. Gemstones, set in an intricate gold design covered a leather tooled book. She carefully opened the cover and tried to decipher the pages.

A few minutes later, Catrin walked into the kitchen. "Sorry it took so long. I needed to change into my gardening clothes." She approached the counter. "What do you have here?"

"You're not going to believe this," answered Iris. "Come here and have a look."

"I don't recognize the writing on the first pages, but the second half of the book is definitely Latin," said Iris.

"Can you read it?"

"I haven't used Latin since college, but I'm certainly going to try."

"This is incredible," Catrin said, shaking her head. "There isn't a title or date anywhere?"

"Not that I can see. It's handwritten, and looks like the hand-bound books from the Middle Ages, judging from the cover, but it may be even older."

Iris stepped back and crossed her arms. "Giuseppe told me that technically, we have to alert the local authorities when something ancient, like Roman artifacts are discovered on your land. But they come in and halt all construction, *everything*. It can take months, sometimes years for them to allow you to proceed."

"Well, this clearly isn't a Roman artefact. Let's just say it's an old family book the owners hid away...for sentimental reasons," suggested Catrin. "There's no need to bring in the authorities and delay our opening."

"I agree," said Iris. "I want to translate the text. If I discover who it belongs to, or if it is something more than a family heirloom, then we'll turn it in. For now, I need to take a photo of each page so at least we'll have copies."

Catrin ran her hand along the metal detail on the cover. "I wonder...."

"What?"

"I wonder if this has anything to do with the woman. The half-sister of the priest."

"What makes you say that?"

"I'm not sure. Something though..."

Albergo Pietra Bella

September, 2013

It was early autumn, and the summer heat was slowly giving way to cooler nights and crisp mornings. The renovations with Pietro were taking longer than Iris would have liked, and she was growing restless. Catrin would be back from the States in October for the opening.

Iris had moved into the room at the end of the hall. It was the smallest room, but it was cozy and had a view of the lake that Iris liked.

She spread the sheet over the mattress and tucked it under the sides. She reached for the spray bottle on the nightstand and misted the bed, allowing the soothing smell of lavender and rosemary to waft around her.

Taking off her clothes, she laid down on the cool top sheet and closed her eyes. She hadn't heard from Ben in weeks. With so much work to get done, she only now felt the absence of his communication.

Iris could feel the blood racing through her veins. Surges of longing electrified her stomach. She felt like one of those static electricity balls she kept next to her bed as a child - the one you would touch the glass, and the electricity inside would follow your hand wherever it moved. Ben was the hand, and she was the electricity.

Iris opened the leather notebook beside her bed and grabbed a pen. She began to scribble whatever words came to mind.

The Phantom Fuck

She opens her eyes

Hand slides between her thighs

Slippery and wet

Proof of your presence

But you are nowhere to be found

She placed it in an envelope and wrote his name and address across the top. Iris would post it when she went into town. She closed her eyes. Sweat dripped from her neck and dotted her chest.

Suddenly, the bell rang in the reception room downstairs, followed by a crashing sound, causing her to jump. Iris didn't recall there being any craftsmen coming today. She quickly dressed and headed downstairs. Iris wiped the sweat from the back of her neck with her palm as she reached the bottom.

The man knelt down and picked up the brass bell that had fallen to the floor. "Looks old," he remarked, turning it around. "There's an inscription . . . *Vocem Meam Audit Oui Me Tangit.*" He looked up at her. "Latin?"

"Yes," she said, taking another step.

"Do you know what it means?"

"It means, *Who touches me, shall hear my voice.*"

"Hmmm, interesting…"

She reached the bottom of the steps and stopped. "It's a common inscription found on old monastery bells."

"Well, I'll be sure to fix it for you."

"We haven't officially opened yet. We're in the middle of renovations. So, if you're looking for a room, I'm afraid there isn't one available," Iris said, shrugging her shoulders.

He stood up. "So, no guests are staying here at the moment?"

"That's right," she replied.

He placed the bell on the reception desk, then laid his duffle bag on the floor. "So," he said, walking up the stairs to meet her, "there's no one around to call in a noise complaint?"

"Not a soul," she said, putting her arms around his neck. "Ben, I can't believe you're here."

"Well, I was in the neighborhood."

"Of course, that makes perfect sense," she said, nodding and kissing his mouth. "Are you hungry? I'm afraid I don't have much…"

"Thirsty, actually," he replied.

"Follow me," Iris said, walking into the dining room. "Have a seat, and I'll pour you a drink."

"You hung it in here," Ben remarked, stopping in front of the large painting hung on the wall.

It showed her kneeling, and her back was facing the viewer. She was wearing a pair of black lace underwear that she was pulling down with her thumbs. Her face was turned to the side, and her eyes were fixed on something beyond the edge of the canvas.

"A little risqué for a dining room perhaps," said Iris, "but I felt like it belonged in here." She placed two glasses on the table and filled them with wine. "Thank you, by the way. It was such a surprise. But I don't remember seeing this one at your exhibition."

"It wasn't. I made this one especially for you," he said.

Words were scrawled down the right side of her back, disappearing around her hip and reappearing around her thigh, then wrapped around her legs and ended on the sole of her foot.

"The scar on the back of your shoulder," Ben said, lifting his glass in the direction of the canvas, "how did you get it?"

"I fell out of a tree house when I was seven and hit a branch on the way down. I earned about ten stitches." She turned her gaze back towards him. "Why are you here?"

"I wanted to see you."

Iris didn't respond.

"Should I not have come?"

"No, I didn't say that. How long are you here for?"

"Only a week, I'm afraid."

"Let's take a walk. Bring your wine," Iris said, standing up.

He followed her out the door. Iris didn't know where they were going. She just wanted to keep moving. They came to a small clearing where the lawn met the edge of the forest, and she sat down on a bed of soft grass and pine needles. She placed her wine glass on the ground and leaned back, looking into the crisscrossed branches that laddered up to the sky.

"I found something," she began tentatively.

"Here, at the inn?"

"Yes,"

"I'm sure there was a whole treasure trove of things you uncovered here. This place is several hundred years old, isn't it?"

"About five hundred," she replied.

"Sounds like a mystery, Miss Drew. What did you find?"

"A book."

"Well, what kind of a book?"

"It's written in a language I do not recognize. But it seems there was a Latin translation that was added at some point later. My Latin is rusty, but slowly, I've been translating it."

"And?"

"And, there's some pretty interesting information. It speaks of a civilization near Venice that worshipped a female deity named Rieta."

"That doesn't seem so far-fetched. There have been a lot of discoveries about the feminine deities and religions that came before Christianity as we know it. Before God was some old jealous dude judging and condemning everyone; there were civilizations that worshipped the female divine. Women are the life-givers, after all. Who wouldn't worship that?" he said, running his hand along her thigh.

"Right, and all of the female statues, with pregnant bellies, all signs of female deity worship. But never before, at least that I am aware, has there been a written record of their ideology. The book doesn't seem to be an original script obviously, but it does appear to be translations of translations."

"A Rosetta Stone of sorts?"

"Exactly."

"This sounds right up your alley. So, what are you going to do with it?"

"I haven't decided yet."

"You'll have to turn it over to the Italian Authorities."

"I know that. I just want to hold onto it for a little longer."

"And did Giuseppe know anything about it?"

"I didn't have the chance to ask him about it. But I doubt it."

"So, can I see this book?"

"Come on. I'll show you," Iris said, standing up.

He remained seated and took her hand. She stood over him, and he pulled her back down on top of him. "Not so fast. There's something about this place," he said.

Albergo Pietra Bella

September, 2013

"This is incredible," Ben said, shaking his head.

Iris picked up the tweezers with her gloved hand and turned another page. "I know. I only work with copies I made from the book, obviously."

"I was talking about the fact that you have white gloves and tweezers."

"Oh, be quiet," she said, nudging him. "You have to be careful with old books. The oils from our skin damage the pages."

"But dirt and moisture under an old staircase is okay?"

"I doubt whoever hid it expected it to be there for so long."

"It's in remarkable condition. But you're right. We would need someone to verify the age. The contents appear to be much older than the book itself." He closed the book and ran his hand over the cover. "These jewels alone must be worth a fortune." He lifted the book and turned it over. "The metal work is remarkable. So intricate," he said, tracing his fingers along the gold edge.

"That's interesting," she said.

"What's that?" he asked.

"This," she said, pointing to a circular metal disk in the center of the cover. "It almost looks like some sort of a lock."

She leaned in closer. "Strange, I never noticed it before."

He tilted the book slightly upward. "Yes, there are tiny threads, almost like gears. This is getting more intriguing by the minute." He turned the book back over and laid it on the table. "So, what have you uncovered with your translations?"

"Well, I searched the original text online, and nothing comes up as a match. But, in the back," she explained, opening the book, "the text is all in Latin. I can only assume it is a translation of the original text. Next life, I'll come back as a linguist," she said.

"Well, what do your translations say?"

"They seem to speak of religion or philosophy. Of life and humanity. But it isn't just philosophical. It seems to give specific instructions on how to live, form social norms, societal structures, relationships, and even the education of the young. It's a paradigm of sorts that speaks of another time entirely. Of personal freedom and personal evolution above all else. But also the importance of cooperation and altruism. It speaks of the whole, and how there is only one of us, one energy. They call it the Light. And how we are only a small expression of that energy, so, therefore, it is in everyone's best interest to act as if we are all one."

"What are these pages made from? They have a very unusual texture."

"I think it's either parchment or vellum. Both are made from animal skins, most likely sheep or goats. Vellum is made from baby calf or sheep and is more expensive. Based on the craftsmanship of the book, I'm going with vellum. Paper didn't replace parchment until the 15th century."

"The graining is really nice," he said, examining the pages closely. "This gives me an idea."

"What's that?"

"I'd like to use the writings in this book for my next art collection. You would be my model if you are agreeable, of course, and then apply the writings to your body in the same way as before. But I would use animal skin instead of canvas."

"Which translation would you use?"

"Probably the original," he said as he looked up at her. "A gallery in Brooklyn is asking for an exhibition. We could work together, and you could pick out which translations you want me to use." He looked up at her, and she could see the excitement in his eyes. "What do you think?"

"I think it's brilliant."

"I need to go back to New York for a few weeks to meet with the exhibition curators. We can get started when I return."

"Great. That will give me time to get through the opening here."

Pietro

Albergo Pietra Bella

October, 2013

He stepped into the shadows, his black shirt clung to his chest, and his wavy hair hung heavy with sweat around his face. He walked with a determined stride beneath the tree branches, cracking twigs and crunching leaves beneath his boots. Clouds blanketed the autumn sky, and the dark water rippled gently on the lake's surface like a blot of ink pooled on paper. But he didn't look at the lake. Pietro's eyes were fixed on the inn.

The windows were open, with a soft glow illuminating the curtains. He could hear jazz playing. Iris would be in the kitchen washing the dishes. Then she would make her way into the front sitting room and select a book from the shelves he had built for her this summer. She wanted the fireplace wall surrounded by bookshelves from floor to ceiling. It was one of the first things she had requested him to do. The project had taken him several weeks to complete, and when it was done, Iris had filled the shelves with books on every imaginable topic - history, fiction, the classics, cooking, art, and satire. Her interests were as vast as her ambition was bold to settle in this isolated territory, he thought. Why she chose to be here when she could be in America, he would never understand, but that's precisely where he was headed. She could rot here, along with all the locals he detested. He was moving on.

He looked at his watch. A few more minutes, and she would be sitting in the corner of the sofa, reading, and sipping her wine.

It was Friday night so she would select a more expensive vintage. Weekend wine, she called it. He had learned her routine well.

Pietro lingered back on the lawn and lit a cigarette. He looked up at the top floor of the inn. It was dark and still. It irritated him that the book was in there somewhere, and yet he hadn't found it over these last few months. But there was hope. In her nightstand, he found a notebook that contained translations from a text in a language he had never seen. There could be only one explanation. He tossed his cigarette. He only had to wait a bit longer, until he installed the safe in her room. He guessed this was where she would keep it. But the safe had still not arrived. He was growing impatient. Perhaps if he chatted with her over some wine, she would give him some sort of a clue. Now, with Ben and Catrin both gone, it was at least worth a shot.

He flicked his cigarette and went to knock on the door.

For two hours they had been sitting in the living room and she hadn't given away any information. Not that he really expected her to,

"Well, I don't want to keep you longer," he said, setting his glass down on the side table. "Thanks for the wine and I guess I'll be headed out."

She stood up. "Wait just a moment. I have something for you. I'll be right back."

He sat back in his chair and crossed his leg over his knee. He was pleased with the bookshelves he had made. Maybe he could do some carpentry work when he got to America. Italian craftsmanship. Americans love that.

"I wonder if she's actually read all of these books," he muttered.

His eyes swept back and forth over the spines, all different colors, widths, and heights. Suddenly his eyes stopped. His brow furrowed as he focused on the corner of the top shelf. It was barely perceptible and could easily be missed. But he saw the difference. His carpentry work had taught him to always look at the details - the direction of the grain of wood, the construction of the joints, the subtle carvings and texture that made a piece of furniture come together. So many minute details and elements most people never bothered to notice when they opened a drawer or sat on a chair. But he noticed. And he noticed the one book on the shelf that did not look like the others.

He stepped toward the shelves and examined the rectangular shape made of wood. Judging from the flat shape, it appeared to be more of a box than a book. Of course, Sherlock; she was hiding something in plain sight, he thought. His heart was beating wildly out of his chest.

"I wanted you to have this," her voice interrupted. He turned quickly, maybe too quickly. Pietro tried his best to control his emotions and not give anything away. He couldn't blow this. "It's a bottle of limoncello," she said holding up the bottle. "I made several dozen bottles this summer. I wanted you to have one, in celebration of our opening next week."

"My favorite," he smiled, taking the bottle from her hand. "And congratulations, it's very exciting. And I'm sure you'll be happy to see Catrin again."

"She arrives the day after tomorrow. It'll be great having her back."

"Well, I'll be going." He lifted the bottle, "Thanks for the limoncello."

She followed him to the door and stepped out onto the porch. "Did you walk?" she asked, looking around.

"Yeah, I didn't plan on being out so late."

"Why don't you take my car back? I'm not using it tonight, and you can return it tomorrow."

He paused, weighing his options. "That's ok, I prefer to walk. And it's a nice evening."

"Ok. Good night."

He stepped off the porch and walked across the lawn. The inn would be open soon. He would take the book then. With the guests around, he would not be suspected, at least at the beginning.

In the blink of an eye, his entire future had changed. His chest expanded as he walked into the woods.

Past the clearing, he stopped abruptly in his tracks. A layer of perspiration dotted his skin. Suddenly, he had the feeling of being watched.

His eyes darted around him nervously. Then, he took a deep breath, cursing his timidness. This is not the quarry, and you are not a child, he told himself.

He quickened his stride and continued on.

Albergo Pietra Bella

October, 2013

A week later, parked cars lined the road. The inn was buzzing with people, dogs, and children.

Pietro entered the small lobby.

"Hey stranger." A female voice startled him from behind.

"Catrin, you're back. We missed you." He leaned in and gave her a quick kiss on the cheek.

"It's great to be back. We're fully booked. Can you believe it?"

"Of course I can. Look what the two of you have done, it's incredible," he said enthusiastically.

"Well, you played a part too," she said, looking around. "The renovations look fantastic."

"I was just the labor," he replied, glancing briefly in the direction of the sitting room. "You two had real vision with this place." He wished she would get out of his way so he could see if the book was still there.

"Are you here to install Iris' safe?"

"Sorry?"

"Iris' safe. It arrived this morning. We put it in her room. Grab the key from her."

"Will do."

"And did you see the baby goat?"

"Baby goat?"

"Yes, a man who lives down the road brought it by the other day. He gifted it to the inn as a welcome present. Said it would bring good luck. I thought she looked like a Glenda, but Iris insisted we name her Mona Lisa. Can you imagine? A goat named Mona Lisa!" Catrin burst out laughing. "I'll catch up with you later. You're staying for dinner, right?" Before Pietro could answer, she darted out the door.

Relieved, he quickly stepped into the sitting room and looked up at the top shelf. He furrowed his brow. He stepped closer, this time scanning the entire shelf from left to right. Anger gripped his chest.

It was gone.

"Catrin said you were here," Iris said, walking into the room behind him. He tightened his fist and took a steady breath to calm his nerves. Then he turned around. "Yes, she told me your safe arrived."

"It arrived this morning, finally. Now I can lock away all those family jewels," she winked.

Yes, your jewels. Only your jewels you don't wear around your neck, do you? he thought. Funny, how people give things away without knowing they are giving anything way.

She stretched out her hand. "Here's the key to my room. You know where the tools are."

"Sure thing," he said, taking the key from her hand. A small terrier bounded into the room and ran a circle around Iris' legs. She knelt down and scratched it behind the ears. Pietro clenched his jaw and walked out of the room.

Pietro unlocked the door to Iris' bedroom and pushed it open. A cool autumn breeze rushed though, carrying the promise of early winter. He took a deep breath in. He had lived in the mountains his entire life and could read the air as sure as he knew his own breath. He read once that Eskimos have a hundred words for snow. He could have a hundred words for mountain air. It didn't just change with the seasons, it changed with the hours of the day, and he knew each subtle shift by heart. Pietro shook the thought from his mind. He did not belong to this place anymore.

He spread his tools on the floor. The box to the safe was lying in the corner. One side of the box had been opened; the instructions were lying on top. He flipped through the booklet. It looked the same as the others he had installed, only larger. He picked up his tools and went to work drilling the holes. When he was ready, he removed the safe from the box and lifted it onto the shelf. He adjusted the alignment of the holes and secured the safe to the shelf, bolting it from the inside. He stepped back and looked at the empty safe. Soon it would hold the passport to his future. And he had to find a way to get to it.

He looked at his watch. It had only taken him twenty minutes. He peered out the window. A flurry of activity filled the lawn and the clattering of dishes and utensils could be heard as the guests enjoyed their aperitivo. He hoped Iris would be occupied for a while.

He worked quickly, sweeping through the closet, armoire, and dresser drawers. He rummaged through the dresser, feeling beneath the stacks of sweaters and shirts.

Nothing.

His eyes darted around the room. He wiped his palms on his jeans, knelt on the floor, and peered under the bed. He pulled out a long plastic box and removed the lid. He swept his hand beneath the folded clothes. When his hand hit something wooden, he looked beneath the clothes.

There it was.

Pietro opened the lid to the rectangular box. His eyes widened at the sight of the encrusted jewelled book. Hastily, he took it out of the box and sat it aside. He threw the clothes back in the box and shoved it under the bed. Now he had to figure out a way to get it out of the inn undetected. He looked around the room, spying the cardboard box. He slid the wooden box inside and closed the flaps. Then he picked it up and walked downstairs.

Half way down the stairs, he bumped into Iris. "Ah, you're finished," she said.

"It's all ready for you."

"Great," Iris said. "Are you staying for dinner?"

"Wish I could, but I just got a call on another job," he said, shifting the box to his other arm.

"Ok. Thanks for coming by today." She glanced at the box. "Just put that out with the recycling."

His hands gripped it tighter. "Sure thing. See you later." And he slipped passed her and bolted out of the door. He did not look back. He would be gone in twenty-four hours.

The sun was disappearing behind the trees. He emerged from the woods and walked along the jagged rocky path, up the mountain in the direction of his hut. He would catch a ride to Trento and take the first train to Milan in the morning. From there, he would buy a one-way ticket to New York City.

He gripped the straps to his backpack and picked up his pace. The wind whipped his face, and a few drops of rain began to fall as he reached the top. He paid no mind to the impending storm; he felt alive and invincible. He walked along the edge of the path where the peaks and valleys stretched out before him, laughing to himself. Where his ancestors had failed, he had succeeded. He would call his contact once he arrived in New York to begin the process of selling it in the underground art market. He was sure there would be a bidding war over this one.

Suddenly, two hands pushed him forcibly from behind, and he felt himself falling, face first, off of the mountain. Then, he struck a boulder, and his body lay twisted, broken over a jagged rock. A sharp pain sliced through his back and head, and he gasped for breath.

A minute later, a nimble figure appeared before him and crouched down near his face.

"That was a nasty fall you took," said Robinia.

She unzipped his backpack and took out the wooden box. He groaned and tried to move, but he could not feel his limbs. She placed her fingers on his pulse, faint and fading fast.

Robinia brushed the hair from his eyes and leaned in. "Sometimes, the Death card…means exactly that," she whispered in his ear.

His body convulsed as he watched her stand up and disappear up the mountain side.

He gasped weakly as a rush of cold air swirled around him and the rain fell harder.

One breath he had never considered, was his last.

Iris

"Where there are many women, there are many witches."

The Malleus Maleficarum, Part 1

Question VI

Heinrich Kramer, 1486

Albergo Pietra Bella

October, 2013

Iris closed the novel and tapped her finger on its soft cover. A restlessness nagged at her, making it impossible to concentrate. She opened her bedside drawer and took out the notebook with her translations and a red pen. She flipped through the pages. Something about the translations seemed incomplete, but she couldn't put her finger on it. Iris went over the words, underlining the ones that caught her attention: one; energy; light; dark. "Light," thought Iris, "has two states, particle and wave." She continue reading and underlining: unity; duality; seen; unseen; feminine. Iris paused.

She circled the word feminine.

She removed her glasses and placed the notebook on the nightstand. Then she stood up and pulled the long plastic container out from under her bed and opened the lid. Reaching beneath the pile of clothes, she felt for the wooden box. She moved her hand to the other side. Panic swept through her body as she pulled the clothes from the box and threw them on the floor next to her.

Nothing.

A wave of nausea swept through her, and she sat on the bed, trying to think. She was the only one with a key to her room. She stood up and looked around. Everything was in place.

She opened the drawers to her dresser. Nothing had been disturbed. She checked her jewelry boxes; nothing had been taken. The person who took it, knew what they were looking for.

The safe caught her eye.

Pietro.

He was the only one who had access to her room. She took out her phone and called him. It went straight to voicemail. She texted him and hit send. Then she called again. The voicemail message came on again. Iris looked at her phone. Ten o'clock. He could be on a train or plane to anywhere by now.

She hurried down the hall to Catrin's room and knocked on the door. "Catrin, it's me. Open the door."

She knocked again, this time a little more loudly. Iris took out her phone and called her. She could hear the phone ringing inside the room.

She went outside and stood on the front porch, cursing herself for being so trusting.

Laughter was coming from across the lawn. She spotted Catrin and ran up to her. "Catrin, I need to talk to you."

Catrin looked at the man standing next to her. "Thank you for the lovely stroll. I'll see you in the morning."

The man nodded and walked in the direction of the inn. Catrin turned to her, "What's up?"

"Did Pietro ever tell you where he lived?"

"He said he was living with a relative. Why?"

"The book is gone, and I think he took it."

"What do you mean it's gone?"

"It's gone," Iris said.

"Well, we have no choice but to go to the police," said Catrin.

"I would rather not bring any attention to myself, especially considering we just opened. It wouldn't look good if word got out we had a robbery our first week."

"Yeah, and he knew that too."

"Bastard," cursed Iris. "I should have been more careful."

"But you have the copies of every page, right?" asked Catrin.

"I do."

"So, I really think we should go to the police and file a general complaint. Maybe they can give us some information on this guy. Say it was a valuable book from your family. They don't need to know anything else. And let's face it, I doubt they really care about the contents."

Iris paused for a second. "Okay," she agreed. "I'll get the receptionist to cover for us and we can go tomorrow after breakfast."

Alpinella

October, 2013

The officer stood up and opened the door to his office in the back of the tiny station. "Thanks for coming by."

"I'm shocked to hear about this terrible accident. I'm sorry I can't give you any more information," Iris said.

"It's unfortunate but not surprising. Trouble followed Pietro since he was a kid. But we don't suspect foul play. Just an unfortunate fall on his way back to his barn. The rocks get slippery after a rain."

"Barn?"

"Yeah, it was one of those mountain sheds for animals. It looked like he was living there after he left home recently."

Iris struggled to appear casual, not wanting to alert the officer.

"Really? He told me he was living with relatives."

"No relatives that I know still talk to him. He had some bad financial dealings, and they all pretty much cut him off."

"This is beginning to add up," Iris thought to herself.

"We found a few of his belongings. Everything was packed up like he was ready to leave. Poor bastard never could catch a break. Well, maybe one last break," he chuckled, amused at his own joke.

"You know, he had one friend he mentioned he was close to. Perhaps he would like to have his belongings. I could give him his things?"

The officer shrugged his shoulders. "Sure, if you like. Just a bunch of dirty clothes and a book."

Iris raised her eyebrows. "A book?"

"Yeah, a book on Italian marble. Guess he was sentimental after all."

Iris' heart sank.

"Roberto, grab the belongings we retrieved from Pietro and give them to this lady, that is, if I'm not interrupting your third coffee break this morning," his voice dripping with sarcasm.

Iris' mind was racing. If he was packed and ready to leave, that means he had planned to steal the book, and he was probably carrying it with him when he fell. That meant the book could still be on the mountain somewhere.

Roberto returned with a plastic bag and handed it to Iris.

"Thank you," she said and stood up to leave.

"The inn is open, I hear," he said.

"Yes, this month."

"How's that going?"

"It's been a good showing so far."

"I'm glad to hear it. It's nice to know people are interested in coming here. We need to breathe some life into this place," he said, shaking his head. "Well, if you need anything, don't hesitate to call us."

"I will."

She stepped out onto the sidewalk and put her sunglasses on. Catrin was chatting up a couple. "Be sure to come by and see us," she said, waving.

"So, what happened?" Catrin asked.

"You're not going to believe this," she said in a hushed tone. "Pietro is dead. A group of rock climbers found his body on the cliff close to the inn."

"He's dead?" shouted Catrin, covering her mouth with her hand.

"Shhh," said Iris, grabbing her arm and steering her down the sidewalk.

"Was it an accident? And did you tell them about the book?"

"The police think he slipped, but I found something out that was rather interesting."

"What's that?"

"The officer said he had been living in one of those little barns. You know, the ones that are in the mountains here, for animals to take shelter during the winter."

"Really?"

"Yes, he said they found his belongings, and it looked like he had been living there, but everything was packed up as if he were getting ready to leave. He gave me this bag."

"I wish we could find that stone hut he was living in."

"Me too. Even if we did find it, I'm sure the police cleared everything out. And since they did not mention it, my guess is, he was carrying the book when he fell off the cliff."

"Which means it's either at the bottom somewhere or if someone pushed him, whoever it was, took it."

"That seems to fit."

"Anything interesting in the bag?"

"I don't think so. The officer said it's just some clothes and a book on marble."

"He did say his family owned a quarry."

Iris opened the backpack, found and pulled out the book.

"A guide to Italian marble," she read and flipped open the book. An envelope fell out.

Catrin leaned down and picked it up. "It looks very old," she said, opening it carefully.

"It's a letter written in Italian. Can you read this?"

Iris examined the paper. "I can. But, with the cursive handwriting, it'll take me a little time to read through."

"I say we try to find that barn. Did the officer give any specifics on the location."

"It was off a mountain trail, not far from the inn. I know the one," replied Iris.

"We still have some time before we need to get back. I say we stop on the way back and take a look around."

They emerged from the woods and made their way along a grassy path that led up the side of the mountain.

"Look, over there," Iris said, pointing across a meadow.

"It doesn't look like an animal hut to me. It looks more like a cabin."

"Let's go take a look," said Iris. "Maybe they've seen him and can tell us something."

They approached a small grey stone house and knocked on the door.

They waited, casting each other uneasy glances.

A woman with long copper curls and piercing eyes opened the door.

"Hello," said Iris. "My friend and I live close to here and we were wondering if you could -"

"I've been expecting you," the woman interrupted.

Iris smiled politely. "Oh, you must have us confused with —"

"Come in," she said, looking up at the sky. "It looks like rain."

Iris and Catrin walked inside. "Sit down," she said, gesturing to the small round table with wooden chairs. "I'll fix you a cafe."

 "I'm Iris and this…"

"I know who you are," she said, pulling out a chair.

Catrin cast a curious glance at Iris, who gave her a knowing nod to keep quiet and play along.

They waited in silence as Robinia prepared the espresso.

"My name is Robinia," she said, and placed two small cups and saucers filled with dark, rich espresso on the table. Then she returned with a small bowl of sugar and two small spoons.

"You said you were expecting us?" Iris asked curiously.

"Yes."

She sat with her back effortlessly straight, her head slightly tilted. Her demeanor was relaxed, yet there was an alertness in her gaze. "You bought Giuseppe's inn."

"That's right," Iris said.

There was something about this strange woman, with her golden eyes and hair that seemed to reflect the surrounding light, that made Iris feel oddly at ease.

"If you can both agree, and I have no doubt you will, can you not ask any questions about what guided you to my door? Then, we can start from here and move forward regarding something of great interest to you."

Speechless, both Catrin and Iris nodded in agreement. "I have come into possession of a book that Pietro had stolen," she explained.

Iris gasped. "You have the book?" she exclaimed in disbelief.

"I discovered him living in a shed on my property. I didn't trust him, so I searched his things, and found a letter that describes the existence of a book I now have in my possession."

Iris took the letter from the bag and laid it on the table. "This letter?" she asked.

Robinia glanced down at it. "Yes. That is the one I saw in his backpack. I had heard about this book ever since I was a little girl growing up in Venice, actually. Everyone dismissed it as folklore or legend. But after reading the letter, I decided perhaps there was more truth to the story. So, I followed him, and that is when I realized he was looking for the book at the inn, as it tells of in the letter."

Iris stirred the sugar in her espresso. "What would Pietro want with a book about a female deity?"

Robinia pulled her hair back and tied it in a bun, making her eyes stand out even more. Then, she crossed her arms and placed them on the edge of the table. "I doubt Pietro was after the knowledge contained in the book. He mentioned that he was headed out of town, and my guess is this book was his ticket out."

"I can't imagine what kind of crooks he would have sold it to. It could have been lost forever," exclaimed Catrin, shaking her head.

"It was a close call for sure," agreed Robinia. "But the important thing is that we have it. Now, this book, is proof that it wasn't a myth. The civilization actually existed. And, now, we must be prudent on how we proceed."

"We?" Iris stopped stirring. "So, what are you saying?"

"I'm saying that nothing in this universe occurs by chance, and there are no coincidences. The universe is not random, but has an intelligence and timing that is perfect and beyond our mortal comprehension. Our brains cannot fathom such an intricate interplay of meetings, timing, and occurrences, but everything is always brought together in perfect harmony." She paused for a moment. "So, to answer your question, whatever our role in this is, if we stay alert and read the signs, then we will know what to do next."

"Wow. I feel like I just stepped into some alternate reality," Catrin said.

"Who knows, maybe you did," Robinia said.

Robinia stood up again and left the room. When she returned, she was holding the wooden box. She opened the lid and removed the book. "Open the book to the last chapter," said Robinia, sliding the book across the table to Iris.

Iris carefully flipped the pages to the end. "I didn't make it this far in my translations," she said.

"I suspected as much," said Robinia. "There, in the last chapter of the book, it explains."

"Explains what?" Catrin asked.

"It explains the origins of the text and how to access the other volumes and artifacts."

"Wait, did you say other volumes?" Iris asked.

"That's right. This is only the first. There are two more. And they are needed to open the cave."

"Cave? There's actually a cave? This is incredible," said Catrin.

"Rieta's people knew the invasion was coming and that they would be overthrown. So, they took care to save the history of their civilization, their written record, and hid the most valuable of their possessions so that they might preserve their past and one day people would come to know it again. This final chapter explains all this, and it says it was included in each volume so that whoever came into possession of the book would know of the existence of the others."

"So, how did this volume end up at the inn?" Iris asked.

"That, we can only speculate. But it was no accident that you came into possession of it. We often receive guidance and help from other dimensions."

"Like guardian angels?" Catrin asked.

"Not exactly. More like other beings, some like us, that exist in other dimensions. Surely you do not believe that we are the only dimension that exists?"

"Of course not. I've just never come into contact with any of them," replied Iris.

"Maybe you weren't paying attention. The Light, as they called it, uses the entire universe and all the means at its disposal to communicate, help, and direct us. And when we decide upon a course of action or desire a particular result, the entire universe arranges itself to make it happen. We change the entire course of the universe, actually, in the most subtle of complex ways, far beyond what our imagination can ever conceive, just by deciding on something."

Iris thought back to the night of Befana. The broken-down car. The visit to the inn. Reconnecting with Ben. Leaving Nico. Feeling drawn back to the inn, almost as if she were following some sort of instinct beyond her control.

"To quote Shakespeare: 'There are more things in Heaven and Earth, Horatio, than are dreamt of in your philosophy'," Iris said.

"Shakespeare was a prophet. Unlike Jesus and the other messengers who were murdered, he wrote books for our entertainment and posed no threat. But unlike Hamlet, this book does pose a threat. If taken seriously, it has the power to unravel an entire civilization by giving the power back to the people. Of course the people *in* power will do anything to make sure that doesn't happen," Robinia said.

"So where do we find this cave?" Catrin asked.

"The Christians knew the best way to erase something was to build on top of it. They built a church on top of her shrine in Venice. Luckily, Rieta's followers moved everything from that location, just further north in the Dolomites. There is a hidden cave, where everything was relocated."

"And no one has found this secret cave in all these years?" Catrin said.

"We don't·know."

"And how are we supposed to find this cave if some explorer hasn't already?"

"They left us directions," Robinia said.

"You can't tell us that we are the first to find this. Someone could have beaten us to it by now."

"Not necessarily."

"Why is that?" Iris asked.

"Because it says that the key to unlocking the vault is here," Robinia turned the book over and pointed to the metal shape on the back cover.

"So, that is a key?" Iris asked. "I knew it had to be more than just a decoration."

"But anyone could have tried this by now," Catrin said.

"Possibly. But it also says that, in order to unlock the vault, there must be a total of three books turned *at the same time.*"

Catrin rolled her eyes. "Well, that throws a wrench in our plan. How will we find another *two* books? It's a miracle we found this one."

"I know it seems impossible and far-fetched. But we've come this far," Iris spoke up. "I can't believe this is the end of the journey." She ran her fingers around the edge of the rose petals, feeling the grooves and smoothness of the metal. "I say we find this cave. If what you say is right," she said, looking at Robinia, "then the universe will lead the way."

"Where do we start?" asked Catrin.

"I think I have an idea based on some of the translations I've deciphered. And luckily, it isn't too far from here."

Val di Luci

November, 2013

The three women walked in silence along the overgrown path. Although none had much to lose from such a seemingly reckless goose chase, Iris still felt the weight most heavily. She told herself it was only a book, but from somewhere deep down, in a place she had only recently discovered and begun to trust, she knew it was more. How much more, she couldn't say.

"Is anyone else thinking this path could be only a figment of our imagination," Catrin asked.

"Did you smoke again?" asked Iris, rolling her eyes and laughing.

"No," said Catrin innocently, "but I'm wishing I had."

"According to the book and the very vague map, it is the most likely place for the cave to exist," Robinia said

"Even if we find the cave, it still worries me that we are supposed to have three books to unlock it, and not to sound negative, but we only have one," Catrin said. "I can't help but think we should have started our search in Venice."

"Everything that would possibly have survived from her old temple has either been pilfered, burned, or succumbed to the canal by now. There would be nothing left," replied Robinia.

"Let's just see what we find, and try to keep an open mind," Iris said. "Look. It looks like the path leads to some steps up ahead."

They climbed the stone steps whose treads were spaced far enough apart making it an awkward gait as they ascended, forcing them to take either one large step or two awkward smaller ones.

At the top of the steps, a village emerged. Large stones lay next to crumbling walls that were overgrown with vines. The majority of the roofs were caved in.

"Wow," Catrin said, looking around. "Even if there were anything left that would lead us to the other books, there's no way we can sift through all this rubble."

"Remember, the book mentioned a cave," Iris said.

"Yeah, a hidden cave that you need three books, not one, to open it," Catrin reminded her.

"We have one book," said Iris hopefully. "Where shall we start?"

"I think it's worth a shot to look around this town. Maybe there is something here that can help us with the other two books. The one place that would conceal it best," Catrin said. "Maybe the church," she said, pointing across the patchwork of stones.

They walked into the small chapel. It was the only building that remained somewhat intact. The walls were solid, and there were a few holes in the roof. The front doors were missing, probably harvested for firewood at some point, and inside, the pews were gone as well. All that remained was a faded fresco of Mother Mary behind the simple stone altar.

The three women walked down the length of the nave.

Iris suddenly felt light headed and she could have sworn she caught a trace of incense wafting through the air, even though they were the only ones inside. She braced for what she knew was coming next. But, instead of the usual visuals of words and images that accompanied her physical sensations, something unexpected happened. A chorus of chanting filled her head. She heard each word distinctly even though she had never attended Mass. She fell behind Catrin and Robinia, taking in the sound that seemed to come from everywhere and nowhere at once.

Then, slowly, the chanting changed into the sound of running water.

"I wonder who used to inhabit this tiny village, and why they left?" Catrin wondered aloud.

"Many of these villages were for miners," Robinia explained. "When the mines dried up, there was no reason to stay."

"It's a wonder squatters didn't come in and take over," Catrin said.

"The winters are harsh up here. With no heat or running water, it would be difficult to live," Robinia said.

"So, if we were trying to hide a priceless artifact, where would we hide it?" asked Catrin.

Iris ran her hand along the top of the altar, and a sudden vision filled her with certainty. She looked up at the two of them. "In plain sight," she said resolutely.

Robinia and Catrin looked around the empty church. "Not in here," Iris said. "Come with me."

They followed Iris outside the church and across the small courtyard. "There's one in every town," she said, thoughtfully, looking around.

"One what?" Robinia asked.

"A well," responded Iris. "They were usually in the center of the piazza, right?"

"Yes," Robinia replied, "but there doesn't seem to be one here." Robinia exhaled and put her hands on her hips. "In these villages, it was common for there to be water spouts coming directly from the mountain rock, capturing the fresh spring water."

"Where were they located?" Iris asked.

"Wherever you could tap into the spring water," Robinia replied.

"Why do you think it has anything to do with water?" Catrin asked.

Iris looked at them. They had come so far on this journey together. They had trusted her. Surely, she could trust them with this, she thought to herself. "Listen," she began. "I'm not sure exactly how to explain this, but my entire life I have had … sensations."

"What type of sensations?" asked Catrin.

Iris put her hand on her forehead, "Physical sensations…and other things. Visions, words. And, now, in this church, I heard chanting and running water very clearly." She sighed, "Maybe I am crazy. But it doesn't seem crazy when everything I experience has pointed me in a specific direction. And when I have followed it, it has never led me astray. When I ignore it, that's when things don't go well." She gave them a sly smile and continued, "I understand if you don't follow me."

Catrin shook her head. "The only thing crazy is not following it. Not listening to it. The universe speaks to each and everyone of us, but I believe the language is subtler and quieter than we imagine. It's not trumpets and banners blaring from the heavens. It's not pastors waving a Bible in the air and yelling into microphones. It is faint whispers, signs, coincidences, and sensations in our bodies. It's that little voice that tells us where to go, based on nothing more than a hunch."

Robinia stepped forward: "Even if people do call you crazy or don't believe you, leave them to their own conclusions. It is not your business to control what others think. It's your business to follow your gut. Do you know the Italians say that your gut is your second brain? I am sure there is a grain of truth to that."

Catrin put her hand on Iris' shoulder. "Come on. Let's go find the fountain."

They turned down a narrow abandoned street where crowded medieval buildings stood on either side of them, empty shells that once contained the heartbeat of life from a very different time. A different time, but the circumstances were still the same, thought Iris.

She stopped briefly and looked up at a broken window on the second floor of an apartment building and imagined the mundane routines of life that the walls had witnessed - lovemaking, a breast offered to a crying baby, bitter words exchanged between a husband and wife, a cold compress held to a child's feverish forehead, birthday songs sung, prayers fervently offered, and death. The same disappointments and triumphs playing out generation after generation. Sometimes, in places like this, when she stood very still, she could swear she caught the slight breeze of someone brushing past or the low murmur of a conversation.

She turned and continued down the cobblestones to catch up with the others.

The street turned into a narrow dirt footpath that hugged the mountain's side. The buildings were fewer and farther apart, giving way to sweeping views of the valley below. Trees shaded the path and provided shelter from the sun.

"Look, moss and algae," Catrin said. "A water source should be around here somewhere."

Encouraged, they all picked their pace and rounded a corner that sloped slightly downward.

"Look at this," said Robinia. They stood in front of a fountain made of pink stone. There was a rusty metal spout that still had a small but steady stream of water trickling out of it.

The water poured into a smooth stone basin with a cut-out, diverting the runoff through a trench that continued down the mountain. Above the metal spout, was a metal rosette. The rosette was set into a deep cove that looked as if it had been carved out of the mountain itself, protecting the rosette from the elements.

Iris leaned in and traced her fingers along the carvings above the faucet. "I never in a million years thought it would be this easy."

"Well, it's definitely a floral shape. It's been somewhat protected by this overhang," Catrin said. "But there's only one way to find out if it fits."

Iris took off her backpack and unbuckled the top flap. Then she removed the wooden box and opened the lid. She carefully removed the book and held it up. "Here we go," she said, taking a deep breath. She placed the back of the book against the rosette and slowly moved it until it clicked into place. Slowly, they rotated the book and, to their astonishment, the small rosette began to turn.

Iris turned the book forty-five degrees.

"It turned," Robinia said.

"Yes, but I don't see anything else happening." Iris pushed on the disk. "Nothing." She tried to turn it further, but it would not budge. She tried to twist it back to its original position, but it did not turn. "It looks like it's stuck now." Iris removed the book and studied the disk. "I think we've reached the end of our adventure. Nothing is budging, and I don't see anything else on the fountain that could move or open," she said, running her fingers along the edge of the stone.

"I'm sorry," Catrin said. "I guess the book was right. There are another two somewhere that we're missing."

"It was a crazy hunch, but worth a shot," Iris said, placing the book in the backpack. "I think it's time to take the book back to Venice."

"Sounds like a good idea." Catrin started down the path, then glanced back where Iris was still standing: "Are you coming?"

"Yes, I'll catch up," Iris said, staring at the dial.

"All right."

Iris took a sip from the fountain and then stepped back and put her hand on the disk.

Waves of tiny pinpricks ran through her fingertips and up her arms, igniting a billion points of light in her eyes.

She gasped and pulled her hand back, certain of what she had seen: three women and two men standing inside a cave, surrounded by a brilliant light.

She turned and hurried down the path, eager to catch up with the others.

A pensive mood filled the car as they headed back to Alpinella. Catrin was the first to break the silence. "I don't think we should feel defeated. First of all, it was incredible adventure...."

"And second of all?" asked Robinia.

"Second of all, I don't feel like this story is over. Iris, what do you think?"

Concentrating on the road, Iris gripped the wheel and slowly braked into the curves that switchbacked their way down the mountain. She could feel her palms begin to perspire. Blind curves always unsettled her.

Iris nodded. "I don't believe any story has a beginning or an end. Look at this book...something must always occur prior to an event that caused the event. And nothing ever ends, given that infinity is all there is." Iris shrugged her shoulders, "It's all one endless journey."

"Who's hungry?" asked Robinia. "I could go for a pizza right now."

"I remember a pizzeria at the bottom of the hill. We can stop there," suggested Catrin.

Iris rounded the next corner and was met head on with a white delivery van that was driving in her lane. "Shit!" Iris screamed as she jerked the wheel to the left.

The driver of the van swerved back into his lane, careening into Iris' car and sending it over the edge of the mountain. The car rolled down the mountainside and landed in a deep ravine before catching fire, burning everyone and everything inside.

Violetta

"Having taken these precautions, and after giving her Holy Water to drink, let him again begin to question her, all the time exhorting her as before."

Malleus Maleficarum Part 3

Question XVI

Heinrich Kramer, 1486 AD

Albergo Pietra Bella

November, 1553

She walked alongside Marco for what felt like hours, each faltering step exacerbating the pain in her legs and body, but they finally reached the inn. They passed the lake that looked to Violetta like a dark bottomless well on a moonless night, and she wished she could disappear into its abyss.

Marco led her upstairs to the bedroom. "Lay down. I'll be right back."

She remained seated on the edge of the bed and stared at the floor. Moments later, he reappeared carrying a tray with a steaming cup of herbal tea and two slices of bread with honey. "You need to eat."

She did not have an appetite, but she was too tired to argue. She took a bite and chewed the bread that felt like a piece of tree bark in her dry mouth. She took a sip of tea to force it down. Marco dipped a towel into the wash basin and rung it out.

He knelt before her and wiped the blood from her face. "I need to leave."

"Where are you going?"

"I have to do something, but I'll be back."

"Tell me, what's going on?" she demanded, her voice cracking and weak.

Violetta looked into his eyes, but, as always, they gave nothing away, and she felt her thoughts pound into waves of confusion.

Exhausted, she lay down, pulled the covers around her neck, and prayed for sleep. She heard the door close softly behind her.

Marco

Alpinella

November, 1553

His stride outpaced that of two men, but he was not in a hurry. He was calculating every detail of his plan. So far, everything had gone as he had anticipated, except finding Violetta in the cell. It could have ruined everything. Now, with that behind him, he would strike the final blow.

He walked across the empty piazza, past the well, and toward the Municipale. The priest would arrive early today, so he needed to prepare. He kicked his boots against the stone wall, shaking the mud off the soles. Then, he unlocked the door and walked down the dark stairwell that smelled of dirt and dampness. When he reached the bottom, he lit the torch and swept it over the long table where dozens of instruments were laid out, but he only needed one.

Marco walked to where the cells were, and made his way toward the end, where an empty desk and chair sat. It was intended for a guard, but there was not enough money to hire one, and besides, none was needed. It was impossible to escape. The only exit to the outside world was a narrow window located above the desk. The prisoners could watch the feet of their neighbors and friends pass by.

 He tossed the rope to the floor. He placed a sheet of paper from the drawer on top of the desk next to the quill and bottle of ink. Then he sat in the chair and waited.

Not thirty minutes had passed, when Marco heard footsteps lumbering down the hall toward the cells.

"I trust the two of you made it through the night." The priest emerged and walked toward the cell, a grim smile on his face. "Let's check on our signorina, shall we?"

The priest paused abruptly. "Why is the gate open?"

The priest peered inside the empty cell that was merely a hole carved into the earth.

With a crash, he flew into the cell, landing on his knees. Marco locked the gate behind him.

The priest stood shakily to his feet and turned around to face his assistant.

"What in God's name do you think you are doing?" he demanded, shaking the dirt from his cloak.

"Let's not bring God into this."

The priest's mouth contorted, and his cheek twitched. He looked around the cell; he was trapped. Sweat beaded across his forehead and ran down his temples.

"You have no idea who you are dealing with." Spit sprayed from his lips. "I demand you release me."

Marco's voice was even. "You are going to listen very carefully. Then, you will do exactly as you are told."

The priest grabbed the bars. "You will not torture me."

"A year ago, there was a woman locked in this cell. You tortured and killed her."

"Is that what this is about?" His mouth twisted to the side. "Justice you're seeking for a woman? It seems like you've gone to an awful lot of trouble for some whore."

Marco stepped forward, inches from his face. "That woman, Francesca, was my mother."

A look of disbelief swept across his face. "Your mother?" he stammered.

"And now you will kill yourself, just as my father did."

"But, I had nothing to do with your father's death."

"You had everything to do with it."

"Your mother was an accomplice to witchcraft. She helped my mother escape with your uncle. They had to be punished. I was carrying out my sworn duty!"

"My mother was innocent, like all the women who have died at your hands. And now you are going to clear their names."

"I'll do no such thing."

Marco opened the gate. "Get out."

Father Enzo backed up. "You will not coerce me like his. I am a man of the Church, of God."

"I said, get out."

The priest sized him up, then stepped past him cautiously. "You won't get away with this."

"Sit down at the desk."

The priest walked over to the desk and took a seat.

"You will write on that sheet of paper, exactly as I dictate, word for word. Understand?"

He shot him an angry look. "And if I refuse?"

"Unlike my mother, you have a choice." Marco stared him down steadily. "But I don't think you'll like the other option."

Reluctantly, the priest picked up the quill.

"A wise decision. Now, begin writing. 'It is in this final act I ask for mercy and redemption, thus, restoring dignity to my victims and clearing their good names'…"

Father Enzo looked up. "I will write no such thing."

"Keep writing. Or we can go the other route."

Father Enzo finished the note. "Now, sign it. And use your ring to seal it."

He did as he was told.

"Now, stand up."

The priest stood, his eyes darting like a caged animal around the room.

"Pick up the rope and tie a noose," instructed Marco.

"You can't be serious."

The assistant didn't speak.

"I will not tie my own noose! It's a mortal sin."

"Like I said, you have a choice."

"What's the other choice?" he demanded.

"The other option is, I kill you myself. And I assure you, it will not be pleasant."

Father Enzo started breathing heavily. His eyes darted around the room again, but the only escape lay behind the assistant. He let out an anguished moan and charged forward toward Marco, head first, like a bull.

Marco swiftly moved to the side, and using the priest's own momentum against him, he grabbed the back of his cloak and thrust him against the wall. Marco walked over to where he was crumpled on the floor, and put his boot on his neck.

"Wait," he said, wheezing. "Wait. I'll tie the knot."

Marco released his boot.

"Get up."

Father Enzo

The priest struggled to his feet and walked over, picking up the rope. Shakily, he began tying the rope around in loops, just like he had done for the animals in the forest. His favorite way to administer death.

He glanced at Marco; he felt the hate raging inside of him. He had been betrayed, but he would not show fear, he told himself. He made the last loop of the rope and then tucked it in.

Marco pointed to the beam above him. "Tie it on there."

The priest, resigned to his fate, did as he was told. He stood shakily on the chair. Perhaps he welcomed death, he thought, as he secured the rope in place. He did not believe in all the fanciful stores about a paradise that lay beyond the confines of this world. He knew they were stories invented to control and manipulate the masses, but he couldn't help but think there must be something that existed outside of this world, even if that something was nothing more than an empty void of nothingness; to him, that thought sounded very inviting. He placed the rope over his head and tightened it around his neck. He stood still on the chair, awaiting his fate.

But nothing happened.

He looked sideways at Marco standing next to him.

"You are kicking the chair out from under yourself," instructed Marco.

The priest stared out the window at the feet walking past, but his own were unable to move. His body began to tremble.

"I can't," he stammered.

"You can. And you will."

Father Enzo gasped for breath. "I tell you, I can't. Please. Don't do this. I beg you."

A long pause of silence filled the space. The priest's hands and knees began to tremble.

As Marco turned to leave, he kicked the chair with his boot and kept walking.

The chair fell over on its side, and Father Enzo's feet kicked wildly about in the air. He felt his throat being squeezed with incredible pressure, cutting off the air supply.

Life had certainly dealt him a twisted fate, he thought in this last moment.

As the priest stared out of the window, he felt his body ripping in two. He lost feeling in his feet, and he felt his torso combust from within. His heart pumped wildly alongside his lungs that were ceasing to function. A great force from his heart and lungs erupted upward, desperate to escape from out of his head, but was blocked by the rope around his neck. His head built up an incredible amount of pressure causing the blood vessels in his eyes to burst, filling them with blood.

As his lifeless body dangled from the rope, a tiny pinpoint of light buried deep within his heart began to spin. It spun faster and faster, rising up with each rotation, its tiny sparks flying out in every direction. The pinpoint of light spun until it merged and became indistinguishable from the waves of light surrounding it.

Violetta

Family Tree
1523 - 1553

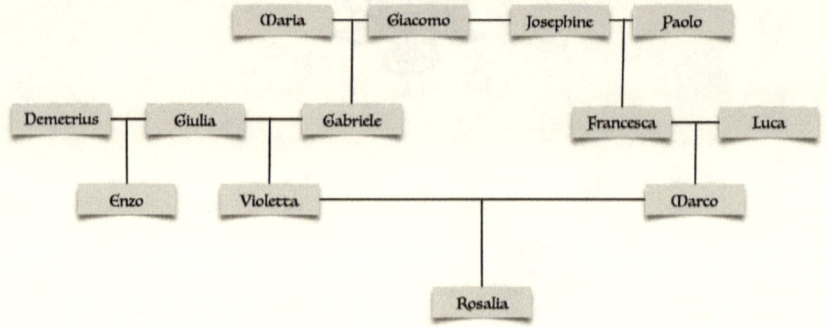

Albergo Pietra Bella, 1523-1557

Violetta didn't know what time it was, but judging from the sun's position in the sky, she was guessing it was late afternoon. She did not know if she were alone in the inn. Marco had not come back, and she had not seen or heard from Chiara.

She heard footsteps approaching down the hall. Violetta knew his gait by heart. She gripped the sheet on the mattress and stared at the door. The handle turned, and Marco walked in.

He sat down next to her and put his forearms on his knees.

"It's over," he said flatly.

"What is over?"

He stared straight ahead as he began to speak.

"When my mother was seven, her mother married the owner of this inn. He was a kind man who had recently lost his wife and was left with a son to raise. His son's name was Gabriele. He and his half-sister, my mother, took over running the place after their parents died. While my mother was pregnant with me, Gabriele moved away with a woman he had fallen in love with. It was sudden, and we never knew where they had gone, and my mother rarely spoke of him, although I remember she did keep his portrait hanging on the dining room wall.

When I was sixteen, a priest arrived who replaced the old priest who was retiring. That's when the trouble started. The new priest, Enzo, was an angry and unsettled man. His Sunday mass was filled with fear and litany, as if he had some sort of score to settle. He was here only a couple of months before he began rounding up women on bogus accusations - all in the name of the Holy Inquisition. That's when old rumors surfaced from the elders in the village.

They claimed that he was the son of the woman who had left town with a man from the inn. Giulia, was her name, a Dutch wife of a prominent local man. Most dismissed it all as idle gossip. Some even said Enzo's father had gone mad and murdered his mother. Either way, neither his mother or the man were heard from again."

Marco stopped and looked at Violetta's hand that was trembling in her lap. "What's wrong?" he asked.

"Giulia," she muttered, "the mother of the priest. A Dutch woman named Giulia." Suddenly, everything fit. Violetta looked up at Marco. "She's my mother."

Marco sat up straight. "Which means that Father Enzo is your…"

"Half-brother," Violetta finished.

"Well, that explains everything," Marco said. "He came to the inn on numerous occasions one summer asking questions. Somehow, he was convinced that there was a connection his mother had with our inn - that the man she had run away with worked there and he was convinced my mother knew who he was. My parents, knowing his reputation, were growing increasingly concerned and decided to send me to Switzerland to live with relatives.

I did not hear anything all autumn, and by Christmas, I demanded that I return here. When I did, I learned that my mother, Francesca, had been arrested, tortured, and burned on bogus witchcraft charges. My father, heartbroken, hanged himself.

I swore I would make Enzo pay for what he did. But the murder of a priest, even in this remote place, would cause an uprising. Hysteria and paranoia were running deep, and more people would be arrested and burned. I had to come up with a plan—something that no one would suspect was murder. I had to take him down from the inside."

"So you became his assistant," stated Violetta.

Marco nodded. "I knew he liked his midday drink at the pub, so I met him one afternoon and chatted with him. In the end, I convinced him that he needed me."

"That day in the piazza. I saw you sitting on the well and then follow him inside the pub. That was the day?"

"Yes. Finally, I decided enough time had passed and that I would be above suspicion. I had planned to kill him that week. I just needed to get him down in the basement alone, which was difficult to do without a prisoner down there. And that's when he came through the door with you. If I had killed him right then, I would have been caught for sure. The only option was the one I gave you, gave us. But I swear I would never have let you die. You have to believe that much."

Violetta gasped, "The book!"

"What?"

"He wanted the book." Violetta jumped up and looked under the bed, but she couldn't see it. Violetta felt blindly, but there was nothing.

"It's gone," Violetta said. "He must have taken it."

"Where's Chiara?" Violetta asked.

"I don't know. I haven't seen her."

"She'll know if he took it," Violetta said. "The priest told the young man with him to find it."

Violetta ran down the hall and flung open the door to Chiara's room. The bed was neatly made and everything was in place. She opened the drawers to the chest to find everything was gone. A feeling of despair washed over her.

"I'm sorry," he said, walking up behind her. "I know that book was important to you."

"I have to find it. It was the most important thing my mother left me."

"Listen, I think we should get out of town for a while."

"But won't the officials want to speak to you?"

"The priest gave me my papers, but I never filed them with the Church. And the suicide note should convince them that it was a willful act." He took her hand. "We will find the book eventually, I am sure of it."

Violetta sighed heavily. She knew he was right; they needed to leave. "We can go back to Venice. I'll take you back to my home."

Albergo Pietra Bella

May, 1554

Tender greens, soft lavenders, and pale pinks dotted the monochrome landscape as leaves unfurled, flowers blossomed, and birds engaged in lively morning chatter, signaling the end of a harsh winter.

There was much preparation to be done before reopening the inn, but being back at the lake filled Violetta's heart with joy and anticipation for the coming season. She and Marco had spent the winter in Venice, deciding it was best to board up the inn and allow the drama to burn itself out.

The townspeople had been shocked by the suicide of Father Enzo. Older women held handkerchiefs to their faces, men buried their heads in their hands, and others held their clasped hands to the heavens pleading for answers; but few, if any, genuinely grieved his absence. Rumors swirled in hushed whispers through shops on Saturday mornings, and, despite the biting cold, parishioners huddled together on the steps of the church after worship to hear the latest waspish gossip, resurrect past grievances, and throw around idle speculations. But, a year later, the townspeople were eager to move on and meet the new priest, who was said to be young and handsome. The replacement had not wanted to stay.

Marco helped Violetta down from the carriage. There was much preparation that needed to be done before the baby arrived.

By the end of the week, the dining room, kitchen, and bedrooms needed to be scrubbed and cleaned and ready to receive the first guests.

Violetta stared down from a guest room window at Marco, clearing the weeds from the vegetable garden in the back. The garden had been neglected the past year and was overgrown with weeds, and most of the plants had not made it through the harsh winter.

Her eyes traveled to the far corner of the yard, where a cluster of bright yellow and white daffodils bloomed in the middle of the stone well. Violetta did not recall daffodils blooming there last year. Curious, she went downstairs to investigate.

The daffodils were beautiful and reminded her of the day Chiara arrived at the inn, a fresh bundle, tied with a purple ribbon in her hands. Suddenly, realization crashed down around her, and she dropped to her knees and started digging with her hands.

Marco ran over, a bewildered expression on his face. "What are you doing?"

"It's here," Violetta said breathlessly. "Chiara left the book for me here."

"You need to slow down," he said, kneeling beside her.

"The daffodils, she left them for me. She wanted to show me where she hid the book."

"Let me," he said.

Marco took the spade in his hand and began to dig, carefully removing the bulbs and setting them aside.

His spade hit a sharp thud, and they both stopped and looked at each other.

He cleared more dirt, "It looks like a metal box." He set it on the grass and opened the lid. He unwrapped the linen rags to reveal the wooden box and handed it to Violetta. Violetta lifted the lid, and the gems sparkled in the sunlight.

"I can't believe it," Violetta said. "She buried the book. She knew I would find it. Marco, what do you think happened to her?"

"I suspect she knew she had to escape."

"I hope she's okay," said Violetta.

"So, did you ever find out where the book came from or why your mother had it?"

"Unfortunately, no. She didn't leave any clues as to its origin or meaning …and you don't remember your mother ever mentioning it?"

He ran his hand through his hair. "I wish she had, but I don't recall her mentioning anything."

Violetta bit her bottom lip and creased her forehead.

"What are you thinking?" he asked.

"I just don't understand what my mother was doing in possession of a book that appears to be from a Venetian society."

"Well, she lived in Venice. Most likely, someone from there gave it to her," he suggested.

"I guess we may never know," replied Violetta. "Anyway, we need to hide this somewhere. Some place safe."

Marco took the book. "I have a place."

"Where?" asked Violetta.

"Beneath the floorboard on a stair. That squeaky one. I used to hide all kinds of things from mother there as a kid."

Albergo Pietra Bella

June, 1554

She put her hands on her stomach and felt it again, stronger this time. She gently shook Marco. "Wake up. I felt him. She's kicking."

"What did you say?"

She grabbed his hand and put it on her belly. "Wait, she'll do it again."

They lay still. "There," Violetta said.

"I felt it," said Marco.

"She's strong."

"Just like his mother," he said, pulling her close and kissing her neck.

"So, the baby will be coming soon," she said. "Four months."

"Yes," he said, sliding his hand down her body.

"And, there are things that I won't be able to do once she's here."

He stopped and looked at her. "How are you so sure it's a she?"

"I just know," she said. "I can feel her."

"If you say so," he said, kissing her.

"As I was saying, the baby is coming soon. There are things I won't be able to do once she arrives."

"Such as?"

"Such as visiting the mountains up north."

"What's in the mountains we should visit?"

"I'm not quite sure."

"I'm not quite sure I'm following."

"I've been reading the book from my mother. The last chapter describes a cave in the mountains, not far from here, where special artifacts from this culture are supposedly hidden. And there was a map inside as well."

"Sounds far-fetched. You don't really know anything about this book. Where did your mother get it from? And why did she never tell you about it?"

"I have no idea. That's why I need to find out."

"I think it's too risky, especially in your condition. Besides, I can't leave now. There's too much work to do."

"But I feel great, and I may not get a chance later. This is the best time to go."

"A woman traveling in these parts in your condition is too dangerous. We aren't married yet. And with the Inquisition that is still dragging on. They're hunting witches for sport in those parts. I won't let you go."

"You won't let me? I'm not asking permission."

"Well, you are carrying my child, and I do have a say in that."

"But right now, the child goes where I go, and I am going to find that cave."

He frowned and threw the covers off. "Why do you need to do this? Why now?"

He got out of bed and put on his shirt.

"Because there's something important in this book, something the priest was willing to kill me for. I need to find out what it is, and I may not get another chance."

"No."

"What do you mean, no?"

"I mean," he said, buttoning his shirt, "you aren't going anywhere."

"I came here from Venice on my own." She could feel the rage taking over.

He tucked in his shirt. "And you almost got yourself killed. We aren't going anywhere until we are married."

"But the new priest has not arrived. He was supposed to be here by now."

"Then we'll wait until he does. The cave will be there."

"I know you're worried, but nothing will happen to me," she continued. "I'll be careful."

He finished buckling his shoes and, without a word, walked out of the room.

Violetta got out of bed and opened the door to her armoire. She reached her hand on the top shelf and pulled out an envelope, the one she had found in the wooden box beneath the book. The handwriting was shaky, but legible. Violetta read the words one last time, erasing any doubt from her mind.

Marco

Albergo Pietra Bella

June, 1555

Early the next morning, before the sun skirted the horizon to sweep the darkness from the land, Marco awoke. He reached across the bed and ran his hand along the smooth sheet. His eyes flew open and he bolted up. He ran and peered out the window. Her horse was gone. He tried to calm himself and recall the map she had shown him with the river and stars. He remembered the red circle drawn in the center. He quickly dressed and hurried downstairs to saddle his horse.

On the desk at the bottom of the stairs, he saw a piece of paper folded in half with his name written across the front. He'd recognize the whiplash lines of her penmanship anywhere.

M,

This is a journey I must take on my own. My first journey was unknown, but this one was clear. I know where I am going, and I am confident I will reach my destination and achieve what I am setting out to do.

I promise to be careful and not do anything that will put our child or myself in danger. I ask you to have faith in me as I had faith in you when you asked.

I will be back soon. We have much to look forward to.

Yours,

V

His face was calm, but the trembling paper in his hands betrayed his fury. He cursed and crumpled the paper into a ball.

Violetta

Val di Luci

June, 1554

..

Down a narrow path, obscured by tall grass, Violetta rode on. The sun peaked through the clouds, and she removed her hood to let the sun warm her face. Adrenaline coursed through her veins as she turned onto a dirt road that led to a small village nestled in the foothills of the mountain. The road was quiet, except for some dried leaves that stirred down the path.

A single crow landed atop a wooden post and squawked incessantly as she rode up to the stone cottage. Violetta checked the note again and knocked on the small wooden door with a wreath of dried lavender hanging from a hook.

A woman with thin, angular shoulders and braided hair tied into a bun opened the door halfway.

"I'm sorry to disturb you. I'm looking for Lucia."

"I am Lucia."

"My name is Violetta. I know your friend, Chiara." She handed her the note. "She said you can help me."

Lucia opened the door wider and motioned for Violetta to come inside.

The fire crackled, and tiny sparks flew from the fire as she cradled a cup of steaming red wine. The saccharine liquid slid down her throat and warmed her stomach. She preferred more spices to cut the sweetness, but she was too tired to care. Lucia placed a light wool blanket over her shoulders and sat across from her. "It gets cold this high up in the mountains at night."

"Thank you," said Violetta, grateful for the cover.

"You are either very brave or very foolish to take this journey. I don't need to tell you they've been burning witches like matchsticks in these parts," warned Lucia. "Forty-three so far in this area alone."

Violetta felt a lump form in her throat. "I'm aware of the danger," she said, and took another sip, swallowing hard.

"You cannot trust anyone. One misstep can be cause for a person to turn you in. A woman was taken in for talking to herself. *Talking to herself.* She told the inquisitor she was reciting the Psalms. Do you think that saved her?" Lucia shook her head gravely and her face took on a somber glow in the dim light.

"I understand. Once I'm done, I will return home."

"My advice is to return home now."

"That is not possible."

Lucia eyed her suspiciously. "Tell me, what is so important in this mountain?"

"I just need to find something. Something that was left to me - an heirloom from my late parents."

She decided to heed the woman's advice and not trust anyone, not even her.

Lucia's face softened a little. "I see."

Violetta pulled the blanket over her shoulders. "When was the last time you saw Chiara?" Violetta thought it was strange she had not asked about her friend.

"It's been a few years since I've seen her. We met when our husbands worked the mines together. She visited me here only once, after I moved in. She was pregnant, just like you," she said, nodding down at Violetta's belly. "But then, nothing. I wrote her a few times, but she never replied."

"Both of you read and write?" asked Violetta.

"Chiara knew. She had been educated in Venice and she taught me while our husbands were away working. I'm no scholar, but I get by. Of course, these days, it would be very dangerous for people to know." A stricken look crossed her face and then disappeared. "So, you know Chiara well?"

"No, not well at all, but she worked for us at the inn. Only a short time."

"I see. And that husband of hers?"

"He passed away. That is all I was told."

Lucia stood up and closed the small window where a lace curtain was blowing in the night breeze. "That's just as well. He was no good." She turned around and smiled. "You must be exhausted. I'll let you get some rest. I'm afraid it isn't very comfortable, but you'll be warm."

"It's fine. Thank you."

Violetta lay on the pile of wool blankets and stared at the fire. Her adrenaline had worn off, and her bones felt heavy as lead. She must have fallen asleep fast and deep because she woke up with a start. Her dreams were as vivid as if she'd lived them. She darted down serpentine paths that dead-ended into stone walls. Footsteps echoed through the shadows, and she knew they were coming for her. She gripped the slippery stones and began to climb.

She blinked and her eyes focused on the stone fireplace, a blanket of silent ash lay inside. A bird squawked loudly, and Violetta noticed the small window had blown open during the night. She kicked off the blankets and got up.

She lit a fire for Lucia and then entered the kitchen and took two jars of herbs from the shelf. Then, she sprinkled a generous amount into a linen napkin and tied it with some twine. She placed it in her pocket and walked out the door.

A small basket filled with bread, fruits, and nuts hung from the post next to her horse, a generous gift for her journey. She mounted her horse and gave him a swift kick. She wanted to make it to the village with plenty of daylight to spare.

Across the field, a farmer with a bulbous nose and a hunched back - formed from years of staring at the ground, watched the lone woman ride off on a horse... like a man. He snarled and turned his attention toward Lucia's house where the smoke ascended from her chimney, twisting and swirling into shapes of nefarious creatures. He nodded his head slowly, then hurried back to his house to mount his horse and ride into town.

Lucia

"I had rather dwell with a lion and a dragon than to keep house with a wicked woman."

The Malleus Maleficarum, Part 1

Question VI

Heinrich Kramer, 1486 AD

Val di Luci

June, 1554

Lucia slowly brushed the top of the dough with a mixture of egg yolk and water. It was her favorite part of the bread-making process. Then, she scooped salt from a small porcelain bowl with her fingertips. Sprinkling a little on top, she put the rest in her apron pocket. Taxes were high on salt, so she used it sparingly. She placed the loaf in the fire and began sweeping the floor. It was her morning ritual she cherished: the smell of baking bread reminded her of her grandmother, and sweeping cleared the worries in her head that had a way of accumulating during the night. As she swept, she sang a song her grandmother had taught her as a child. She recited the words, but she did not understand their meaning as the language had long since disappeared. Still, the sounds resonated with a familiarity she felt in her bones.

She had come to the tiny cottage on the outskirts of town to start over in the private light of the mountain valley. She longed for a new beginning and was eager to plant her seeds of intent. Her grandmother had taught her that one should always transform, taking what is and turning it into something new. Just as she believed in the power of nature to transform seeds into plants, she believed in the power of transforming dreams into reality. So, she packed a bag of seeds, some fresh cuttings, her favorite spade, and her grandmother's book of recipes and set off in search of fertile land.

It did not take her long to stumble upon the abandoned little cottage; over four seasons, she transformed it into her home.

Lucia opened the front door and swept the dirt out. Then, she turned the broom upside down and leaned it against the door frame. It was bad luck to rest a broom on its bristles. She checked to ensure no one was coming down the road and that no eyes were peering at her from across the field. She always had the sense of being watched - especially in these days. Satisfied she was alone, she took the salt from her pocket and sprinkled it along the threshold.

Suddenly, the broom fell onto the floor. She froze. A fallen broom meant a visitor would soon arrive. Her heart started racing: one unannounced visitor brought good news, but two in a fortnight portended trouble.

Lucia rushed to her bedroom and began packing. She hastily fastened her small bag and hurried to the door. Pounding of hoofs could be heard coming down the road. She peered out the window and saw two men on horseback fast approaching her house. Fear ran down her spine. She knew what they were there for. Whom they were there for.

Violetta

Val di Luci

June, 1554

Violetta stopped at the fork in the road and read the wooden signpost. She was only a few kilometers away. Her back was beginning to ache, so she decided she would walk the rest of the way. She dismounted, pulled her coat around her belly, and began leading the horse down the road.

A pair of shutters creaked open. Glancing up she didn't see a face but could feel eyes bearing down as she walked along the deserted street. A chill ran up Violetta's arms. Suddenly, a feeling of dread swept over her. But if the last months had taught her anything, it was to control her fear. If she could control her fear, she had a better chance of controlling the outcome.

She would find the lock and return to Lucia's house before nightfall.

The town was much smaller than Alpinella, with only a few stacks of tightly clustered buildings. She passed a small chapel in the center of the town with two wooden doors that stood open. Halfway, she told herself. Just keep walking.

A priest stepped from the shadows of the doorway of the church, causing her to jump. He couldn't have been much older than herself. His eyes were youthful and matched his light blond hair.

"Can I help you?" he asked.

"No, thank you," she replied, lowering her head.

"Please, come inside."

"I'm sorry, but I'm rather late."

He stepped to the side of the door. "This will only take a moment."

Reluctantly, she tied her horse. Casting a tentative look behind her, Violetta stepped inside the church. The priest closed the doors and slid the iron bolt into place, causing a shiver to run down her spine.

"Where do you come from?" he asked.

"I come from Val di Luci."

"And what brings you here to our small mining town?"

"I am visiting a friend in the country. She grows herbs for the herbalist. She isn't feeling well, so I am delivering her herbs to the apothecary for her," she explained, taking the bundle of herbs from her pocket and showing it to the priest.

"It's lunchtime. The apothecary is closed," he replied.

"Of course, then I can come back another time," she smiled, glancing around the modest church. The walls were unadorned except for a few crucifixes, and a thick layer of dust coated the floor and benches.

"They are looking for you."

"Who is looking for me?" she replied, taking a step back.

"A man from the country filed a report this morning." His eyes narrowed. "About a suspicious newcomer."

"I told you. I am only visiting a friend."

"It isn't safe for you to be traveling alone."

"I'm leaving," she said, brushing past him.

There was a knock at the door, and she froze.

"I'm sure they've seen your horse. Quickly, go in the back and stay there until I tell you it's safe to come out."

There was another knock, louder this time. "Go on!" the priest urged.

Hidden behind a thick velvet curtain, Violetta strained to hear the men's voices. All she could hear was the blood pounding in her ears. Placing her hand on her belly, she closed her eyes. She should not have asked fate to favor her twice.

Lucia

"First, that her house should be searched as thoroughly as possible, in all holes and corners and chests, top and bottom; and if she is a noted witch, then without doubt, unless she has previously hidden them, there will be found various instruments of witchcraft, as we have shown above."

The Malleus Maleficarum Part 3

Question VIII

Heinrich Kramer, 1486 AD

Val di Luci

June, 1554

Lucia ran to the back of the house and climbed out the window. The field to the woods was too big to make it across without being seen. She thought quickly. The only way to go was up. She spent hours in nature as a girl, swimming in lakes and climbing trees. She was as good a climber as the other boys her age, and even after all these years, her limbs were still strong. She slung her bag across her chest and began to climb the tall oak. She reached the branches toward the middle and clung tightly to the trunk. She eyed the roof, but it was too late. She could hear the men inside. Pressing her body to the trunk, Lucia waited for them to leave, thankful for the cover provided by the leaves.

She strained to hear the words coming from inside.

"Check under the bed, in the cupboards, rip up the floorboards if you have to," a raspy voice ordered.

Through the open window, she heard the slamming and crashing of pots and pans. Then she heard glass shatter. She closed her eyes.

The purple vase.

She breathed into her anger, just as her grandmother had taught her. When the other girls made fun of her clothes. Or the boys stole her favorite doll, tossing it back and forth in a game of keep away. Her grandmother would braid her long locks and tell her that anger was like a bolt of lightning. It could strike and split a tree in two, or it can strike and transform sand into beautiful pieces of glass.

One day, when Lucia had reached her breaking point, her grandmother took the vase from her shelf. "I want you to keep this as a reminder to channel your anger into creating something of beauty in this sometimes not-so-beautiful world." She placed the vase in her hands. "Remember that everything in this world we call good and evil, flows from the same source, like water through a spout. Most of the time, it flows as an even stream. This makes up the bulk of life and fills our days with alternating moments of pleasure and discontent. Sometimes it flows at full force. These moments are gifts. Treasure them. But sometimes, it is shut off. This is what we call evil, but it is nothing more than the absence of God. Judgment falls away when you understand this, and you will see all things as holy. You will see all things as one, coming from the same source. Only then will you see through the eyes of God."

Lucia breathed deeply again, but the peace her grandmother spoke of was not found. She imagined the broken vase, and all she wanted to do was take a shard and drive it deep in the neck of those men.

Suddenly, one of the men emerged from around the side of the house and walked across the grass. He stopped under the tree and scanned back and forth. She could feel her left foot slipping. Gripping the tree tighter, she kept her eye on him. Animals in the forest could detect when they were being watched, but she doubted these men possessed such finely tuned senses.

A shorter man with black greasy hair joined him.

"You think she could have escaped so quickly?"

"No. There was no one to tip her off."

"Maybe she left with the other woman he saw her with."

"That woman left the house on a horse. And she left alone."

"It looks like she dissolved into thin air. Maybe she is a witch after all," he said, laughing nervously.

"Don't be a fool, Angelo. She'll come back. And when she does, we'll get her." He disappeared around the house.

Lucia watched from the tree as the two men rode away. Then, she climbed down and went inside to survey the damage. Pots, pans, and dishes were thrown about the kitchen. Blankets were ripped from the bed, and clothes were strewn across the room. She stepped over broken dishes and knelt down beside the broken vase. Jagged purple pieces lay scattered around her. She frowned. Her grandmother was wrong. There was not one force, there were two; and one was always trying to destroy the other.

Tears stung her eyes as she gathered the broken pieces into a pile.

Lost in thought, she did not hear the footsteps that belonged to the shorter man, who had forgotten his knife.

"Well, it turns out you didn't dissolve into thin air after all." He cracked his knuckles, a nervous habit he had developed as a boy. "You're going to have to come with me."

She should have felt panic. Instead, in the space between the inhale and exhale of her breath, she found the peace of which her grandmother had spoken.

A tingling warmth engulfed her body, and she felt light as air.

Angelo took a few tentative steps toward her. She continued staring at him as she ran her palm along the shards until she felt a long pointy piece. She wrapped her fingers around it.

"No," he said. "You don't want to do that."

He curled his fingers into a fist. Many men beat their wives. It was as common as beating a dog. He did not look like the type; but this time, it looked as though he might make an exception.

"Did you hear me?"

She did not react, and he wondered if she were mute. Still, something in her gaze unsettled him. Memories from his childhood flooded his mind. Never show fear, Angelo. His father's words came rushing back to him. He remembered being on the front porch, hands on his knees, breathless from running. Now, go back out there and show them you are not afraid. And, because he did not want to disappoint his father, he left. But, he did not return to the field where the boys were waiting with their sticks and taunts. Instead, he went to his grandfather's bakery, where he helped him prepare dough for the next morning's loaves.

Angelo slowly reached out his other hand. "Get up, and come with me," he repeated, softer this time.

Still, she did not respond. Instead, she studied him as if she had all the time in the world. As if the end was not upon her.

Suddenly, every detail of the man before her became vibrantly clear. She stared at his face as if looking at a face for the first time, with all its dents and contours. The way the pale, smooth skin stretched over his high forehead and soft cheeks. The way his rounded nose turned pink at the tip. She marvelled at his eyes that, beneath their cloudy surface, danced and laughed with the gentle wonder of a child.

She noticed a smudge of white powder on his left temple and white specks on the ends of his dark lashes. She looked at his hand, frozen in mid-air. White flour was caked around his cuticles and under each nail.

It's a pity, she thought, in another time and place, she would love to have spent more time with him.

She rose to her knees. Angelo pulled back his fist. A smile spread across her lips, and she plunged the glass into the side of her neck in one sweeping gesture.

Angelo

Val di Luci

June, 1554

Angelo's stomach churned as blood poured from her neck and pooled onto the floor, staining her copper strands a deeper shade of red. He couldn't think, and his body went numb because his senses had stopped working - all but one.

He stepped around her body and hurried to the kitchen, where he grabbed a towel and wrapped it around his hand. The intoxicating aroma of yeast, flour, and water, filled his nose. Carefully, he removed the loaf from the fire, wrapped it in a towel, and hid it beneath his coat.

He spotted his knife on the way out but left it where it was. He did not need it. He would break the bread with his hands.

Outside, clouds were gathering, and a cold breeze nipped at the bottom of his coat.

"Shouldn't she be buried?" Angelo asked.

Salvatore narrowed his hawkish eyes. "Always the romantic, aren't you, Angelo. Your grandfather was right. You aren't cut out for this," he snorted in disgust. "But, it looks like I'm stuck with you."

"It's just that if we leave her, she'll be eaten by wild animals." It was all he could say, and all he could think about. He thought he would be sick. He pulled his coat tighter, afraid the smell of the bread would give him away.

"A proper ending for a whore," Salvatore laughed. "She killed herself. There will be no Christian burial!" He adjusted himself in the saddle, "Come on, you idiot. We will come back later for the other one." He inhaled deeply. "Suddenly, I feel quite hungry."

Violetta

Alpinella

June, 1554

Footsteps approached, and the velvet curtain flung back. "I think it's best if you tell me why you have come here."

Violetta stared at the priest. Her nerves were obstructing her ability to see his light.

"You don't have any friends in this town, so unless you tell me why you are here, I'm afraid you won't get very far."

"I'm not here to deliver herbs."

"I gathered as much."

"I'm here to find a fountain."

"A fountain?"

"A lock on a fountain," she gripped her bag tightly.

"I think you'd better come and sit down."

Violetta finished explaining the book. "I think this tells me where to find the lock that uncovers the other books."

The priest reached for the book uttering, "May I?" He turned the book over and traced his fingers along the metal ridges.

"I believe the fountain mentioned in the book can be found near here."

The priest sat quietly.

"I don't have much time. I need to leave now," she said, standing up.

The priest stood up and handed her the book. She placed it in her satchel and fastened it.

"Thank you for your help. I'll be on my way."

"I do not need to tell you that you are in grave danger. Evils abound."

"Yes, I am aware."

She could feel a wave of anger rising in her. "Evil lurks everywhere in this world. But there is also light," she said, eyeing him steadily.

The priest folded his hands in front of him. "Heh, light. A fickle trick of the eye that eludes the best of us. It cannot conceal the evil that lurks in the places we think not to look. The cleverest amongst us know that the best place to hide evil is to cloak it in virtue and parade it in plain sight. People will be drawn like a moth to a flame because even the lowliest creature gravitates toward light - even if that light is a flame born of Satan and burns in Hell."

Violetta stared at him in disbelief. "I'm not sure what you are saying."

He leaned into her. "You see this Light in people, don't you?"

Violetta shifted, unsure if this was some sort of entrapment.

His face softened and he nodded. "Of course you do. And, it is wise not to speak of such matters."

Violetta turned to leave, and the priest reached for her arm to stop her. "Violetta, I want you to understand that no matter what happens or what doesn't happen, do not judge by appearances. The ripple effect of actions cannot always be seen, but only felt, often times long after the act is done and forgotten." He let go of her arm.

"I understand. Just one thing though," she said.

"What's that?"

"I never told you my name," she replied, staring defiantly back at him.

The young priest shifted his eyes down. "I'm sure that you must have," he said.

"I'm sure that I did not," she fired back.

Violetta walked down the nave and stopped at the holy water.

She looked up at the priest. "It's empty," she stated.

"Excuse me?" asked the priest.

"The holy water, it's empty. Would you not have noticed when you entered the church today?"

The priest stared back at her but did not speak.

"Who are you? Because, I doubt you are an actual priest," Violetta said accusingly.

He stepped towards her. "You are correct. I am not who I said I am."

Violetta could feel her pulse quicken. So, it was a trap, she thought desperately.

The priest held his hands up in the air. "Don't be alarmed. My name is Liber and I also come from a different … place," he finished.

"I don't understand," said Violetta, taking a step back.

Liber lowered his voice, "I am here to help you."

Violetta stared at him, trying to make sense of the situation.

"No one accomplishes anything alone," said Liber.

"I don't need your help," she said emphatically. "And you still haven't told me how you know my name."

Liber walked up to her. "I promise to explain everything once we find the fountain. For now, you'll have to take my word for it."

"We? I'm not going anywhere until you explain," retorted Violetta.

"Listen, we don't have much time, and we really should leave now," Liber urged her.

Violetta wanted to think, but she knew she did not have time. Instead, she scanned him from top to bottom, but saw nothing. Confused, she shook her head.

"You're looking for the seen," Liber told her.

"What?" asked Violetta.

"Truth does not lie in the seen, but the unseen."

"You speak in riddles! What does all of this have to do with me?" Violetta clutched the strap to her bag. "I don't know who you are, but I'm leaving," she said.

She began walking toward the door when she stopped abruptly. Suddenly, she saw things differently. Light was pulsating all around her. Some areas in the church were vibrating at incredibly fast speeds, while others were vibrating more slowly. The areas where physical objects had been a moment before, were barely vibrating at all, but nothing in the room was standing completely still.

"It's all around us," muttered Violetta.

"Yes," said Liber. "Everything is made of the same stuff."

Violetta glared at him and the room came back into focus. "You said you were sent here to help me. Who sent *you*?" she demanded.

Liber paused for a moment. Then, he let out a long breath. "You wouldn't know her," he said. "Her name is Adolphina."

Violetta gasped and her covered her mouth with her hand.

"You know her?" the priest asked, cautiously.

"Ummm, no," Violetta stammered. "I just …remember the name. From a dream I had, before I left Venice."

"I see," Liber said. "Well, that is not surprising. The Light takes many forms and communicates in many ways," said Liber. "We need only to pay attention." He reached toward the door.

"Shall we leave?"

Liber walked at a steady pace next to her along a narrow rocky path.

"So, will I meet Adolphina?" asked Violetta.

"I'm afraid that is not possible," he replied.

"I am not afraid to travel. I have taken dangerous journeys before," she said.

"This is a journey you cannot reach by horse."

"Okay. Well, I have always wanted to travel by boat," she pressed.

Liber laughed. "You cannot reach it by boat either."

Violetta frowned, "Why are you always so vague?"

"There are some things I cannot divulge."

Violetta stopped and turned toward him. "You said you were from a different place. Where?"

Liber stared over the horizon. "I was not honest. I am from here, actually."

"Why would you lie?"

"It's not so much a matter of place, but time. Have you ever gotten the feeling that you were two places at the same time?

Or that you have been in a place or certain situation before?"

Violetta thought back to the torture chamber with Enzo and how she felt herself leave her body and travel to the bed with Marco.

The wind began to pick up and she swept her hair behind her ear.

"I have," she replied.

"Well, that is kind of what I am doing right now," he stated.

"But, how is that so?" she asked incredulously.

"The how is not important right now." He put his arm on her shoulder. "We should pick up our pace."

Annoyed, Violetta reached for the map inside her satchel. "We should check the map. It's rather vague, but there are some markings on here that could be useful."

Liber raised his eyebrows. "There's a map?"

He took the map from her hand and tucked it inside his pocket.

"What are you doing?" asked Violetta. "We need that."

"We don't. I do."

"This is all crazy. Everything you have said is outrageous," she shouted.

"Is it? Is it any crazier than seeing the Lights your mother taught you about?"

"I'm through with this. I'm going on without you," she screamed, and turned around to leave. Then, she stopped in her tracks. "How do you know that my mother taught me about the Lights?"

Liber ran his hands through his hair. "This was not supposed to go this far. But, given what has already transpired, I guess there is no harm in telling you the rest."

Violetta narrowed her eyes. "The rest of what?"

"I know that your mother taught you about the Lights the same way I knew your name."

Violetta crossed her arms tightly around her stomach and waited.

"Violetta, I know your mother. Your mother is Adolphina."

The wind picked up again, sending dust and leaves swirling up into the air.

"That's impossible," she exclaimed. "My mother was named Giulia, and she died."

"The body of your mother, Giulia, died. But think back to the moment of her death. What did you see?"

Violetta's mind raced. "I saw her die. *That's* what I saw." She took a step back toward the edge of the path.

Liber stepped forward. "It's okay," he said reassuringly. "Think harder. What did you *un*-see?"

Violetta pictured her mother in bed, her breath slowed, then stopped. She stared into her mother's eyes, waiting for death to come. "It did not," she said aloud.

"What?" asked Liber.

Violetta swallowed. "Death did not come. Her body died, but she did not."

"That is correct," he jutted his chin forward, "and neither did I."

He held out his hand. "Now, give me the book," he commanded.

Violetta eyes widened in terror as she grasped her satchel tighter. "Enzo," she muttered.

"It's 'Liber' these days."

"That's why I couldn't see your Light back in the church," she exclaimed. "But how is this possible?"

"Give me the book. You're in no position to argue," he warned.

She glanced backwards. A steep cliff was only a few inches behind her.

"You won't get away with this," she said bitterly, removing the satchel from her shoulder and handing it to him. "I'll tell the authorities, I'll tell Marco. We'll find you." As soon as she said, it she regretted it, realizing how foolish it sounded.

He laughed as he snatched the satchel from her hand. "That's the funny thing about truth and lies. People always find an outlandish lie more believable than an outlandish truth." He slung the bag over his shoulder and took the map from his pocket. "That's why you don't speak of your precious Lights, am I right?" He gave her a wink and a wicked smile.

Violetta clenched her fists. "Why didn't you just take the book from me in the church? Why bring me this far?"

"Simple. I want what is inside the cave, and I was hoping you would lead me to it. But, now there is a map, and I don't need you anymore."

Violetta's eyes widened as he stepped forward, so close she could smell his stale breath.

He raised his hand and placed it in the center of her chest. "Don't do this," she said, holding her belly.

His lips curled into a sneer. "Don't worry. I think living out your days knowing that you have failed is the better form of…torture," he sneered.

He turned and walked down the path. "Don't follow me," he called over his shoulder.

She squinted as the wind whipped her hair around her eyes, and she heard him laugh as he disappeared around the corner.

Violetta stopped in front of Lucia's cottage. Her back and feet ached, and she was eager to sit in front of the warm fire and try to make sense of everything that had occurred on the mountain. Defeat hung heavy around her neck, and felt like a weight that was dragging her under water.

As she walked up the path to the stone cottage, she noticed the front door stood ajar, causing her unease. She paused at the threshold.

"Hello," she called out.

She stepped inside, scattering salt across the floor with her shoes.

She gasped and ran over to kneel beside Lucia lying on the floor, in a puddle of blood, a shard protruding from her neck.

She took a blanket from a chair. Gently, she laid the blanket on top of Lucia, stopping at the shoulders. She stared at the glass dagger buried in her neck. She instinctively knew they would return to take her too, but she did not feel fear.

She felt rage.

Carefully, she pulled the shard from Lucia's neck, closed her eyes, and covered her head with the blanket. Suddenly, she heard a clamour of footsteps behind her.

"Well, what do we have here?" Salvatore asked, and took a step closer. "A dead body."

Violetta slipped the piece of glass into her cape pocket and stood up to face them. "I just found her."

"This woman is wanted for witchery."

"She wasn't a witch. She's my friend, and she was murdered."

"You are not the authority on such things," shouted Salvatore. "The Tribunal will decide on such matters," he walked up to her and spat in her face, "and you are her accomplice. Arrest her, Angelo!"

"You can't arrest me."

"I can and I will arrest you. Angelo!"

Angelo hurried forward and grabbed her by the arms.

"In the name of the Holy Roman Church, you are officially under arrest for murder and witchery," Salvatore said. He turned to Angelo: "Take her outside at once."

They walked down the path, stopping in front of their horses. "Tie her hands, Angelo."

"Sir, I didn't bring any rope."

"God, you are worthless. Go back inside and try to find some," he ordered. He turned toward Violetta, glancing at her belly and grimacing. "Just sit tight."

Violetta watched Angelo disappear inside the house, a faint trail of pink light following behind him. "I don't much care for all the witch-hunting business, but you women need to know your place and learn to stay home."

Salvatore turned toward his horse and adjusted the reins. She gripped the shard of glass in her cloak pocket, letting all the rage in her heart travel down her arm and pool in her fist. Then, she took her hand out, and with one quick strike, she drove the glass deep into his back.

Salvatore let out a cry and dropped to his knees. Violetta mounted her horse and rode as fast as she could in the direction of the inn.

Angelo

Val di Luci

June, 1554

Upon hearing the commotion, Angelo emerged from the house and ran up to Salvatore, twisting and contorting on the ground like a wounded snake.

"Help me, Angelo," he moaned. "Get this out of me, and then go after her!"

Angelo was unable to speak.

"What are you waiting for? I said take it out, you bastard!"

"Hold still," he muttered.

Angelo leaned down and put on his leather glove before gripping the glass.

Suddenly, from the recesses of his mind, the familiar taunts from his childhood emerged, and he saw himself stumbling through the field, trying in vain to outrun the other boys. He tripped and fell face-first into the grass. He heard the boys fast approaching from behind. He grasped at the tall grass as he struggled to his feet, but it was too late. The other boys were upon him. The tallest one was holding a large rock above his head.

"Look at dough boy," the boy hollered. The other kids began chanting, "Dough boy! Dough boy!" Angelo put his arms up to block the blow he knew was coming. Terror seized his body, and he trembled uncontrollably. The tall boy raised the rock higher above his head, then brought it down, smashing it into the earth next to his head. He laughed, "The look on your face was worth it." He turned to his friends: "Come on, let's go hunt some real prey."

"Hurry up," Salvatore shouted.

Angelo shook his head and gripped the glass tighter. "I'll count to three. One, two,"

"For God's sake, just do it!"

"Three," and he drove the glass shard deep into Salvatore's back, twisting it as Salvatore cried out in anguish before collapsing in front of him.

Angelo wiped his hands on his pants and walked back to his horse. He unwrapped the bread, sank his teeth into the crusty loaf, and chewed slowly. He would give her a decent head start before returning to town to report the unexpected ambush they had encountered.

Aster

"But the devils cannot interfere with the stars."

The Malleus Maleficarum, Part1

Question I

Heinrich Kramer, 1486 AD

Venice, Italy

2110

There was a knock at the door.

Aster stopped slicing the carrots and looked up from the cutting board.

"Are we expecting anyone tonight?"

"It's probably the security team from the museum. I believe the book is still in the city, so I'm having a full search conducted on every building and home," Theo said as he brushed passed her.

"You didn't tell me about that," she said, but he had already disappeared down the corridor to answer the door. Her hand started shaking. She placed the knife on the counter and wiped her palms on her pants. She walked around the kitchen island, but it was too late. Two men dressed in navy suits with the Lion insignia on their breast pocket appeared in the room.

"We're sorry for the inconvenience," the taller one said, "but your orders were to search every house in the city."

"It's not an inconvenience, gentlemen. Don't mind us, we were just preparing dinner," replied Theo, leading them into the apartment.

"We won't be long," the shorter one said, and they began their systematic search of the apartment.

Theo opened the long glass doors to the wine fridge and, without turning around, said, "Can you put the water for the pasta on the stove? I'll open a bottle of wine for us."

Aster slowly walked back into the kitchen. Her head felt lightheaded as she filled the pot with water. This is it, she thought. They'll find the book, and I'll have to confess. And I will be arrested.

Aster didn't know what the punishment would be for the theft of an ancient relic, but given the state of things, she knew it would be severe.

She placed the pot on the stove and walked toward the bedroom. She wasn't going to wait until they found it.

"Aster, where are you going?"

She stopped and turned slowly around. "I'll be back. I need to do something."

"You need to come over and have a glass of wine with me."

He walked up to her and held out the wine glass.

Her arms felt like lead as she reached for it.

He held up his glass and looked her in the eye. "To conviction."

Her mouth went dry. "Conviction?"

"You know, seeing things through. It's been a long and tedious journey turning this city into a museum. I didn't think we'd ever get those old canals drained and converted to pathways." He brought his glass up to his mouth and paused. "What conviction were you talking about?"

He took a casual sip and swirled his glass. A wave of nausea overcame her; she needed to sit down.

"We hate to disturb you again, but one last thing - could you open the top drawer to the chest for us? It has an identity lock."

"I'd be happy to," he said. Then he looked at her. "You stay here. I'll be right back."

She placed the glass down and steadied herself. Then she took a deep breath and stood up straight. Aster walked toward the bedroom.

"We'll keep looking, sir. There's still a lot of ground to cover," said the guard.

"I have no doubt we will find the book," replied Theo.

"Have a good evening, sir."

"I'll show you out."

The two men walked past her and nodded. "Good evening."

Aster walked to the chest. The drawer was still open. Inside, it was empty except for a folder. She picked it up and flipped it open. The identity chips.

She closed the drawer slowly and walked back into the kitchen, where Theo was standing over the boiling pot of water. "A few more minutes," he said casually stirring the pasta with a wooden spoon.

"Why did you do it?"

"Do what?"

"You know what," she yelled. "And why were you fucking with me this whole time?"

He looked up from the pot. "Listen, I don't need to know why you stole the book. I assume you have your reasons, and knowing you, they're good ones. So, how about you give me the same consideration; and we end this discussion here?" He went back to stirring the pasta. "And I fucked with you because you are technically a criminal. I think you deserved some sort of punishment. Besides, it was also fun seeing you sweat."

He turned toward her, daring her to challenge him.

"Borrowed," said Aster.

"What?"

"I didn't steal it. I borrowed it," she said through gritted teeth.

"Listen, I don't give a damn about the book, just like I don't give a damn about this city. It's all greed disguised as altruism. This is my job and I do it, but I am not going to do this forever. So, whatever is going on with the book is your business, but other people won't see it that way. So, I took care of it."

He put his arms on her shoulders. "Hey, you have to understand I just saved our asses. You put us both in danger. This is Italy. The powers that be trust no one. *Everyone* is suspect."

She squared her shoulders and brushed his hands off of her, determined not to show she was affected by his antics. "We need to talk about where to go from here," she said matter-of-factly.

"Ok."

"So?"

"So what?"

"You know what. Where is it? And will you give it back?"

"That depends."

"On what?"

"On what I get in return."

She stepped in closer and could feel the adrenaline coursing through her veins. "I think I see where this is going. You're talking about extortion."

"Your words, not mine."

She paused for a moment. Then, she laughed and slipped off her dress letting it fall around her feet. She hopped on the counter and pulled him in close, wrapping her legs around his waist.

"What about the pasta?" he murmured.

She turned off the burner, and the boil rolled to a stop. "The pasta can wait."

He grinned and took off his shirt as she unbuttoned his pants.

The following morning she put the espresso on the stove and poured the pot of water and soggy pasta down the sink. She grabbed two cups and saucers from the cabinet and placed them on the bar top. Then she grabbed six eggs and a block of cheese from the fridge.

Theo appeared in the kitchen and walked up to her. "You're up early," he said.

"I'm starving." She cracked an egg and tossed the shell in the sink. "I imagine you're hungry as well," she said, shooting him a sly grin.

"Famished," he said, pouring two cups of espresso.

They sat at the counter and ate their eggs, sipping their coffees. The sun was streaming through the windows, and the morning felt lazy and warm.

When they finished eating, she picked up the dishes and took them over to the sink. He stood up and walked over to the wine fridge, opened the glass door, and pulled out the middle drawer.

"It's a little early, don't you think?"

He removed the drawer, and placed it on the counter. Then he turned back toward the fridge and reached his hand toward the back. She heard a faint beep and a stainless steel drawer popped open from the back wall. He reached inside once again and pulled out the book.

"I believe this is what you want," he said, handing it to her.

"I guess I earned it last night?" she said, taking it from his hand.

"I would have given it to you either way."

"I know you would have."

She stared down at the book. Its jewels sparkled in the morning light.

"What about my hat?"

"That hat is the most wanted hat in the city."

"So, what did you do with it?"

"I oversee construction for the largest concrete job since the Hoover Dam. What do you think I did with it?" He gestured toward the book. "If you need to get it out of the city, I can help. I'm a very important man with clearances, you know," he said, giving her a playful wink.

"Thank you. But I'm not taking it from the city. It belongs here - just not locked inside a glass case in some museum for visitors to walk by and not even bother to read."

She held the book tightly to her chest. "Rieta's followers were people who lived by simple truths and believed in honesty, fairness, and equality - true equality, not the kind we love to talk about but don't bother to practice."

"And now, you're going to start a cult?"

"Not a cult, a revival - a modern Renaissance."

"And how do you plan to pull this off? You can't just parade a stolen book around the city."

"There's a cave beneath the church. It's near where her temple stood. I'll start there, hold meetings for those interested in learning about her."

"What if you get found out?"

"I won't."

"How can you be sure? There's always a rat."

"Not this time. I can't explain it, but I feel like I'm being protected or guided in some way."

"Well, what about me?"

"What about you?"

"Well, what if I want to be a part of this underground movement of yours too?"

"You're a man."

"So what?"

"So, all the trouble started with you."

"But you forget I'm a different type of man."

"True," she sighed, shaking her head, "you are different."

"And you said 'equality for all'."

"You're a good listener too."

"And good listeners make for very good students."

"Perhaps…"

He stepped in closer and put his hands around her hips. "If you really are determined to start another Renaissance, don't you think you'll need some allies on the other side?" He grinned, "I think I've proven myself worthy and loyal."

She looked into his eyes - deeper than she had looked before. Trapped inside the bottomless well of his pupils, a shadow twisted and churned. It was only a flash, but she was certain of what she had seen. She placed her hand on her stomach. And, as if reading her thoughts, he pulled her in.

She placed her hands on his chest and leaned back from him.

"I need you to help me," she said.

"What can I do?"

"You need to help me smuggle the book out of Venice."

"I thought you were keeping it here."

"I am. I plan to. It's just that there's something I feel like I should try to find out first."

"What's that?"

"Well, to be honest, I wasn't sure I wanted you involved, but I need you."

"I see. Go on."

"As you know, I've been translating the texts, and I came across one passage in particular that caught my interest. It speaks of a hidden cave in a mountain town not far from here. According to the writings, the senior counsel members moved all of their most precious artifacts to a hidden location when they were being overtaken."

"That's all very interesting, but don't you think someone would have found this cave by now?"

"That's where it gets interesting and a little out there. Supposedly, the engraving here on the back is a key. A key that unlocks the door to whatever is inside the cave."

"This is beginning to sound very far-fetched to me."

"I know, but just hear me out. It's written that there needs to be three books, with three locks."

"But you only have one."

"Yes, thanks for pointing that out."

"I'm just being realistic."

"Except I feel like I can't be realistic. Not about this."

"Even if what you say is true, how are we supposed to find this cave?"

"I believe there is a map contained in the last chapter. I've been piecing it together and I think I have enough figured out to get us there. It's not a typical map though. It's a...here, I'll show you," she said excitedly.

She opened the book and unfolded the piece of trace paper tucked inside. She placed it on top of the page. "I noticed that there were patterns, a certain cadence to the language, but only on this last page. The passages on this page changed. It's subtle, but if you read it aloud, you can detect a stark contrast in the writing. It turns more ominous, almost. I think it was written after the other passages, perhaps when the invasion was beginning. So I began looking for patterns in the phrases and drawing connections between the words. And look," Aster ran her fingers along the lines drawn on the vellum connecting the words beneath, "there are words in the passages that seemed to refer to the four elements: fire; water; earth; air. I isolated each element and connected the words of each element in a different color. See, I drew the water in blue, earth in brown, and air in yellow. And look what emerged - the water element created the river - it's the river that flows from the mountain range I mapped out here in brown. And, look at the air element, it's the position of the stars in the sky. Stars in the summer sky this time of year."

"And what's this," he asked pointing to a red circle in the center of the page.

"That's the fire element, and it encircles the one mountain in this range that is a dormant volcano. This is where I think the books are hidden."

"Why do you think they hid the books inside a volcano?"

"Because Rieta was represented by the element of fire. Her temple had blazing torches surrounding the perimeter of the rooftop."

"Fire? That's surprising. I would have thought a female goddess would be represented by water."

"Only in the current male dominated mythology. According to this text, fire was attributed to the female. It symbolized the sun, warmth, and light - the nurturer of life itself. It also symbolized rebirth and regeneration. Fire represented her power to destroy a forest and renew the land with fertile ground - the circle of life. The Light of the world.

When men took over, they turned fire into the symbol of the Devil and the flames of Hell. In fact, the word "Gehenna" is translated as hell many times in the Gospels. Gehenna is the English transliteration of the Hebrew word 'Hinnom'. Hinnom and Gehenna was the name of a valley just south of Jerusalem's walls. In the context of Jesus's sermon, He is referencing a place where trash and the carcasses of dead animals were burned. It is also likely where we get the term 'burning in Hell'. People would say, 'If you don't behave, you'll burn in Hell.' Again, a reference to Gehenna, where at one time, they burned the bodies of murdered heretics. Over time, fire also became strongly associated with the caricature of the Devil. How fitting that they used fire as the number one way to kill women during the Inquisition. So many layers of meaning."

Theo tapped his finger on the map. "I get the fire reference, but how can you be sure the books are inside that volcano?"

"Because it's written in the stars."

"I thought you didn't believe in fate," he said.

"I don't. It's *actually* written in the stars. This," she pointed to a cluster of yellow dots she had drawn above the volcano, "is the constellation Aquarius. He pours water from his vessel. And look, he's pouring the water directly into the volcano. It cannot be any clearer."

Iris looked at Theo. "Honestly, I doubt I'll find anything, especially with just one book. But if I don't try, then I'll always be left wondering, what if." Aster paused, then added, "You know I'll go either way."

"I know you will. And I'm going with you."

"Are you sure?"

"When do we leave?"

"If you get caught with this…" she warned.

"I know all about consequences. And I'm aware of what kind of woman you are. I'll get burned with you either way. I asked you, when are we are leaving?"

She knew there was no time to hesitate. "We leave tonight."

"That is quick."

"Yes. I can't explain it, but I just feel like it has to be now, or never."

"Then we leave tonight."

They stood in the bedroom, sorting through the clothes spread across the bed.

"How do we get out of Venice undetected? Our security chips track our every move."

"That's why we aren't going to use them."

"But we can't clear the security points without them."

Theo continued packing, placing his folded shirts inside the backpack. "That's why we aren't going through the checkpoints." He zipped the bag and flung it over his shoulder. "Are you ready?"

"I'm not sure. I only packed a few changes of clothes and a coat. Do I need anything else?"

"Only your resolve that this is what you want to do."

She nodded. "Let's go."

"Ok, grab your bag and follow me."

They walked to the most northern end of the city and stood in front of the entrance to a large gate.

"Where does this lead? I don't remember seeing this on any city plan," said Aster.

"It's an abandoned shipyard. They used to make gondolas here. Now it only stores them."

They walked through the gate and down a narrow road with red brick warehouses on either side of them. Through the large glass doors and windows, Aster could see rows of gondolas stacked floor to ceiling. "There must be thousands of them," Aster said.

"Venice had 30,000 in operation at one time," said Theo. "Later, there were only a few thousand used mostly as novelties for tourists. Now, with no canals, there is no need for them."

Aster could see a look of disgust pass over his face.

"It sounds like you disapprove of turning the city into a museum."

"I disapprove of anything that bastardizes greatness and turns it into a novelty. We've turned Venice into an amusement park," he replied, with a level of disdain she had not heard before.

"It was already an amusement park. Very few people actually lived here anymore. The city was under siege by tourists. It was the only way to protect what was left."

"There were other solutions."

"Such as?"

"There was a simple solution. We should have given the city back to its people. But greed always trumped reason, and now here we are."

"Here we are," she said, looking around shipyard. "So, I'm assuming we leave by gondola?"

"No, we could never pass through the laser detectors that surround the city."

"I didn't know the waterways were secured by lasers."

"It's basically an electric fence. They have secured the entire perimeter."

"So if we can't leave by road, and we can't leave by water, how are we going to leave? Miniature submarine?"

"You're not too far off," he replied.

They arrived at the far end of the shipyard. He slid open a heavy iron door and stepped inside. Aster followed him.

He switched on a light.

"What in the world is this place?"

"My warehouse."

"It looks like a medieval laboratory," she said, walking to the center of the room. There were long wooden tables filled with every imaginable gadget and tool, most of which she had seen only in movies. "Where on earth did you get all of these things?"

"I've collected them over the years. Whenever I come across something that interests me I purchase it."

"What do you do with all this stuff?"

"It's mostly a hobby. I enjoy tinkering with it, restoring some of it, building new stuff out of old parts."

"I had no idea."

"No one does."

"So why are we here. It doesn't look like any of this stuff is going to get us out of here," she said, picking up and turning over an old clock gear.

"Come with me."

She set it back on the table and followed him through another metal door in the back. The room was vacant except for a large piece of black circular fabric laid out in the middle of the floor. Next to it, stood a tall basket.

"Is that what I think it is?"

"That depends on what you think it is."

She turned toward him. "Is this a hot air balloon?"

"That's right."

"Have you gone mad?"

"If you want to get out of here undetected, this is the only option we have."

"But I've seen these in old films. They are quite loud, not to mention large."

He walked over to a garage door and opened it. "Not this one. I've modified it. It generates the same amount of heat but is virtually silent. I've also modified the size. This one is much smaller than the originals. No one will detect us, especially out here. With the cloud cover, we'll be all but invisible." He walked over to the basket. "We will make our way over to the lagoon and land in the foothills of the mountains. From there, we go on foot to the village."

"Hot air balloons and walking? You were born in the wrong century."

He folded the fabric and placed it inside the basket. "If you don't want us to be stopped and searched, then this is the way we have to go. Especially if they realize we are both missing."

"It's a three-day weekend. No one will know we are gone before Tuesday."

"Then let's get going. Help me with the basket."

They lifted the basket and carried it outside. "Why do you have this, may I ask? This doesn't look like a simple hobby to me."

"Because I trust no one. And I rely on no one." He flipped a switch, and a small generator hummed. "Stand back until it's finished."

They watched the balloon fill with air. "Are you nervous?" asked Theo.

Just then, a man stepped out of the shadows and walked across the dock, pointing a gun at Theo's chest.

"William," Aster cried.

William Blankship turned his gaze toward Aster. "Did you really think I wouldn't figure it out? That you were the one who stole the book?"

"Listen, William, I have the book right here. You can have it, just put the gun down."

William turned his attention back toward Theo. "You know, it's quite fascinating, the similarities between a gun and a paintbrush. Both require finely tuned motor skills. One has to be so careful with a paintbrush, mindful of using the most delicate strokes, the most subtle controlled movements. The same control is required for handling a gun. One careless move, a little too much pressure on the trigger, and —" he pointed the gun at a bottle sitting on the dock and fired. His hand flew up in the air, and the bullet hit a lamp post and ricocheted off into the lagoon.

"For Christ's sake, William," Theo said. "You're going to kill someone."

William aimed at another bottle and closed one eye. He fired and the silenced bullet shot through the night, missing a second time.

Aster held up her hand and calmly asked, "William, why don't you tell us why you are here? What is it that you want?"

"What do I want? Since when has anyone ever concerned themselves with what *I* want?" He dropped his arm.

"If you don't want the book, and you obviously haven't turned us in, then why are you here?" Aster asked.

"I want you to take me with you."

"You've got to be kidding me," Theo said.

"You heard me. I want to go with you."

"William, that can't happen. You can't involve yourself in this," replied Aster. "You'll lose your job, or worse."

"My whole life, I've been told what I can and can't do. Now, I'm telling you. Take me with you, or I'm one command away from sounding the alarms on the two of you. Don't think I won't," William threatened.

"But, why? Why are you risking everything for this?" Aster asked.

"Do you know what it's like to spend your entire life being afraid to die? And you know the only thing worse than being afraid to die? Being afraid to live."

Aster sighed and turned to Theo: "Can it hold three of us?"

Theo looked at William. He held out his hand. "Give me the gun, William. And, please, stick to painting."

The balloon rose above the lagoon, silent and dark. From above, the skyline looked the same, eternal and untouched. The bell tower and St. Mark's Cathedral distracted from the ribbons of concrete curing in the canals. Slowly, the fog obscured the rooftops, and eventually, the city disappeared below them and gave way to a soft moonlight above.

Theo removed a small brass box from his pocket.

Aster raised her eyebrows. "You carry around an astronomical compendium?"

"Technology fails and becomes obsolete." He opened the box, flipped past the first two compartments that contained finely engraved details of the lunar calendar and a sundial. In the third compartment, a delicate arrow spun on a needle. He held it up. "But a compass will always point you in the right direction."

Aster took a closer look. "Where did you get it? It looks in perfect condition."

"I took it from a museum in Florence," Theo replied.

"You did what?" exclaimed Aster.

"I liked it," replied Theo casually. He shot her a grin. "You think you're the only thief around here?"

"You stole it?" she asked incredulously.

"Relax, it's a family heirloom. It belonged to the Grand Duke of Ferdinand de Medici."

"So, we are in the presence of royalty," William said, not bothering to conceal his sarcasm.

"Medici? You're related to the Medici?" Aster asked.

Theo chuckled. "Isn't everyone?"

"Not everyone," William grumbled.

Aster shook her head. "Unbelievable," she whispered.

They drifted in silence through the still night, floating over the flat plains. A gentle rain began to fall as they approached the mountains.

"Can this balloon fly in the rain?" William asked nervously.

"I guess we'll find out," Theo said.

"Maybe we should land. It looks dark ahead," Aster suggested.

The rain began to fall harder, and Aster moved to the center of the basket.

"The rain isn't so much the problem. The problem is wind or lightning," Theo explained.

"Let's land. Death by balloon is the last ending I had for us," Aster said, steadying herself.

"Us?" asked Theo.

Aster looked at him. "What?"

"That's the first time you've ever said 'us'. Granted, I wish it weren't in reference to death, but it's a start."

A low thunder rumbled in the distance. "Would you two stop talking and start landing," William yelled.

"Hold on," Theo said. "There's a clearing below, just beyond that grove of trees. I'll try to land there."

"Try? Have you ever flown this before?" William demanded to know.

"We don't want to know the answer to that," Aster replied.

A gust of wind whipped at the balloon, and the basket rocked to the side, knocking Aster into William. She gripped the edge of the basket and steadied herself as the rain beat down on her face, and Theo steered the balloon downward.

"Grab this rope and hold it steady," he said, handing Aster the knotted end.

She took hold while Theo wrapped the other rope around his arm. He adjusted the generator, and they dropped another ten feet, the bottom of the basket skimming the tree line. She turned her attention to the field directly in front of them.

"I have to drop her hard, or we'll go back up, so hold on," Theo yelled.

He cut the generator, and the balloon swooped toward the ground, landing with a crash and turning on its side, sending Aster and William skidding across the grass.

"Are you ok?" Aster heard Theo yell from across the field.

"Theo, I'm here."

Theo reached Aster as she was standing up. "Are you ok?"

"I'm fine," she said, dusting off her pants. "Where's William?"

"I don't see him. William!"

They scanned the field. Then they heard, "I'm over here!"

They turned in the direction of the grove. "He's by the trees," Aster said.

They ran across the field and found William on the ground, holding his leg.

"Are you all right?" Aster asked.

"I think it's broken," William grimaced.

Theo leaned down and examined the leg. "It's not broken."

Aster looked around the field. "Do we have any idea where we are?"

"Not a clue," Theo said, checking the GPS on his watch. "I'm not getting reception."

"What about your compendium?" William asked slyly.

"Then I say we climb under the balloon and wait this storm out," Aster suggested.

"Good idea," Theo agreed.

"I can't make it," William said, letting out a moan.

"You have one good leg," Theo said, swinging his arm over his shoulder. "Stand up and we'll help you."

They turned the basket on the side and pulled a portion of the balloon over it, creating a makeshift tent, and the three of them crawled underneath.

Aster opened her backpack and pulled out clothes and a scarf.

"What time is it?" she asked.

Theo checked his watch. "21:20."

"We weren't in the air for very long, but it feels like we left Venice ages ago."

"Time dilation," Theo stated.

"What?" Aster asked.

"Moving clocks run more slowly than stationary clocks. The effect becomes more pronounced as the moving clocks approach the speed of light," Theo explained.

"At which point do we stand still? The one eternal moment of now," said William.

"We don't know that yet," Theo replied.

Aster looked at him, an amused expression on her face. "So, are those the kind of things you ponder in your warehouse?"

Theo glanced up toward the sky. "Among other things."

Aster gave him a quizzical look. "What other things?"

He put his arm around her and pulled her in close. "You should rest." He turned to William: "How are you holding up?"

"I think it's just a sprain."

The early dawn streaked the sky as the clouds cleared. Theo and Aster folded the balloon and placed it in the basket.

"We're coming back for it, right?" Aster asked.

"So, you enjoyed it," Theo said.

"It was peaceful up there. Up to the point where we nearly died."

He looked at his watch. "I'm getting reception. There's a town a few kilometers down the road."

"I don't think William can make it," she said, looking at him.

"I think she's right." William rubbed his leg.

"You're going to stay put. We'll come back and get you as soon as we find a car." Theo slung his bag over his arm.

"Aster," said William, rubbing his leg, "listen, sorry about—"

Aster smiled. "I'm glad you came along, William."

Theo sat next to Aster on a bench as she studied her map. "Let me see our coordinates," she said.

Theo lifted his wrist, and a holographic map beamed from his watch.

"I think this is the town we are supposed to be in," she said.

"Really?"

"Yeah, look at this. My map isn't to scale, but according to this position, there isn't anything else around here that fits as well as this place. I guess the wind blew us further than we thought."

"This is encouraging, but I feel like we're still looking for a needle in a haystack."

Aster looked down the street. "They must have left some other clue. I wish I could figure it out."

"Unfortunately, we don't have much time if we want to make it back to Venice before Tuesday. And don't forget about poor old William. He's not exactly a survivalist. That guy couldn't find true north with a compass."

Aster exhaled slowly and tried to think. "Wait a minute. A compass."

"Yeah? What about it?"

"Let me see that compendium of yours."

He took it out of his pocket and handed it to her. "How is a compass going to help you? You already know the directions."

She flipped to the first compartment. "It's not the compass I need. It's the lunar map and the sundial."

"Listen, first I'm going to check you into a hotel room so you can shower and wash all the blood off your cuts. While you do that, I'll find a car and go pick up William."

"But I feel like I'm on the verge of something."

"Yeah, it's called a precipice, and you're about to fall off if you don't get cleaned up and eat something." He stood up. "Let's go find a hotel and I'll get going."

Aster stepped into the shower and let the hot water run down her skin. It stung the scrapes that had cut her arms and legs, but she hardly noticed. She squeezed the shampoo onto her hand and began massaging her scalp. A sharp pain sliced through her abdomen. She reached for the grab bar to steady herself. That's when she saw it, a small ribbon of red flowing toward the drain.

She got out of the shower and towelled herself off. She had planned to tell Theo about the pregnancy after this was over. Now, she would wait until she took another test.

She shook the thought from her mind and got dressed. Then she walked downstairs to meet Theo and William for breakfast.

"All right," Theo began, "do we know where we are going?"

Aster spread the butter on her toast. "I have no idea. We are looking for a fountain with a rose on the outskirts of town."

"That could take a while," replied Theo.

"And don't forget, according to the book, we need two additional keys. That's what concerns me the most," she pointed out.

"What was your idea about the sundial and lunar calendar earlier?"

Aster laid the compendium on the table and opened it to the sundial. "I don't know. It was a flash of inspiration. It's probably not going to lead anywhere."

"Well, we don't have much more to go on," William said. "Anything's worth a shot."

"What you said about time dilation made me think that there might be some correlation between time and space. I just don't know what." She tapped her finger on the dial.

William leaned in. "Let me see that."

"What is it?" Aster asked, handing it over.

"I studied these as a child. They were very popular in the 1500s. Galileo and all the great inventors had one. Look," he said, opening each compartment like pages of a book. "The sundial. The lunar calendar. The compass."

"I can see that," said Aster. "So?"

"All forms of measurements. As artists, we create in three dimensions: length, width, and height, but we often fail to consider the other dimension that is just as vital." He closed the box. "Three dimensions stacked on top of each other, existing simultaneously inside the fourth dimension."

"Time," Theo said.

"I wouldn't worry about those other two keys, if I were you," William suggested.

"You mean we are working with other dimensions, in other times?" asked Aster.

"Why not? We now know that time unfolds vertically, not horizontally, so stranger things have occurred," said William.

Aster stared at the box. "The one eternal moment of now," she said thoughtfully.

"So, say this is true," Theo pondered, "that still leaves us with the task of actually finding the rose fountain."

Aster folded the map. "I think I've been staring at this for too long. If it is true that we are working within the construct of one time, that means there must be overlaps, and it's possible to access information, or even events, in other times."

"Overlaps in time is certainly a theory, although it has yet to be proven," Theo said.

Aster's eyes lit up. "What if our future selves can use these overlaps to guide us by sending information, like clues or signposts? What if they are doing it now, and we need only to pay more attention?"

"Speaking of time, we're wasting it. Let's get going," said Theo.

Aster, Theo, and William had scoured the dormant volcano for two days and now, they stood in silence before a stone fountain with a metal rosette carved into back.

Aster was the first to speak. "Well, the rosette looks like it could fit, but there's only one way to find out."

She placed the book upon the rosette and rotated it until it locked into place.

Nothing happened.

Theo stepped forward and ran his hand along the edges of the fountain, inspecting the sides.

William scrunched his nose. "Well, it certainly goes together like the yin and the yang, like black and white. I really thought something would happen though." He scratched his head. "Maybe I was wrong about the fourth dimension. "

Aster turned toward him. "What did you say?"

William gave her a quizzical look. "Maybe I was wrong about the fourth dimension?"

"No, the other thing."

"I said it goes together like the yin and the yang, like black and white."

"Black and white." Aster grabbed her bag and pulled out her notebook. She flipped to the back where there was a pouch, stuffed with several photographs. She removed the photos and started going through the stack.

"You carry photographs of Rieta with you?" Theo asked.

"I like to reference the statue while I do my translations."

She flipped to the next one. "Look! Here it is," she exclaimed excitedly. "I remember seeing these black markings on her forearms. And, look closer, I always thought her forearms were oddly shaped. Everything on her is perfectly proportioned except for the forearms, which have two indentations in them, both slightly narrowing in the center."

William scratched his chin. "So what are you trying to tell us?"

"The way her forearms and palms are facing upward, and her hands are open, yet slightly curled, as if they are gripping something." She shoved the pictures and notebook into William's hands. "Hold these, for a second."

Aster held out her arms, forearms facing up. "Theo, place your arms on top of mine and encircle my forearms with your hands.

Theo placed his arms over hers and gripped her.

"Geez, not so hard."

"Sorry," he said, loosening his grip.

"See?" Aster stared down at their arms, her heart beating out of her chest. "This is how I think they interlock. Do you know what this means? Rieta did not rule alone. She had a mate."

"This definitely makes sense," said William, nodding slowly in agreement.

"If this is true," said Theo, "you just made a discovery that changes everything."

Aster let go of Theo's arms. "There must be her counterpart somewhere, possibly in black marble, based on the scratches on her arms. Which means, most likely, he would also have had a temple."

"Like the Taj Mahal," said William.

"The Taj Mahal?" asked Aster.

"Yeah, according to the story, which most dismiss as a myth, only half of the plan was ever built. Supposedly, Emperor Shah Jahan wanted to build a mausoleum in black marble on the other side of the Yamuna river, across from the white one he had built for his favorite wife. They would have been connected by a bridge. The grounds were designed as a garden paradise, reflecting the heavens, and was to be his final resting place, alongside his wife. Except, the king's son had him imprisoned in a tower and took all of his fortune. The poor bastard died in a room with one window that overlooked his wife's mausoleum, one last cruel card dealt by his son. Or so the story goes…"

"That's some serious family feuding," remarked Theo.

"Black and white…" Aster said to herself, thoughtfully. She looked up. "In the translations, it said a woman was writing atop a black temple with pillars of fire on top the night she was taken."

"Her statue is white and she had a black temple. Maybe, he is represented in black marble and his temple is white," suggested William.

"Possibly," Aster mused. "I don't know, but it looks like we have a lot to figure out."

Aster ran the pendant that hung from her neck back and forth along the silver chain, deep in thought.

"Interesting necklace," commented William. "What is that exactly?"

Aster glanced down at the oblong silver pendant. "It's silkworm cocoon. I purchased it at the gift shop in the Cairo Museum, where I used to work."

"You worked in Cairo?" asked William.

"Only briefly," replied Aster. "I was cataloging a collection of lepidopterans. One of the largest collections in the world."

She froze momentarily, still holding the cocoon between her fingers. A bewildered expression crossed her face.

"What is it?" asked Theo.

"The Madagascar moth," Aster said slowly. "From inside the book."

"What moth?" asked Theo.

"I found a moth inside Rieta's book. I thought it was odd that a moth from Madagascar was flattened inside. They are marvellous, one of the most beautiful moth species in the world. They're also diurnal and their wings reflect sunlight in every color of the rainbow. Jewelry makers have coveted their wings for centuries."

"Would that be so unusual for a moth from Madagascar to be in a book from Venice?" asked Theo. "The Venetians were tradesmen, after all."

"I think it would be somewhat unusual. The Venetians traded mostly with the East, along the Silk Road. And this moth is not migratory," explained Aster. "There has to be a reason that particular moth was inside the book. Something that has to do with that island."

"Why do I get the feeling we are going to Madagascar?" asked Theo, cautiously.

Aster dropped her pendant and looked at Theo. "It's the only clue I have to go on, and I can't think of anywhere else to begin. Not to mention…"

"What?" asked Theo.

"If there's another statue, there might be another book." Aster's eyes widened. "We have to get to Madagascar."

"Well, do I get to come?" William asked, crossing his arms.

"Oh, William. Of course, you're coming, too," Aster said.

"It's getting late," said Theo. "Let's head back to town. We need to prepare for the trip, which means I need to get that balloon functional."

"Are you insane?" yelled William. "I'm not getting back in that thing!"

"Don't worry," Theo assured him. "Obviously, we can't take a balloon to Madagascar…which is why I'm turning it into a raft."

He slapped William on the back. "Let's go."

Theo walked off and William turned to Aster, his face panic stricken. "He's crazy. You know he's crazy, right? A raft will never make the trip to Madagascar. We'll capsize and drown for sure."

Aster shook her head and smiled. "You gotta relax, William. He was only kidding."

She hurried to catch up with Theo.

"I hope," she muttered under her breath.

Adolphina

Val Di Luci

2110 AD

"Is Violetta on time?" Adolphina asked.

Abacus crossed his arms. "She had a close call, but we put Thantos in her path, disguised as a priest, and she's safe now."

Adolphina furrowed her brow. "A priest? Wasn't that risky, given her prior experience?"

"I wanted to give her an opportunity to learn not to condition herself."

"Not exactly a good time for a lesson," she retorted, "but it worked?"

"It did. They left the village and he's on the path with her now."

Adolphina frowned.

"Is something wrong?" asked Abacus.

"What do you know about Thantos? It makes me uneasy that I haven't met him."

"His record is solid, and he was eager to take on the assignment."

"And what about Aster and Iris?"

"There were fluctuations in their energy fields; but, in then end, both acted on their impulse." He nodded his head and smiled, "It looks like it's all coming together, Adolphina."

"Only time will tell. And that time is very soon," Adolphina straightened her shoulders and lifted her chin, "and we've spent enough time here in Val di Luci. Let's go to the fountain and see what happens."

They walked briskly along the narrow path that snaked around the side of the mountain. The golden threads in Adolphina's gown shimmered and contrasted against her skin that her mother said reminded her of the volcanic soil from her home. Although she grew up in the mountains with the majestic peaks and silent snowfalls, Adolphina longed for her mother's homeland in Madagascar, a place born from violent volcanic eruptions that gave way to fertile land. She was certain that she shared the same destiny.

When she took physical form in Val di Luci, her father said she arrived like a bolt of lightening. He had taken one look at those emerald eyes, that seemed to already have the ability to focus, and felt a surge of love and wonder. They named her Adolphina, meaning kind and noble wolf.

Adolphina stepped in front of the fountain that was worn smooth and appeared to have become a part of the mountain itself. "It can't fail," said Adolphina. "We have neither the time nor the resources to wait any longer. If they don't unlock it…"

"They'll unlock it," said Abacus. "We have studied the texts, and this is the only way to get three books to unlock the cave. When three books turn the key *at the same time*, the lock will open. Timing is everything."

"We're putting a lot faith in a construct of time that has been proven not to actually exist," she insisted.

"Maybe, but they don't know that. They are your three lives that are most open to receiving our message. I'm confident we made the right decision."

"Check on Thantos again," said Adolphina.

Abacus pressed his temple and a lens covered his right eye.

"Well?" asked Adolphina.

"This doesn't seem right. Thantos is headed in the direction of the fountain, but Violetta is walking in the opposite direction," he replied.

Adolphina faced Abacus.

"What just happened, and, more importantly, what is he up to?" she asked.

"It's hard to tell," he said.

Adolphina turned back toward the fountain, her coal-lined eyes widening in anticipation. "I guess we'll find out," she said.

Within minutes, Adolphina and Abacus watched as the marble rosette above the spout slowly rotated and then stopped with a loud click.

The only sound came from a hawk that screeched in the distance.

"It worked," Abacus said. "It actually worked."

She removed the rosette and reached her hand inside, gripping the edge. With all of her strength, she pulled the fountain toward her. It budged slightly. She pulled again, harder this time. It moved a few more inches. Abacus reached in and pulled on the other side. Inch by inch, they pulled it toward them until, eventually, the entire fountain broke free from the mountain and they pushed it aside. "I need a light," said Adolphina, looking inside.

"Here," Abacus said.

She held it inside, and Adolphina peered through the opening.

"What do you see?"

"More than we could have hoped for," Adolphina said. "Come on."

She entered the cave, and the other women followed. It was filled with statues and artifacts.

"Look," said Abacus, pointing to a black granite case with gold engravings. Adolphina walked over and removed the lid. Inside, lay a single book covered in jewels. Adolphina traced her finger along the gold rose.

Two other women joined her. "They'll have to believe us now," said Abacus.

"Yes," Adolphina said, smiling down at the book.

"Actually, I'll take over from here," a man's voice interrupted. They turned toward the entrance to see a halo of light shining from the outside and outlining his body, casting his face in a dark shadow, but she would recognize that energy anywhere.

"Liber," exclaimed Adolphina stepping toward him. "What are you doing here?"

Liber grinned. "So, you remember me?"

"Of course I remember you. You've been a thorn in my side for lifetimes."

"Where's Thantos?" demanded Abacus.

"Thantos? The guy you sent disguised as a priest to meet Violetta? It turns out he wasn't up for the job." He glanced around the cave. "I have to say, I did not expect to end up back here, meeting the two of you … I guess we haven't worked out all the kinks with this time travel business."

"You entered a wormhole where two of you cannot exist simultaneously. You were flung back into the time from which you originated," said Abacus between gritted teeth.

"Whatever you say," said Liber. He walked forward and peered inside the case. "It's taken me lifetimes to find this. But where are the other two books?"

"There's only one, and it doesn't belong to you," Abacus warned.

"Huh. Well, no matter, I have what I need in this case." Liber turned toward Adolphina. "You've gotten a little darker and taller with each life," his lips curled, "but those eyes remain eternal."

"How did you find us?" Adolphina demanded.

"That's your problem. You have always thought that only women have access to the Light. It never occurred to you that men can be just as powerful."

"You'll never be powerful as long as you stand alone."

"Really? I found you didn't I?" He gestured toward the case. "You really think you can save all of humanity with this one book?"

"It's the message contained within it."

"And what message is that, my dear? That we are all one? That we are all individual manifestations of the Divine? That each of us holds the keys to our own reality, destiny, etcetera, etcetera, the same message since the beginning of time?" he mocked, narrowing his eyes. "Do you think any of that is new? That it hasn't been said before and fallen upon deaf ears? People are blind, Adolphina, and they like it that way. In fact, the more rigid, simplistic, and intolerant the message is, the better. The less room for questioning, the more appealing it is. People will believe anything if they don't have to overthink it. In fact, the less thinking they have to do, the more fervently they fall in line. You should know this by now."

"That's not true," said Adolphina. "People are tired of the old way of living. They want to hear the truth."

"I admire your optimism. I always have. But, people are weak. They enjoy festering in their emptiness and feeling sorry for themselves. They like feeling hopeless and thinking that they've lost before they've even begun - that way, they don't need to try. They've become addicted to self-pity and their sad little poor me stories." Liber smirked and shrugged his shoulders. "Who are we to break that cycle?"

"They only believe those things because it's the only story they've been told," said Adolphina.

"Correction. It's the only story that resonates with them. Is it our fault they have no imagination? That they see their lives as they are and believe that they have had no say in creating them? Is it my fault they have lost the ability to reason? That they can only recite the same paralytic responses that they've heard from those who have told them *what* to think, instead of *how* to think?" He ran his hand along the edge of the granite case. "They repeat the message because another person's words sound more intelligent than their own, and it makes them feel smarter for a moment ... until they have to elaborate, of course."

"The people are ready. It's time for a new way. There is no right or wrong. There's only what works and doesn't work, given what we are trying to do. And what we have been doing clearly isn't working," retorted Adolphina.

"Spoken like a true visionary," he held up his hand, "and I don't disagree. But I'm not here to fix this world."

"True awakening can only happen when first, you reject everything you see and know... the physical world," she said. "Liber, you're awakening, so don't go backwards. It's time for you to move forward."

"You can spare me your moral conjecture. I have studied the same things as you, but I have arrived at a different conclusion. The physical world has served me well," said Liber.

"The physical world is not reality. It's the remnants of old thoughts born in the minds of blind men who came before us; yet we hold tightly to these physical things as if they were sacred treasures - even as they crumble in our hands."

"The only thing crumbling right now is your dream, *your* vision for a new world," he scoffed. "My world is real. And now that I have this book, and I can control—"

"You will be greatly disappointed when you discover there is no reality to control," she interrupted. "We are doing nothing more than spinning an ephemeral dream, and the spinner is what is real... not the dream. The creator, *not* the created." Adolphina stepped toward him.

"You are still living inside the old paradigm of an old God, and that paradigm is a house of mirrors reflecting everything you think and believe. Don't you think it's time to shatter that prison?"

Liber pointed a weapon at Adolphina's chest. "A single shot from this laser has the power to burn a hole straight through your heart. I suggest you stop talking and step aside," he said, placing the book inside his bag. As he walked toward the entrance, he paused. "Let's hope this is the last time we meet," and stepped out of the cave.

Adolphina stepped behind him and whispered over his shoulder: "You didn't think we would do this alone, did you?"

A dozen women stepped into a circular trench in front of the fountain, flowing with water. They held hands as they encircled Liber and focused their attention on him.

"Give me the weapon and the bag," Adolphina said.

He turned around. "You really think I'll just hand it over?"

"It's over, Liber," said Abacus.

"You're right, it is over. I'll take all of you out, beginning with you." He pointed the gun at Adolphina.

Before he could press the trigger, his arm flew up. "What the hell?" he yelled.

Abacus stepped behind him, taking the bag and slinging it over his shoulder.

Liber fought to move his arm, but he could not overcome the force that was holding it in place. "What the hell is going on?"

"Simple. We are using the energy generated in our hearts to control your electromagnetic field, which is weak and susceptible to influence," said Adolphina. She gripped Liber's arm and took the gun from his hand. "It happens all the time when people are weak-minded and allow others to dictate their thoughts and beliefs. Now, we have figured out how to do the same with the body. We are all energy systems, after all."

"Let me out of this!" demanded Liber.

"We will let you go, but not yet."

Liber's mouth contorted into a snarl as he tried to twist his shoulders.

Adolphina clasped her hands behind her back and began to walk in a circle around Liber.

"You have misused and misdirected your energy for some time. We will never interfere with your free will to do so, as it has been a crucial part of your journey and development thus far," she continued making a circle around him, "but we believe you are ready to move beyond your self-imposed limitations.

To harness the energy inside of you more intentionally, with purpose. You only need to be shown…a different way. And we are eager to help you along in your journey."

Adolphina completed the third circle and stopped in front of Liber.

She took a step towards him. "Shall we begin?"

Adolphina stepped forward and addressed the group gathered in front of her and Abacus. "There are those of us who have come to this life with the purpose of shining our Light upon the darkness and lies of the world - sometimes, from inside the misguided institutions in which we serve. You can find us everywhere. Our work is diligent and steadfast. We have not come for praise, vanity, or recognition. We do not scream our message. We live it. All the while, our Light neither dims nor fades. And those in our path are either blinded or ignited by our Light, depending on their level of awareness."

She raised the book high and it sparkled brilliantly in the sunlight. "We hid this book centuries ago, in hopes that we would find it again. I wrote the last pages atop Rieta's temple as men came for me with their torches and shackles."

Adolphina turned toward Abacus and continued. "I entrusted this book to Abacus, who was by my side that night, in hopes that it would remain safely hidden until such time that we were ready to spread our eternal message once again. It is time. We are prepared. We are strong. Now, we begin."

Madagascar

2154 AD

They stood on the balcony looking across the sea. "Do you really think Liber will change his ways and embrace our teachings?" asked Abacus.

Adolphina nodded. "I do. Change is an inevitable, unstoppable force. We can fight it all we want, but it'll always have its way in the end."

"I worry his ego is too firmly established. He certainly thinks he knows everything."

She sighed. "Unfortunately, arrogance is an impediment to progress. We think we are the pinnacle of human evolution. The final product. We fail to consider that we will stand alongside the caveman in a museum one day, visitors remarking how primitive we homo sapiens were," she laughed, "and, oddly, this thought gives me great comfort."

"I've been wondering…why didn't you tell them about the other half?"

Adolphina kept her gaze forward. "The other half of what?"

"The other half of the story."

Dawn was breaking over the horizon.

Adolphina liked this time best, when light and dark divide the heavens, when the sun shared its glory, for the briefest moment, shining alongside the other stars in the sky. Adolphina could not think of a better way to start each day. She turned toward Abacus.

"Well?" he asked expectantly.

"Everyone's journey unfolds in its own time," she said, reaching for his arm, cradling his forearm in her hand, "and so does the truth."

Coming soon…

Maidens of the Eastern Star

"And so in this twilight and evening of the world, when sin is flourishing on every side and in every place, when charity is growing cold, the evil of witches and their iniquities super-abound."

The Malleus Maleficarum, Part 1
Question II
Heinrich Kramer 1486 AD

"And so in this dawn and sunrise of the world, when enlightenment is flourishing on every side and in every place, when charity is increasing ten fold, the virtue of witches and their goodness super-abound."

The Light of all Things
Book I, Part I
Adolphina

Delphine

Istanbul

August, 2110

"Once upon a time," she read, beginning the story as she did every night.

But on this particular night, her voice trailed off as she stared down at that single phrase. Her eyes focused on the second word. Upon.

Delphine had heard the line countless times as a child. Now, she recited it to her son - words so familiar, they flowed effortlessly from her mouth with little thought or emphasis. But tonight, for the first time, she understood the phrase in its entirety. The most profound truths have a way of hiding in plain sight.

Her son rested his head on her shoulder. "Mother, are you going to read?"

She blinked, and the words came into focus.

"Once upon a time," she read slowly, "in an ancient city that stood atop a petrified forest, where mazing streets flowed with water that carried both the life and the rot of the sea, lived a hunter of wayward beasts and a gatherer of untamed things."

Late that night, in an apartment overlooking the Bosphorus Straight, Delphine lay awake in her bed. The silk sheets clung to her legs like honey to a comb. She didn't know if it were her nerves or the heat, but she felt as if she were suffocating.

She kicked the sheets off and stepped onto the balcony. The silhouette of the darkened cityscape pierced the midnight sky - another power outage. Or, at least that's what they wanted everyone to believe.

She looked down at the flowing water. She swore she would never return to the city. The city that once pulsed with energy, color, and vibrations had made her dizzy with excitement.

But, she had come back.

Only now, everything was different. Tonight, the moonlight reflected off of the water that looked like a gelatinous mass moving toward the sea. "The entire city has succumbed to inertia," she muttered.

She checked her watch; still no word from Adolphina.

A small red flicker caught her eye beneath the canopy of a tree. She leaned over the balcony as he stepped onto the sidewalk. Her pulse quickened. "You've got to be kidding," she whispered. She grabbed her robe and quickly headed toward the front door.

"How long have you been out there?"

"Not long," he said.

"Get inside," she demanded, opening the door and motioning him in. "Someone could have seen you. How can you be so careless as to come here? For God's sake, you're a wanted man!"

"Fuck them," he retorted, plopping down on the sofa.

"You need to be quiet, Alexander is sleeping."

"Well, isn't that convenient? It's been ages since I've seen him, but I guess that's how you like to keep it."

"You're drunk."

"Quite drunk." He stood up and stumbled across the floor. "Why don't you pour me a glass of whiskey? I know you keep a stash of the good stuff in here somewhere."

"You can't have anything." She grabbed his arm and steered him back toward the sofa. "I swear, sometimes I think you have a death warrant out on yourself."

"I remember a time you found my reckless antics sexy." He reached for her hand, and she swatted it away. "I see," he remarked, "and they say absence makes the heart grow fonder." He stretched his back and put his feet on the coffee table, "but in your case, it only made it wander."

"You don't know what you're saying."

"Don't I?"

"No, you do not. I'm going to get some water. And, don't move. I swear if you wake up Alexander, I'm going to lose it. I don't want him seeing you like this."

"You don't want him seeing me at all."

"Enough."

She returned with the glass, and he took a sip. "Why don't you just come clean?"

"We aren't starting this again."

"You and Gregory. Why can't you just admit it?"

"There's nothing to admit, that's why."

"I don't believe you. And I don't believe him either."

"Well, there's not much more to say then, is there?"

"Well, there's Alexander."

"Keep him out of this."

"Come on, you can tell me now. Is he really mine?"

"Believe me, there are times I wish he weren't." She took the glass from his hand. "You know where the spare bedroom is. Go sleep it off, and we'll talk in the morning."

Delphine waited until the door to the bedroom closed before stepping outside onto the balcony to dial Gregory. "He showed up outside my apartment, Gregory, I can't believe how stupid he can be. He's going to get us all killed."

Suddenly, a rapid succession of knocks was followed by a man's warning on the other side of the door. "This is the police. Open the door."

"Shit. They're here. I have to go," she said, and hung up the phone.

She opened the door, and three officers stormed passed her, sweeping flashlights from side to side across the room.

"Search the bedrooms," one shouted. Then, one of them walked up to Delphine. "We received word you are harboring a wanted man. Where is he?" he demanded.

His breath smelled of cheap vodka. Delphine remained silent. She knew better than to speak.

"Mommy, what is happening?" Her son stood in the doorway to the living room, rubbing his eyes.

She ran over and picked him up. "Quiet, honey," she whispered in his ear.

The two men returned to the living room. "No one's here."

"You searched every room?"

"Yes, Sir. It was probably another false tip. We've been getting a lot of those lately."

"These bastards think it's funny to lead us on wild goose chases." He gave her a once over and snarled. "Come on, guys. Let's get back to our card game."

Delphine hugged Alexander tightly. "It's ok, sweetie. Everything is ok now. Let's go back to bed."

Delphine walked into the guest room. The bed was still neatly made and the window was closed. Delphine shook her head and turned to leave when something caught her eye. A single gold band lay on the nightstand. She picked it up and walked over to the window. Beneath the tree, a tiny red spark flared and disappeared. She waited, but it did not return.

She took her necklace off and slipped the ring onto the chain. Then, she fastened it around her neck and tucked it beneath her shirt.

Outside, beyond the trees, the dark water pressed on, stirring the sand and silt that lay beneath the Bosphorus, revealing five black marble fingertips the size of Doric columns. They stretched upward. Longing, waiting to lock hands once again with his eternal beloved.

Gratitude...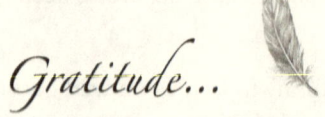

First and foremost, to my mom. With unshakable love and encouragement every step along my journey in life, thank you for your support.

Those who helped me through the editing process. My editor, Victoria Straw, my mother, and friends Rebekah Ellis and Silvia Pepe.

And to every person, place, and experience I have encountered along the way. A culmination of inspiration I hold close to my heart, unfurled itself, in some form, on these pages.

i love connecting!

You can find me usually on Instagram, rarely on Facebook, and often enjoying a spritz in a piazza in Verona. Shoot me a text, send me an email, or join me at my table.

lisa_arriola_neidhardt

lisa.r.arriola@gmail.com

www.ingramcontent.com/pod-product-compliance
Lightning Source LLC
Chambersburg PA
CBHW022235020726
47496CB00004B/915